Dekker, T.
Outlaw.

PRICE: $30.00

NOV 2013

CENTER
STREET

LARGE
PRINT

OUTLAW

TED
DEKKER

CENTER STREET

LARGE  **PRINT**

New York Boston Nashville

Copyright © 2013 by Ted Dekker
Ted Dekker is represented by Creative Trust Literary Group, www.creativetrust.com.

Center Street
Hachette Book Group
237 Park Avenue
New York, NY 10017

CenterStreet.com

Book design by Sean Ford
Printed in the United States of America

RRD-C

First Large Print Edition: October 2013
10 9 8 7 6 5 4 3 2 1

Center Street is a division of Hachette Book Group, Inc.
The Center Street name and logo are trademarks of Hachette Book Group, Inc.

The Hachette Speakers Bureau provides a wide range of authors for speaking events. To find out more, go to www.HachetteSpeakersBureau.com or call (866) 376-6591.

The publisher is not responsible for websites (or their content) that are not owned by the publisher.

ISBN 978-1-4555-7612-8 (large print hardcover)
ISBN 978-1-59995-415-8 (hardcover)
Library of Congress Control Number 2013939391(hardcover)

OUTLAW

My dearest son, whom I was allowed to birth for reasons far beyond my own understanding:

You must know the full truth of who you are and from where you came. I have carefully written down our story through many nights alone, lost to the world, to be read only by those who would seek the truth as I myself do.

I pray that in reading our account, you will finally understand. Listen with your heart and surely you will be among the rarest who live, as will be those who one day awaken from their stupor and follow in your footsteps.

I wait for you, my son. Find me, the one whose womb gave you breath and blood. Search me out so that we might summon all those who would hear the distant beat of our drum and see, with new eyes, the world as it really is beyond the law of flesh and bone.

Hear my voice calling to you through these pages now. Come to your mother. Let my words guide you home. Awaken, my son. Come out from among those bound by the law of this world and find new life.

I wait...

CHAPTER ONE

THE STORY of how I, Julian Carter, and my precious two-year-old son, Stephen, came to be on that white sailboat, tossed about like a cork on a raging dark sea off the northern tip of Queensland in 1963, is harrowing, but it pales in comparison to being abandoned in that tempest.

One moment we were in the hands of a capable captain; the next he was gone, swallowed by the storm, leaving us utterly alone and at the whim of nature's crushing fury.

Before leaving Thursday Island, I'd been assured that the captain—a congenial and talkative man named Moses who'd agreed to take us out for a leisurely afternoon sail—was the best. I suppose he might have been, but not even the most experienced pilot can control the hand of fate. In this case that hand was nothing less than a fist, perhaps a large log or a whale, and it slammed into the hull, jerking me from my dead sleep below deck where I'd dozed off in gently rising and falling seas.

The boat lolled dangerously to my right, then pitched in the opposite direction. I cried out and clambered to the adjacent bench seat, thinking little Stephen had surely been thrown across the galley. To my relief I saw that he hadn't been bothered at all. He slept peacefully, unaware of the waves crashing against the craft.

How long had we been sleeping? In my panic I left Stephen and scrambled up the narrow ladder to the main deck.

The sight that greeted me stopped me cold. Dark, ominous clouds pressed low like a cave of black boulders. We were in the maw of two towering waves with jagged, wind-whipped crests that looked like bared teeth. The serene seas that had beckoned us out for leisure had become a monster and we were in its jaws.

The captain twisted from the wheel, sun-leathered face now ashen and drawn. I saw the fear in his eyes, two open wells that sank into the abyss of uncertainty. I felt myself being swallowed by the darkness in his eyes, sucked deep into a place that could not be rightly navigated.

For the space of no more than a heartbeat, we

shared a common, terrible knowing: we were in dreadful trouble.

Whether distracted by my sudden appearance or lost in his own fear, I don't know, but he was oblivious to the sudden swing of the mainsail sweeping toward him. I thought to cry out, but before the words could form in my mouth, fate dealt its blow. I watched, speechless, as the boom struck the side of his head with bone-crushing force. He lurched to his left. A sudden wave heaved the boat, and he toppled over the side and into the boiling sea.

I stood frozen at the hatch, clinging to the ladder, unwilling to believe what my eyes had just shown me.

Thinking to rush to the rail and save the man, I released my grip, but my legs were not accustomed to walking a bucking deck and I grabbed the ladder again, sure that I would only be thrown over as well, leaving my helpless son alone.

I cried out and frantically searched the foaming water but there was no sign of the captain. The ocean had swallowed him whole and shoved the boat far from where he'd gone overboard.

I felt a moment of dread for the man and whatever family he'd left behind, but the thoughts were quickly crushed by the singular terror of my own abandonment.

The empty deck before me looked like a scene from a nightmare, disconnected from reality, a single cruel image meant only to horrify. I saw the full scope of our danger as the boat rose to the top of a colossal wave. We were alone in the throat of a yawning ocean, a mere speck in that towering sea so far from the distant American shores I'd left to answer God's call in the wake of a sunken marriage.

Even during my tumultuous relationship with Neil, my family had always been a strong fortress of refuge. My whole life, mother and father and sisters and servants had always been at my beck and call. Even during the darkest nights, the land had always been solidly under my feet.

But in that sea north of Queensland I was free-falling into bottomless chaos and death. The God I had come to serve was nowhere to be seen.

The boat tipped dangerously onto its side and my mind snapped to the crash I'd heard. Something had broken.

The rudder? The keel. Or worse, the hull.

Salt water crashed over the railings as I spun toward the open hatch behind me, grabbing for purchase, sopping wet. The water spilled through the doorway.

I threw myself down the ladder, reached up and

slammed the door shut, then jerked the lever down to lock the door tight, muting the sound of pounding waves.

Stephen slept in peace.

I began to shake.

For a long moment I allowed myself to imagine that it was all a mistake. I was still asleep beside my son aboard the Pan American flight high in the sky, angling toward Australia, enduring a nightmare from which I would soon awake. Safe.

But then the boat lurched wildly, hurling an empty stainless coffeepot from the shelf to the floor, and I knew it was no dream. Large raindrops began to pelt the windows.

Amazingly, Stephen breathed evenly in a peaceful sleep. It was the only blessing of that moment. My maternal instincts demanded that I protect my son at all costs. He would continue to sleep without a hint of discomfort or fear—this became my sole purpose in the galley of that boat.

Pushing away all thoughts of the pounding storm, I dropped to my knees and scrambled under the table. A single latch locked the tabletop to the stand. I clawed at the lever, popped it open, then jerked the top off the stand and stood it on end, bracing it against the cushions where Stephen slept so he couldn't roll off. I'd seen a box of canned goods along the wall behind me, and I fought for balance as I hauled it into place to secure the tabletop.

In truth, nothing could possibly be secure in that storm.

I knew nothing about making a sailboat go or turn or stop, even in a glass sea. The boat's mainsail was straining in the wind. Looking out the round porthole window, I could see that we were being flung over the waves, tipping first one way and then the other in a dramatic fashion. The power of the storm would surely capsize us unless I could find a way to lower the sail. From what I could see, there was no way to accomplish that task from inside the hull.

I had to go back up and face the storm.

My mother and father were eccentric but made of iron. Some of that mettle had found its way into my bones. Faced with what seemed like certain death, I was finally able to set my panic aside.

I can't tell you that I had any idea what I was doing or that I had any real hope for accomplishing it, but I knew I had to do something.

I staggered back onto the main deck, the memory of Moses being hurled overboard large in my mind. Why he hadn't lowered the sail was beyond me. Perhaps he had been desperate to get out of the storm using as much wind power as possible.

Seawater soaked my blouse and capris to the skin, but the rubber soles of my canvas shoes didn't slip. I grabbed one of the ropes to steady myself and pulled myself to where the sail was tied into the mast. There was a metal crank there and I tugged at it, but the lever refused to budge. Spray slapped my face. I could hardly see, and if not for my firm grasp on the rope, the bucking deck might have thrown me from my feet.

I searched in vain for a locking mechanism. I couldn't figure out how to release the crank. It came to me that I had to cut the rope.

Lightning ripped jagged lines in the sky. Thunder crashed over my head. Angry clouds unleashed torrents of stinging rain, forcing me to squint to protect my eyes. The sail was dragging us over the crests, threatening to capsize us at any moment. Maybe I could release the sail by cutting the line. There had been a red bucket and a filleting knife on deck earlier, but no more. Both were long lost to the sea.

I clawed my way back to the hatch, descended the ladder without falling, retrieved a knife from the galley, and returned to the deck. With each step I took, the waves seemed to rise higher, like rolling mountains on either side. I had to get the sail down!

But the moment I tried to saw into the rope, I realized that it wasn't rope at all. It was a cable. Thick strands of steel wire.

I stood there, frozen by indecision. I didn't know how far out to sea we were. I didn't know the direction in which we were headed. I didn't know where the sea ended and land began.

We were in the Coral Sea, I knew that much. The boat might have been blowing west into the Pacific, north toward New Guinea, south toward Australia, or east, back toward Thursday Island. I could only hope that it was the last. Thoughts of the open Pacific filled me with the certainty of death.

Screaming at the wind, I lunged for the sail and thrust the blade at the stretched canvas. Repeated jabs rewarded me with a small tear in the material before a large wall of water threw me to my knees. The knife flew free.

Grasping at any surface that gave me a hold, I managed to crawl back into the galley and close the hatch. Stephen still slept—how, I'll never know.

Only then did I think to secure him to the cushion using the strap from a life jacket so that he wouldn't be thrown off the seat if the ride grew worse.

After I did so, there was nothing else I could do

but crouch over my boy and beg God to save us. We were ants on a piece of driftwood being pummeled by crashing waves. Each clap of thunder rattled the metal stove.

The wind ripped into us with a savagery that left the boat groaning and screeching. My only hope lay in the fact that we hadn't already been torn apart or flipped under the waves. The crash that had first awakened me must have been the rudder rather than the keel.

The beating seemed endless. Minutes dragged into what must have been an hour and then what might have been several hours.

I can't fully understand how the boat held together under those pounding walls of water. I only know that somehow we made it through the storm's worst. The wind finally began to ease. The waves weren't as high and the rain lightened.

After hours of terror, a calm began to settle over me. Real hope for our survival slowly edged back into my mind.

The moment the storm finally destroyed us came suddenly, with a deafening crack below us, much louder and more jarring than the one that had broken the rudder. At first I thought the hull itself had split in two.

But as soon as the boat began to tip, I knew that the keel had somehow snapped. The long underwater wedges that keep the wind from pushing a sailboat over are normally the sturdiest part of a boat, so I don't know why the keel broke before the hull.

What I do know is that one moment the boat was upright, and the next it had been pushed all the way over on its side. The impact forced part of the mast through the window.

I find it nearly impossible to relate the full horror of our capsizing at sea. The floor jerking up to my left. That coffeepot smashing into the ceiling. The tabletop flipping away. Water gushing into the cabin.

I could see the cabin collapsing around me, but my mind was swallowed by what was about to happen to Stephen. I instinctively grabbed for him, releasing my hold on the table post. The instant my hand came free, I was thrown across the cabin.

I remember screaming, a pitiful cry as my body flew through the air. I remember thinking that all of this had happened because of a recurring dream that had drawn me halfway across the world. Then my head slammed into one of the low-hanging cabinets and the world vanished.

CHAPTER TWO

EACH OF our stories begins long before any event that suddenly and often irrevocably catapults us onto a new path.

My story began with a dream.

But really it began with my father, who guided my understanding of the world, and with my mother, who influenced my every waking moment. I will write here only what will give you a general context for my life before I was ripped from the bosom of one world and thrust into another, all because of that simple, recurring dream.

My mother, Ellen Carter, was a proper British woman from London who met my father in New York, married him a year later, then moved to Atlanta in 1933. She soon gave birth to my older sister, Patrice, then to me, Julian, and finally to Martha. We lived in Georgia with all the Southern belles, but Mother brought us up as proper English. We were referred to as "the Brits" by many in our social circle. My accent was far more British than Southern drawl, and I preferred hot tea to mint juleps on summer afternoons.

Our estate consisted of a mansion and four smaller homes, and to hear Mother talk, you would think she was the queen, our estate her country, and we her subjects. Anyone not part of our family was a foreigner who did not belong on her soil for more time than it took to have tea or play a game of croquet, and she saw no harm in making her opinion known.

Her eccentricity grew as she aged and eventually gave way to a disposition that might be considered senile. Her choice of words made foreigners cringe, but we knew her heart was golden.

She got it in her mind that the servants, all of whom were colored, were slaves, and she had no problem saying so to their faces. "Slave Regina, what have you done with my slippers?" Or, "Where are the rest of the slaves, Jacob?"

Our servants were with us for many years, and Mother was thoughtful of them on all occasions, particularly at Christmas. She was the first to bandage up their scratches and send anyone with the smallest cough to the doctor.

And yet my mother was distant. Her own mother and father had shipped her off to boarding school for a proper education and were barely present in her life. I suppose she was only doing what she knew. I often thought she was more present for the servants than for me.

If my mother was distant, my father, Richard, was almost entirely absent. And when he drank, he was downright obstinate—which was most of the time he was home. We learned early to stay clear of him to avoid a smack or a verbal lashing.

Furthermore, he was a racist. His great-great-grandfather had been one of the wealthiest plantation owners in Georgia. The family no longer farmed cotton, having traded cotton farms in the South for oil fields in Texas, but Father still hadn't shed the bigotry that ran thick in his blood. He could talk the proper line and work up some kind words for Martin Luther King if required, but his veneer vanished after a couple of drinks.

Nevertheless, as is the case with many children, I grew up under his spell—a daughter desperate to be accepted and loved without achieving either. As I grew older, I swore that my own children would receive my full love and attention. Like many young girls, I dreamed of an idyllic marriage to a loving man who would shelter me in a beautiful mansion surrounded by lush green lawns and a white picket fence. There, in bliss, we would sing around the fireplace with our children, because singing had always been my most treasured escape when things became difficult.

We would have picnics with our children, tell them delightful stories, and tuck them into bed to dream beautiful dreams. How I looked forward to finding this man with whom I would birth wonder and love.

Despite my father's apparent self-confidence, he secretly depended on my mother for his security. When she became sick with pneumonia and died, part of my father died with her. We all mourned her loss, but Father came unglued. He barricaded himself in his room for nearly a week. When he finally came out, he emerged with a new vision for his life.

During that week of solitude, weeping for his loss, Father fell under the deepest conviction that he had to have a grandson. He called together his three daughters—Patrice, Martha, and me—and begged us to consider him in his last days. He would soon follow our mother to the grave, he said, he could feel it in his bones.

He instructed each of us to marry swiftly, keep our maiden name, and produce a son to whom all the wealth and prestige of the family could pass. After all, Father had no brothers.

Perhaps it was his way of making good. Having been dealt such a blow, he wanted a second chance at love, and for him that meant having a son, which he could only have through one of his daughters now. My only true value to him seemed to be my potential to give him a son.

"Keep our maiden name?" Patrice objected. She was already married and had moved to Houston, where her husband, Henry Cartwright, managed Father's oil wells. "I'm already married. Besides, I was under the distinct impression that you wanted me to keep an eye on Henry, not raise a family."

"And you *should* keep an eye on that parasite, before he sucks me dry!" Father rasped, pointing a crooked finger at her. "But you have to change your name back to Carter. Give me a son. A good-looking boy who has the Carter blood in him. It's the least you can do after all I've sacrificed for you."

Having made his plea with Patrice, Father turned his desperate eyes on me. I was twenty-four at the time and had no lasting love interest.

"Please, Julian, have mercy on your father and give me a grandson. I'm dying, for heaven's sake."

"I'm not even married," I protested.

"But you could be! Like that." He snapped his

fingers. "We have to find you a man. Someone with looks and brains, not like the dolt Patrice got."

We all knew there was at least some truth in his words.

"And you, dear," Father said, turning to Martha, who was only nineteen. "You're the spitting image of your mother. You have to bear me a grandson. Soon. Before I die. Promise me." His eyes begged us all. "Promise me this one dying request."

"I don't think you'll die anytime soon," I said.

"I'm half-dead already! Promise me this one thing. It's all I will ask."

For a moment no one spoke; he had us all under his spell. I had been very particular about whom I would eventually marry, looking as I was for the perfect man, you see? But it struck me then that my expectations had failed to bring me any satisfaction.

And I had always dreamed of having a son or a daughter who might finally correct what was wrong with my life. Perhaps I should honor my father. Really, any fine man could make a good husband or give me a beautiful child.

"I promise," I said.

He fixed his look on me. "That you'll quit being so picky and find a man."

"I'm sure—"

"That you'll keep my name," he pressed.

"Maybe I could—"

"And give me a baby boy. A grandson. To carry on my name and my legacy."

The idea began to blossom in my mind.

"Yes, Father."

"Promise me."

"I promise."

He threw himself at me and hugged me tight, thanking me as if I had just given him his only reason to live. And I had, I think.

But I knew that marrying wasn't like snapping fingers.

"If I can," I said.

"I'll help you, my dear little songbird."

He never called me his songbird, even though he said that I was the one who'd inherited Mother's beautiful voice. She and I often sang duets at the First Baptist Church, where we attended Sunday morning services.

I married Neil Roberts a year later, when I was twenty-five.

He died when I was twenty-six.

If I had known Neil's true nature I never would have allowed myself to be impressed by his charming smile when my father invited him to our estate as a potential suitor. Many said that I was a fool for marrying him, but he gave me Stephen, and for that alone I am eternally grateful.

I can't remember exactly when I began to dislike my husband—perhaps when he began refusing to come out of his room, cowering under deep depression less than four months after we married. He was a tortured soul. I suffered as well, but not as deeply as he did. Despite his mistreatment of me, I had compassion for his misery.

He often sank to the bottom of emotion's darkest well, particularly when he drank too much. At times he would stare at the horizon for hours on end, as if he were hardly more than a corpse. At other times he ignored me for days, refusing to acknowledge me even when I spoke to him.

On one occasion, when I spilled flaming oil on the stove and nearly burned down the house, he refused to acknowledge my cries for help, and I became so frustrated that I threw a frying pan at him. It struck his shoulder, but he hardly gave me a glance.

Honestly, I don't know how he became this way—he wouldn't speak about it. Even worse, I don't know how he managed to hide his true character from me until after we were married. He was a master of the shift, as I called it. Put him with men discussing an oil deal in South America, and he could shift into smooth talk on the fly. But at home he had few words for me, even on the best of days.

At times I wondered if my father had paid my husband to court me, marry me, and offer his seed for a son. Once that job was done there would have been nothing left of the arrangement to interest Neil. Father would never confess to such a thing, naturally, and I never wanted to burden him with the question.

Within six months of our wedding, I woke up realizing that I despised my marriage. Despite my family's disapproval of divorce, I think I might have left Neil in the first year if I hadn't learned that I was with child.

The change in me was nothing short of a radical conversion. As soon as I grasped the notion that a baby with fingers and toes and a tiny nose was growing inside my womb, I became obsessed with love for the child. Nothing else really mattered to me, only the life that moved in my belly. I dreamed only of my healthy baby cooing up at me with round eyes, suckling at my swollen breasts before falling into sweet sleep.

The day Stephen came into the world, a part of me found heaven.

And it was on that same night, while I was still in

the hospital, that I first had the dream that would change the course of my life forever—the same dream that landed me on the white sailboat in the middle of the raging sea.

I wasn't one who normally remembered her dreams, but the next morning the details of the jungle I'd seen while sleeping were still so vivid that I forgot I was in a hospital.

In the dream I was looking down at a large valley filled with a tangle of trees and vines the thickness of my forearms running all the way to the ground. Flocks of red-and-blue parrots took flight and flapped over an endless swamp at the valley's far end. The landscape was both savage and idyllic at once.

As I watched, thinking what an enchanting place this was, a single sweet high tone began to reach out to me, wooing me. A presence seemed to have taken notice of my own and was calling in an unbroken, haunting note.

I looked around, wondering where the song could be coming from, but I could see no one. The singular, evocative tone grew in volume, and birds from all corners of the jungle took flight, not away from but toward the sound.

And then I too took flight, as one sometimes does in dreams, sailing above the trees, up the valley.

A low tone joined the higher one then, a deeper note that seemed to reach into my bones. I wasn't afraid—on the contrary, I found the sound exceedingly comforting. It seemed to wrap itself around my whole body and pull me forward.

And then I was rushing, faster and faster, headed directly for a barren hill. It was there on that hill that I saw the form of a human. I couldn't make out if the person was clothed or naked, man or woman, but I knew that the song was coming from him or her, and in my mind's eye the singer was majestic. An exotic creature from another world called out to me in a voice that was unearthly, both high and low at once.

Come to me, it sang without words. *Find me. Join me. Save me...*

Before I could see the singer's face, the dream faded, taking the song, the jungle, and the figure with it. I awoke with eyes wide open.

The images and sounds of that dream lingered for half an hour before I forgot about it in favor of holding my newborn baby.

But the dream returned a week later. And then again, several days after that. Every few days the dream would return to me, a haunting call that beckoned and gave me peace despite the plea to be saved, all of which I felt more than heard. My initial interpretation of this dream was that it was somehow my own son calling to me—after all, it had first come to me the very night of his birth. Stephen needed his mother to show him the way to a garden called Eden. Together we would always be safe, full of life, love, and beauty.

I fussed obsessively over my baby, ignoring the suggestions from more experienced mothers that I not jump at his every sound. *Let him cry on occasion rather than grab him from his crib to nurse him*, they would say. *For heaven's sake, smack his hand when he touches things he shouldn't.*

But I was ruined for my son. I simply couldn't let Stephen cry, and I could *never* smack his hand, because then he would surely cry even more and I could not bear his suffering. I could, in fact, do nothing but spoil him. He was life to me.

Heaven on earth.

He was my Eden.

And he was life to my father, who poured his love into Stephen with an abandon that completely bypassed me.

Stephen was the most adorable bundle of joy a woman could dare wish for. I know mothers often say this about their babies, even if they are quite homely, but Stephen really was a perfect doll. Everyone said so. He could easily have been featured on television to sell baby food. Mothers would surely flock to buy whatever they saw him eating, subconsciously hoping that their own babies might look as healthy and precious as my little Stephen. He had a full head of dark hair and pale blue eyes, taking after me. And he was contentedly chubby, because I gave him all the milk he could possibly drink.

I treasured my baby more than my own life. He was, in more ways than one, the only life I had: my only true identity as a daughter, a wife, a woman.

And yet, apart from my child, I still felt an emptiness. I was aware of my longing to be accepted and loved for myself, not for my place in society or for what I could offer.

It was during this time that my church attendance grew from a cultural obligation to an honest search for meaning. As an unloved wife and a mother to a small child, I found myself reconsidering what I'd learned about God in my early years. I can't say that my faith was profound—it was simple and childlike. But I took great comfort in believing that I was being watched over by a loving God.

It was during this time that my recurring dream of the jungle, which still came to me every few nights, began to take on new significance. Rather than thinking of the song coming from my son, I began to think of it as the voice of an angel calling out to me. And I started to wonder if the notes held specific meaning that would one day become clear to me. The dream was always with me, if only in my distant awareness.

I began to share the dream with those in my immediate circle—my sisters and my pastor. They smiled graciously, but I saw only dismissal in their eyes. I was not, after all, the Virgin Mary. Dreams were flights of fancy. Naturally I agreed, but secretly I wondered. Even hoped.

For his part, Neil paid no more attention to religion than he did to me or Stephen, and when I finally told him about the dream one evening, he only offered me a blank stare. He spent more and more time on long trips and remained totally detached when he was at home, preferring to spend most of his evenings at the local bar.

His disdain for God only pushed me closer to the church. As my love of religion grew, I felt less attached to the rest of my life in Georgia. Except where Stephen was concerned, it had brought me no fulfillment. And always there was the dream with its haunting song, beckoning me.

In the summer of 1962 a missionary visited our church and spoke of a land far away called New

Guinea, where life was both pure and lost at once. I didn't think much until he began a slide show. When I saw the jungle and the images of the natives on the south coast of that island, my heart leaped. Could the figure in my dream be one of these natives?

I sat in the pew, sure that I was staring into a corner of my own dream. Surely I was only making wild associations, but I couldn't shake them all that afternoon or into the evening.

That night, when I dreamed of the jungle again, I was sure there had to be a connection. Was this God's way of calling me to a land far away? But this too must be my overactive imagination, I thought, and I dared not tell a soul about my feelings. I was too young to cross the ocean, surely, and I had a child. I'd been brought up on a diet of tea and crumpets, not coconut milk and grubs. The idea terrified a large part of me.

But the call of those dreams refused to leave me.

In the fall of 1962 my husband's dealings in oil exploration took him to Indonesia for what was to be a two-week trip. He was still in a deep place of depression, and I was grateful to see him go, as much for his own sake as for my own.

He never returned. One week after his departure I received word that he'd been found shot dead in

Jakarta. A terrible tragedy. They said that bandits had mugged and killed him. I have my doubts, but it's not for me to say.

I was surprised at the grief his death brought me. He was my son's father, after all, and for that alone I think I loved him. I felt as if a cord that tethered me to ordinary life had somehow been severed.

I was a single mother.

But it wasn't until February 1963, when my father died of a heart attack, that my world was finally torn in two. If my sorrow at having lost my husband surprised me, the profound sense of abandonment that swallowed me at my father's passing shook me to the core. I felt like a lost little girl. My mother, my husband, and now my father were all gone, leaving me alone with my son.

For a week I sat and rocked my child, feeling hollow, sure that I could never offer Stephen the kind of love I wanted to give him, having never experienced it myself. My father's, my mother's, and my husband's failures were sure to became my own. I may have appeared strong to the other mourners, who all shed their appropriate tears, but inside I was in free fall without a line to anchor me to any solid rock above.

The only constant in my life besides little Stephen was my dream. The same dream, over and over. The same jungle, which I now associated with the images I'd seen of New Guinea. The same figure, singing to me without words or melody.

I begged God to show me more, if this was his way, but I had only that same dream. Only that long, low, high, beautiful note reaching down the valley to me as I rushed toward it with the wind in my hair.

Come to me. Find me. Join me. Save me...

The haunting call would not leave me. The dream became my hidden obsession, calling to me without reprieve every few nights. I made no attempt to silence it. Instead I began to look forward to it each night, to soak in its promise and long for its fulfillment.

Three months after my father's death, the call of that distant land became too loud for me to ignore. Many said that I was only looking to run away, to cast off all the suffering of my former life, and to find a new one. Perhaps there was some truth to that.

But those same people did not know how real my dreams felt. And I didn't try to make them understand. They only would have branded me a lunatic.

My sisters thought I was losing my mind when I first spoke of my interest in becoming a missionary. Did I want to be celibate?, they wanted to know.

Wasn't I just chasing wild imaginations of distant paradise in the wake of hardship? Didn't I have an obligation to raise Stephen on the estate left by Father? I had a good life in Atlanta, they insisted. Why throw it away?

But in my way of thinking, it was Atlanta that had become nothing.

Soon I could think of nothing other than leaving Georgia. At the very least, I reasoned, I should visit that far part of the world to see for myself if my dreams were more than flights of fancy.

As it turned out, mission agencies rarely accepted single mothers for service in the field abroad, so after much consideration and numerous discussions with various experts in such matters, I made the decision to take a trip to see for myself what the possibilities were. I certainly had no shortage of resources, having received a sizable inheritance.

A World War II veteran at our church had served on Thursday Island, off the northern tip of Queensland, Australia, just south of New Guinea. He spoke of the island in such endearing terms and with such assurance that there was no danger there that I decided I would visit. Perhaps I might then venture north into New Guinea. Just an exploratory trip, you see? I had to know for myself, and I would take the journey cautiously, one step at a time, just in case my sisters were right about my state of mind.

I packed two large suitcases for me and an even larger one for Stephen. Everything but his crib went into that elephant-size bag. I remember laying out half of my own wardrobe on my bed before figuring out a way to squeeze all of it into my two cases.

All the talk of Queensland being paradise notwithstanding, I prepared for every eventuality. Pants for any jungle trek. Shorts for the beach, more pants in case the others got soiled or eaten by cockroaches. Blouses of all varieties, dresses for the casual stroll and for any dinner party. And shoes. Shoes for the dance floor, shoes for the beach, shoes for walking around town, shoes for traveling home, and shoes for blazing trails through the tropics. The shoes alone took up half of one bag.

Then there were my lingerie, toiletries, makeup, jewelry, and books. I packed enough clothing, diapers, and formula to last Stephen a week. The airline had a weight limit for each passenger, but paying the fines posed no problem. Stephen and I flew into Sydney on a Pan American flight and then up to Horn Island on a twin-engine airplane.

There we boarded a boat for a fifteen-minute hop to Thursday Island.

If you look on a map of the world, you will see that Australia looks rather like a small pig without feet—snout on the left looking down at the Indian Ocean. On its back is one spike above the large territory called Queensland. Just north of this spike is a string of tiny islands, and a hundred some-odd miles north of those islands is the huge island called New Guinea, which looks something like a bird.

Thursday Island was a tiny jewel in the Coral Sea roughly one mile wide by two miles long. Aqua waters gently lapped white-sand beaches frequented by adventurous vacationers from all over the world. For a week I took it all in, nearly delirious with the notion that I had found paradise. The people were extraordinarily friendly and welcoming and I quickly made friends, both among the locals and at the mission that I visited on several occasions. Here was a world that was color-blind, filled with cheery voices and wide smiles.

It wasn't the same as my dream, but I felt as though I was finding myself.

On the seventh day I worked up the courage to venture out to sea, a prospect that was both exhilarating and a bit frightening, seeing as how I had never actually been on a boat before this trip.

Following the recommendations of Father Reuben at the Catholic mission, I contacted a local captain named Moses, who agreed to take me out the next afternoon for a reasonable price.

So it was that I boarded that little white sailboat with my two-year-old son and headed out to sea on that fateful day.

I chided myself relentlessly in the hull of that battered boat. I begged God to put me back in the safety of my home in Atlanta. I felt like Jonah in the belly of a whale, having made an error of my calling, which was surely to anywhere but there. Or, more likely, I had naively made absurd dreams out to be more than they were.

But I now know that there was also perfect reason to what seemed madness in the belly of that whale. If my mother had not died when she did, my father would not have gone into a depression and demanded I marry. If I had not married Neil, I would not have given birth to Stephen. If I hadn't given birth to Stephen, I might have never dreamed of that distant jungle. If both Neil and my father had not died when they did, I might not have been predisposed to pursue that dream across the ocean.

And if I had not visited Thursday Island and gone under with that white sailboat, the harrowing events that followed would not have allowed me to see what I was meant to see.

Which, as it turned out, was a place of terrible loss and death.

CHAPTER THREE

IT WAS dark when I awoke in the sea. Pitch-black. For several seconds I hung limp, lost to any understanding of where I was or what had happened to me. My head throbbed. Slowly details filtered into my mind.

I was floating on my back, staring up at a vast empty space. Or I was dead. But no, I could feel something pressing into my back, keeping me from sinking into the water. I was alive.

Other details drifted into my mind. I had been on a boat. A white sailboat. We had sailed into a storm. The captain, Moses, had been swept overboard. The boat had capsized.

Stephen had been in the boat with me.

I jerked up and tried to steady myself by kicking my legs and flailing my arms. My feet found nothing but water beneath me. My head, however, struck something solid only a foot or so above me. I was under the hull?

I spun, searching for my baby, but I could see nothing.

"Stephen!"

My scream sounded hollow in the body of the overturned sailboat. The sea was calm, which meant I had been under this bubble long enough for the gale to subside.

"Stephen!"

Visions of my baby being lost in those towering waves immobilized me. He'd been dragged into the depths. Consumed by sharks.

Then I remembered that I'd secured him to the seat with a strap so that he wouldn't be thrown about. I sucked in a lungful of air and dived, straining my stinging eyes.

I could see nothing below but dark water. I twisted back and up and saw the surface—green water filtering daylight around the dark hull of the boat, most of which was nowhere to be seen. Air trapped in the bow had kept afloat the section that saved my life.

But there was no sign of my Stephen.

In my panic I sucked in a mouthful of salt water. It burned my lungs and I was immediately aware that I might drown. I struck out toward the lighter water, cleared the edge of the jagged hull, then surged straight up.

My head broke the surface and I coughed up the water, desperate for oxygen. But my mind was on Stephen, and even as I gasped for air, I twisted back and forth, looking for my baby.

I saw that I was in a glass sea in early dawn light. A thin layer of fog perhaps six inches deep drifted over the water.

"Stephen!"

But how could any baby have survived such a pounding? He'd been tied to the bench seat. Unless that cushion had come free of its frame, he'd surely been dragged under and drowned.

If Stephen had drowned, then I too was dead, lifeless in my mind and soul, because he was my life. I spun around and screamed his name again.

"Stephen!"

The morning sea swallowed my cry. I twisted and yelled at the top of my lungs.

"Stephen!"

I first set eyes on them then. The seven tall dark figures towering over the fog twenty feet from the broken hull looked like wraiths. Black vultures watching me with unblinking eyes, waiting for their turn at my carcass.

Then I saw the dugout canoe beneath them, and the sharpened paddles in their hands, and I knew they were human. They were naked from head to foot, without any covering except for bright yellow and red bands woven from some kind of palm bark, then wound around their muscled arms and thighs. Their skin was as black as midnight. Each wore a head covering made from the face and snout of a brown furry animal unknown to me.

They stood in stoic formation, silent and unmoving, without a hint of emotion. Behind the canoe floated a second, this one holding only two men and cargo heaped in the space between them.

I might have experienced some relief in being found, even if by savages such as these. They were in long canoes scarcely two feet deep; surely they had come from land nearby. But I was still in a state of dread. My mind could not process relief.

"My baby!" I cried. I doubted they could understand my words, but such considerations weren't at the forefront of my mind. "We have to find him."

The canoes were slowly drifting my way, I realized. I trod water close enough now to see the whites of the warriors' eyes. Several wore curved bones through their nostrils. All of them watched me with the same expressionless stare.

Not a shred of concern. No fear. No aggression. No hint of either amusement or sorrow. They might have been dead.

But one look into their steady eyes and I saw that the beings before me were pillars of life. Like gods watching a lesser being at their feet. A new kind of fear edged into my mind.

The first dugout canoe slid forward like a serpent, parting the blanket of fog in silence. I had seen photographs of natives before, certainly. But the man who stood on the bow of that canoe filled me with an awe and dread I had never experienced. I knew immediately that this man was their leader.

Part of my reaction was to his unabashed stance—his perfect form, his boldness and unwavering confidence as he stared directly into my eyes. He was a tower of brute strength and poise, void of emotion at having found a woman alone in the sea. By the set of his jaw and his bearing, I knew that in his world he was master and I the humblest slave.

A long thin scar ran down his left side, from his chest all the way to his hip bone. He'd survived someone's attempt to gut him and looked no worse for the wear.

Two of the men behind him gently lowered their paddles into the water to slow their drift. Water gurgled over the carved blades. It was the only sound beyond my own breathing as I continued kicking and clawing at the water to stay afloat.

They came within arm's reach of me, looming above the fog with brazen dignity. I cannot possibly do justice to that first encounter with the gods of the earth, as I quickly came to think of them. Tears swam in my eyes. I opened my mouth, desperate for their help, but only a whimper came out.

The warrior on the bow lifted his eyes and gazed at the horizon, perhaps to a distant shore, though I could not see one. The men behind him dipped their paddles beneath the water again, as if responding to an unspoken order made by the single shift of his eyes. The sleek dugout slid past me, floating through the fog. Not one of the seven men in the canoe gave me another glance. Their eyes were fixed on the horizon.

I stared after them, confused by their indifference. I was a white woman from an important family, flailing in the ocean next to a capsized sailboat, and they had shrugged me off as a bull might shake off a fly.

The object that struck my head then could only have been a paddle, swung by the first of the two men in the second canoe as I stared after the first. Sharp pain flashed down my neck, and I felt myself falling beneath the sea once again.

CHAPTER FOUR

IT WAS dark when my mind crawled from unconsciousness. Pinpricks of light that I first mistook for stars spotted my field of vision. I lay on my back in a puddle of warm water that sloshed gently around my legs and elbows. The strongest scent of rotting mud filled my nostrils and I found it hard to breathe.

Only then did I realize my predicament. I was bound up like a mummy in the bottom of a dugout canoe, and the pricks of light were tiny holes in some kind of bag that covered my head.

My first reaction was to cry out, but the moment I tried to open my mouth I learned that I was gagged as well.

The canoe rocked under the thrust of heavy paddle strokes, pushing the dugout forward in unbroken cadence. I might have struggled, but I had the sense to know that any attempt to break free would be pointless. Clearly the men who'd taken me were not given to my concerns. If they'd asked me to climb into their canoe I would have been in no position to refuse. They could have thrown me a rope and dragged me to shore and bound me up there.

Instead they'd smashed my head and hauled me aboard like a large fish. For all I knew, they thought I was dead. Showing my discomfort now might only earn me another blow to the head.

So I lay still and focused all my will on suppressing the waves of terror washing over me.

The air was hot—no August in Atlanta could possibly compare to that heat. A steady chorus of insects surrounded us, punctuated by the calls of birds as we passed their perches. Trees. I could hear no crash of waves on any nearby shore.

We weren't out to sea. We were on a river driving into the jungle. To what end, I couldn't begin to comprehend. Were we in Australia? I doubted it. These natives were vastly different from any photographs I'd seen of aboriginals.

The only possibility I could think of was New Guinea, north of Australia, the fanciful paradise I had dreamed of.

The eastern half of the island was hospitable, yes, but the southern coast of western New Guinea, known as Irian Jaya, was vastly unexplored and reported to be one of the most forbidding regions on the planet, inhabited by a mysterious and harsh people.

My dilemma felt surreal to me. That I, an American citizen from Georgia, could possibly be bound and gagged in a canoe like cargo, refused to rightly align with my reality.

That I had lost my son aligned even less.

An image of Stephen's tiny form drifted through my mind. He was lost to the sea, consumed by the deep, gone from this world. Had he struggled? I prayed he hadn't awakened before drowning.

The men whose cargo I'd become could burn my body, cut me into pieces, feed me to their dogs—it hardly seemed to matter. In fact, I think I might have preferred it. My life without my son was no life at all.

Still the paddles gurgled through the water. Still the canoe surged forward.

Grief and exhaustion finally coaxed me to sleep and only then did I find any peace.

I dreamed that I was back in Georgia, a young girl playing tag around the large cottonwood in our backyard, chasing my sisters, who squealed with the certain knowledge that I would catch one of them, because I had always been the fastest runner.

A spring breeze sweet with the scent of peach blossoms rustled through the tree. The grass was cool under my bare feet. We were joined by Betsy, the eleven-year-old colored daughter of our maid, who could outrun even me. She became it and then I joined my delighted cries with my sisters'.

I was in church Sunday morning, wearing my favorite yellow dress, holding the microphone with a white-gloved hand, singing a solo of "Amazing Grace," my mother's favorite hymn. The enraptured congregation of two hundred faithful watched me, awed by my pure, angelic voice.

"She's even better than her mother," they whispered. "And she's got the looks. She's going to be a star one day, you just watch."

We were on the south porch, Stephen and I, he cooing while birds chirped in the cottonwoods, I sipping a cup of hot tea with my mother, who had died before Stephen's birth. Dreams could not hold the dead in their graves. Father sat across from us, smiling around his pipe.

I was lying in the bottom of a dugout canoe driving deep into the jungle, but in my mind I was in Georgia, eating peaches and singing like a bird and holding my baby as he stared into my eyes, both of us lost in a world of wonder and love.

It was all that I'd ever wanted.

The next time I opened my eyes it was raining. We had stopped and I was being pulled from the canoe. I jerked against my restraints in a sudden panic.

A gentle, low male voice spoke in a language that sounded garbled. Even so, its fluidity struck me as perfectly mathematical, like that of a master percussionist's drum roll. I could not mistake his tone—he did not want me to struggle.

A soft chuckle from the others reached me. They dragged me up a muddy bank by my ankles, then dropped my legs onto marshy ground.

The bag was removed from my head and I blinked up at pouring rain. Lightning slashed through the sky and for a stuttering moment I caught a glimpse of my new world.

The jungle rose in jagged angles on all sides, crawling with vines, and leaves a hundred times the size of any I'd seen before. We were at the bend of a muddy river. Rain poured from the sky in long unbroken strings. A tall, dark-skinned man stood over me, his scarred chest bulging, arms limp by his sides.

It was a staggering canvas, here on the edge of the world that tested the bounds of human sanity. And then the lightning was gone and I was in darkness once again.

The form remained still for a moment, then squatted, pulled the gag from my mouth, and tilted a gourd to my lips. Cool water flooded my mouth. I choked and sputtered, then lifted my head and gulped.

When he thought I'd had enough, he removed the gourd, replaced the gag, and dribbled water on it so I could suck at it. Then he pulled the bag back over my head and threw a covering over me. At the time I thought it might be plastic, but later I learned it was thatched palm leaves. Rain pelted the hood over my face.

They made no attempt to feed me. If they had, I doubt I would have eaten. I was too heartbroken, too exhausted, too ill to eat. There was nothing I could do but lie still in the steady downpour and cry, mind filled with thoughts of my son.

I knew that Stephen hadn't been found by these men, at least not alive. I would have heard his cry by now. There was no way to silence such a young child indefinitely. The image of his limp body, bound up in one of their bags, haunted me for a long while, but I finally reasoned that they would have no use for a dead baby. In this I found a sliver of comfort. I much preferred him returned to nature than seized by cruel hands.

I, on the other hand, was alive and worth their

taking. To what end, my imagination knew no bounds. I begged God to save me, but he remained utterly silent. I felt betrayed, abandoned, and a fool for having thought a dream could be more than wild fantasy. My sisters had been right. And now my son was dead.

And yet I clung to the barest hope that God would somehow rescue me.

Little sleep came to me that first night. I re-played the dream in my head, desperate to find the beauty of that song that had lured me from safety into the jaws of death. But each time I recalled the dream, the once-enthralling and -haunting tones sounded more and more like a mocking melody.

Calls and howls from unseen creatures in the jungle replaced that song, and I soon found myself hating, even cursing the once-loved call in my dreams. I could not stop imagining leeches and snakes crawling over my legs and belly. My captors had wrapped me like a mummy, but slippery crea-tures could surely find a way in through the seams.

I had just slipped into an exhausted and thank-fully dreamless sleep when I felt the wrapping on my legs being unwound. The rain had stopped. Daylight dotted the tiny holes in the bag over my head. Words were mumbled, melodic and low. The man caring for me began to prod my legs with a hot stick. But the hiss of burning, wet flesh wasn't of my own. It took me a few minutes to realize that he was burning leeches off my skin.

When I was twelve I tried out my mother's razor on my legs. The blade was loose and I managed to scrape a strip of skin off my shin before pain convinced me to jerk the razor away. By then it was too late, and blood seeped out of a two-inch wound. After firmly scolding me, my mother took the greatest care of my wound.

Now I was at the mercy of a native jabbing at my beautiful legs to burn off engorged leeches. The thought of it nauseated me.

My caretaker pulled the worms off one by one, and despite being burned they did not come off easily. I could feel their tenacious grip on my skin. Leeches do not squeal, but in my mind they put up a horrid fuss when forced to let go. I imagined that each took a chunk of my flesh with it. When the man dug into one on my inner thigh, a full foot above my knee, I felt I might pass out.

Job completed, he coated my arms and legs with a cool mud and bound me up again. He was only protecting his possession, but to the extent that a Southern belle from Atlanta was able to appreciate such generosity, I suppose I did. Somehow I got it into my head that the mud's awful odor might keep carnivores larger than leeches from taking a bite out of me.

Hood still over my head, I was hauled back into the canoe and we pushed off the bank. Then we were sliding through the river once again.

I could hear the steady breathing of the two men on the canoe that carried me, otherwise only an occasional cough or the sound of spitting betrayed our journey through the infested jungle. I guessed that they saw no need to advertise their passage along this river, perhaps because it was enemy territory.

It's interesting how the mind can dredge up the most hidden bits of knowledge when left to itself for long stretches. I knew next to nothing about Irian Jaya, because the missionary who'd first spoken of the island had come from New Guinea proper, the tamer, eastern half of an island the size of California.

That night the bag was again removed from my head in a heavy downpour. Again a gourd of water was tilted to my lips, and again I sucked at the water in long, deep drafts. For the second time since my capture I was able to see the leader, who tended to me. It was he who first gave me food.

I say food, but at the time I wondered if it was the mud scraped off the bottoms of his feet. The gray paste that he held in his fingers and pushed into my mouth tasted like a flour glue that had started to rot. Something squishy was mixed with the starchy compound. I know now that it was a sago grub—a thick white worm half the length of a finger that feeds on the pith of the sago palm.

My mother had always claimed that I was the pickiest of eaters. I was the last of her daughters to try fish, the last to taste escargot—and then only once, after my uncle coaxed me into it with a bribe of twenty dollars. I liked my meat well done and my hamburgers plain. I could barely handle biscuits and gravy, and mashed potatoes were passable only as long as they weren't too smooth. With these exceptions, no gooey thing ever went into my mouth.

But I hadn't eaten in nearly three days, and so I stared into the man's brown eyes and swallowed his offering whole, desperate for any kind of nourishment.

The leader returned my stare without interest before pushing another handful of the paste into my mouth. He then pulled the sack over my head and left me free to breathe without the gag.

Despite the heavy rain, I slept that night.

The next morning my caretaker repeated the procedure. Off with the leeches. On with the mud.

He replaced the gag, this time over the hood. Back in the canoe. Up the river.

No speaking, no chanting, no laughter, nothing but the steady breathing and gurgling of paddles as they were drawn through the water.

I was only half-alive. Deadened by sorrow over my child's fate. Suffocated by self-pity. Barely strong enough to lie still, knowing that any attempt to change my predicament would surely worsen it.

The men had come a very long way—that much was now clear. I found moments of comfort in the likelihood that they would only carry very important cargo for so many miles into the jungle. They didn't act like warriors celebrating any great feat, nor like mindless savages given to causing disturbances.

They carried themselves with utmost assurance and purpose, sure of their every move, contained and unruffled. They dominated their world without fear. Indeed, they seemed rather bored with it all.

When it seemed to me that nothing would ever change, our journey upriver came to an end sometime after noon on the third day.

For the first time since I'd joined them, my captors began to speak freely as they pulled the canoes up the bank with me still aboard. Their tones were low, and the speed of their speech rather than its volume expressed a new enthusiasm among them.

I'd surrendered my exhaustion to the unceasing murmur of paddles dipping into water, and to the gentle, musical quality of their voices, comforted by the fact that they had not killed me. But now any semblance of peace ended and my skin prickled with the uncertainty that faced me.

Two men hauled me out of the canoe and dropped me onto firm ground. I landed with enough force to knock the wind out of my lungs.

One of them gently nudged me with his foot and spoke what I assume were instructions. When I failed to respond, he nudged me again and presumably asked if I'd understood him.

Still gagged, I offered him the only thing I could, a mere grunt.

This seemed to satisfy him. My hands and feet were loosed, then strapped securely to a pole. In less time than it took me to grasp their intentions, they had me hanging from the pole between them and were marching into the jungle.

My sore neck couldn't support the weight of my head, so I let it hang. My skull struck objects on the ground twice. Both times I cried out into my gag.

Both times the carrier at my feet expressed surprise and lifted the pole higher for a moment before setting it back on his shoulder.

This is how, in August of 1963, I came into the valley known as Tulim: strapped to a pole like a bag of beans, carried like a bundle of bananas, swinging above the ground like a slain pig.

Surely I had been presumed lost at sea along with Stephen. Someone would find the shattered pieces of sailboat, and after a cursory search along the coast my sisters would weep and hold our funeral in the graveyard behind the First Baptist Church. My father would weep, my mother would cry.

But my father and mother were already dead.

And now so were my son and I.

I knew by distant cries that we had reached a village. At first there was only one utterance, a long whooping call that I briefly mistook for that of a bird.

Within moments the single cry was joined by a dozen more, and then by hundreds of voices whooping in unison, and a stampede of bare feet. They began to pound the earth with their heels, carefully in time with the chanting, making a kind of music of its own.

Uhm, uhm, uhm, uhm.

Deep and guttural, the sound shook me to my bones. This was the warriors' welcome home.

Inside the bag my eyes were wide and my breathing was frantic. Imagined or not, I could feel hundreds of eyes staring at my cocooned body as my captors marched me through the throng.

A single voice silenced the others, calling above them in a long, melodic string of words. Within a few seconds the caller stopped and the chorus resumed.

Uhm, uhm, uhm, uhm.

We marched on.

I began to tremble in my sack.

Then the solitary melodic voice again, followed by the chorus and the pounding agreement. *Uhm, uhm, uhm, uhm.*

Children ran alongside us, whispering and giggling. Women joined in with high cries between the lower chants, like cymbals between drumbeats.

And then the pinpricks of light vanished from my hood. The rhythmic mantra fell away. The darkness deepened and the air grew slightly cooler, thick with an earthy scent. A door or a gate of some kind was closed, muting the voices to a distant burble. I was marched deep into the earth and dropped into a large hole in the ground.

No parting words of instruction, no encouragement, no sign my carriers either cared or did not care that I'd been brought into their village.

They simply left.

I was in my new home.

I was in hell.

CHAPTER FIVE

AN UNCLE had taken me and my sisters camping once. I'd spent only one night on the lumpy earth before deciding that I hated tents. The ground was hard, the smoke was rank, the night was cold, the bugs were everywhere, and I was not a happy camper. Only my sisters' willingness to brave the harsh environment convinced me to stay the second night.

Compared to the dank holding cell into which I'd been thrown, that tent was a palace.

The air was cool underground, but I couldn't appreciate the reprieve from the oppressive heat. At least in the boat I'd had gentle rocking and bird-calls to settle my thoughts.

In that dungeon I had nothing but my own mind to keep me company, and it was clogged with impossibilities that had somehow, through the most cruel twist of fate, become certainties.

The sea had taken my life. The jungle had stripped me of my dignity. The gods of the earth had taken my soul.

During those three days on the river, my mind had frequently gone to God, begging him to deliver me, clinging to the vaguest hope that there might be more to my faith than mere fantasy. But there in that hole, a seed of bitterness took root deep in my heart.

The dream that had drawn me across the ocean felt like a smudge on the edge of my consciousness. I cringed every time it slithered back into my memory, though the dream itself had not returned since I'd left Atlanta.

Destitute, I lay still and tried to shut down my mind. In the wake of my son's death, filled with fear and anger, I began to believe that no distant God who would allow such suffering would rescue me.

I had left my home in good, obedient faith, eager to discover and offer wholeness and light. And I had found only wretched anguish and darkness.

It was the first time that I'd dared curse God for my misfortune.

"Hello?"

My eyes snapped wide.

"Is anyone there?"

The voice was male. Raspy. It spoke English. My mind refused to process the sound as a reality. I was hallucinating.

But then it spoke again, in a hushed tone from another cell that seemed not so far from my own, this time in a broken form of the language the natives spoke. I knew then that the man was not a figment of my imagination.

I cried out, but I couldn't form any words around the gag.

The prisoner must have assumed I was a native, because he mumbled something in their tongue before falling silent. I cried out again, and then again, until my throat was raw. All to no avail.

But I was no longer alone.

My body began to tremble with hope. I lay there, bound like a cadaver awakened from death, flooded with life. Waves of elation washed over my mind.

I was not alone!

I was alive.

Even more, the man spoke their language, which could only mean he'd been alive long enough to learn it.

They say that once broken, a person often willingly subjects himself to the master who has broken him. My ordeal had shattered my strongest resolve. The men who had taken me had become my gods, and I their slave. But now I had heard the voice of another slave.

I wanted to rush out and throw myself into his arms. I wanted to kiss him and beg him to tell me that everything would be OK, that this small interruption in my life would soon fade into the distant past, that my son was still alive and my sisters eagerly awaited my return, that my family and friends were preparing a sprawling lawn party for our reunion on the far side of the world. I would tell them of my most magnificent adventure and they would all cry and hug Stephen and me. Then they would beg me to sing for them.

I refused to listen to the other voices whispering in my mind. The ones that asked why, if the man had been here long enough to learn the language, he was still captive in this pit. The ones that wondered if these gods would treat a woman as kindly as they had treated a man.

I tried to rouse the man's attention again. And yet again. It was pointless. Maybe his voice had been a hallucination after all.

THEY came for me several hours later and woke me from a heavy sleep full of indecipherable dreams. Two men pulled me from my hole, then hefted me over one of their shoulders. The realization that they were taking me away from that place of safety near the man who spoke English jolted my mind. I made a pathetic protest into my gag and tried to kick, but I was nothing but a squirming pig in their grasp.

It was dark outside, and a chorus of insects announced my passing. Bare feet slapped at the earth as I bounced over my carrier's shoulder. No rain—that was new. Night had always seemed to bring rain.

Even then my mind was beginning to register perceived facts about my new life. Such as that I was a pig. That it rained most nights. That the man's shoulder under my waist was powerful and his stride strong under my weight.

We must have traveled a mile before the man ducked through a doorway and set me in a sitting position on a hard floor. Soft voices were exchanged, and the men who had brought me left.

A fire crackled. The air was hot, but a chill tickled my flesh with anticipation—of what, I could not know.

When I didn't think I could hold still in that silence for a moment longer, the bag was lifted off my head and I found myself staring up at a man

I immediately recognized by the long scar on his left side: the tall leader on whom my eyes had first fallen in the ocean fog. His skin looked even blacker by the dancing flames. The fire pit was at the center of a round hut with a low, charred ceiling. His dark eyes studied me, still emotionless.

He was dressed more stately and his skin glistened clean now. But when I say dressed, I mean only as the gods can dress, naked except for what could be called jewelry. Thatched golden arm- and thigh bands. A yellow-and-red collar nearly an inch wide wound around his neck. Two white bone hoops through his earlobes. No longer covered by the furry headdress, his hair was longer than I'd imagined, and wet with some kind of oil. The orange light cast deep shadows between his muscles. I was sure that this man could snap my neck with a simple, quick twist if he was so inclined.

I found it difficult to breathe in his presence.

He wasn't alone. Behind me hands carefully unwound the wide lengths of woven fibers that that had secured me for the last three days. The yellow of my sleeveless blouse had turned brown, and my canvas shoes were gray with mud. My black capris were torn at one knee.

I sat on a bark floor surrounded by thatched walls lined with no fewer than thirty human skulls.

I turned my head to see who was behind me. A woman, perhaps in her late teens, knelt at my back. I could not see her face in the shadows.

Like the man, she wore bone earrings and woven bands around her neck and arms. She was naked except for a lap-lap, flaps of red- and yellow-dyed fabric that hung from a string around her waist.

Having completed her task, the woman stood up, squared her shoulders, and stepped to one side.

"*Mitnarru.*" She motioned for me to stand.

I slowly pushed myself to my feet and stared at the woman's face, struck by her beauty. Her dark cheekbones rose high, brightened by two streaks of a light blue paste or mud that wrapped around her brown eyes and rose like wide, pointed vines on her forehead. Her shoulders and breasts were accentuated by woven bands of blue and yellow.

Both she and the man were clean despite the environment. From what I could see, other than the hair on their heads, both had either plucked or shaved every strand from their bodies.

The man nodded at the woman. "*Bo purack.*"

She motioned for me to remove my blouse. When I stared back, unsure, she repeated the man's order.

"*Bo purack.*"

To say that I was not given to public displays of

nudity would be to grossly understate my disposition at the time. Even in the face of terrible danger, human pride is not easily sacrificed, at least not among those with refined character. Being made to disrobe in front of them suddenly struck me as inhumane.

The man mumbled a short word and spat into the fire. When I still did not move, the woman stepped up and began to pry at the buttons on my blouse.

I hated myself in that moment. I hated that I stood trembling with neither the strength nor the resolve to resist. I hated being forced to disrobe.

It's strange how the simplest things, like nakedness, can be so debilitating. How the fear of being seen for what she really is can render a person so powerless. We humans protect what is ours to the bitter end, and when it's forcibly taken from us, we no longer feel human. This is an absurdity.

Even so, I was given a small gift in the hut. The woman trying to undress me was as unfamiliar with buttons as I was with public nakedness. Before she or the man resorted to more strenuous means, I made the decision to help her. I would undress for them, of my own free will.

Pushing back my anxiety, I lifted my hands and unbuttoned my blouse for her. She slipped my shirt

off, then stepped back and stared at my bra, blink-
ing.

The man's eyes settled on my chest. It was as if
neither of them could quite believe that I was en-
cased in yet another layer of protection.

I was too dense at the time to realize that their
curiosity was motivated by incomprehension as to
why any woman would want to hide her femininity and perhaps be mistaken for a man. In their
eyes I was not unlike a cross-dresser. An outer gar-
ment was bad enough—surely they'd seen
Western clothing before. But from their expressions I gathered that they'd never seen a bra.

For several long moments, neither seemed to
know what to think of it.

The woman reached out and plucked my shoulder strap. Then she pulled one of the bra's cups
aside to make sure it wasn't attached to my flesh.

She giggled and turned to the man, who shared
none of her amusement. He mumbled something
that elicited a high-pitched diatribe and unbeliev-
ing scoffs from the woman. The man let her rave
for several seconds, then cut her off with a single
word.

She nodded and waved her arms at me, motion-
ing me to take it off. *"Bo purack."*

Needing no further encouragement, I quickly removed my bra and handed it to the woman, who examined it carefully. When she motioned to me to keep going, I took off my shoes and pants.

I stood naked except for my underwear, once yellow, now brown. They continued to stare at me. Once again the woman broke into an amused diatribe. Once again the man silenced her.

The man shoved his chin at me. *"Peked."*

She began to inspect me as if I were something from the market. Without any regard for whether I might care, she examined my hair and my scalp. She pulled open my lips and flicked my teeth, then peered into my mouth. At this both of them mumbled in amazement.

Satisfied, she moved on to a cursory examination of the rest of my body. There was no mistaking the matter: I was not her equal. I was her lesser, her slave.

In a strange way the realization gave me strength as she examined my belly, my thighs, my toes. When she'd finished, the man stepped forward and gently squeezed my mouth open again. He stared at my teeth for a few seconds, then grunted and stepped back. It was my teeth that impressed him the most. In fact, he seemed interested in nothing but my teeth.

Then he released my face, spit one last time into

the fire, mumbled something to the woman, and left the hut.

I could not know it at the time, but I had just been touched by one of the three most powerful men in the Tulim valley, and he'd left me unscathed. His name was Kirutu, fearless leader of the Warik, one of three valley tribes coexisting in a fragile balance.

Never again would I be so fortunate.

As soon as he left, two older women entered the hut through the same door. For a brief moment the three women stared as if unsure what to make of me. Then they approached and touched my skin, expressing their astonishment.

The eldest, a woman of about thirty with heavy breasts and a scarred chin, began to speak in a harsh tone. She was lecturing me, waving at my body and then at the skulls on the wall, scrunching her nose and pointing accusingly at my skin and my hair. With each exclamation, the woman who'd accompanied her voiced agreement. I didn't know any of the words, but their eyes and gestures spoke a language shared by all women.

Clearly these savages who were as black as midnight and wore little more than colored mud for clothing did not approve of the way I looked or smelled. But their opinion outweighed mine. I was at their mercy and I quickly felt as ugly and stinky as they seemed to believe I was.

The eldest must have decided to correct my flaws, because she scooped up a handful of black soot and began to rub it over my belly and chest. The other newcomer joined in, heaping the soot on my head and my shoulders, smearing it over my whole body.

The show came to an abrupt end when the youngest, the woman who'd helped me undress, picked up a burning stick from the fire and threatened to burn the other two if they did not leave. They argued with her for a moment, then left, uttering their disapproval.

At first I thought I had been spared, but it soon became clear that the gods of that earth were fickle, and there were only very faint lines between salvation and damnation.

The young woman walked around me, frowning, then tapped me on my head and pointed to the line of skulls. She snapped a clear warning, threw the stick back into the fire, and followed the others out.

I was alone with the fire. Alone with the human skulls. Naked and shivering, but unbound.

Free.

CHAPTER SIX

MY FIRST thought was to run, but before I could properly consider where I might run to, three men stepped in, hastily shoved the bag over my head, and marched me out of the hut. I was confused, I was in shock, and I was terrified.

But another thought gave me a hint of hope as they steered me down the path. Although the hole they'd thrown me into was its own muddy hell, I'd found some solace there. Now without the gag, I could speak to the man who'd called out to me.

And yet they weren't taking me to my hole. That much became clear five minutes later when we began trudging up a steep incline that I couldn't remember.

I had difficulty walking on the stony path barefoot, but I wasn't exactly in a position to complain, so I stumbled forward as best I could. When I tripped on a rock that sent me to the ground with a sharp cry, the men argued for a few seconds, then pulled off my hood.

"*Naneep.*" They motioned up the path. This could only mean "go" or "walk."

I could see the trail well enough by moonlight to avoid most sticks and rocks, but the bottoms of my feet were already bruised. The underbrush on either side was thick and the trees a tangle of branches. After three days I'd seen only brief glimpses of the land itself, and I imagined the worst. It didn't matter that I had yet to see a snake; I was sure they were there, just out of sight, as were crocodiles and lizards and every other kind of crawling creature. Truly, I was surprised that I hadn't been attacked.

I struggled on, panting and sweating.

It took us at least an hour to reach our destination on a barren hill that overlooked two draws, one on either side, just visible by a three-quarter moon. Now I could see more of the terrain. We were nowhere near the river, which I assumed lay far behind us where this sweeping valley met the swamps we had crossed in the canoes. Beyond each draw, tall mountains eclipsed a starry sky.

Ahead, under a grouping of massive trees, stood a

large shelter without walls, perhaps forty feet to a side. Firelight cast a glow into the surrounding foliage.

I could see dark forms silhouetted there as we approached, but my escort stopped under the closest tree. They tied a rope around my neck and secured the other end to one of a dozen posts. I was obviously not the first to be brought here, and fears of what awaited returned my mind to a state of frenzy.

I couldn't shake the feeling that I was a goat about to be slaughtered.

One of my escorts wagged his finger in my face, uttered a stern warning, then motioned at something to my right before leaving.

When I first laid eyes on the girl who waited in the moonlight twenty paces away, I thought we'd been followed by the woman who'd helped me undress. But as she approached I saw that she was much younger, perhaps twelve or thirteen. The simple bands around her arms and neck were fashioned from woven vines, and she wore no colored accessories.

Something else caused me to wonder if she was of a lower class than the three women I'd met earlier. The split skirt hanging from her waist was made from some kind of woven grass or thin bark rather than from dyed fabric, as the others had worn. And as she walked toward me I saw something even more distinctive about her. Her skin was a milk chocolate, not the near-black of the others'. Her hair wasn't as curly. In fact, she looked altogether racially divergent, from her tiny stature to the roundness of her face.

She stopped a few paces off and looked at me with round brown eyes. After a moment she addressed me.

"Are you English?"

I was too stunned to answer. Her accent was heavy, but I refused to believe I'd misheard her words.

"I am Lela," she said. "I will speak for you."

"Speak for me?" My voice was hoarse.

"I will speak for this trial." She shoved her chin toward the square structure.

Tears flooded my eyes. "You speak English!"

The girl named Lela stood still. "What is your name, miss?" she asked.

My breathing was heavy. "Julian."

"Yulian?"

"Julian. I'm an American."

"I attending English school. A long time past. I forgetting this words."

"No, no, you speak perfectly!" I cried. Then, eyes

darting in fear that I'd been overheard, I lowered my voice. Words rushed from me like water from a spigot. "You have to help me! This is all a mistake! My boat...I was taken but I'm an American. We have to leave before they kill me! This is a mistake, I don't belong here!"

"It cannot leave this place, miss. Anyone leaves this place, they will be sick and die. It is the way, this *purum*. This evil spirit."

"No, that's only what they tell you." Her earlier words caught up to me. "What do you mean, trial?"

"This lords. It is the way of *wam* who come to Tulim. This three tribes will decide if you will be with a man."

I couldn't process what she meant.

Lela looked at the council just out of earshot, then back at me. "You must make pretty or I think you will die."

Oddly enough, the girl's suggestion that this tribunal had gathered to decide if I would be married or taken or whatever *with* meant, unnerved me more than the possibility that they might kill me. My life had already been snatched from me. My child had drowned. What was left for me?

"I..." Words couldn't keep pace with the revulsion flogging my mind. "They will force me?"

By her expression I could see that she still didn't

comprehend. But of course she was hardly a woman who could understand such things.

"They will hurt me?"

Slowly a smile nudged her mouth. "No, miss, you do not understand. They will not hurt you if you are beautiful," she said. "It is great honor to be with this great lords. This are princes of this Tulim."

"I don't *want* to be with these lords!"

She looked shocked. "But you must, miss!"

I was nearly hysterical. There on the hill my circumstances became too much for me—the leeches crawling up my legs, the stench of mud and rotting river, the sweating black flesh. An image of Stephen sinking below the waves flooded me with anguish. I felt I couldn't breathe.

"No! No, I will not be taken by any man, you tell them that!" My breath came hot and heavy as I marched in front of the astonished girl like a red-faced schoolteacher.

"You tell them that I will cut it off and feed it to the crocodiles if one of them even touches me!" I thrust my finger toward the gathered council. "Tell them that!"

Her eyes went wide and her lips tried to form a response but she was too shocked to voice it. I lowered my face into my hands and tried to regain my composure, but I couldn't stop my tears.

"No, miss, this is not a good thing," Lela said. "You must not cut this off. They cannot make baby if you cut off this."

The sincerity in her voice shocked me out of my fear. I lifted my head and stared at her.

"You must make yourself beautiful and try to make a baby or you will die," she said.

I realized then that I was seeing the world through a completely different set of lenses from this young girl. My head was abuzz with this simple thought: being taken by any man who gathered around that tribunal fire would be a great honor for Lela. In this context, being forced did not compute in her mind.

Lela was trying to help me. This young girl was a friend who spoke my language. English! If the men who'd taken me captive were gods in their world, then I was their slave and this girl was my only angel.

Shaking, I sank to my knees and pressed my palms together as if praying to her. "Please...please help me. I'm sorry. Please help me."

She glanced over at the council, quickly stepped up to me, and pushed my hands down. "You must not do this. I am not this lord."

I quickly lowered my hands.

"You must ask the spirit to help you look beautiful to this lords, miss. If you can make baby, then you will be safe."

"My baby died," I whispered. I'd become like a little girl myself.

"You already make baby?" she asked, surprised. The revelation seemed to impress her more than anything I'd yet said. "What you are saying is true? You can make this baby?"

"Yes ... but my child is gone."

"You can make more baby?" she asked.

"I don't *want* to make another baby!"

She lowered her voice. "No, you must! I will say and this will save you." The excitement in her voice was infectious. "There is little possible to make baby in this place. A woman who make baby is much good! You must make yourself pretty and I will tell them you make a baby."

She seemed to be implying that pregnancy among the Tulim was not easily achieved.

Lela grabbed a handful of grass, wadded it up, and began to rub my skin. The heat and humidity coated my body with moisture, and the black soot that the women had applied earlier smeared. She shoved the grass into my hands and grabbed more.

"Quickly. You must clean. It is very important to clean if you want to make a baby."

My every instinct told me to rub *more* dirt on my skin, to make myself as offensive as possible, but reason dictated that staying alive was, at least for the moment, the higher value. So I followed her lead and tried to wipe the soot off my belly and arms as well as I could without the help of soap and water, which hardly amounted to more than moving the stuff around.

Lela squatted and worked on my legs, smearing the soot over my exposed skin rather than cleaning it, a fact I quickly pointed out.

"You're making me dirtier."

"No, miss. You must not look ugly."

Clearly they did not prefer white skin. The older women in the hut had made as much plain when they'd heaped soot upon me in the first place. This was only the jungle's version of a good tan.

I nearly reverted to my impulse to look as ugly as possible. Instead I followed her lead.

"Are you sure they will like this?"

"It is better," she said. "I will tell them you will make a baby."

To hear Lela, children were the most precious commodity in that valley. I shoved from my mind any notion of how I might actually go about making a baby and assisted her in her attempts to spread the dirt on my skin. My arms, my legs, my belly, my chest, my back, my face—all of it was soon tinted brown.

"I will too soon make a baby," she said, working on my feet.

"You're too young!"

She stood and grinned wide. Two of her bottom teeth were missing. "No, miss. I already give this blood. I will be chosen." She said it as if nothing could possibly make her more proud. I wasn't sure whether to reprimand her or cry for her.

It was then, standing under the tree as I awaited my trial, that the raw humanity of the inhabitants in the Tulim valley first overshadowed my fear of them, if only for a few moments. Lela was only a girl doing her best to belong, like any girl her age in any social circle anywhere in the world.

I assumed that she, like me, had been brought in from the outside. What was more, she seemed to have come to terms with her place in this world.

She lifted a slender hand to my mouth, pulled down my lower lip, studied my teeth, and *ahhed*.

"It is very pretty," she said, and released my lip. "It is very healthy, this teeth. I will tell them."

"Where are you from?" I asked.

"I am from this Tulim."

"But where did you come from, before this Tulim?"

She hesitated. "I am *wam*, miss. I come from this Indonesia. It is where I learn English."

"What is wam?" I asked.

"This is offspring of animal and Tulim, many years past. You are wam, miss. Only this lords and this people are not wam."

A voice called to us from the council, and Lela hurried to untie me from the tree. "They call. We go. I will tell them, miss. You will make this baby."

CHAPTER SEVEN

THIS LORDS, as Lela called them in her broken English, were positioned around a massive rectangular slab of gray slate about a foot thick set upon four stumps. I say positioned because I immediately saw that each side of the table hosted a unique group.

These were the leaders of the three tribes that occupied the Tulim valley, and as a group they looked as imposing as the scarred man who'd plucked me from the sea.

I couldn't shake the certainty that I was walking directly to my death. The script was already written and I was only following the same path many others had taken before their demise.

I should run now. I should spin and flee into the jungle to face whatever fate awaited me there, beyond their reach.

And yet I walked confidently. One foot in front of the other, captive already in a world that offered no escape.

I stopped at the edge of the thatched roof. To a man, they stared back at me. It was as if I were not only in another world but in another dimension altogether, a newcomer to an alternate reality.

My head swam with a sense of déjà vu and my heart, beating quickly already, slowed to heavy beats.

Maybe this was all a horrible nightmare. An illusion that was swimming through my head as I slept peacefully in the white sailboat, still in calm seas. Perhaps at a single prod from the captain, or at my son's fussing, I would wake to find all well.

Lela gave me a gentle nudge. I looked at her. The plain reality of my predicament returned, free from illusion. But of course I'd known the full certainty of it already. My mind, so strained by terror, had offered me a moment's reprieve, however absurd.

She gave me an encouraging smile and glanced at the one side of the table that was unoccupied. I faced the council and edged forward into a yellow glow provided by the fire pit in the middle. Smoke drifted up to the blackened ceiling high above.

Each group consisted of five men, four of whom

stood on the ground or sat on rocks behind their spokesman. Another twenty or thirty warriors from each tribe stood idly in the dark beyond the structure, peering in with interest.

They were all fully clothed in their own way. That is to say they were naked except for woven bands around their thighs, arms, waists, and heads. Piercings graced their nasal septa and earlobes, some accented with pieces of bone, fangs, or claws. They all wore headdresses of colorful feathers or animal carcasses—bird heads, fox-like heads, boar heads. Each of the men in the group to my left wore a human skull on his back, suspended between his shoulder blades on a cord.

I stood in my own near-naked glory, trying to present myself as beautiful and fertile and worthy of bearing a child. According to Lela, this was my only hope for survival, and I had no reason to doubt her.

I stood quivering, trying to be strong and failing miserably. The spokesman to my left began to speak, a long rumbling sentence that sounded dismissive. He wore a thick bone through his nose and was missing three fingertips at the first knuckle. Bright yellow feathers fanned out above his head. I thought he must be the master of ceremonies here.

Head bowed, hands together in a praying position, Lela stepped forward and addressed the speaker, stopped immediately when he interrupted, and then continued in a similar fashion through several exchanges, which ended with a collective mumble from a number of the men.

The scarred warrior who'd taken me from the sea was seated cross-legged on a flat rock behind the speaker. Around him squatted three other warriors, but none with shoulders squared or jaw fixed to display the same authority as he. My captor wore a human skull on his back and the top half of a boar's head on his head. As soon as my eyes met his, I was convinced that he was indeed one of the princes and I felt compelled to look away.

The three groups launched into a short but pointed discourse that ended with all three staring at me. I looked down at Lela.

"Miss, this lord wish to know if it is true, what I have said."

I cleared my throat. "What did you say?"

"As we have spoken," she said. "You must not be ugly spirit."

"Yes. I mean, no. Tell them I am not a spirit. I am a woman from America."

She spoke to them and the first speaker scoffed.

"This lord says that all peoples is spirits. You are white and this must be evil spirit."

"Tell him he is wrong. Where I come from nearly everyone is white and they are not evil spirits."

Lela's eyes grew at my request. "You cannot say this is wrong, miss. This is lord."

"You tell this lord what I said, you hear me? I am not an evil spirit."

The speaker followed with a command that I took as agreement. *Tell me what she said.*

Lela faced the council and spoke, this time with some trepidation. I looked around the council with more boldness, realizing that after days in their possession, I was finally in a position to be heard. That I was as free as I might ever be. That standing before the council might be my last opportunity to be fully human here in their realm.

When Lela finished, the man snapped back his response, which she quickly interpreted.

"He says that you are wam and can know nothing."

"And he's a savage!"

She blinked. "What is this?"

I rethought my remark, grasping for something that might give me an advantage, however slight. The courage I'd found helped me rise from the immobilizing fear, and I clung to it.

"I will only tell them who I am if I know who they are."

She looked confused. "This is lords, miss."

"Who are lords? All of them are lords?"

"All this people is lords." She pointed to the group on my left, my captors. "This Warik clan." Then to the tribe on my right. "This Impirum clan." Then to the tribe directly across from me. "This Karun, the keeper of this spirit. There is three princes, one from Warik, one from Impirum. One from Karun tribe." Her eyes drifted to a figure to one side and behind the Karun tribe and I could see immediately by the fear on her face that she was afraid of the man.

"This Karun tribe has shaman," she whispered.

I followed her glance. Behind the Karun clan, just beyond the fire's brightest reaches, stood an old man with wrinkled flesh covered in glistening black pigment or grease. He wore a darkened mask made from plaster or mud with large white pig's tusks that jutted from the mouth and deep holes drilled for eyes.

The deep pits in his mask seemed to look through me.

For a moment I found myself swallowed by those black holes. I was suddenly so terrified that I couldn't move. It was as if they were sucking me into an abyss of horror deeper than my fear for my own life.

What kind of evil hid behind his eyes I could not know, and I forced myself with great difficulty to avert my stare.

It took me a moment to settle my mind. I had just found some courage. I couldn't afford to lose it so quickly.

Three tribes, three princes, one shaman. I wanted nothing to do with the last.

"Tell them I must know who's the most powerful among the three princes," I said.

"I think this is not good."

And yet I knew most leaders to be brokers of power above all else, and I knew that if my father had found himself in an argument among three powerful men, he would have played them against each other until he saw some weakness to exploit.

"It's the way of my people," I said. "I can only address the most powerful when telling my secrets."

The speaker demanded to know what was going on and Lela gave them an answer. They discussed the matter briefly.

"Did you tell them?" I asked.

"No, miss. I only say that you have very important secrets."

"Why didn't you say what I asked?"

"This is not good. There is much trouble for you."

"Tell them I need to know their names before can I tell them my secrets."

When she told them, the speaker for the Karun tribe objected in the most strenuous terms, spitting on the ground to accentuate his point. When he'd finished, Lela was visibly shaken.

"What did he say?"

"He say you are evil and will use names to speak evil. He say your eyes are the color of the sky where this evil spirits fly."

A somber silence settled over the gathering. Again I had a strange sense that everything I was seeing was a mistake. This could not be happening to me. I was in a world in which talk of spirits and evil trumped all else, and I had firmly planted myself on the wrong side of that world. I silently begged God to save me, though he hadn't paid any attention to my prayers thus far. I felt utterly powerless.

A soft but certain voice spoke to my right. One of the Impirum.

All eyes immediately turned to a man with strong cheekbones and gentle eyes. Well muscled without an ounce of fat. Wide woven bands wrapped around his biceps, his neck, his waist, his thighs, and his calves, each bordered by blue body paint. His headdress was exquisite, fashioned with blue and black feathers that protruded from a beaded yellow band.

But it was the way he looked at me, with a sure yet amused expression, that struck me the most. Here was a man who found me interesting. Perhaps only in the way a cat might find a ping-pong ball interesting, but that was far better than the way a cat finds vermin so.

In that look I found comfort. And I was sure that only a very powerful man could command such respect.

The man looked at the ancient shaman behind the Karun tribe leaders and asked a question. To a man, those gathered stood in perfect silence. After a moment's pause the masked man dipped his head just barely, but enough to make his approval clear.

"This shaman says I will tell you their names," Lela said.

She quickly asked the council something, heard the answer, then told me.

"I will speak. At this time the chief is called Isaka, from the Impirum. This two prince of Isaka blood."

So the leader of them all, this chief, wasn't present.

"They are his sons?"

"Yes, miss, only two Isaka sons. They may be chief."

Princes by blood.

She pointed to one of the Karun leaders opposite me. "This Karun peoples has this prince. He is Butos. Not son." The man she indicated was shorter than the others and laden with beads. He was the Karun prince but not as powerful as the shaman behind him, I guessed.

Lela looked at the man with the scar on his chest, the one who'd captured me. "This prince is Kirutu of this Warik tribe. He is great warrior and kill many, many peoples."

Kirutu, the man who'd taken me captive. I did not let my eyes linger on him.

"This Wilam prince of Impirum." She indicated the man who'd convinced the shaman to let me hear their names. "This son of Isaka."

I began to make sense of the council. The Tulim valley had one chief who had authority over three clans, the Karun, the Warik, and the Impirum. Each clan was controlled by a prince. They were Butos of the Karun clan, Kirutu of the Warik clan, and Wilam of the Impirum clan. Kirutu and Wilam were vying for their father's title.

I doubted my learning this much helped my case, but I had gained a small victory in being heard. So I pushed further.

"And what about the other one?" I asked. "The shaman."

"This spirit man is called Sawim. He is very important leader. You must not look at him."

There it was. What to say next, I had not a clue.

"I will now say this secret, miss," Lela said. And then, before I could stop her, she offered them my secret, whatever that could be. They watched me with new interest.

"What secret?" I whispered, when she had finished.

"That you will make this baby, miss."

Yes. There was that. Seeing no good alternative I went with my advocate's suggestion.

"Tell them that I am the only white woman to enter their valley because white women are rare and made only from good spirits."

She told them and received a harsh rebuke from Butos, one of the three princes.

"This lord say not to think they are fools. They know this white peoples. But this white peoples is not too smart. They die quickly in this jungle."

"But am I not the first white woman in this valley?"

She nodded but asked them anyway. "They say yes."

"Then what they cannot know is that a white woman may be stupid because white women are not made to think, but to make babies. This is good, not evil." I said it only for their sake, naturally.

Lela's translation went on far too long, but it held their rapt attention.

"What is it?" I asked.

She looked up at me, beaming. "I say you have made baby. I know this. You say to me in secret. You will make many babies with this lords."

Butos, prince of the Karun, objected again, spitting with disgust.

"This prince say it is forbidden for this lord to make baby with this ugly animal."

Up until this point I don't think I fully understood that the Tulim really did perceive me as a kind of animal. I wasn't human to them. Furthermore, I was also too ugly to touch.

"I'm not an animal," I said with renewed fear. "Tell him that."

As she translated, I thought it wiser to play into their way of thinking than try to change it.

"I am wam," I said. "Which is more than only animal."

Lela nodded and repeated my claim with pride, because she too was wam.

"And I am proud of it," I said.

Lela translated and I continued.

"Who is the most powerful among you?"

"It is this black one," she said, and I could see the fear in her eyes. They darted toward the shaman.

But the shaman wouldn't be vying for the throne.

"Besides him, which prince is the most powerful? Ask them."

She did, haltingly.

By their sudden stillness I knew that by returning to the issue of power I had struck a chord.

"Who will be the next chief here?"

"I cannot say this, miss."

"Ask them——"

"I am afraid! I must not say this. The one who is strong will be this chief. If he can make babies."

So then, I had stumbled upon the conflict between them. The strongest would take the throne when the current chief died. Among other considerations, children were a sign of strength because producing offspring was difficult.

Lela suddenly hopped up onto the stone table, stood to my height, and pulled open my lips. She showed them my teeth and spoke in excited terms. She turned and beamed at me.

"I tell them you are very healthy, miss. You have made baby and are still young and strong. You must speak only of making this baby."

I resigned myself then to the mere task of survival.

"It's true," I said. "I am very healthy and can make many babies."

Kirutu, prince of the Warik tribe, stepped forward, spoke three words, "*Ti an umandek*," and set two clamshells on the stone.

Lela hopped down, grinning wide. "This lord will take you. You will be saved."

The idea terrified me. "I don't want this lord!"

Lela's smile vanished, replaced by a genuinely frightened look. "No, miss, you must not say this! It is great insult."

Seeing Kirutu's glare, I knew he could not have misunderstood my tone. His eyes darkened.

But I saw something else in his face. Pain. He was wounded. This prince wasn't accustomed to being turned down. He likely couldn't understand why anyone, particularly one as lowly as me, the white wam, would object to the prospect of marrying him. It should be the pinnacle of my existence, a great honor.

Again reason came to my aide. I cast my gaze into the fire. "Tell Kirutu, the great prince of Tulim, that I am overwhelmed with gratitude at his choosing," I said.

Lela quickly told him and listened to his response.

"He says you will suffer most painful death if you lie to this lord."

"Tell him I have not lied."

She did and gave his response, once again smiling. "You will bear him many strong children."

The thought of allowing Kirutu to touch me was deeply repulsive, but I managed to hold the feeling back, thinking that I would agree then and make myself revolting to him later.

"Yes."

The prince Kirutu addressed the others and nodded at the two shells. The clans discussed his offer for a minute, then nodded in agreement, all but Wilam, son of the Impirum chief, who didn't seem interested in the talk of payment.

"This is very good price, miss," Lela informed me.

"He's paying two shells for me?"

"This is this trade. They must pay the chief."

I caught the eye of the prince called Wilam, who studied me with a curious expression that made me wonder what he was thinking.

He spoke without taking his eyes from me, then turned to Kirutu and exchanged several words with the man. I wondered if he was making a bid for me as well.

As one they turned to me. Wilam nodded at Lela. "*Yoru.*"

"This Wilam says you are making them fools," Lela said. "He says you lie to this lords. That you don't want to be with this prince. This is insult. The prince will not force any woman."

Wilam had exposed me, and I felt as though I had no choice but to offer my honesty. "What does he expect from me? To want this? I was taken from the sea by force. I've been bound for three days in a canoe, like a pig. They've thrown me in a hole and hurt me and they expect me to be thankful!"

"This is very dangerous to say, miss," Lela whispered.

"It's the truth."

"I think this lord Wilam does not want the other to have you. Maybe he not like you making this babies with Kirutu. It gives Kirutu power."

"Then tell Wilam to take me."

"No, it cannot be. All must agree."

For the first time the shaman with the mask asked a question, to which Wilam responded. The exchange between them came to an end. Without further delay, each one of the three tribal leaders spoke the same verdict.

"*Kamburak.*"

Nothing about these people met my expectations of the word *savage*. Their ways were not characterized by boiling pots and chanting. This was a calculated affair driven by complexities and cunning. I was only a pawn to be taken or sacrificed in some chess match far beyond my understanding.

Kirutu picked up the shells he'd offered and stepped back. Only then did I see the horrified expression on Lela's face.

She looked up at me, stricken. "This prince Wilam say you cannot live."

I felt my heart stutter.

"They say you must die tomorrow."

CHAPTER EIGHT

THERE in the jungle, I understood fully what it meant to be worthless.

In America good health was a basic human right, and if the family could not bear the cost of extending life, the state would step in to spend millions of dollars on the infirm, all with the hope of adding a day, a week, a month, or a year to a person's life.

And yet in the Tulim valley I was purchased for two clamshells, then rejected and sentenced to death so that one man wouldn't gain an advantage over another.

The council dispersed and two warriors pulled me away from the table. My struggling only made things worse. They gagged and bound me and carried me down the mountain without fear that I would cause them any more trouble. Once again I was only a pig on a pole.

An hour later I was back in the hole.

Only then, after the slapping feet of my carriers had faded, did my mind settle enough to form coherent thoughts.

I hadn't been kidnapped by savages as I'd first assumed. Instead, I had been collected by highly skilled hunters and traders. In their world none of my rights had been violated, because I was wam and therefore had no rights.

Tomorrow I would die.

I lay on the damp earth, breathing into the bag they'd left me in, and slowly drifted into oblivion, wholly defeated.

A soft thump prodded my tired mind. But only a few hours had passed and so I was sure I'd imagined it. They hadn't come for me yet. Tomorrow was still a long way off.

My eyes snapped wide when I felt hands tearing at my bonds. I was instantly awake. It was morning already?

Someone was over me, breathing hard, freeing the knots that bound my hands and feet. The bag was unceremoniously pulled off my head and I turned in time to see the bare outline of someone vanishing over the hole's rim. And then they were gone, leaving me in the earth, my heart pounding like a drum.

They would come back?

But they didn't come back, and after a several minutes I dared to think the impossible: someone had freed me! Who or why I had no basis of understanding, but their actions had been deliberate and they had not returned to collect me.

I saw something else. My blouse, my capris, and my shoes lay beside me in a heap. Everything but my bra. They had known I would need some covering to survive an attempt at escape? My feet needed protection from the jungle floor, and my skin a barrier from sharp branches and leeches.

I ripped off the gag wound about my head. Trembling like a twig I scrambled to my feet, frantically pulled on my pants and blouse, and made an attempt to pull on my shoes. But I staggered off balance and decided they could wait. I had to escape before anyone else came. So I flung the shoes out of the hole and climbed up after them.

The structure's layout slowly emerged by moonlight seeping through an opening roughly thirty paces to my right. I was in a long thatched house with a dirt floor, a prison for slaves or enemies, I guessed.

I ran two steps, made a hasty retreat to collect my shoes, then turned and sprinted toward that faint light, desperate to be free.

"Ta temeh?"

The hoarse voice swirled around me. They were coming! I had to get out! Never mind that I had not the slightest notion of where to go. Never mind that they would only discover my escape and fetch me as if I were but a pet turtle who'd crawled under the table. I only wanted out.

"Ta temeh?"

I was halfway to the opening before it occurred to me that I recognized the gruff voice. It came from the other prisoner. The one who'd spoken English. In my gagged haze, without the means to call out, I'd forgotten about him.

"Hello?" My speech sounded hollow, suppressed by hard breathing.

His call came back, just ahead and to my right. "Hello?"

I hurried to what I now saw as a cell of sorts, made of timbers set in a framework of poles. Twine was knotted around a piece of wood that kept a rough-hewn door shut.

Breathless, I spoke again, in the thinnest voice. "Hello?"

"Who is it?" Even through his whisper I could hear that his accent was American, though not Southern.

"Julian," I managed.

The steady song of cicadas came through the opening ahead. Nothing more.

"Hello?"

"You're an American?" he finally asked.

"I'm from Atlanta," I replied.

The moment still stands in my mind as utterly surreal. There in the deepest unknown jungle I had indeed stumbled upon an American, like myself, and I was so overwhelmed that I could not yet think to set him free.

"Who…who are you?" I asked.

"I'm Michael," he said. "Can you open the door?"

Dropping my shoes, I tugged at the knot with fervor, managed to unwind the twine, and yanked open the door.

There stood a man taller than my five feet and four inches, looking half my width, and I was a small woman. His hair was thin and receded, tangled and sticking out in every direction. A dark beard hung low enough to make me wonder if he'd shaved in the last year.

His nose and cheekbones protruded from a gaunt face covered in days of well-worn dirt. He was dressed in tattered slacks and a filthy shirt that might have blown away in a strong wind.

He stared at me with eyes that looked too large

for their sockets and tentatively offered me a thin hand coated in dried mud. "I'm Michael."

"We have to go!" I said. I knew that I wasn't reasoning properly, but I was so eager to be out of that clammy place that I made no attempt to slow myself down. "They're coming! Hurry."

"You've finally come?" he said. "You're her?"

"Who? No. My boat was wrecked. They found me and forced me here."

"You're an American?"

His eyes twitched in their sockets and I could see that his mind wasn't fully coherent. But the fact that we were both alive and together buoyed my courage and I tugged at his arm.

"We have to get out."

"Where are we going?"

"Out! We have to get back to the coast."

"The coast?" His eyes darted to the opening on his right. "No, we can't. That's not the way it goes."

"The way what goes? We have to! I've been sentenced to death."

"Sentenced?" He lifted his crusty hand and ran his fingers through his hair. It was clear to me that his captivity had affected his mind in a profound way.

"This may be our only chance, we have to try," I said.

But he didn't come. "You don't understand..." He stared at me, eyes searching mine, as if lost in a trance.

For a moment I felt as if I were disconnected from my own body, watching insanity unfold beneath me. I had no context for what was happening to me. I was lost between worlds.

But then the moment passed. I wasn't lost at all—I could see, hear, smell, and feel that much with every cell of my body. I was trapped. A slave against my will, suffering through a horrible tragedy that would surely end in my death.

As was Michael.

Even in my own frenzied state I could see that such a fragile man could be as much of a liability as an asset in any escape. But I also knew that any journey through crocodile-infested swamps would be impossible without help. There was no telling what this man might have learned during his time among the Tulim. He spoke their language, didn't he?

"How long have you been here?" I asked quickly.

"What date is it?"

"August. Nineteen sixty-three."

He stared at me. "They only put me in the hole when they think I'll be a problem."

"You've been free here?"

"No. Yes. Not without a guard. But…" He kept looking at the moonlit opening and now whispered what seemed to be a great secret to him. "I don't think I can leave the valley."

"Why not?"

He tugged at my arm and struck out toward the opening, suddenly and fully alive.

"Hurry!"

I hurried after him as he quickly hobbled toward the exit.

The sounds of the night exploded in my ears as we rushed from the structure they'd imprisoned us in. Tall trees, many meters high, blotted out the stars above and blocked any view of the houses in the main village I knew to be near.

"This way! This way!" Michael ran in a half crouch, back hunched, straight up a jungle path that quickly ascended a hill. I followed on his heels, not daring to say a word. He seemed to know where he was going and I was so relieved to be free of the hole that I didn't think about what lay ahead.

It took us ten minutes to reach the knob of a barren hill that rose above the surrounding canopy. Michael doubled over, hacking, hands on knees.

I was more worried about pursuit than my lungs. He saw me searching the jungle behind us and waved it off.

"We're good." *Pant, pant, cough.* "Trust me, if anyone saw us leave we would be back in the hole by now."

"You're sure?"

"I'm sure." *Cough, cough.* "I'm going to die." *Cough.* "How did you get out?"

"Someone cut me loose," I said. "They brought my clothes and untied my bonds."

"Cut you loose?" He straightened. "They *intentionally* set you free?"

"They must have. Yes, why else would they untie me?"

He stared back at the section of the jungle we'd fled. "Hmm."

"So what do we do now?" I asked, gaining my breath.

He turned to me. "Eh? Not we. *You.* I can't. I'd die before we reached the sea."

I stared down into the dark valley, toward the lowlands. Moonlight glinted off patchwork swamp water miles distant. The screeches of a million creatures daring me to enter the black tangle of jungle sent shivers down my spine. Thoughts of trying to navigate the rivers alone filled me with dread. Surely I stood no better chance than he.

"Are you sure you can't make it out?" I asked. "Whatever the risk, it would be better to die trying to escape than to die here."

He scratched at his head and paced, considering the matter as if tormented by the choice set before him. What was I missing?

He made for a boulder to our right. "Just let me rest a second."

I felt naked on that hill under a bright moon. "Are we safe here?"

"There is no safe place," he said, waving his hand about. "We would have to get to the cliffs and get down to the swamps. Roughly ten miles that way." He pointed westward. "The tidal surge reaches all the way in and reverses the flow of the river currents each day. Hundred miles in places. The alluvial coast makes one heck of a swamp…nothing but mud and mangroves for hundreds of square miles." He was babbling. "I'm not sure if this is one of the Catalina tributaries that eventually meets the lower Balim River, or if we're farther west. I've been trying to figure it out by the stars ever since I got here, but it's near impossible without my glasses."

"Slow down." He was dumping details on me that might be invaluable. "You're speaking too fast. How am I supposed to remember any of this?"

Michael stared at up me. I wrapped my arms around myself and paced in front of him, sure that at any moment the Warik would appear at the clearing's edge. But he didn't seem to share my concern, and I was desperate for more information about where I was, so I pressed him for more.

"Michael? Michael who?"

"Stevenson. I'm an anthropologist."

"How did you get here?"

He spoke quickly. "I was on a trip to collect carvings and skulls. My boat was swamped by a tidal flood. I made it to shore but was stuck in all that mud by the river. They took me."

"Where? Which river where you near?"

"The Eilanden. Along the Casuarina Coast in the Arafura Sea. They had a bag over my head most of the way and I was handed off twice but I'm pretty sure we traveled northwest." He paused. "If you ever make it to the swamps, you'll have to stuff your ears and nose with something when you sleep to keep the bugs out. That's primarily why they use the head bags when they take slaves. When your hands are tied, you can't swat them away."

I knew then that there was no way I was going out alone.

"The rivers are a meandering maze of mud and silt, changing—"

"And I'm supposed to do this alone?" I said. "With cotton in my ears and nose?"

"I can't go," he answered without a missing a

beat, shaking his head. "They would hunt me down."

It was nearly hopeless—he caught in his own fear; I still frantic from my ordeal. So I drew deep breaths and tried to still my hammering heart.

A comment he'd made when he first stumbled out of his cell returned to me and I turned to him. "You asked if I'd finally come. If I was her. What did you mean?"

He studied my eyes, thinking. "I'm not sure. Are you?"

"Am I what?"

"I've been having dreams," he said, voice so very quiet. "I was meant to come. So is she."

Dreams? My mind was filled with the dream that had haunted me in Atlanta. But by now I was so loath to accept its validity that I rejected any serious consideration. If my captivity and Stephen's death were party to that vision, it had come from hell.

And what if that was true? What if I had died on that white sailboat and was now paying for my failure as a daughter? Was God like my earthly father, capable of such torturous abandonment?

I shivered and shifted my stare. I think the final doorway to that dream closed then, with the terrible fear that I had been lured into hell, not figuratively, but literally. I simply could not hold that thought in mind without breaking down.

So I didn't. I blocked it out.

"Whoever she is, it's not me," I said.

Michael gazed at me for a few long moments. "Don't know." He grinned, baring dirty teeth. "Just crazy dreams. I know that I was meant to find Tulim. This is my home now. Somehow my wanton mind calls for a woman." He shrugged. "Not for me. For this valley. Something much bigger than me or you. And I'm not saying it's you or anybody, for that matter. But I've learned some things."

He sounded like he looked—unhooked.

I made a conscious decision then never to regard the absurd dream that had first persuaded me against good judgment to leave Atlanta. The foolishness of my naïveté angered me.

"What have you learned?" I asked.

He nodded, suddenly in his element, and I listened as Michael told me "some things."

He'd been taken captive by the Tulim, a previously unknown tribe who lived a hundred miles inland, just north of the better-known Asmat people whom he was studying. The valley system we were in contained several small peaks within a massive depression bordered on three sides by cliffs, and to the south by a swamp.

He began to speak in more lucid terms now. There seemed to be two parts to his psyche, one that dipped into his academic prowess, and one that had been broken by his imprisonment.

He was well versed in the entire region, having already spent several years traveling all of Irian Jaya. Did I know that all early attempts to make contact with the indigenous people along the south coast had failed miserably? Captain Cook had met with death and disaster when he tried to land in 1770. Even though Dutch missions had been set up along the coast long ago, the inexplicable ways of the Asmat deeper inland were hardly known.

"So then the Tulim are from these Asmat?" I asked.

"No. Heavens, no. Not alike at all. Well, in many ways, yes, I suppose they are similar to an unstudied observer. But the Tulim ancestry is a mixed bag. Influenced by crossbreeding with their slave trade over the centuries, which, to my knowledge, is unique to the Tulim in this part of the world. They are ethnically distinct from other tribes in the region. Taller, darker than the Asmat. Even some of their customs and names have been influenced by far reaches. It's extremely rare. Staggering, actually. Hidden away here north of the Asmat live an undiscovered people that would deliver any anthropologist to heaven."

He coughed.

"But they don't accept change easily," he said. "They reject most notions suggested by the outside. Whether it was the Japanese soldier they took during the Second World War, or a Chinese merchant, they judge most new ideas of advancement as the foolish talk of wam. And frankly, they might be right."

"This is all good, but we need to talk about how to get out."

"Just hear me out, you'll see," he said, lifting his hand to calm me. "You'll see. You need to know what you're up against if you expect to survive. There's nothing but hundreds of square miles of Asmat territory between here and the coast."

I sat and let him continue, though it was clear that the anthropologist in him was more interested in sharing his rare discovery than in discussing an escape he clearly thought was impossible.

While the Asmat were certainly fierce survivors, they lacked the natural resourcefulness that had allowed the Tulim to grow into such a formidable group. The people here were hidden not only from the Western world but from their Asmat neighbors, who consisted of nearly a dozen ethnic subgroups that spoke several languages.

Did I know that there were well over eight hundred distinct languages in New Guinea?

No, I did not. Neither did I care. But he was adamant that I hear him out.

Only a handful of the languages had any alphabet or written form. He was certain that he was the only Westerner who spoke Tulim. Many tribes had lived in complete isolation for centuries, particularly the peoples of the south coast, where the terrain was too forbidding for humans less skilled than the Asmat or the Tulim to navigate.

There were three other factors that kept the Tulim hidden from the world, he said, holding up as many fingers.

The first was that, in addition to the treacherous swamps to the south, the terrain leading into the mountains to the north was as impossible to traverse as the swamps.

Had I seen the documentary *The Sky Above, the Mud Below*, he wanted to know. It was the fascinating and detailed account of a joint Dutch-French attempt to cross this very territory by any means possible. Disastrous. Seven months and numerous deaths later, all but a few of the party were finally airlifted out.

He told me that 80 percent of soldiers involved in campaigns here during the war had perished, not at the hands of the Japanese, but at the hand of the greater enemy, the land itself. Crossing mountains such as these was, as the army engineers had learned, the ultimate nightmare.

The revelation only deepened my anxiety. The man seemed bent on making my case unmistakably certain: I was hopelessly trapped between the mountains that towered against the night sky to my right, and the impassable swamps to my left. I had the distinct feeling he was out to persuade me that I, like him, should just accept my fate here, in the Tulim valley.

He didn't know me. I hadn't been raised in privilege to die so far from home.

But then I saw another reason for his presentation. He was an anthropologist paying homage to the land and those who had conquered it. In some respects these included him, and he found some measure of pride in that fact. He could not hide the wonder in his eyes and the slight curve of his lips as he touted the land's threats.

In some ways Michael was finally giving his report to the only Westerner he believed would ever hear it. This was his opus.

A second factor in the Tulim's isolation, Michael continued, had to do with their animistic beliefs, which demanded they stay hidden from the evil spirits above. It was forbidden to build any structure under an open sky. They lived under the jungle's thick canopy and avoided open spaces.

"Clearings like this?" I asked.

"Oh no, they would never build a path directly through this clearing. They would follow the tree line."

"But the council—"

"You were there?"

"I...my trial, or whatever that was."

"Neutral space," he said, waving it off. "But the court is built under trees, yes? And they only meet at night."

It explained why he wasn't as eager as I to leave this knoll. We were under open sky, hunkered down among the rocks.

"And the third reason?" I asked.

"All these questions drove me crazy, you know. Why these people have remained unknown. You would think they could have been observed from the air, or that the surrounding tribes would spin rumors of their existence. I eventually understood why that couldn't happen. But what surprised me more was that no one had ever escaped this valley and lived to tell."

"No one?"

"No man, woman, or child, once entering the

valley, may leave alive. It's at the heart of their law. They believe they're the only true descendants of the first humans, created here in this valley. Their protection from evil spirits is limited to this valley. The belief is so ingrained that no one dares try, and any who do are quickly hunted down and killed to appease the spirits."

"What about the traders who took me?"

"Ah yes. But you were taken by traders who consumed *tawi* in a ceremony that protects them from certain death if they leave—up to ten days at most. Only Sawim, the old shaman, knows the ingredients taken during a ceremony. And only those among the Warik tribe are allowed to ingest it. It's part of the intricate balance of power among the three tribes that make up the Tulim. So you see, I can't go."

"You're not making any sense. That's only folklore."

"Still, they would hunt me down. I would be dead."

"And so would I if I tried to go alone."

He stared at me, then nodded. "Yes, there is that."

"Then there's no way out for either of us?"

He thought. "No. No, come to think of it, there isn't."

He had surely known that from the beginning. This had just been his own way of making it clear to me.

"So I'm stuck. And I will be killed."

"If they've condemned you, then yes. Although you could try."

"How?"

"You could get into a canoe and hope for the best. Maybe an Asmat party finds you and helps you to the coast. Or they might just take your head."

"That's it? That's your solution?"

"Or you could make an effort to change the council's mind. Why did they condemn you? You're too ugly?"

The events of the trial spun through my mind. "Apparently. But Kirutu, the prince from one of the tribes—"

"The Warik. He's the one who condemned you?"

"No. He made a bid for me. Two clamshells."

Michael looked astonished. "Kirutu did? Then you're saved!"

"No. I think I offended him."

"You *what*?"

"He wanted me to bear him a child."

"But of course! Do you have any idea how valuable children are in this valley? Can you bear children?"

"I have a..."

I caught myself and turned away, doing my best to suppress the horror of my loss. But I could not stem the emotion easily and this wasn't lost on Michael.

"It's OK, my dear," he said in a soft voice that sounded as if it might belong to an angel. "We all have our crosses to bear."

The last comment sparked anger in me, but I knew he meant well.

"Better not to resist it," he said.

This proved too much for me.

"How can you be so insensitive?" I snapped. "My son drowned out there!"

"I feel your loss. And I also know that you've arrived at exactly at the right place at exactly the right time. As have I. Resisting that truth will only cause you to suffer."

"I already *am* suffering!"

"Then you will suffer more."

He was suddenly sounding far too lucid and I wanted none of his stoic philosophy.

"This isn't the right place at any time!" I said, shoving my hand at the jungle. "I'm nothing but an animal here! One of their wam. That may be fine for you, a man who made the choice to investigate these people, but I don't belong here."

"And yet you *are* here. We both are."

I dismissed his childish view outright but held my tongue. How cruel that my only hope for freedom was in the hands of a man who couldn't value my right to it. For a brief moment I think I despised him.

"Well, then," he finally said. "If you can't see the world through their eyes, you will die." His tone had turned matter-of-fact.

"Then why did you agree to help me?" I demanded.

"I *am* helping you. And at great risk, I might add."

"By telling me that my only hope is to accept my fate here? They're going to *kill* me tomorrow!"

"By helping you understand what we have here. Someone freed you, am I correct? You're in a world bound by laws and beliefs that haven't changed for centuries. There's conflict brewing among the tribes that you could use to your advantage. A power struggle could blow this place wide open, and, like it or not, you have some of that power."

"Not if I'm dead."

"Are you? Dead, that is? No. You can worry about being dead when you're dead," he said. "Until then, use the power you have."

"What power? Having a child?"

I meant it as a preposterous suggestion. Michael did not.

"Naturally." He stood and walked a few steps to the right, then back again. "But you can't see it that way, can you? No. And frankly, I'm afraid it might be too late. Changing the council's mind would be impossible. Maybe a month ago, but things are too hot between Wilam and Kirutu. The chief is practically on his deathbed, and one of the princes will take power when he dies. Kirutu has something up his sleeve. He's a very powerful man."

"Now you're throwing in the towel, after setting me straight?"

"You don't seem to want to be set straight," he said.

"I want to live!"

"Then *live!*" he stormed. "Bring life!" The volume of his voice stood me back. Then softer: "Bring life, not death, my dear."

Bring life. His conviction was so great I almost believed him.

The memory of Wilam staring at me with his look of amusement filled my mind.

"It wasn't Kirutu who condemned me," I said. "I think the other prince, Wilam, was behind it."

"The prince of the Impirum," Michael said. "It

makes perfect sense that Wilam wouldn't want his greatest rival, Kirutu, to come into possession of another slave who could bear him children. It's quite a status symbol."

"Having a pregnant slave?"

"Fathering children. The women in the Tulim valley are plagued with infertility, something that is either hereditary or perhaps results from their diet, but without testing there's no way to know. Suffice it to say only one out of three women ever becomes pregnant. Fertile women are highly valued, as you can imagine. I would say it's a wam's only leverage."

The whole thing bothered me to my deepest core. It went against my convictions as much as my desire.

I set my elbows on my knees and lowered my head into my hands.

"You are no longer bound by the laws of a foreign culture, my dear. Bring life into this valley. Love them. After all, I'm sure God does."

"I don't even know who God is anymore."

He sat back down on the boulder and stared at the jungle ahead of us. "Then perhaps you will learn."

What happened next is still rather foggy to me. My mind was split between my loss of Stephen and the last words spoken by Michael. A soft crack sounded in my right ear and I jerked up, startled. Michael slumped over and toppled off the rock.

A bag was slipped over my head from behind; a muzzle over my mouth and nose smothered my cries. In mere moments they jerked my arms back and bound them. Powerful hands plucked me from the rock and threw me over a shoulder. And then they were running.

But not a sound. Not from Michael, who I assumed was either unconscious or dead. And not from the men who had found us on the knoll.

I hadn't been recovered, I thought. If they'd only meant to recover me, they would hardly be running or keeping so silent. Why would they see any need for stealth?

My abductors ran on bare feet that slapped lightly on the muddy earth, perhaps a dozen of them, a small army of men. I had been cut free in my pit. My clothes had been returned to me.

Maybe Michael had been right. Perhaps I was meant to live.

I clung to the thought as their feet pounded through the screaming jungle.

CHAPTER NINE

The warriors who had collected me carried me on their backs for an hour at a steady pace before slowing, ducking into a house, and setting me gently on a seat. Since being taken from the sea, I had been treated as so much cargo, being traded back and forth between houses and pits and trials, and once again I was bound up and dumped into a holding place.

But the differences in my new environment were not lost on me. The jungle had grown quieter as we'd traveled, if only slightly. I thought it might be because there were fewer insects farther from the swamps, assuming we were headed north, toward the mountains that Michael had pointed out. In addition, the room in which they'd dumped me had a crackling fire and a wooden floor. I could make out very soft whispering from my left, but after a while this abated.

I was alive. I hoped Michael was as well. His words whispered through my mind, urging me to live. To live because I was still alive.

I spent most of that night, my fourth in captivity, in a fitful doze with pain in my joints due to my awkward position. When I finally crawled from sleep the sound of children playing outside was the first to reach me.

The faint giggles of three or four children over-running each other with exuberant discussion were incongruous with the dark savagery that had characterized the past few days.

My mind filled with Stephen and my eyes with tears. I was surprised at the severity of my pain as I lay there thinking of my poor child lost at sea. There is no picture so perfect as a sleeping baby after a bottle of warm milk, and I had Stephen's image indelibly etched into my memory. His tiny pouting lips, his long lashes, his soft cheeks and miniature nose. That fine dark hair, floating with the slightest breeze.

The sound of giggling children outside brought it all back, and I began to cry softly. Gone was the hope of life Michael had instilled in me the night before. I found myself both desperate for God and cursing him. For my loss, my predicament, the un-doing of all that I had held sacred. Hadn't the very

God I'd given my life to, in heart and deed, turned his back on me?

A sympathetic female voice called my thoughts back to the hut. "*Aye, at eeniki andi, oh. Aye, aye.*"

The floor creaked as she walked in. She *tsk*ed and repeated her expression, which I took as one of consolation.

The bag was lifted off my head and I saw that I was in a round hut perhaps twenty feet across. Like the one in which I'd first met Kirutu, this too had a bark floor, timber walls bound together with vines, a central fire, and a blackened ceiling. But instead of skulls, there hung from the wall carved wooden masks and tall painted shields etched with intricate patterns. They were spaced evenly, one every few feet all the way around.

Three women had entered the hut. The one who'd muttered her sympathy knelt beside me and repeated herself. Then she wiped the tears from my face, helped me sit up, and quickly untied my bonds, now grumbling on and on about something. Perhaps the way I had been treated, though that might have been wishful thinking on my part.

The other two women stood by the fire, watching with fascination. Like some of the women I'd met earlier, they were young and covered only by woven skirts and woven armbands. Their hair was trimmed short and a yellow band perhaps one inch wide hugged each of their necks.

Their skin was black, not merely chocolate brown, and their teeth were white like their eyes. If they were older than twenty, I was judging them wrong. They held themselves upright with that same unabashed stance that I'd come to associate with the warriors who'd taken me. But they seemed nonthreatening. Even amused.

"*Amok. Amok.*" The woman behind me helped me to my feet. She stepped back and shook her head, *tsk*ing as if to say, *No, no, this just will not do.* She reached out and pulled at my blouse, asking me something. She plucked at my capris and the other two women giggled.

The sight of those women laughing, eyes sparkling as they studied me, struck me as altogether absurd, and suddenly, without warning, I saw some humor in it.

"*Koneh pok!*"

At the order the women immediately swallowed their amusement. A warrior stood at the door, scowling. He motioned at me, barked another order, and ducked back out. The woman who'd untied me shrugged and offered me a sheepish smile.

They guided me out of the hut into the morning sunlight, and it was there that I first laid eyes on a Tulim village. The sight made me stop. I say village, but it was really more of a small town with hundreds of homes that spread out far beyond my line of sight. The whole community was built under the jungle canopy far above us, which allowed streams of light past its leaves which dissipated the tendrils of smoke rising from the roofs. Ahead and to my right lay a large meadow, but there were no structures in the clearing that I could see.

Most of the thatched dwellings were square, not round like the hut I'd been held in overnight, and they were elevated off the forest floor several feet. The ground around each home was built up and flat, forming a kind of grassless yard.

Long wooden pathways built several feet off the forest floor ran between the homes. This, I assumed, was to keep the mud out of the houses. The large spaces between the boardwalks were cultivated. Gardens. I saw that sunlight fell on the leafy vegetables in the gardens but not on the adjacent homes, and I realized that the branches above had been pruned to allow light in only where it was desired.

"*Naouk.*"

I was nudged from behind and moved forward, still taken by the sight.

So then, this was how the natives lived. It was

all muddy and dirty on one level, without the benefit of concrete and green lawns, but surprisingly clean and orderly at the same time. Thatched palm leaves covered each dwelling, and painted carvings were affixed to the outer walls near most doorways, which were covered by rough planks fitted into slots, rather than hinged doors.

We passed several naked children who were squatting just outside a hut in a patch of bright sunlight. Between them sat a black beetle the size of my thumb with a thin string cinched around its body. These were the children I'd heard laughing, now staring up at me with big round eyes.

As I watched, the beetle took flight, circled them at the end of its tether, then settled on one of their heads. The young boy holding the other end of the string did not break his stare. Snot ran from his nose but he seemed not to be bothered by such trivialities.

Everywhere I looked my gaze was returned with curious fixed stares. The people were outfitted with woven bands and sometimes body paint, some with feathers in their hair or tucked into the armbands. The women wore either grass or woven skirts that left their thighs bare all the way up to a rolled cord around their waists. All the men were naked.

The children with the beetle pattered along the wooden path behind us, whispering and arguing. They were soon joined by a few others, then a dozen, all hurrying along, jostling for a better view of me. When I looked at them they fell silent and grinned from ear to ear.

But I was too entrenched in my own predicament to appreciate the children's obvious wonder.

The walkway rose and fell with occasional steps that followed the change in the forest floor's elevation, but coming to a steep rock cliff, it rose up a flight of stairs made from seventy or eighty steps. We left the children behind and I made it halfway up before stopping to rest my burning lungs and aching legs. Once again I was the subject of amusement for the women who escorted me. I guessed they couldn't comprehend how anyone could tire with such little effort.

The moment we stepped onto the upper landing, I thought that we had left one plane and entered another, this one built for royalty.

The manicured cleanliness of this large section of forest reminded me of a botanical garden I'd once visited. The canopy was thinner here, allowing more light to reach the ground than in the village below. A fence of perhaps fifty meters per side surrounded a large round structure in the midst of seven or eight smaller ones. Later I would learn that this was their *Kabalan*—the lords' royal courts. I assumed the central structure to be their palace, although the Tulim's version of a palace, which they called the *Muhanim*, was like none I had seen or imagined.

We passed under a tall archway to which were affixed twenty or thirty human skulls. My escort motioned me through but withdrew as I stepped between two tall men who studied me without expression. It took my eyes only a moment to adjust to the dim light, most of it from a large fire at the center, which revealed a floor covered by thatched mats and walls lined with shields, spears, and bark paintings. Tall round timbers, at least a dozen of them, rose from the floor to beams that supported a pitched roof.

Warriors stood or squatted on either side of the fire, watching me as if interrupted by an unremarkable distraction. I don't know how I had such little effect on the Tulim men in comparison to the women's and children's interest, but not once had they seemed either interested or put off by me.

"Amok."

My eyes darted to the end of the room. There, on a platform holding a large stump surrounded by drums, shields, and hides, sat the man who'd spoken. I recognized him immediately.

This was the prince named Wilam. So I was among the Impirum tribe at the north end of the valley.

Two women sat near him, outwardly unimpressed but unable to hide the curiosity in their eyes. Another knelt in front of the prince with her back to me. I saw the prince's eyes watching me and I felt chilled by his stare. The quiet in the room stretched out. He'd commanded something but no one was moving.

"You must come, miss."

My heart jumped at the sound of Lela's voice as she turned her head. She was the one kneeling.

I hurried forward, pulled by the comforting sound of her voice. All the men and women here were well appointed with golden bands and all of the women wore dyed skirts. The feathers they used were more colorful and the bones on their necklaces whiter than what the villagers wore. But Lela, the young girl from Indonesia, was dressed simply in a grass skirt without any appointments. I could only guess it spoke of her status. As she'd said, she too was wam.

Reaching her side, I didn't know what to do, so I knelt.

Wilam mumbled something, which was returned by soft chuckling from the men behind me. I kept my gaze directed at the woven floor mats.

"You must stand before this prince," Lela said quietly.

"Stand?"

"Yes, miss."

I pushed myself up in front of the platform, which I now saw was made of planks covered in the hides of small foxes. Wilam sat on the large stump, which was topped by the same hides.

He spoke again and Lela quickly stood.

"You must look at this lord," she whispered, looking up.

I lifted my eyes. He was darker than I remembered. Perhaps his color was accentuated by the bright bands on his biceps, forearms, and thighs. The men in the village below were all fit and healthy enough, but the warriors here, led by their prince, looked supremely healthy. But if Wilam was royalty among these savages, he likely had better food.

He leaned forward and rested an elbow on his right knee, studying me with that look of mild amusement. Then he shifted his eyes off of me and lowered them to Lela, who stood still under his long, firm gaze. Long enough to make me wonder whether she was here only to translate.

He demanded something of her. She answered. Another question. Another answer.

They went back and forth for several minutes, he demanding answers, she humbly offering them, until my curiosity could bear it no longer. My fate was at stake, and I was lost in the dark.

"What?" I asked during a pause.

Lela kept her eyes on the prince. But then he nodded and she looked up at me.

"This prince say I must now die with you."

I was aghast. "Why would you have to die?"

"He say it was I who set you free, miss."

"Was it?"

"It is good to take another slave if they escape. This too will give this prince power."

"But did you free me?"

She didn't respond, and I knew she had.

"And what about the man? Michael."

"This Impirum no want that man. He not good for work or for fight."

So Lela had told the warriors from the Impirum that I had broken free and they'd retrieved me, which was evidently allowed under the tribal code.

"Why would Impirum men want me?" I asked.

Her eyes shifted. "To make this babies, miss."

The prince cut in, and they spoke for another minute before Lela turned back to me.

"This prince say I make you free and Kirutu will want blood. But I say you escape and I tell to his fighting man to get you. I say he now has new wam with power to make this babies, and this people will see Kirutu not as strong as this prince."

About the making babies I wasn't sure in the least, but she seemed to have talked some sense into the man and for that I was relieved.

"So then it's good," I said.

"No, miss. He not believe me. This prince say I lie and now I too must die."

Contemptuous. That's what my father sometimes called me as I was growing up. I knew even as heat burned my face that I wasn't in a position to assert myself, but good sense did not redirect me as I turned to the prince.

"It's not her fault," I snapped.

His brow arched. I at least had the satisfaction of gaining his full attention. And I wasn't done.

"She's just trying to save me and give you a good thing. Because of her you look strong, you should be thanking her."

"*Koneh.*"

But I wasn't ready to *koneh*, which I assumed meant "shut up."

"You want babies? I can give you babies."

Lela translated without waiting to be told.

The prince studied me for a few seconds, then began to chuckle. Lela smiled and returned a tentative laugh as I watched. Seeing Wilam so close, I saw that it was muscle, not fat, that covered the sharp edges of his bones. Kirutu was tall and as wiry as a vine tree, but Wilam was as tall and perhaps the stronger man.

He said something and Lela's smile faded.

"What did he say?"

"He say that I am very clever and you are wild cassowary."

"Is that good?"

"Yes, miss. But it does not change his mind. He say because I have tricked him, and you have tried to tempt him, he will give us to Kirutu when this man come."

"Then he is an idiot," I said.

She repeated the word slowly, with an odd pronunciation. "Idi-out?"

"He's a fool."

Her round eyes questioned me. "I will not say this. I tell him what this Kirutu cannot hold, Wilam can master. This people will see he is very strong chief."

"And?"

"He say he cannot master cassowary who will peck out his eyes when he is sleeping."

"So he will just turn us over?"

"I think he is afraid of you, miss," she whispered.

I wanted to ask if Wilam knew of Michael's condition, but the situation didn't warrant the question.

The prince demanded something of her and she answered quickly.

Wilam stood up and spat to one side. Amusement was gone from his face. He issued a verdict that sounded ugly, spat once more, then strode from the house.

"What did he say?"

Lela stared up at me and for the first time I saw real fear in her eyes. "I tell him you must be so happy to make many nice babies with him. But he will not make this babies with you. Now this Kirutu will come with many fighting man and he will take us."

CHAPTER TEN

Lela and I spent the rest of the day bound on opposite sides of the hut they'd first held me in, but it wasn't until darkness approached and she began to cry that I fully appreciated what she had attempted to do for me.

I tried to talk to her, but she informed me that she'd been ordered not to speak.

A single lean guard with several pronounced scars on his chest and a single rattan band around his waist milled about the hut watching me with curious eyes as he carved the shaft of a spear. I was beginning to see the divisions among the savages' classes, primarily in the sophistication of their dress. There also seemed to be distinctions in the ways they groomed themselves. Wilam, for example, took meticulous care of himself, while my guard, who was plain, had grimy fingernails and unruly facial hair. Nevertheless he looked as healthy as a tiger.

At one point the guard withdrew a bundle of palm leaves from a platform above the smoldering fire and peeled back the layers to reveal a white paste that reminded me of plaster of paris. He apportioned the paste onto two leaves and set them on the coals. When the food was baked, he set one portion before Lela and untied her hands so that she could eat, before approaching me with the second portion. Rather than untying me, he squatted before me and brought the food to my mouth with a dirty hand.

They'd fed me their disgusting paste on the river, but when it was cooked its smell wasn't terribly different from that of toasted flat bread. Still, I was unsure.

The guard grinned wide, showing stained teeth, two of which were broken. He cackled and looked back at Lela. She glanced between the guard and me, then nodded at the food.

"This is sago, miss. You must eat this food."

The man pushed the baked sago close to my mouth and muttered something that brought forth another cackle. I let him push it between my teeth and took a tentative bite. It tasted like half-baked bread.

The guard fed me the rest with some pleasure, as if he were feeding a new baby pet. Then he retrieved his own food from the platform—several strips of meat, which he enjoyed eating while watching me, wearing that same jagged smile. I was struck by his relatively charitable disposition.

When I told Lela I had to use the bathroom she informed the guard, who snapped at her, perhaps for speaking, because he surely couldn't blame me for needing to do what even animals must do. I wondered if he expected me to urinate on the reed floor, but after staring at me for a while he motioned for me to stand. He then led me through the doorway.

The moment I stepped into the bright sunlight, a cry went up and no fewer than twenty children of all ages descended on the hut, whooping and hollering with glee. The guard tried to shoo them away with flailing arms and angry shouts, but the children's enthusiasm wasn't tempered until several other adults joined in the guard's rebuke.

He led me down the boardwalk, then out into the forest, as the swelling crowd of children followed curiously at a distance of no more than fifteen paces. The thought that I would have no privacy superseded the horror of my impending fate.

Rather than send them away, the guard led them with square shoulders, as if enjoying his position as the caretaker of such a popular oddity.

I was struck by the sight of one young girl who carried a piglet. The baby pig had dried mud on its snout and grunted, but otherwise seemed content to rest in her arms like a pet. I had been hauled through the jungle like a condemned pig, surely worth less to my captors than this animal. And yet even a pig could be treasured, could it not?

When we reached a dense patch of underbrush, the guard motioned to the bushes and said something that I took to mean, "There you go, do your business there."

I looked back at the flock of naked children watching my every move with wide eyes.

"You expect me to go in there? With all of them watching?"

He turned on the children and began to yell at them, then scooped up small sticks and hurled them in their direction. The children dodged the missiles and retreated a few yards.

Evidently satisfied, the guard grinned and motioned for me to go on. But I couldn't seem to make my legs move. Not only was the audience completely unacceptable to me, the thought of wading into the brush where spiders and snakes had surely gathered proved too much for me. I lost the urge to relieve myself.

After a bit of an argument during which I tried to express my desire to be returned to the hut, my guard reluctantly led me back, this time with- out issuing any order for the children to stay back. They hovered like a swarm of buzzing bees.

Within half an hour my bladder was painfully complaining. It's interesting how attitudes change when one is confronted with stark choices. Tor- tured as I was by my body, I began to accept the fact that nakedness was not an issue in the jungle.

Once again I told Lela that I had to urinate.

She looked confused. "You did not do this, miss?"

The guard, who had settled back into whittling, tried to shut her up but she told him anyway. Hear- ing this he stood and spit to one side, then let loose with a tirade that must have clearly expressed his displeasure at having to take me out yet again.

Nevertheless he did take me out. Once again the children cried out with excitement and swarmed us. Once again he chased them back to a safe dis- tance. Once again we all marched out to the bush, but this time, when we arrived at the selected spot, my guard picked up a long stick and ran at the children, beating the trees in a ruckus, yelling his threats in no uncertain terms. The children fled.

I pulled my pants down and quickly relieved myself while they were fully engaged, not bothering to climb deeper into the underbrush where the snakes waited.

When the guard returned I was already pulling my pants up. He took one look at the ground, then up at me, and muttered what could have been a scolding for not following his instructions. I wondered if I had somehow desecrated a part of the forest floor that was not made for soiling.

We marched back to the hut, I, my guard, and the children, who had returned in full force and were chattering with even more excitement.

Two warriors with set jaws and wearing golden bands came for Lela and me near dark. Our heads were bagged, and we were pulled to our feet and wordlessly guided out of the hut.

They walked us along the boardwalks, then out onto a grassy field and up a slope. The numbness that had settled over me was replaced by a terrible sorrow. Images of Stephen cooing in my arms as he groped for my face flooded my eyes with tears.

I was being marched to my execution, that much was painfully certain, and my basic need to survive raged through me. Where this instinct had failed to prick my deadened nerves for most of the day, it now raked them with a vengeance.

I and the girl breathing beside me were stopped on a patch of barren earth. The bag over my head was pulled off and I found myself staring at the side of a hill. If there was grass on the hill, I could not see it, because a sea of dark bodies covered it.

We stood under a tree that stretched out its ancient limbs like a mother eagle sheltering her young. Beyond the tree stood two slopes. The hill on our left was filled with several thousand natives seated behind three or four hundred squatting warriors, each armed with spears, shields, or tall bows.

Another armed group had gathered on the opposite slope, standing, and I saw immediately that these "fighting men," as Lela had called them, belonged to Kirutu because he stood before them, not fifteen paces from me.

There was no sign of Wilam, only several of his guards, now standing near the mat.

All eyes watched me. Only some of the Impirum children who were jumping around and somersaulting at the top of the knoll were distracted. Otherwise I was the sole focus of the valley.

A call went out over the valley, delivered by a man whose face and chest were covered in ash, running back and forth in front of the Impirum warriors. He stopped and began to hop up and down as if he were on a pogo stick, crying out, "*Wege, wege, wege!*"

As one the Impirum stood. I followed their stares to my left. Wilam had arrived.

He was flanked by four armed warriors who, like Wilam, wore feathered headdresses and were heavily appointed with golden bands. Mud or paint colored their jaws and brows in wide swaths of red and white. I felt hands on my shoulders, pushing me to my knees next to Lela, who was trembling.

Wilam stopped opposite Kirutu without giving us a glance. He gestured with two fingers down by his side and the Impirum on the hill all squatted, followed by the Warik warriors when Kirutu nodded once. Only the guards remained standing next to the two princes, who had come to conduct their business.

What was spoken next I later gathered from a nearly hysterical Lela. Though I can't be certain as to the exact words chosen for the exchange between Wilam and Kirutu, I am confident that what follows captures its full essence.

"You have what is mine," Kirutu said, eyes steady on his adversary. Wilam was the only threat to his taking power when the current chief, Isaka, passed.

Wilam seemed cordial enough. "So you have

said." He looked at the Warik leader's warriors on the hill beyond Kirutu. "And yet I see no trade. What have you brought me?"

Kirutu didn't immediately respond. The air changed with Wilam's demand for payment. My and Lela's lives were at stake, but these two were negotiating for their own power, like two challenging lions.

"There is no trade for what is already mine," Kirutu said evenly. I saw the tension in his taut belly muscles, marred by that single scar running up to his chest.

"How can something not in your grasp be yours?" Wilam asked. "How did this wam come to me if she was in your hands?"

"You took her by force," Kirutu snapped, spitting on the ground.

"And which of my warriors used this force to kill your guards?"

"Your little pig cut the woman free."

Wilam looked at Lela, eyebrow raised. "You expect me to believe that a young girl fooled your guard and plucked this wam from your grasp? My warriors found the white wam free, on the hill with that old white fool you keep."

"That old fool is dead."

"And the white woman is not."

The skilled politician in Wilam had already backed Kirutu into a corner. If the Warik prince admitted that Lela had foiled him, he would look weak before the people. But Kirutu was no less practiced in the ways of power.

A cynical smile twisted Kirutu's lips and he stepped toward the people and addressed the entire gathering. "So now Wilam will play games with his words to make me look weak before you all. The matter is simple. I found this white woman in the sea four days ago. It is said that some white wam are as fertile as mice. So I took her."

They watched the Warik leader lay out his case.

"But white wam are forbidden without the full consent of the council. So I took this one before Wilam and Butos, and it was Wilam who rejected my payment to the great Isaka. It was he who condemned her."

His voice was steady, with little emotion. This was not a man easily ruffled or compelled to impress.

"Naturally I agreed. Wilam was right. Bringing this ugly wam to the Tulim was wasted effort. I agreed to put her to death on the cliff, as required by our laws."

Four hundred Impirum warriors stood as one, glares fixed on the Warik warriors. I was certain then that I was to be caught between two armies in full battle.

Kirutu faced Wilam. "The law requires that what you take without permission must be returned with payment," he said. "I have come to collect what is mine. The men who guarded this wam have been put to death. What more trade do you require?"

"Ten boars," Wilam said.

A murmur went through the crowd. The question had been rhetorical, but Wilam hadn't even hesitated to state his price.

Kirutu grinned. "Ten boars? For two wam whose heads will be smashed within the hour?"

"Nevertheless, I will have ten boars for the trouble to my men. Let this be a lesson to you. Keep what is yours close and do not blame me if you lose it."

"The girl took what was mine."

"Then all Tulim know how weak your guard is. Give me ten boars and you may take them both to kill before sunset."

The entire hill had stilled once again. Somewhere a baby cried and was immediately quieted. Beside me Lela gawked at Kirutu, whose grin had softened.

The Warik leader slowly raked his piercing glare over the tribes awaiting his decision. His was the look of someone resolved to take what was his. It was a beginning, not an ending. Surely it took Kirutu's full strength to restrain himself, knowing that he'd been outwitted not merely by Wilam but by Lela, the runt wam who'd sneaked past his guards to set me free.

Kirutu's eyes settled on Wilam. "Then I will play your game, son of Isaka. You would do well to remember that his blood is no thinner in my veins. You may make your play for this floating fish I found in the sea, but the council has judged." He spat the last word. "She must die."

"You will not pay ten boars for my troubles?"

"No more than I would pay ten boars for a fly."

Wilam stared at his adversary. "Then I will take these flies you cannot hold as payment enough."

"You will kill them as agreed."

Wilam dipped his head. "As I see fit."

A cry went up from the back of the Impirum tribe, not one of objection or agreement, but one of abject fear. As one they all turned and looked up the hill.

There on the crest a hundred yards away stood a man with furs about his waist and ankles, leaning on a spear. I could see immediately that the man was from a different stock than any I'd seen in the Tulim valley.

They stared up at him in gripping silence, as one might stare at God himself if he suddenly appeared. I felt a chill wash down my spine, more from their reaction to him than from the man's appearance.

For several long seconds no one moved.

"Leave us!" Wilam snapped.

Immediately the gathered tribes, both Warik and Impirum, began to scatter toward the cover of the trees. They ran without a cry, like a thousand spooked horses.

I watched in amazement as the hills emptied, leaving only Kirutu, Wilam, and four guards each alone with Lela and me. Both of the princes had their eyes fixed on the crest.

When I looked back up, the man was walking toward us with even strides, spear held lightly in his hand. No other weapons, no body paint or adornments, just that one spear made of wood and bone.

The air seemed to still. Even the birdcalls stopped. I couldn't know whether the princes saw the man as a threat or whether this was Isaka, their chief, but there could be no doubt that he commanded a respect they dared not challenge.

The man walked toward us in no hurry, eyes not on the two princes but on me. My heart hammered and I found myself wondering if he'd come to execute me.

But as he drew within ten paces, I saw that he didn't have the eyes of a killer. His were a deep brown and brimming with mystery. I found myself immediately put at ease.

When I looked up at Wilam and Kirutu, my hope surged. They were clearly uncomfortable. Which meant the stranger held some power over them, and any man with such an understanding gaze might be a benefactor.

Beside me Lela was trembling. Not Isaka, then, I thought. She'd spoken of the chief with pride, not fear.

The man stopped five feet from me and for a minute he searched my eyes. He shifted his gaze first to Wilam and then to Kirutu.

He stepped up to the prince of the Warik. Slowly lifted his right hand and laid his fingers on the man's scar. He slid his hand up, tracing the scar, *tsk*ing softly.

His back was to me so I couldn't see his face, but I watched Kirutu's reaction. Saw the bitterness in his dark eyes. The trembling in his fingers.

The man's hand left Kirutu's chest and rose to his face. Followed the lines of the prince's cheek to the back of his head. The stranger's strong hands gripped Kirutu's neck and pulled his head forward so that they were cheek to cheek.

He whispered something into Kirutu's ear and I watched the prince's face quiver as if he was resisting and terrified at once.

The man slowly drew back from Kirutu, gave him a barely perceptible nod, and, without ceremony, turned from us and walked back the way he'd come, in no hurry.

I watched him go, stunned by the strange exchange, struck by how little I understood of what was happening in this mysterious dark valley.

Only then did I see the silhouette of a lone figure behind Kirutu on the slope. I couldn't mistake the man coated in black. The shaman I'd seen at the council, Sawim. The one who'd struck such fear into my soul.

Two shamans? If so, they were not of the same character.

The black one, Lela had called him.

The fur-clothed stranger paid him no mind. He simply walked away as if he had no care in the world.

When I looked back to where Sawim stood, he'd already turned and was walking away, beyond the hill's crest.

Michael had said there was a war brewing in the

valley, but it was a contest for more than Isaka's throne, I thought. There was a deeper struggle at hand—one that stirred the same unspoken cry to God that I had been uttering since waking in the bottom of that canoe.

Save me. Please, I beg you. Save me!

A cry that he had not yet heard. If he was even listening.

"So be it," Kirutu said.

He turned his back on us and walked south with his guards.

"So be it," Wilam said. He nodded at his guards and headed west, toward the Impirum village.

Two of the men who'd remained by his side hauled Lela and me to our feet. Shoved us down the path.

"Who was that?" I asked, hurrying to keep pace. "What's happening?"

"This Kugi," she said. "Evil spirit man."

"A shaman?"

"More maybe."

But her face was lit with hope.

"We're free?" I asked, hurrying to keep pace.

"No, miss," Lela said. "This Wilam our master now. But we not die, I think."

I prayed that she was right. That whereas Kirutu had not been able to hold me captive, Wilam would now show the whole valley that he could.

He'd kept me to spite Kirutu publicly. Kirutu had just as publicly called for my death. What this Kugi had said to Kirutu, I didn't know, but I wouldn't argue with the outcome.

A new hope swept through my mind.

And then I remembered where I was.

I remembered the people I was with—the nakedness of their bodies, the savagery of their ways.

I remembered that I was still in hell, and my heart sank.

CHAPTER ELEVEN

I LEARNED that night who the stranger was, and my confusion deepened. Not because of what Lela shared with me, but because of what she didn't.

They called him *Kugi Meli*, which means "evil spirit," a name they gave to many things of a spiritual nature, I learned. The man had appeared from the mountains two years earlier and walked into the chief's hut without being seen by the guard. He'd told Isaka that he would be dead in less than three years' time. The valley would embrace a new king who would tear down all that was sacred. And then he'd left.

Filled with fear, the Tulim had immediately set out to kill him, but the man had proven impossible to track down. Why? Because he was an evil spirit—there was no other explanation.

Word spread that killing the man would anger

the evil spirits. The man was untouchable. No one knew where he lived or came from. After that he was seen every few moons, usually at a distance, watching. Then vanishing. Like a ghost.

"What about the shaman?" I asked.

"Sawim," she whispered. It was clear that she wasn't comfortable speaking of these matters.

"Is Sawim evil as well?"

She grabbed my arm, eyes wide. "No, miss! You must not say this evil!"

"They are enemies?"

"This is not for me to say. These prince very afraid of both."

It was all she offered me. Neither of us had any idea what words the stranger had spoken to shift Kirutu's position, convincing him to leave me with Wilam, unharmed.

I set aside my attempt to understand their myths. Of more importance was my new status among the Tulim.

I was to be a free woman.

Truly my guard—Momos, the same lanky man who'd watched over me earlier—was only there to ensure my safety, knowing that I was at risk of being taken captive by any of Kirutu's more ambitious warriors. The Impirum placed no restrictions on where I might go or whom I might talk to, excepting their Kabalan, which was reserved strictly for the *muhan*, or lords, as Lela called the class connected to the chief and his bloodline.

But when I was set free to live among the Tulim, the reality of my situation rose up and swallowed me whole. My eyes were opened to the terrifying prospect of actually living among them.

It began that first night of freedom, when Lela took me by the hand and excitedly led me to her hut. "Come see, you live with me!" As darkness claimed the jungle, we wound our way to the south side where the lowest and poorest lived.

I could understand Lela's excitement as she stepped into her home—she was proud of her dwelling, and even prouder to have proven so useful to me and her prince. But when I stood up in the hut I saw only darkness. The fire was out, the air smelled like smoke and mildewed dishrags, and I felt desperately alone.

Lela was already on her knees, bending over the fire pit, blowing at the coals still smoldering there. With a few splinters and some dried bark she coaxed up flame, then heaped up some wood.

"We are very good, miss! It is very special."

I stood by the door, at a loss, consumed by a simple question that had not presented itself to me until that moment.

Now what?

Enslaved in a hut awaiting execution was one thing, but living freely in a smoky hut with only straw for a floor and charred poles with cracks for walls...

It was not me.

The food wasn't me. The stench wasn't me. The dress, the language, the insects, the snake-infested bushes calling to my bladder...none of these were even remotely me.

I can't adequately describe the hollowness I felt as I stood there watching Lela. I can still see it all: the rough-hewn poles, the mounds of ash in the fire pit, the bare ground showing beneath the straw, the dirty sparseness of the hut. I should have been grateful for the incredible risk she had taken in saving me.

I should have hugged her and danced around the fire in celebration. But all I wanted to do was curl up in a gunnysack and let sleep shut down my mind.

The only reprieve from my misery was Lela's announcement that I was forbidden to have contact with any man but Wilam, and then only if and when he called.

My memory of the next week among the Impirum tribe of the Tulim is still somewhat clouded.

I managed to survive, but my mind was under a savage and alien sea, struggling to rise out of deep hopelessness, thinking always that there had to be a way home but knowing all the while that there was not. The strange sights and sounds pummeled me into a kind of oblivion that left me too stupid to think properly and too numb to cry. I slowly began to shed the layers of my own identity.

I was terrified of going outside where every eye would turn to me, but I had no choice when needing to relieve myself. I cannot tell you how disagreeable each experience proved to be. Lela suggested that I bathe in the nearby creek, and I needed to wash, but after trudging down to that creek I took one look at the muddy, infested water and demanded we go back to the hut. The children who'd discovered us leaving the village found my behavior amusing. I only found it mortifying.

The village was relatively clean, in part because of the Tulim's pervasive boardwalks built among their small garden plots. When the pigs outgrew their place as pets, they were tied up in small corrals outside the village. Still, there is no way to keep pigs clean. Their nature is to root in soft soil and mud. The children treated them like babies and the adults chased them from the gardens with sticks.

I could not eat anything but plain sago cakes

and the vegetables from their gardens, which consisted mostly of squash. Lela preferred sago mixed with meats, but the moment I saw the makeup of their protein, I blanched. She took great pleasure in making a meal with cooked sago worms, baked insects, cooked lizards, snakes, rodents of all kinds—anything that squirmed, crawled or flew, none of which seemed remotely edible to me.

No more was said of the stranger, this evil spirit who'd apparently facilitated our release.

I spent most of the days thinking of Stephen and my home in Georgia. Strange thoughts crisscrossed my mind, daydreams of the simplest pleasures. What I would have done for one glass of milk or one bite of an oatmeal cookie. How far I would have walked for one pair of clean underwear. In those dreams I would be a queen and Stephen would be at my side. Our servants would bring us a tray of cookies and milk, and we would relish each bite as the court watched. Then we would throw a party with milk and cookies for all.

At night I listened to the distant sound of chanting as the natives beat on hollowed carvings skinned with crocodile hide. Then Lela would lie beside me in the dark and stroke my long hair, telling me not to be afraid because it would all be nice. Soon we would both make babies.

But I had a hard enough time getting used to their nakedness, much less any thought of making babies. Even after living among so many men bared for all to see, I found the sight unnatural.

It all amounted to me staying in the hut, alone. More than once I dreamed of wandering out into the jungle at night, knowing that I wouldn't last until morning. Perhaps I was better off dead.

My entire existence was consumed with only *I*. I this, I that, I the other. Not once did I truly think of *them*. In the world of I, they hardly existed except as savages who were hardly human. I was wam to them and they were all wam to me. The only exception was Lela, but she was only a teenager who couldn't possibly understand my world. Truly I was awash in self-pity.

And then, a little more than a week after I was put under the protection of Wilam, my world began to change.

I had taken to sleeping late and Lela usually let me sleep, using a stick to ward off any curious onlookers who might want to poke their heads in and take a look at the white wam. She'd become a woman of status in her own right, being the keeper of me, a position she held with great pride and delight despite having to put up with my melancholy.

On this morning, however, she shook me awake,

chattering excitedly about bathing in the river. Not just any river, but the Konda, which fed into the Tulim valley two miles upstream. Lela had received permission from Wilam to take me so that I could bathe.

"Bathe?"

"You must go to clean water and make this smell goes away."

I sat up, horrified. "Smell?"

"The people say this smell, miss." She indicated my clothes.

I sniffed at my underarm. Musty, yes, but not half as smelly as the Tulim, at least from my perspective. But what about from their perspective?

I held out my arm. "I smell?"

Lela took a polite whiff and covered her small nose. "This skin very bad smell, miss."

"Just today or always?"

"Always, this white skin very smelly. You must clean."

I had not thought about what the world looked or smelled or tasted like from the Tulim's perspective. But the very idea that I was walking around smelling like a cesspool was enough to offend my sensibilities even in my state of despondency.

Their distaste of me extended to the color of my skin. And my long straight hair. And the fact that

I wore dirty clothes. And my strange language. In Georgia I was considered a beautiful woman; in that jungle I was hardly more than a pig.

Unless I could give them a child.

"Is it safe?"

"It is very safe, miss."

Half an hour later we were making our way through the village with Momos, my lanky, broken-toothed guard.

At first sight of me, the children came running, whooping and hollering their delight. *The wam is coming, the wam is coming!* By the time we skirted the grassy slopes with the lone tree under which Lela and I had been set free, no fewer than twenty children were in tow. I tried to tell Lela to send them back, knowing that they wouldn't be bashful about watching me bathe, but she only shrugged.

"No, miss. This children not go away."

Momos stayed at my right heel, also ignoring the children. I looked back at him and he offered me a crooked grin. Despite his earlier frustration over my refusal to urinate as instructed, Momos seemed somewhat enchanted with his charge.

We walked on like that, Lela and I abreast, with Momos a step behind to my right, followed by twenty chattering children who hushed and smiled wide the moment I glanced back.

A flock of white cockatoos took flight overhead, eliciting a few cries of delight from several of the children, who mimicked their calls with remarkable precision. Others chimed in with lower calls and within seconds, like a pipe organ, they were performing an ethereal yet melodic tune in perfect harmony.

When I looked back, I saw that the girl who led them with her high-pitched call was hardly more than three feet tall, idly dragging a thin branch behind her as she hooted with pursed lips.

The moment she saw that I was watching her, she broke off her birdcall and offered me a face-splitting, toothless smile. I could not look at such an innocent vision and not return a simple smile.

When I turned and trudged on up the path, the children broke out in a chorus of excited voices. Clearly my smile had made an impression.

"What do they say?" I asked.

"They like this teeth, miss," Lela said. "This children like you very much."

Then Lela did something that took me off guard. She placed her hand in mine and we walked hand in hand. Something deep in my spirit began to break, but I could not recognize it, not yet.

The sound of so many feet pattering behind me on the hard-packed path still resonates to this day.

Birds were calling above us, reptiles and small creatures rustled in the brush on either side, and here I was, walking down the middle of it all like the pied piper, leading a band of dark-skinned children.

For several minutes I walked with Lela's hand in mine, unsure why her simple gesture stirred up so much emotion.

Then I felt small fingers slide into my left hand, and I looked down to see that the child with the pure, high voice had caught up and followed Lela's example. She grinned up at me, barely able to contain her joy at my acceptance of her.

"Yuliwam," she said.

Yuliwam. It took me only a moment to hear my name. Julian had become Yuliwam.

The little girl said my name again, beaming. "Yuliwam."

I nodded. "Yuliwam." The fact that *wam* was in my name mattered not to me.

I walked on, holding her hand tightly, aware that the small girl was looking back at her siblings and friends, glowing with pride. My world started to cave in on me as I walked. Where I was seen by the adults as an ugly wam, I was the object of fascination and pride among the children.

We've all seen the pictures of children making

mud pies in the middle of a concentration camp, oblivious to the terrible suffering around them.

In that moment the Tulim children became, to me, the same picture of innocence in the midst of savagery. I walked for a hundred yards, treasuring both hands in my own, when it suddenly all became too much.

I remember the moment clearly. We had just come to the edge of a clearing that Momos insisted we skirt, but I couldn't think to turn right or left. My heart was breaking.

I glanced down at the little songbird who beamed up at me with big brown eyes and rounded cheeks, and I began to sob. My grief and regret and desperation settled over me and I sank to my knees under their weight. I threw my arms around the child and clung to her tightly, surely terrifying her, although I can't be sure because I could not stop sobbing long enough to look.

There for the first time I pressed innocent Tulim flesh against my own as if it were my own, because in that moment the little girl became living, breathing hope to me. For a long time I wept on my knees, and none of them—not Lela, not Momos, not the children—made any attempt to discourage me. They stood still, silent, watching.

If I had not broken down, and they had not gone

so silent, they might not have heard the drone of an aircraft flying far above us. I certainly wouldn't have, crying or not. My ears were not trained to hear such a distant, abstract sounds.

There was a mumble of questions and then a cry of alarm: *Woruru, woruru, woruru!* The children scattered back into the forest, led by Momos, who was running and yelling at Lela to bring me.

I jumped to my feet, spinning around, fearing an ambush. "What?"

"Hurry, miss! This woruru evil spirit!"

The airplane's distant drone reached me then, a faint sound similar to their name for this evil spirit in the sky. *Worurururururu...*

The little girl beside me was now crying, frightened by the others' panic. I swept her up in my arms and fled back into the jungle, half-convinced myself that I must not let the giant metal demon in the sky see me.

Even as I did, another thought occurred to me. Were they looking for me? I should make a scene! But as soon as I thought it, I realized that the plane was far too high to see a human on the ground.

When the danger had passed, Momos and the children returned with glee, sure of having avoided a close call with certain death from the sky. It was no wonder the Tulim had never been identified from the air as a unique indigenous group.

Five minutes later we were past the clearing. Once again I walked with Lela. Once again the little girl hurried along beside me, hand snuggled in my own.

"*Yellina! An Yellina!*" she announced to me, smiling wide. *Yellina, I'm Yellina!*

She was the vision of a treasure.

"Hi, Yellina."

She pointed to me with a tiny finger.

"*Yuliwam! Kat Yuliwam!*" *Your name is Yuliwam.* And so it was.

For the first time since being taken captive, I felt truly human.

CHAPTER TWELVE

BATHING AT the river with the children that day washed me of more darkness in one sitting than I knew was possible—so much that I came to think of it as a kind of baptism. My newfound freedom taught me many things, both about myself and about how the Tulim saw the world.

I learned how effective body language can be in bridging language barriers, particularly the use of hands.

I learned how absurd my clothing appeared to their eyes. Was I an animal that needed a coat to hide my flesh? I saw how proud Momos was to have charge over me, directing orders at the children with far more bark than bite. Seeing me naked had absolutely no effect on him. He might have seen my hand and been as impacted.

I learned that the evil spirits that live in crocodiles are also known to hide in the deepest parts of swimming holes and pools.

I learned that the Tulim use soft fuzzy leaves from the *mbago* plant, the jungle's version of soap, to wash their bodies. I learned that a fibrous stalk with a biting, minty taste, called *rapina*, cleaned teeth quite effectively when rubbed vigorously over the enamel.

I learned that there were two ways to rid the body of unwanted hair—a requirement for cleanliness among all Tulim. You could either pluck your hairs one by one, a decidedly painful prospect, or you could use a sharpened piece of bamboo, nearly as painful.

I learned from Lela that when Tulim women had their menstrual period, they used rolls of tightly bound moss. And here I had thought Procter & Gamble had invented tampons.

I learned that in a far part of the jungle there existed tiny men no taller than a finger who lived in small, square logs. This they knew with certainty, having heard them firsthand. Lela knew the name of this square log.

It was called *radio*.

I learned that the Tulim love color, especially when applied to the body. Indeed, the body makes a better canvas than any flat object, because it lives and breathes, they explained.

But mostly I learned that there are bonds tying all human beings together in ways we cannot fully understand, and those bonds are never more obvious than between children. For those few hours I spent with the children, I became one myself, stripped of my misery and my sense of self-importance.

In the weeks and months following my baptism in that river's pool, I gradually came to accept the fact that, although I could never thrive with the Tulim, I could survive.

I had new friends among the Tulim now. The children, who were more taken with my novelty than my ugliness. The little girl Yellina, who was an orphan. She lived in a hut on the far side of the village. Whenever I emerged from my hut she was nearby, and always one of the first to run over to place her small hand in mine.

Without any particular intention on my part, I gradually began to learn how to live among the Tulim, at least from my perspective. From theirs I'm sure that I looked the complete buffoon.

I could not dress like them. That would be too much. The closest I could bring myself to nakedness was to cut the legs off my capris and crop my sleeveless blouse to deal with the heat. Along with my canvas shoes and underwear, they were my only clothes, and I had to wash them every other day. There was positively no way to keep the soot from the fires from blackening them.

I did not eat using all of my fingers as they did, but picked at my food using only one finger and my thumb, afraid I might inadvertently consume some live creature like an ant; some piece of ash that might have drifted onto the food; some sliver or dirt that might have fallen from the ceiling.

I did not walk about barefoot or scamper through the underbrush as did the children, but chose each placement of my feet cautiously, like a soldier stepping his way through a minefield.

I butchered their language, rarely managing to deliver a full sentence without granting the children some amusement. Heaven only knows what kind of lewd or ridiculous statements came out of my mouth those first weeks. But as the months passed I learned, more each day.

I was too far removed from their customs to understand or engage in any of their ceremonies or dances, which seemed to be the central focus of their passion once the sun set.

Apart from their politics, which I knew little about, and their animism, which I knew even less about, the Tulim way of life was profoundly simple. They collected, prepared, and ate food; they fashioned and maintained their dwellings; they slept; they danced and sang; they warded off evil spirits; they obsessed over babies, and they talked ceaselessly about all of the above.

But in these ways, wasn't their life similar to the life of the tribe I had left upon boarding the jetliner bound for Australia? With limited resources, the Tulim used much simpler devices to accomplish their tasks, but the knowledge and sophistication required to live was no less in the jungle than anywhere else in the world.

Take, for example, the harvesting and preparation of the starchy staple sago, which Momos had formally introduced me to. The food is in the pith of the palm tree's massive trunk, and getting it out is a chore.

The trees are a closely guarded treasure. Fell a sago tree belonging to another and you might pay with your life. I watched from a boulder with several of the younger children as three men and four women went to work on one of Momos's sago palms. Little Yellina was kind enough to explain every detail of their labor, rattling on nonstop despite the fact that I understood only a fraction of what she said.

They felled the palm, stripped off the copious thorns, and split its thick bark with an ironwood wedge. But that sweaty task was only the start of the process. Over the next few hours they dug out the pith and beat it to loosen the starch. Using water retrieved from a nearby creek, they washed the fibers over a screen that caught the starch as the water flowed through into a trough they'd built on the spot for the harvesting of that single tree.

The end result was a paste, which they rolled into banana leaves for transport back to the village, a good hour's hike, two hours with me in tow.

Simple. But who had been the first to cut down such a tree, cut it open, beat and wash the pith for the tiny bits of sago growing between the fibers, and then consume the bland starch as we might eat bread?

My only contribution to the Tulim those first weeks was in my offering of fashion. It started with the legs that Lela had convinced me to cut off my capris. Left with two tubes of black polyester, it occurred to me that I could cut off a band with a bamboo knife and give it to little Yellina to wear around her head. The lower class had no golden bands to encompass their foreheads, but polyester stretched easily enough and might make the perfect bandanna for my new little friend.

To say the black headband was a hit with Yellina

understates just how much delight she took in her new headpiece. In the next twenty-four hours I had cut the legs of my slacks into thirty-one similar bands, half of which I gave to clambering children before Lela suggested I trade the rest for food.

I can't tell you how many places I saw those bands over the next few weeks. What started out as head-bands soon became armbands, thigh bands, bundle carriers, slings, washcloths, sago wraps...the Tulim's inventiveness knew no bounds. I saw strips of my slacks around the necks of two different piglets with a leash attached; at least one woman used that cloth as a sanitary napkin.

I steadily progressed in my understanding of the Tulim language as I began applying every waking hour to learning it. As a wam who had learned Tulim as a second language herself, Lela was a patient and effective teacher. As were the children, who prided themselves on being the first to teach me a new word or point out a new bird.

Day by day my appreciation for their way of life grew. That which I had once found horrifying, like the Tulim's grubs or their nakedness, became tolerable and then ordinary, then acceptable. As my vocabulary expanded, so did my appreciation for many of their customs.

They recalled their history through dances and

long, hypnotic songs and chants that sounded more like speeches put to music than the kind of melodic choruses I had learned to sing. They spent hours on carvings, using stone chisels to cut stories and beliefs into their shields and their spears.

Their many taboos took some patience to understand, but given the Tulim worldview they started to make some sense. It was forbidden for any man to sleep with a woman during her menstrual period because she could not conceive when bleeding, and the only purpose of copulation was to produce children. Neither could any man sleep with a girl who had not yet bled, for the same reason.

No woman could enter battle or kill any boar or crocodile lest she be injured and unable to bear children. If a woman pleased the spirits and her husband, she would conceive. If she still did not conceive, it was because one of her ancestors had offended the spirits, and she would only be cleansed with the river of life, which came from a man.

As in most cultures, men lived by a different standard. The stronger the man, the stronger his urge to father children. To produce the rivers of life necessary for fathering those children, a man had to stay strong by killing wild pigs, or by taking the

lives of his enemies, which included anyone outside the Tulim, particularly those who attempted
to enter the valley. Furthermore, men should not
plant food or harvest it, because these actions
robbed them of the energy they needed to hunt
and kill the enemy and to pass life on to their
women.

I still had not been called to Wilam and for this
I was thankful. I rarely even saw him, and when I
did I went out of my way to avoid him. In many
ways I felt like a forgotten piece of luggage, and I
didn't mind.

My only real use to them was in childbearing,
and I wasn't interested in fulfilling this function.

Lela, on the other hand, was.

She was bleeding now. This meant she could be
taken as a wife. A young man among the royal
muhan had been eyeing her. Her days were filled
with anticipation and excitement. My lack of enthusiasm confounded her. For fertile Tulim
women, not bearing children was like not eating or
breathing.

I was finding my way among the Tulim, but I
was grateful not to be Tulim. I think deep down inside I still hated them.

It was nearly sixty days from my capture before
my world was turned on its end once again.

I had learned to sleep reasonably well on a bedding of grass, using dried leaves bound by twine as a pillow. The nights did not get cool enough to merit any covering. My only frustration was the insects that braved the hut when the fire died; they crawled over my body as I slept. Unless I wanted to spread the smelly mud on my skin to ward them off, I had no choice except to tolerate them.

The pervasive smoke that had once bothered me so much became my friend once I understood that insects were repulsed by it as well. Indeed, all sago and other foods were stored on racks above the fire and so remained insect-free, a rather ingenious storage system, I thought.

I had settled into a light sleep late when a disturbance awakened me. Lela had pulled out several out of the horizontal boards that formed the door and was speaking to a warrior at the entrance. I knew enough of the language by that point to understand his request.

"She must come now."

"Now?" Lela said. "To where?"

"Wilam's home. Bring her now."

Then the warrior was gone.

Lela became quite frantic, rattling on about Tengan, who was Wilam's most magnificent warrior. His coming to our hut was very important indeed.

All of my fears came roaring back, and for a few moments I sat frozen by thoughts of being taken to the cliffs to meet my fate.

"Isaka has died?" I asked.

"Hurry! You must be clean!"

She grabbed one of the gourds filled with spring water and shoved it into my hands. I splashed my face and wiped the grime off with my rag. As usual my hair was braided—I had always worn my hair long and couldn't bring myself to cut it despite the tangled mess it easily became.

"Is this good?" I asked. "Should I wash my body?"

Lela, who was frantically changing into a new grass skirt with red-dyed tips she'd made with great care just that week, glanced at my face. Then at my yellow blouse, which was now brown, and ragged at the bottom where it had ripped on a broken branch.

"We must hurry," she said.

"What about my arms and legs? They're filthy!"

"We don't have this time, miss. We must run!"

Fifteen minutes later we stood in the lords' courtyards. Wilam lived in two houses, a spousal home he shared with his wives, and one reserved for his more stately business. The latter was a men's house, or *jeu*, where he slept when he didn't want to be with his wives, or wife as it was now. Tengan, the warrior who'd brought the message, delivered us to Wilam's spousal home.

I didn't know if the hut's decor reflected the tastes of Wilam or of his wife, but the comforts that greeted us took me aback when I set foot inside.

The walls were covered with boar hides, crocodile skins, furs, and groupings of brightly colored feathers from parrots and birds of paradise. A cooking fire burned near the entrance of the room. The back half of the long, cave-like hut was relatively free of smoke and much cleaner than most huts I had seen.

The sleeping bed stood a foot off the floor and was covered in furs. Tall, intricately carved shields lined the walls around the bed.

A woman sat to one side, leg folded back, watching me with interest. This was Wilam's wife Melino. She had been pointed out to me from a distance once before.

Her dark, silken skin was unblemished in any way that I could see. Her lips looked soft and her cheekbones rose high, giving her a majestic appearance. But Melino's defining feature was her eyes, which were tainted with blue, just enough to suggest a mystery behind her gaze.

For a fleeting moment I surprised myself by coveting her skin and her hair. Perhaps even her standing among these people.

The prince sat on the bed, cross-legged, arms on his knees, staring at us.

I brought my hands together in a sign of respect, bowing slightly.

"Come closer," he said. "I would see what has caused me so much grief."

Lela translated everything, even what I understood from the terms I knew and the context in which they were spoken. What she didn't translate on the spot, she explained later that night.

We approached and stopped several paces from his bed. His skin was dark and clean; his nails were white and manicured; his hair was oiled, and sparkled like a starry night sky. He wore no golden bands or rattan, no jewelry at all. His well-muscled body was naked.

I remember staring at him and thinking that he was a beautiful man, particularly his face, his strong square jaw carved in black, his deep-set eyes. He was truly a lord in this jungle.

"Whatever grief we have brought you, we will repay a hundred times," Lela said, dipping her head.

"Do you have a hundred lives to give? Then I might ask for a hundred deaths."

He said it with the authority of one born and bred for nothing less than a throne, but I heard more in his voice. There was note of admiration in his reprimand. A hint of respect.

"Yes, my prince," Lela said.

"My advisers demand I have you both taken to the cliffs tonight."

With this single announcement my world crumbled. I felt panic well up in my chest. I should have known, of course. It had always only been a matter of time. I threw all caution to the wind and bowed to my outrage.

"Then you would lose the greatest treasure that has come into your valley since any of your advisers were born," I said. "Tell him that."

Lela hesitated, but did.

Wilam drilled me with a strong stare. "You know nothing of our ways. Kirutu's hand was held back because he fears the spirits, but his bitterness knows no end." He paused and drew a steady breath. "Butos will present Kirutu with a new wife tomorrow. The two tribes have threatened war if I don't kill you before the feast."

I held his gaze. Everything I had seen in Wilam told me that he recognized and admired strength.

"It was you who saved me, not them," I said.

"Now you will tell the world that you were wrong?"

"Watch yourself," Melino said, but her tone wasn't condemning. She was sincere.

Wilam offered a shallow smile. "I was curious, nothing more. But now Kirutu forces my hand and threatens to make me appear weak."

"Then you called me here only to tell me that you're going to kill me?" I asked. My mind was flaring with offense, and I knew I was speaking out of turn, but the desperation I'd felt upon first arriving was coming back, and strong.

"If not for my wife I wouldn't have called you at all," he said.

"Then your wife is wise," I said. "You possess a great treasure in me. You must take full advantage of this treasure if you wish to defeat Kirutu."

He chuckled. "So now the one our children call Yuliwam thinks she commands me?"

Melino mumbled something that I couldn't understand. Nor did Lela translate.

Wilam stood from the bed and paced before me, arms across his chest. "Then speak. Tell this muhan how to conduct his affairs. Perhaps you could also tell me what food to eat, how to dress, how to produce many sons."

"I could offer you a son," I said.

"You believe I need you to produce a son?"

True. He was a prince. Surely he could have his pick of Tulim women.

"No. But a son from the slave you plucked out of Kirutu's grasp."

He eyed me, then went on, resolved.

"If I kill you as Kirutu demands, then he redeems himself and I look weak. If I don't kill you, he has just cause for war. So I will neither have you thrown from the cliffs nor keep you. Instead I will present you to Kirutu tomorrow, as a wedding gift."

My heart left me. I saw his reasoning immediately. By doing this he would appear both clever and compliant to the laws that governed them.

"Giving me to Kirutu—"

"Silence!"

"Let her speak before you consign her to her death," Melino said.

Wilam hesitated. Clearly his wife had a voice.

"Speak," he said.

I glanced between them, fully unnerved.

"You were right in seeing that I would be dangerous in Kirutu's hands. If he has this treasure instead of you, he would surely—"

"Enough!" he snapped, snatching his hand into a fist.

"If you were going to kill me, why didn't you just throw me from the cliffs long ago?" I demanded. "Your law demands that any wam who comes into the valley can live only if the council approves. Kirutu did not approve, but you showed great courage by defying him. Now you would throw away all of the value I offer you?"

He stepped up to me, took my cheeks between his thumbs and fingers, and squeezed.

"Remember whom you stand before," he snapped. His eyes darted down to my mouth and I thought he might be looking at my teeth. He was showing his dominance, but there was also curiosity in his eyes. A softness that defied his tone, his grip.

"The value you once had to me has become a liability."

He released my jaw, retreated to the bed, and sat down facing us, arms limp on his knees once more.

"Leave us. Both of you."

Melino took a step forward and spoke before we could react.

"Is it true that you lost a son in the sea?" she asked.

I dipped my head. "It's true. His name was Stephen and I loved him more than I loved my own life. He drowned."

"Kirutu took his life?" she asked, surprised.

"No. The storm took his life."

She nodded slowly. "My heart aches for you." She cast a sideways glance at Wilam. "The child came easily?"

I knew what she was asking. "I was with child the first month," I said.

For a few moments no one spoke. Wilam was watching me without interest. Melino seemed satisfied to let the statement work its own magic. I was thinking it would make no difference.

"Now I will bear Kirutu a son," I said.

"Leave," Wilam snapped. "Now."

We left.

CHAPTER THIRTEEN

I MADE the journey south with two thousand radiantly painted and adorned Impirum men, women, and children, and with each step my worry grew. A hundred times I looked at the heavy jungle, thinking that I could make a run for it, knowing that I wouldn't get fifty paces before they hauled me down.

Tulim law was sacred, based on spiritual beliefs that ordered every aspect of their lives, particularly when it came to outsiders. To wam.

Lela had explained this to me. The Creator of all life was pierced in the side by Purum, the maker of evil spirits, as they battled high above the Tulim valley. When the Creator's blood spilled to the ground, the first humans sprang to life in his image.

Seeing his offspring, the Creator sealed the valley for protection. Evil spirits could not enter the Tulim valley, where all humans lived. But Purum, which also means crocodile or snake, tricked a woman into fleeing the Tulim valley. The woman was impregnated by a pig. Now the earth was full of her evil offspring. Wam. In their eyes I was one such descendant, and as such not fully human. Killing any outsider was only an act of justice. This is what they believed, to their core. It explained their bigotry and their isolation.

What had I ever done to deserve the terrible events of these last months? Why had God taken my son? Raised by parents who could not show me love, and then married to a man who'd treated me with disdain, I had sworn to give Stephen all the love that had been withheld from me. I had believed in a God of love and committed my life to all the right prayers and intentions. Although I had stains on my conscience, as everyone has, my heart was a decent one. Even a good one.

Was God angry at me, his child? Was this his punishment because he couldn't love me the way I loved Stephen, without condition?

The questions whirled through my head.

We traveled in two primary groups: the lords

and their entourage had gone ahead to prepare the way; the rest followed with great celebration. Only those too old or too ill to travel remained at the village.

Lela's face looked like a blue butterfly outlined in white with her own eyes trimmed in red where the butterfly's eyes might be. Yellina held my hand most of the way, skipping beside me with the three yellow-and-blue flowers she'd collected from the underbrush tucked into her hair.

I felt like a stone.

The trek was a long dance in and of itself. Men ran back and forth hooting and hollering; women sang and swayed, catching the men's eyes; children hopped and skipped in their best impersonation. Ten warriors flanked me, along with Momos, who barked many orders to the children around me. Despite his self-imposed air of authority, his grandeur could not compare to that of the muhan warriors, who strode stoically, eyes always on the jungle.

But my mind was far away and my legs were weak, as much from fear as from the trek.

We were close to the Warik village and could see the smoke from its fires when a warrior ran back to us and spoke quietly to Lela, who pulled me away from the main group.

"This wife, Melino, must speak to you, Yuli-wam." She grabbed my hand. "Come, come!"

Wilam's wife. To what end?

Momos sent away Yellina and the other children who tried to follow with a stomp and a yell. Surrounded by the warriors, we made our way down a separate path on a ten-minute walk that brought us to a clearing at the top of a knoll.

Below us the Tulim valley gave way to the flat swamplands I had once traveled bound and bagged in a canoe. They stretched out as far as I could see, so vast that I was at once reminded of the futility of any escape. Ever.

I was so disturbed that I didn't at first see the throngs gathered along the edge of a large meadow far below us. They stood in two large groups opposite each other, close to the trees, thousands adorned in ceremonial dress, like a black sea topped with red, blue, and white foam. I could just hear the distant percussive drums and their low chant above the constant cry of cicadas and birds.

Kirutu was down there. When he learned that Wilam had brought me, he would surely fly into a rage.

"Melino must speak with you, miss," Lela whispered.

I turned and saw that Wilam's wife had made her appearance from the trees to my left. Her headdress stood a foot above her gilded forehead, a magnificent display of red and yellow feathers taken from a bird of paradise. A single band had been painted across her eyes and ran past her temples, and she wore a brightly colored red skirt made from the finer muslin-looking fabric reserved for the muhan. Otherwise her skin was her only covering. But what lovely skin it was, unblemished and smooth in contrast to the coarse jungle.

Among all birds in the jungle, the bird of paradise is the most royal, with its long, brilliantly colored plumage. But the male, not the female, is by far the most decorated among these rare birds. In keeping with nature, the Tulim men, not the women, wore the most makeup and jewelry. A woman's glory was to be found primarily in her natural beauty.

Looking at Melino, I could see why Wilam had chosen her for his bride.

She stepped to one side, away from her entourage, and Lela led me to her. Her brown eyes settled on mine.

"You look like a wam who has come to meet her death," she said.

"Perhaps because I am," I said.

She nodded and turned to Lela. "What I say now, no one must hear."

"I will tell no one," Lela said. "I am only here because she does not speak Tulim so well."

Melino shot a glance toward the others. "Walk with me," she said.

We stepped gingerly up a path that led into the jungle. Above us a flock of parrots squawked. Sweat etched trails down my neck and my back.

"I can see that you are a wise woman with soft eyes," Melino said. "The children like you."

"They are beautiful children."

She nodded. "As are you." She stared up at the trees. "Among the muhan there is a knowing that one day a great warrior will come to reclaim the land beyond this valley and end the threat of Pu-rum as far as the eye can see. Have you been told this?"

"No."

"They say that the Nameless One is an evil spirit," she said. "Sawim has declared it."

"The Nameless One?"

"The man who spoke to Kirutu under the tree. Do you remember?"

"Yes. Kugi Meli?"

She frowned. "Did you see his eyes?"

I looked into hers. "Yes."

"He came to me once. No one knows except Wilam and no one must know. It could be dangerous for me, you understand?"

Lela's voice held a slight tremor as she translated for Melino.

"I understand."

"He did not speak to me. He only laid his palm against my face. But I saw."

We remained silent, bound by the mystery in her voice.

"He was not evil. He was something very different and very powerful. Something very good, I think. Perhaps he is the one."

"The great warrior who will come?"

"Or perhaps he values your life because you will bear that great warrior. On more than one occasion I convinced Wilam to keep you. But he refuses to hear me any longer. He has his own power in his eyes, you see?"

So then Melino had been my greatest advocate all along. In that moment she became my savior.

"The power to rule," I said.

"Yes. To rule. The thirst for power blinds them all."

"Do you know what the Nameless One said to Kirutu?"

"Enough to make him leave. But Kirutu is blinded by his own power. Whatever he heard has been long forgotten. He sees only vengeance now. If he accepts you as Wilam intends, he will either kill you or force you to bear him children."

I harbored no doubts.

She stopped and looked back at the warriors who were eyeing us, a hundred yards distant now.

"Wilam's a strong man, bound by the ways of his father. His mind isn't easily changed. There is only one way to save yourself now."

A sliver of hope sliced through the darkness in my mind.

"Tell me what to do," I blurted. "I'll do anything."

She eyed me thoughtfully, then nodded at my blouse. "Let me see your body."

Lela was already unbuttoning my blouse. "This is good, miss. You must show your beauty."

My blouse fell open and Melino looked at me for a moment before making the reason for her request apparent.

"You don't look like a woman who has suckled a child. I must know the truth, how is it that you've given birth to a child?"

I understood the issue immediately. Wilam had seen me at the council meeting and had concluded the same.

"I bore a son but was unable to produce enough milk. I used a special…gourd…a gourd to feed my child."

"And you were impregnated in your first month, as you say?"

"Yes."

"Then you can bear another child?"

"Yes."

"And the first child…it is dead?"

Two months after his death, the truth of it was still a knife in my heart. I could barely manage the answer.

"Yes."

After a moment she nodded once, satisfied. "Then you must make yourself beautiful. And you must win Wilam's favor before all the people."

"I am wam with white skin!" I objected. "He sees me as ugly."

"You are a woman! I know my husband, and although he pretends not to notice you, he is fascinated by you. I would have you become his wife."

"His wife?"

The Tulim took many wives and concubines, naturally, but I'd been told that my being wam precluded me.

"There's a way," she said. She paced before me slowly, thoughtfully. "The rivalry between Wilam and Kirutu began when Kirutu was sent to the Warik by their father, Isaka."

"Kirutu was once Impirum?"

"He is the son of Isaka, Wilam's blood brother from another wife. His heart has been turned black with jealousy because Isaka sent him, rather than Wilam, away. Neither will bow to the other. If you are seen as something truly valuable, Wilam may risk war to keep you. Kirutu doesn't know that you are intended as a gift. We must not allow Wilam to give you away."

"You would approve of Wilam taking me as his wife?"

"I fear that I will never bear a child," Melino said, staring off into the jungle. "I will always be the lesser of any Tulim wife who does bear him a child." She set her jaw and turned to me. "But if he has a son from you at my request, I will be as worthy."

Melino was as shrewd as her husband.

I didn't understand the complexities of how childbearing influenced a woman's status within Tulim society, but I caught the essence of her suggestion. She stood to gain considerable prestige if I could bear Wilam a child. I would be her surrogate.

My child might be more important than any

other child in her view. The great warrior who was to come.

"Then tell me what to do," I said.

"My servants will make you beautiful. You must win my husband. It's the only way."

"Then I will try," I said.

CHAPTER FOURTEEN

IN THE SPACE of an hour I was transformed from the proper, albeit filthy, Southern belle who'd grown up in Atlanta, Georgia, into a Tulim woman. My skin was still white and my hair was still long and straight, but in every other respect I began to believe that I could be beautiful.

They disposed of my blouse, but rather than blacken all of my skin with pigment, they accentuated my femininity with wide blue swaths down my chest to my belly button, where they came to a point, like a blade. Blue streaks brightened my cheeks and eyes. A light oil that tanned my flesh was rubbed over my entire body so that it shone in the sun. They fixed tiny red beads along the ridge of my shoulders and on the backs of my hands.

Like a group of chattering, giggling girls half

their age, Melino's servants decorated my body as I stood still with my arms spread. The necklace they placed around my neck was made from seven mother-of-pearl shells that flashed in the sun. Using golden bands for my arms and legs, and an elaborate headdress made from red and black seeds and beautiful cockatoo feathers, they changed me into a woman who might make any Las Vegas chorus dancer stare with envy.

The skirt they brought for me was nearly identical to the one she wore. Melino was attempting to present me as a version of herself, as magnificent and royal as any woman in the valley save for my white skin, and even that looked purposeful, as if applied as a part of my makeup.

I emerged from the forest with Lela and the servants, where they presented me to Melino, who looked me over with a critical eye. I admit, I felt utterly self-conscious. My mother would have turned in her grave.

But then Melino smiled and nodded her approval. "Now I see a true Tulim woman, the envy of Kirutu."

The servants covered their mouths and giggled at such an audacious statement.

"Do you like it?" I asked. "I don't look too odd?"

"You look like a rare treasure from the most secret place," she said. "A forbidden fruit that no man can resist."

She laid her palm on my chest. "Now you must become Tulim in your heart. Let no stray thought steal this from you. We must go, the feast is underway."

I recalled her encouragement a hundred times as we made our way down to the pounding drums. I was at a complete loss as to how I might impress Wilam, but I knew that I would leave the feast either with him or with Kirutu, and the faintest thought of being handed over to Kirutu filled me with dread.

The moment we stepped from the tree line and looked out over the celebration, any thoughts of seducing Wilam fled my mind and I knew that I was doomed.

The field was sloped on either side, similar to the one near the Impirum village, cleared by hand with one massive tree at its center. Hundreds of women bent over smoking pits near the bordering trees. Here boars and vegetables roasted, waiting to be eaten at the end of the ceremony. Several thousand warriors danced on both sides, close to the jungle, bobbing and chanting to percussive drums. Their dark bodies were greased and painted, topped with feathers and furs. The field had become a canvas for all of nature's glory.

But it was that very rudimentary, naked magnificence that struck terror into my heart. Where I had found a semblance of belonging in the Impirum village, I now felt fully alien. This sweating sea of humanity would take one look at me and call me out as an imposter.

I immediately saw the marked difference in ceremonial dress that divided the Impirum from the Warik. Both adorned their bodies with armbands and shells, preferring mother-of-pearl above all others. Both used carefully applied pigments to mark their faces and bodies with intricate designs, some terrifying, some delightful. Both wore headdresses and piercings through septa and ears.

But many of the Warik also wore human bones and favored headdresses formed from the carcasses of large black fruit bats or foxes. Skulls hung from the backs of many, and even more wore the lower jaw of a human as a necklace. These skulls came from their enemies, I guessed, not from deceased relatives.

Beside me Lela had already begun to move with the music, grinning from ear to ear. Her eyes were locked on the large tree, where several small groups of lords had gathered beneath its branches. Tengan, the muhan warrior she hoped would choose her, was there. As were Butos and Wilam.

And Kirutu. All three in ornate splendor. A young woman sat on the ground next to Kirutu. His new wife.

A caller's voice rang out: "We are the people of the Tulim, and these are our muhan."

Although I could understand some of his words, Lela repeated them for my benefit as five thousand voices thundered approval in tandem with pounding heels. "*Whoa, whoa, whoa, whoa!*"

The ground shook under my feet.

"We are the people of the Tulim and the evil spirits flee at the sight of our shields."

"*Whoa, whoa, whoa, whoa!*"

The guttural sound of their resounding mantra filled the valley and sent a chill through my bones. I felt terrified and awed at once.

"We are the people of the Tulim and the whole world fears our name."

"*Whoa, whoa, whoa, whoa!*"

"Now our muhan Kirutu will receive his bride and his seed will bring new life."

"*Whoa, whoa, whoa, whoa!*"

Another cry went up, this one from an elderly man who ran toward us, then doubled back, shaking his long bow at the sky. "Our muhan is Wilam and he will bring great power through his many wives."

Eyes turned toward Melino. Her arrival had been noted.

The response rumbled. "*Whoa, whoa, whoa, whoa!*"

The man ran again. "Our father is Isaka and the sky bows to his name."

"*Whoa, whoa, whoa, whoa!*"

Of all the muhan, only Isaka was absent. I was told that he was still alive, but asleep. I wondered if he was in a coma.

"Our muhan is Butos and he will send the spirits to the sea," the runner cried.

"*Whoa, whoa, whoa, whoa!*"

"Our muhan is Kirutu and he will gather the wam like insects and cook them in his fire."

"*Whoa, whoa, whoa, whoa!*"

They were singing of their muhan, but all eyes seemed to have turned in our direction, and it occurred to me that they were now looking at me, not Melino.

"It is now in your hands," Melino whispered. She stepped away from me and walked toward her husband, who stood under the tree with his back to us.

The first caller's voice rang out for all to hear once again. "Now we will show our bodies to the spirits of the sky and show that with our muhan we have no fear."

This time the throng edged forward, stamping the ground with their feet as they chanted agreement. "*Whoa, whoa, whoa, whoa!*"

Melino's entourage moved closer, taking me with them. Like a noose, the gathering closed around us. I kept my eyes on Wilam's powerful back, refusing to return the stares of so many who had singled me out.

I was far too terrified to glance in Kirutu's direction.

Like a tidal wave, anxiety swamped me. I was stepping forward with the rest, moving ever closer to the ceremony under the tree, but I felt as if I were alone on a sea that would swallow me at any moment. I was numb. I did not belong.

The drumming and chanting intensified. Warriors encroached, bending forward as they pressed in, closer, closer. Their voices echoed through the valley: *whoa, whoa, whoa.* But I only heard one word: *wam, wam, wam.*

A new thought suddenly filled my mind. What if Wilam had already told Kirutu his intentions? What if any attempt on my part was already a moot point?

Melino had reached her husband and was speaking into his ear.

Still the warriors tightened their circle, and I

with them. Still the drums pounded. Still the chants rumbled through the jungle. Sawim, the witch doctor from the Karun clan, stood to one side of Kirutu, watching me with flat eyes.

We were only twenty paces from the ceremony when I dared a glance in Kirutu's direction. Panic began to blind me. His unwavering eyes stared, void of expression. But in them I imagined hatred and rage. His tall, muscled form glistened with oil and sweat, and with each breath his body swelled like a knot of angry black vipers. A long, stained cassowary beak hung from his neck, splitting his chest down the breastbone.

I couldn't seem to tear my eyes away. Here was the man who would rape me and then drag me for crocodile bait. Only Wilam could save me.

The chanting suddenly stopped; the drums ceased. The throng stood still. All but me.

I was breathing hard, lost in fear, and I was sure that every eye was fixed on me, the lowly white woman who had dared approach their powerful muhan as if she herself were Tulim. Or was I only imagining such direct attention?

I glanced around frantically and saw their eyes watching me in silence. But there was Melino with her gentle eyes. And Wilam, staring with some curiosity.

In that moment of raw dread, a simple thought dropped into my head, like a gift from heaven.

Sing.

That mad dream that had first prompted me to leave Atlanta skipped through my mind for the first time in weeks. The form in that dream had sung. I had long dismissed any real connection between the dream and my new reality. In fact, I had never again had the dream. But now I remembered the pure, clear note sung in that distant dream as I had first heard it, not as the mocking howl it had become in my more recent memory.

I could sing. It was central to Tulim culture. How often had I delighted the children with my soft song? And I knew no other way to present myself.

So I began to sing.

At first my voice sounded like a pitiful cry from a strangled bird. No song in particular, only a tune, and no tune that I knew.

If any of those near had not been staring, they were now. My voice strengthened and my tone became a little clearer.

My eyes shifted to Wilam and with one look at his soft eyes my tune found melody, and my melody lyrics. A familiar song that I had sung to an audience before warbled from my throat, then found its wings and rose, sweet and high, like a lark sent to the heavens.

"Amazing grace, how sweet the sound..."

The stage was now mine and mine alone. It was as if my entire life had somehow pointed to this moment. I forced my legs forward and stepped out from the circle of teeming Tulim.

"That saved a wretch like me..."

My feet carried me into the clearing. It was an intimate call to Wilam, for in that moment I was indeed the wretch, begging for his grace. He couldn't know the meaning of the words, but neither could he mistake the desperate longing for mercy in my eyes.

"I once was lost but now am found/Was blind but now I see."

And with those words I let myself believe that I indeed could see.

I could see the beauty of the children laughing with me at the pool; I could see Lela begging me to make this babies; I could see Melino telling me how lovely I looked; I could see Wilam watching me with fascination.

I stepped forward, carried by the music, light like a feather as I slowly approached Wilam.

Surely he'd never heard such a tune. It was in no way superior to their own form of song, but music is its own magical language. For the first time he was really hearing me. They were all hearing me.

My song soared through the air, heard by the farthest warriors, the wives, the children on the hills, all who had come to celebrate this wedding. It was my gift to the Tulim, but even more my promise to Wilam.

See me, hear me, and know that I will intoxicate you with far more than a mere song.

Still I sang, with even more clarity, in perfect pitch, embellishing the melody with gentle runs of my own, running through another verse of that glorious song.

When I was only a few steps from Wilam I glanced at Melino and I smiled with her. My voice carried into the Tulim jungle and beyond, for all the world to hear.

"When we've been there ten thousand years..."

I turned slowly and swept my arms, enraptured by a power I had not felt for many years. I was no longer merely wam, but an angel that must be heard to be believed. They were in awe of me. The bond of music had made us one.

My gaze settled on Wilam as I came to the end of the song, and when the last note was gone from my lips and quiet settled around me, I stood still, breathing hard, intently watching his steady eyes.

The whole celebration had been robbed of its breath.

I don't know what consequence I might have faced if my bid for Wilam's heart had ended there. But then from the stillness came a small, crystalline voice that pierced my heart. Several short notes, as high and as pure as a sparrow's call.

I turned to see Yellina standing on the edge of the crowd, crooning at the sky, mimicking my own tune.

"Da, da, dada, daaahhh..."

The blue butterflies on her cheeks bunched as she stepped out toward me, grinning.

My dear, precious Yellina! I rushed up to the little girl, laughing, and I swept her from her feet. Together we spun around singing the tune, like a ballerina and her little apprentice, enchanted by our song.

"Da, da, dada, daaahhh..."

I twirled with her in my arms and the sound of her giggling bubbled over the Tulim like a rippling brook.

Not to be outdone, three, then four other Impirum children ran out and began to hop around, trying their best to join with a chant of their own.

"Whoa, whoa, whoa, whoa."

Sounds of delight and laughter spread through

the gathering. Nothing was so treasured among the Tulim as children, and the children were commanding their hearts.

I set Yellina down, took her tiny hand, and danced around with her, first one way and then the other. I lost myself in her beaming face and for a few moments I forgot I was only a wam trying to be Tulim. This tiny girl was all that mattered to me. If there were angels, she was surely one, sent by God years before my arrival to give me comfort when I arrived.

The crier who had led the people only minutes earlier began to run before the warriors, issuing a new exuberant chant.

"We are the Tulim and these are our children!"

The air filled with a thousand voices in one accord. "*Whoa, whoa, whoa, whoa!*"

"We are the Tulim and our children love us because we are great!"

"*Whoa, whoa, whoa, whoa!*"

The children danced with me, their pied piper, as the crier immortalized us with his verse.

"We are the Tulim children and we love those who love us."

"*Whoa, whoa, whoa, whoa!*"

"We are the Tulim and we love the ones who love our children."

"Whoa, whoa, whoa, whoa!"

Because the crier rattled his words so quickly I hardly knew what this poet was announcing until Lela told me later, but I was aware of the electric charge that elevated us all to the heavens in that moment.

"We are the Tulim and the spirits have sent us a woman who loves our children," the caller cried.

The reply came, but with far fewer voices.

I knew immediately that something had shattered their enchantment. I glanced at Kirutu and saw that he stood with one hand raised.

As if overcome by a passing thunderstorm, the dancing ceased and the voices stilled.

Yellina giggled and hugged my legs, oblivious to the sudden change. One of the mothers called out and motioned her back. The children ran back to the circle, leaving me alone with the muhan once again.

Kirutu pointed at the crier. "You have said too much!" His voice echoed through the crowd. "This is no woman, but a wam who has come to steal our children."

I turned to Wilam and saw that he was still fixated on me. I silently pleaded my case to him, willing that he save me from the monster by his side.

The crier lowered himself to one knee. "I spoke not of this wam, but of another woman," he said.

"No." Wilam lifted his hand, eyes still on me. He stepped out and scanned the massive ring of Tulim watching with fascination. "No, Unnanip did not sing of another woman but of this white woman among us. And yet only I can speak of the truth about this woman because she is under my care."

The three gathered tribes—Warik, Impirum, and Karun—stood with brittle poise, aware of brewing conflict. Sawim, the shaman, drilled me with a terrible stare that brought a shiver to my arms. My eyes darted back to Wilam.

"Today we celebrate Kirutu's wedding, and what better way than to bring him gifts?"

No response.

"Melino, my young wife who is wise beyond her years and as clever as a serpent, brought this woman as a gift for Kirutu. If she were only a wam to be traded like salt, I would never have allowed it. Kirutu is far too noble and respected to be given a mere wam at such an auspicious occasion."

Agreement peppered the gathering. "*Aboo aret. Aboo aret.*" *Very true.*

I couldn't tell if Wilam was destroying me or defending me, but he was clearly a consummate politician.

He lifted his finger and studied the Tulim. "But today I have seen as a child sees. I have heard the voice of our ancestors telling us to love our children. I have seen the smile of the littlest one and I see that my wife Melino was right. This white woman is indeed worthy to be in Kirutu's presence."

Wilam glanced at me, then faced Kirutu, who appeared unaffected by the words. If Wilam was truly offering him a gift, he obviously didn't trust that gift.

Wilam nodded at his brother. "Accept this gift of song and dance from me, your brother by blood." He indicated me with his hand. "As she has drawn the love of many children, may your new wife draw your love and bear you many children."

Kirutu glared at him. "I will accept your gift and take this woman."

"No, Kirutu. The white woman is mine. But her song and her dance are from the spirits, a great gift for this great day."

For a moment Kirutu did not react. But as understanding of Wilam's calculated defiance settled into his mind, his eyes darkened. Such bitterness I had never witnessed on a man's face.

He ripped the beak from the twine around his neck and threw it to the ground. The jungle went still.

"You defile me and all that is sacred," he snarled.

He jerked his head to his right and stared at the shaman, Sawim.

"Speak what is true for all to hear."

Sawim's eyes were still on me, unwavering. I couldn't tear my eyes away.

"The blood of the Tulim will be on Wilam's hands," he said in a low, rasping voice.

With that single announcement my fate was sealed, but so was Wilam's. He'd staked his claim. To yield now, even at Sawim's declaration, would leave him with a terrible deficit in the people's eyes. What kind of leader made a claim only to retreat when that claim was threatened?

Certainly not a leader worthy of ruling the Tulim valley.

I saw all of this written on their faces as Kirutu and Wilam faced off, two brothers vying for power.

"Wilam."

It was Melino. She was staring up the slope to my left, north.

"Wilam!"

There on the hill stood the same man who'd once come to my aid. He was too far away to recognize by face, but his casual stance, leaning on that spear, and his furs could not be mistaken. The Nameless One.

Wilam saw him. So did Kirutu. As did all gathered, following Melino's stare.

But this time they did not flee. Kirutu stilled them, hand raised. His order rumbled over the crowd. "Stay."

They stayed. Motionless.

As if satisfied that he'd done what he'd come to do, the Nameless One slowly turned and walked out of view, spear in hand.

Wilam and Melino exchanged a furtive look.

Kirutu turned to his brother. "So be it," he said.

Wilam nodded at his guard. "Bring her."

And then he loped from the clearing, up the path that led to the Impirum village.

As one, his people fell in behind him.

I was going home.

My new home.

CHAPTER FIFTEEN

A FULL DAY passed before I stood before Wilam again. I was sequestered in the upper courts, in a clean but sparsely appointed hut, guarded at all times. A servant brought me food and water, but no one else came and the servant refused to speak to me.

I understood this much: I was the cause of a great rupture in the Tulim valley. A part of me regretted having made such a bold play for my life. How many lives would be lost on my account?

But the better part of me was grateful to be alive.

On the evening of the next day, I was summoned and taken by a warrior to the Muhanim, that great meeting place reserved for the lords in the upper court.

Melino cut us off as we approached the towering

entrance. She took my hand and dismissed the warrior. The man scowled but held his place along the path. The tension between them was unmistakable. I might have been saved from Kirutu, but my actions had earned me new enemies among the Impirum.

"Remember only one thing," Melino whispered as we stepped up to the entrance. "If you do not conceive soon, all will be lost. Think of nothing else. Only a child can save you now."

Then she led me into the Muhanim.

Wilam sat by the fire, etching markings into the shaft of a spear. Four other muhan warriors watched me from across the room. Not a soul spoke.

I stood with hands at my sides, tickled by a bead of sweat that ran down my neck and broke over my collarbone. Wilam stared at me for few moments, then set his spear aside and stood.

"Leave us."

The warriors made for the door immediately, followed by Melino.

Wilam and I were alone.

The fire lapped at the stuffy night air inside the Muhanim, casting its orange hue over menacing faces carved into shields and over figures painted on the walls.

Wilam stood tall next to the platform, watching me, surrounded by drums and weapons and cured boar hides. Every detail of his body was imprinted on my mind. His white eyes, fixed upon my face like twin moons; his coal-dark skin, glistening in the firelight; his powerful muscles strung along his frame like cords of black steel; his firm jaw and fully fleshed lips; his large hands and carefully manicured nails.

I saw it all and I began to tremble.

For a long time we just stared at each other. When he did speak, my as of yet limited understanding of the language slowed our conversation considerably more than what I will convey.

"Do you understand what kind of trouble you have brought us?" he asked, voice low.

"I don't remember bringing anything. I remember being taken by force."

His eyes remained on me, glistening. "Isaka can no longer hear or speak. The future of the Tulim rests on my shoulders. If Kirutu seizes power, he will rule with a spear."

"You won't let that happen," I said, but it was desperate thinking. I had cast my lot with him, but Kirutu would have his day. My whole existence rested on Wilam's ability to protect and save me.

"It's no longer in my hands," he said. "I was won

by my wife's whispers. Melino has placed me at the whim of your womb."

I was at a loss. In many ways he was right.

"You're too strong to be so easily fooled, my lord," I finally managed. "You saw in me a path to power. Do you now doubt your own judgment?"

That gave him a few seconds' pause.

"My advisers doubt. You are as slippery as Melino."

"Too slippery for your advisers, perhaps. But not for Wilam, the lord who would rule."

"Maybe more slippery than Melino," he said.

"And you have more wisdom than your advisers," I returned.

He returned my stare. In the space of under a minute we had achieved an understanding that surprised even me.

Wilam walked up to me. His body smelled of sweet lotion that reminded me of the white orchids that grew in the surrounding jungle. Or was it the scent of coconut oil? But I could also smell the musky odor of man and flesh beneath it all.

He reached out and touched my hair, gently raking his fingers through it.

"It's soft," he said.

I suddenly couldn't speak.

He walked around me, touching my shoulders

and the back of my head. Only once did he feel my flesh, and then only with a soft pinch along my side to measure my fat.

He stood before me again. "You need to eat more," he said.

I looked down at my body and saw a lean, youthful form. Without sugar in my diet and with far more exercise than I was accustomed to, I was thinner than I had been in Atlanta, but not by much.

It occurred to me that Wilam was only like me, trying to come to grips with a situation that was foreign to him. In his lifetime he'd surely never encountered a woman who would not count it a great blessing to be with him.

He retreated to the reclining platform covered in boar hides, sat atop it, folded his legs one over the other, and touched the platform beside him. "Sit."

Without hesitation I approached him and sat, folding my legs like his own.

Wilam stared at the fire in the center of the large room. "I want you to teach me the ways of your world. What Melino says is correct: the Tulim will be crushed as the Asmat are being crushed by the coming of the foreigners."

"I will teach you."

His head turned to me. "These canoes in the sky we call spirits, they have great power?"

"Enough power to destroy the Tulim."

"Kirutu would make war on the wam."

"Then he would be foolish," I said.

Wilam looked at me, perhaps struck by my audacity. But he accepted it without rebuking me.

"You must protect the Tulim from the ways of the wam, not fight them."

He offered a slow nod. "My only concern now is Kirutu. His heart is blackened by Sawim."

"And what of the Nameless One?" I asked.

He went still for a moment.

"Melino spoke to you about this?"

"She said she doesn't think he's evil. And that if I have a son with you, the child may be special." I paused. "What did he say to Kirutu under the tree?"

Wilam averted his eyes, clearly uncomfortable. "The ways of the spirit are best left to shamans." He spat to one side. "My place is to wage war, not bend magic." Then he added, for my benefit: "No one knows this man or why he has come."

"Do you fear him?"

"I fear no one."

And yet I saw fear in his eyes.

"You don't know what he said to Kiru—"

"Enough!" he snapped.

I felt slapped.

He settled and continued in a more gentle tone. "No one will ever know what was said. Kirutu is too proud. What matters is that I chose you before all Tulim. Now I must show them that my choice was wise. Do you understand this?"

His choice to claim me. Melino's words flowed through my mind. The values of the Tulim were still strange to me, but I was beginning to understand. In their world I was simply a means to an end. Yes, Wilam had some attraction to me, but desire to possess and to bring forth a child was what raged through his blood, not any intrinsic desire for me.

If I could bear a child, I would be seen as a valuable asset, one that Wilam had cleverly taken for himself. If I could not, he would appear the weaker, fooled by desire for a woman. A white wam at that.

But I wasn't in a position to complain.

"I understand," I said.

"The course is set—we cannot fail."

"No, we must not."

Even saying it, I felt fear rise through me.

"There's no time. I must show my people that my choice is right."

"Yes."

"Immediately."

I wasn't sure what he meant by that.

Wilam looked at the door and let out a long breath. "You will now be my second wife. I have informed the elders."

I blinked. "Already? There's no ceremony?"

He looked at me, confused. "You are wam. There is no ceremony, we are wed at my word. And make no mistake, you are lesser than Melino. My *akawi*." Which I took to mean something less than a full wife, like a concubine. "You will do only what she commands." He paused. "And you will teach me the ways of the wam who fly in canoes."

I nodded. But my mind was already on conceiving a child, because it was the last thing I wanted to do. In the wake of losing Stephen, I was in no frame of mind to conceive, certainly not with a native I hardly knew.

And yet no remotely reasonable alternative presented itself to me. In the way of the Tulim, being named Wilam's wife was a great honor. Matters of choice and love had nothing to do with it. To bear a son for him would be perhaps the greatest honor known in the valley.

Thinking anything less served neither me nor the Tulim.

"When was your last blood?" Wilam asked.

He was wasting no time.

"Three weeks ago," I said.

Wilam clearly knew the meaning of a woman's cycles.

"Then you will come when I call."

I KEPT telling myself that this was the only way. I had been delivered into the Tulim valley against my will, but I was no longer a slave to be forced. I was the wife of a prince, and my place as that wife was of my choosing. Hadn't I chosen to be his wife rather than be handed over to Kirutu? Yes. And so I would be his wife.

But my fears still rode me like demons as I frantically prepared myself for Wilam should he call. I feared that he would reject me. That I would break down and reject him. That somehow I would be violating my principles despite good reasoning to the contrary.

Within minutes of my leaving Wilam, Melino hurried to the hut they'd assigned me and presented me with two of her finest skirts. She quickly went to work on my hair.

"He will call tonight," she said. "You must not be afraid. Wilam may sound like a boar among the men, but alone he is a gentle man." She glanced up at my eyes. "You are certain that you can conceive?"

It was all too much. I promptly stood and walked away from her.

"Not with this kind of pressure!" I snapped.

She stared at me, stunned.

Tears seeped into my eyes. "I'm not from your jungle, Melino. I hardly know who I am anymore! Now I'm expected to be with your husband and conceive a child at the snap of his fingers?"

Her features slowly softened. She walked to the bed and sat down, then patted the woven bark beside her.

"Sit."

So I crossed to her and sat, knowing already that my course was set.

She took my chin and turned my face toward her.

"Now listen to me, Yuli." I felt some comfort, hearing her call me that name. "First of all, you must know that he is now *your* husband as well. You are afraid, I know, but you are honored now and your honor will know no end when you miss your blood. It is a great honor to conceive the son of a prince. You must wipe your tears away."

I nodded, but my eyes must have told a different story.

"Wilam is a very beautiful man," she said. "When I was still young, I used to watch him strut through the village and dream he would choose me one day. When he did, the whole valley heard my cries of joy."

"Yes, Melino, but this isn't my way."

She couldn't know the courting ways I was accustomed to, but we did have one thing in common, and she had no trouble pointing to it.

"I can see how much you love the children. Yellina is like a little sister to you."

The memory of little Yellina singing with me filled my mind.

"Think of the children. If you don't know how to do this for Wilam, then do it for them. Give Wilam the power to rule and protect our children. Do not think of yourself in this. Think of the people."

Her words cut to my core. It struck me, sitting there on the bed of that hut, that I was seeing my predicament all wrong. I should be delighted at the turn in my fate, not fearful of something that could bring so much beauty. I was thinking only of myself and seeing only through the lenses that had no meaning here in the jungle.

As if a switch had been thrown in my head, my perspective on the path before me shifted.

"If you must know, Wilam is secretly terrified of you," Melino said, smiling.

The revelation surprised me. But then, why wouldn't he be? I was as foreign to him as he was to me.

"He is a kind man?"

"The kindest," she said.

"And gentle?"

"Like a dove." Her eyes twinkled.

"Then make me beautiful."

She did, in her own way, and I began to let all of my fears fall away.

I asked Melino what I should expect of the imminent encounter, what customs I ought to be aware of. She only smiled and said Wilam would be more interested in my own customs.

As promised the call did come, later that very night, and my first thought was to run away into the forest. Instead I followed the servant obediently.

Fifteen minutes later I stood outside Wilam's spousal hut, took one deep breath to calm my jitters, and, at the prompting of the man who'd fetched me, ducked through the entrance.

Wilam sat on a mat by the fire, arms on his knees, staring absently into the flames. The servant quickly boarded up the entrance.

We were alone.

"You've come," he said.

"You called," I replied.

He dipped his head.

"Sit."

I recalled Melino's advice. I had no idea what

was customary among the Tulim in these situations, but I knew my own ways. Wilam had married me, not a Tulim woman. I was a woman, not a slave. A treasure, not a piece of property. That's what I told myself as I remained standing.

"Do you find me beautiful?" I asked.

His eyes lingered on mine, then swept down my body.

"I am honored to be called your wife," I said. "It would be easier for me to conceive if I knew that you felt as honored to be my husband. And that you find me beautiful."

For a long time Wilam said nothing, but I could see by the light of the fire that he was not displeased with my boldness. I knew then that I had as much power here in this hut as he did.

When he spoke, his voice was gentle.

"Sit down beside me, Yuli."

I rounded the fire pit and eased down with my legs folded to one side, leaning on one arm.

"Look at me," he said.

I lifted my eyes and saw no aggression, no hint of wariness, no awkwardness whatsoever.

"You are a woman and you want to know if I find you beautiful," he said.

"Yes."

A slight smile formed on his face. "I find you

more beautiful every day I see you. Even when I first saw you at the council, I was struck by your simple beauty. Others talked about the paleness of your skin, but I saw only the blue magic in your eyes. I refused to confess this, even to myself. Perhaps it is why I refused Kirutu's bid to purchase you."

"And sentenced me to my death?" I smiled.

"If I had not you would be dead. We will thank Lela."

I nodded and looked away. "We will thank Lela."

I had not seen this side of Wilam before. He was nothing like the man I had imagined, throwing his women down to ravage them as he pleased. And yet he had more power than any man I'd ever known.

I was his wife! His wife, imagine that.

Sitting beside that fire, I let the last of my fears slip away and allowed a smile.

"So you are telling me that you are ready?" he asked.

I turned to him, startled. My face blushed. But his bluntness actually put me at ease. I had to remember that I was in the Tulim valley, not playing coy with a man in Atlanta. As with all Tulim, talk of sexuality was almost as free-flowing as talk of food.

"Did I say I was?" I asked.

"Tell me that Melino did not speak with you."

"She did."

"And she told you that I was nervous."

"As nervous as I am."

"And we both know that Melino is a wise woman."

"Very wise indeed."

He sighed. "I think when I become chief, she will rule through me."

"I think she may indeed."

"I won't allow it."

"No," I said. "I'm sure you wouldn't."

"So then let me be a man and tell you what I think, so you will know."

He picked up a stick and poked at the burning coals, searching for the right words.

"I was troubled by you until I saw you dancing with the children. I knew then that you would be mine, but it is a strange thing. I saw that you speak with a whip, but in your heart you are a delicate flower, and I had no desire to see Kirutu harm you. You might give me a son, yes, but I saw more than a child." He shifted his eyes to me. "I saw you."

"Hmm…" His words were a sweet song to my ears. Spoken for my benefit, surely. The prince was offering his own seduction.

He dropped the stick in the fire and set his forearms on his thighs.

"So we should begin," he said.

It wasn't my kind of seduction.

"Begin?"

"Yes."

"Just like that? Right here, on the floor?"

"If you like."

I knew that the Tulim expressed their sexuality
in a fairly utilitarian fashion, but I hadn't been prepared for such a casual approach.

"When you see a delicate flower, do you chop it
off with a stone?"

"I assure you, I won't hurt you. Melino will tell
you, I am very gentle."

There wasn't a hint of humor or insincerity in
his manner. Wilam was being as thoughtful as was
natural to their ways. He simply wasn't compre-
hending my desire to be wooed. I wasn't sure if I
fully knew what I wanted myself. Perhaps I was
only stalling.

"You are afraid?" he asked.

"No. No..."

He stayed quiet for several breaths, then stood
and turned away. "Then you don't desire me."

"Did I say that?"

"How foolish of me," he said, crossing to the

sleeping platform. "You have no longing for the Tulim man."

My intention hadn't been to hurt or reject him, and yet how else was he to interpret my response? I pushed myself to my feet.

"You're wrong, Wilam. I do desire you."

Did I?

He faced me and motioned at me accusingly. "And yet you play with me!"

As I saw it, there was only one proper way to proceed, and I was suddenly resolved to take it. I closed my eyes for a moment and let my restraint take flight. Then I looked at him, intent on seducing him in the only way I knew how.

"Wilam..." I made my approach to him slowly. "You must know that where I come from the way of a man and a woman is different than among your people. It is not that I don't desire you, because I do. I see you and I see a powerful man whose eyes and body call to me and rob me of my breath."

His face softened.

"If you are willing I would show you my way."

The tension in that hut was palpable and the moment I placed my hand on his broad chest, all awkwardness fled us. Behind me the flames lapped the night air softly; outside the cicadas sang. Melino had said she would know if I'd delivered on my pledge. Perhaps she was watching. It hardly mattered.

I drew my finger over his muscles. "If you will allow me, I will show you a new world."

I could smell the sweet rapina bark that had cleaned his teeth, the aroma of the salve he applied to keep his skin dark and healthy. The scents pulled me in.

"Tell me you will not resist me," I whispered, leaning closer. "I will not peck your eyes out like a cassowary. I will make you the father of a son."

He did not respond.

"Tell me that I may do whatever I wish."

"You must."

In that moment I, the white woman scorned by my captors and rejected for two shells, became the most powerful woman in the valley, for I had Wilam, son of Isaka, envy of every man and woman in the Tulim valley, under my command.

And with that power I would serve Wilam in a way he had not dreamed possible.

I placed my hand over his heart.

Under my palm his chest rose and fell as his breathing thickened. His reaction to my touch made me dizzy with desire. The hut was hotter than it had been only moments earlier, and my skin prickled with anticipation.

Leaning into him, I brought my finger to his mouth and traced his lips.

"Where I come from we use our mouth to speak more than simple words," I whispered.

"Show me," he breathed.

The Tulim did not kiss. It simply wasn't a part of their tradition. But we were both beyond tradition. All that mattered now was the fulfillment of need and duty.

I slowly lifted my lips to his, and I kissed him. Gently at first, allowing him time to find pleasure in the new sensation. Then I dipped my tongue into his mouth and I felt him shudder.

The sounds of the night faded and time stood still for us. I had intended to gratify Wilam, but I had not anticipated how deeply I would drink from that same pool. For long minutes we kissed, with increasing passion.

With a sudden groan deep within his throat, Wilam seized my waist and lifted me as if I were a doll in hands of iron. Until that moment deep in the jungle, I had never wanted to be loved so badly as I wanted to be loved by Wilam.

Perhaps because I had been a slave and was now the master, if only in that hut.

Perhaps because he had saved me from certain death.

Perhaps because I wanted to feel fully alive again after living on the ragged edge of death for so long.

Or perhaps because I wanted to create new life.

CHAPTER SIXTEEN

THE DAYS that followed were a dizzying whirl-
wind. Yes, my purpose was to bear a child, but
I had sparked more than the desire for a son in
Wilam's heart—of that I was quite sure.

When a woman is the subject of such utter preoc-
cupation to a man as I was, she cannot help but feel
like a queen. I was caught up in the joy of Melino
and the other muhan, who now treated me with
new respect.

I was tempted to believe that Wilam was falling
in love with me. Perhaps even I with him. Everywhere I went, the people knew. I was Wilam's
second wife. Lela was ecstatic and wrestled far too
many details from me.

But I was duly aware that I was that queen only
because I bore the promise of a child. My power
grew in my belly, not in my heart. I kept telling

myself that this didn't matter, I should only be grateful. But the thought nagged at me when I allowed it.

I was loved for what I could offer, not for who I was.

And who was I? I didn't rightly know anymore.

Melino became my confidante. That first night I was certain that I would quickly become the object of her jealousy. How could she see Wilam's face and not wonder if she could bring such a smile from him? But the very next day she called for me and put my fears to rest.

"What else do you know about pleasing a man?" she asked.

"What do you mean?" I asked, blushing. "No more than you."

She pulled me up the path and spoke in a hushed voice. "I have never touched Wilam's mouth with mine! This isn't our way and yet he will not stop talking of it."

"He told you that?"

She looked at me, confused. "You did not do this?"

"No... I mean yes, I did." That Wilam would be so candid with her took me off guard. I still didn't understand the Tulim's transparency. Of course Melino was Wilam's wife and privy to every aspect of his life, to the finest detail.

"You must show me this so that I can try."

I learned later that her attempt was a great success, and that made me laugh.

Melino and I talked regularly after that, not once exchanging an awkward moment regarding our shared love for Wilam. She had welcomed me into their marriage as was customary, and she suffered no lessening of attention from him.

She was the first among the Tulim with whom I shared my own rudimentary spiritual beliefs, perhaps because for the first time I began to feel as though perhaps God had not forgotten me. The details of all the stories I'd learned growing up seemed disconnected from this jungle, so I spoke only of a Creator of love who had sent his own warrior of sorts, his son, to rescue the world from hatred and jealousy and strife of all kinds.

I realized as I told it that this story was similar to the prophesy Melino hoped might be fulfilled through my child. She found all of it curious and quite delightful.

My faith felt distant to me. It was still there but submerged by my harrowing experience.

A week passed and I knew that one question occupied their minds more than any other. Would I bleed? Melino asked me every day, reminding me of my true purpose. But no, I had not bled. It wasn't that time yet.

Ten days passed and still I had not bled.

Eleven. Then twelve. Then fourteen.

I would never have imagined in my wildest dreams that my bleeding would be the fixation of so many people. They knew, all of them. The wind itself was whispering—Yuli has not bled.

My period, in fact, became a large part of my identity. My brain and my heart seemed to be present only in supporting roles. With each passing day I seemed to be treated with more respect, as though I'd become more valuable.

This fixation with my bleeding began to bother me, and I finally made that frustration known to Melino by snapping at her. She merely looked at me with a stern face and told me to quit being selfish. I had nothing more to say.

On the morning of the sixteenth day I awoke to nausea.

The word spread like wildfire. Yuli was with child. Wilam was going to have a son!

I was immediately elevated to a status not unlike that of a goddess among the Tulim. Where I had been met with knowing eyes and smiles over the past two weeks, I was now greeted with accolades of awe and tender touches.

I was a white girl from Atlanta living in a jungle that had nearly claimed my life, but for the next two days I felt as though God had indeed heard my cry and come to my rescue. Perhaps not in the way of my choosing, but he'd come after all.

The feast that Wilam threw to celebrate was a massive undertaking that saw the slaughtering of one hundred pigs. The scent of their hair burning over open fires filled the entire village and watered Impirum mouths with the promise of meat and yams and squash and steamed pandanus fruit.

Melino saw to my dressing and I walked among them like royalty, colored in red and blue pigments with a crown of towering bird of paradise feathers that might have fetched a month's salary in the Western world. As dusk fell, nearly four thousand Impirum sat or squatted on the slopes, watching Wilam present me to Melino as the bearer of his child, whom he proudly announced would one day rule the Tulim.

As was their custom, he milked the red, soupy paste from the pandanus fruit onto my belly, then fed it to Melino. The congregation's thundering cry scattered a thousand birds from the canopy above. By consuming this symbol of blood, Melino became as much the mother of my child as I was.

The tribe ran back and forth, dancing and

singing, and I with them, until I could hardly stand.

Wilam led me away from the celebration late, followed by Melino and two of his ranking warriors. Much ado was made of how great the feast had been, but as we approached the Muhanim the air became quiet.

When we stepped into the hut, the elders were seated along the walls, watching us with somber eyes. I knew immediately that something was wrong.

Wilam guided me around the smoldering fire. "Get her a soft mat," he ordered one of his warriors. "Get her some water and some meat. Hurry." He looked at me. "You are hungry?"

"I just ate. What's happening?"

His hand touched my belly. "The child is good?"

I was growing accustomed to their hovering and Wilam's unyielding concern for my well-being. "All is well," I said.

"You shouldn't have danced so much."

"Then you should have thrown a smaller feast."

"You must not sit too quickly or run too much."

"Don't be silly. I've been with child less than a month."

"And I will see to it that you're with child another eight months. Now sit."

Melino had seated herself with her legs folded to one side. "Sit beside me, Yuli. Don't pay Wilam any mind, he's only a man who knows nothing about being a woman. He thinks you're made of flowers and will blow apart in the wind."

Normally this would have earned her a chuckle from the warriors and a scoff from Wilam, but tonight there was no mirth in the Muhanim.

I settled to my seat.

Wilam paced on the bark floor like a caged lion. This was not his typical calm behavior. "Because now you must know that everything has changed."

"Not so changed that I don't know what to do with my own body," I said.

His eyes darted to Melino, and by the concern etched on his face, I knew that something was indeed wrong.

She nodded once. "Listen to him, Yuli."

"What is it?"

Wilam faced me. "The Warik are wearing the black grease."

I glanced at the elders and saw the glint of fear in their eyes.

"What is the black grease?"

"We must not speak of this," one of the elders said.

Melino flashed a harsh glare at the men.

"She bears Wilam's child! She has the right to know."

Wilam crossed to the platform and sat, facing me with steady eyes. For a while he said nothing, but that silence worked fingers of terrible fear into my mind.

"The Warik know you carry my child. It was my hope that they would see my wisdom and strength and harden their hearts against Kirutu. This is the way of the Tulim, to offer greatest respect to those who bring life. They saw your beauty when you sang and danced with the children." He stopped.

"What is the black grease?" I asked again.

"But Kirutu and the witch of the Karun tribe have turned them with the black grease. It is made from the fat of a crocodile mixed with Sawim's blood. With this ceremony they call on the power of the evil spirits."

The fear in that room was palpable. I could hear the fire crackling and the night creatures crying in the jungle, and my ears heard the sounds of hell.

"But spirits are only spirits," I said, trying to believe my own words. "They can't overpower the mighty Impirum."

His eyes shifted to Leweeg, the elder who had spoken. He was the closest the Impirum had to a shaman. Among the three clans—the Warik, the

Impirum, and the Karun—a true shaman could come from and live among the Karun only, but each tribe had spiritual elders.

"She is incapable of understanding," the old man said. "She is a woman and she is wam."

"She is my wife!" Wilam snapped.

They exchanged a long look and the elder finally dipped his head.

"Forgive me."

I had been told that, compared to most tribes in the region, the Tulim regarded women with respect. But some biases are not easily washed from the hearts of men.

It was the least of my concerns at the moment.

"Sawim has declared our union and our child invalid," Wilam said.

"And you will tolerate this?" I demanded.

His eyes flashed with hatred. "I will see a thousand Warik die before I see any harm come to my son. The rule of the Tulim must not leave the Impirum clan."

With those words reality once again settled around me like a thick fog. My value to them was still a matter of political power. We had celebrated as if heaven itself had fallen to earth, but the celebration hadn't been for me. It had been for my unborn child.

Even more, it had been for Wilam.

For his river of his life that would extend his power for yet another generation. I was but a vessel.

I felt Melino's hand settle on my thigh. Tears welled in my eyes.

"You have nothing to fear, Yuli," Melino said. "Wilam will raise a thousand warriors to protect you. Our child will be born."

"It has been a hundred years since any have taken up the black grease," the elder said softly. "There will be war."

"Then let there be war," Wilam spat.

He turned to me, face stern.

"You will sleep in the spousal hut alone. You may never come or go without my men. There is nothing to fear. My men will protect you. We have heard that Kirutu is only making noise. This will take time and we will be ready."

His words should have been comforting.

Instead I felt utterly alone.

"Take her to the hut," he said. "Bring me my warriors." And then to me, meaning well, I know: "You will be safe."

Wilam was wrong. I wasn't safe.

CHAPTER SEVENTEEN

—~⚊⚊⚊—

AFTER BEING delivered to my hut alone it took me two hours to drift into a fitful sleep. When I asked Melino to stay with me, she informed me that she could stay only until I slept and would then be otherwise occupied. It was crucial that I sleep. Nothing must disturb me.

The night was quiet and the three warriors stationed outside my hut spoke only occasionally in soft tones.

I don't know how the dark ones slipped through the perimeter guard Wilam had stationed around the village.

I don't know why the three warriors at my door didn't put up a fight or call out a warning.

I know only that I was in deep sleep when a crushing blow struck my head. I remember thinking that the roof had collapsed before darkness swallowed me completely.

But the moment I awoke I knew that a falling roof was not my problem. My being wam, on the other hand, was.

I was bound hand and foot, hanging from a pole. A bag was over my throbbing head and a gag cut deeply into my mouth. I had been in that position before, swinging a foot off the ground between two Warik warriors who rushed me through the jungle.

I struggled and cried into my gag, thinking we might still be close enough to the Impirum village to be heard, but my resistance only earned me a hard blow to my head and a harsh grunt of rebuke.

"*Koneh.*" *Shut up.*

A hundred thoughts badgered my mind— nightmares of the worst kind. Surely Kirutu would not allow me to live.

If only it had been so simple.

Only one thought gave me a moment's hope as I hung from that pole and silently cried into my bag: I was alive. I should have died with Stephen in the sea, but I was alive. I should have been executed the day after entering the valley, but I was alive. I should have been given to Kirutu at his wedding and paid him back with my life, but I was alive.

If Kirutu had wanted me dead now, he could have instructed his warriors to kill me in my hut.

But then even that hope was quickly dashed, because being alive in Kirutu's hut would be only a different kind of death. Whatever his plans for me might be, they could not be favorable.

The vines they'd used to bind my hands and feet to the pole dug into my skin with each bounce as they ran. If we had gone on much longer, my arms might have come out of their sockets, but we were much closer to the Warik village than I had assumed. Indeed, I briefly wondered if we hadn't gone south after all, but to the house of an embittered Impirum villager.

No more than twenty minutes after I'd awakened to find myself bound, my carriers hauled me into a hut, dumped me on the bark floor, and left me prone with a crackling fire near my feet.

My every thought cried out to God. And for Wilam to come before Kirutu could begin whatever harm he intended.

And yet I knew even as I lay bound and gagged, like one of the pigs my prince had slaughtered to honor the life in my womb, that Wilam could not save me from Kirutu. The man was too shrewd and too angry to allow his enemy another victory. He'd been scorned and mocked, and his revenge would be carefully orchestrated to end his shame once and for all.

If Wilam had failed to keep me safe in his own fortress, he could do nothing here, even if he knew I was missing.

The only thing I could do was play Kirutu's game with the thinnest hope that I, not Wilam, could foil him long enough to give my prince the time he needed to find me and save our child.

"I have heard it said that the children of some wam have blue eyes because they are evil spirits." The man spoke in a low tone, only feet from where I lay, and a chill washed down my spine. I could not mistake Kirutu's voice.

"But when I see your child, I do not see an evil spirit," he said. "I see only a child who does not know where it belongs."

The Tulim often spoke of unborn children as if they were already walking about the village, and they used metaphors regarding the ways of the spirit world. But his meaning hardly mattered; I was still consumed with the sound of Kirutu's haunting voice.

"But if I am wrong and the child is evil, then the mother must also be a demon. Only this would explain how you have escaped my grasp and bewitched the Impirum."

You must be calm, Julian. For the sake of your child, you must still your mind and think very carefully.

A hand snatched the bag from my head. I blinked and saw that I was inside the same hut I'd visited during my first night among the Tulim, presumably one belonging to Kirutu, perhaps one on the outskirts of the village reserved for liaisons or for hunting.

Kirutu stepped into firelight, unadorned except for a rattan waistband and a necklace of cowrie shells bearing a single boar's tusk. The scar on his side stood out angrily on his shiny skin covered in black grease—crocodile fat and Sawim's blood mixed with whatever other ingredients turned it black. He watched me with dark eyes set deeply into his hardened face.

"I should have crushed your skull with my paddle in the sea where I found you," he said. "But now I have the pleasure of crushing your child's head as well."

It was to my benefit that he hadn't yet removed my gag, for I would have lashed out at him then. Instead I took great pains to calm myself. My sole objective became to stall him as long as I could, even if that meant compromising myself.

He leaned over, grasped the gag with strong fingers, and jerked it over my chin, freeing my mouth. "You will now wish I had left you dead."

"Then you were foolish for not killing what you could never have," I said. "Now all the Tulim see that Wilam made what you could not."

His eyes lowered to my belly. "So they tell me."

"Any man can take a woman, but only the strongest can win her heart the way he wins the heart of all Tulim," I said.

A wicked grin twisted his mouth. "Your intelligence surprises me. It's true, I will never be favored in a struggle for the people's affections. But I won't have to. Your offspring will give the people to me."

He was playing games, I was sure of it. I had no power over the people.

"I am not so weak."

"No, I hope you aren't. You will need to be strong to kill Wilam."

Again, a game. But there was something in his voice that frightened me. His composure was not that of a bluffing man.

"I would die before I killed Wilam," I said.

"Yes, you would. But would you also take the life of your child?"

"The life of my child is no longer in my hands."

Kirutu smiled. "No. The life of your child is now in my hands."

"What did the Nameless One whisper in your ear?"

The question seemed to rob all sound from the hut. Kirutu's jaw clenched, bunching taut muscles along his cheek.

"You think I would bow to the whim of the one Sawim fears? Then you don't know my heart."

"I know only that your heart has been turned black with hatred. This isn't the way of the Tulim."

"This is my way!"

He snapped an order and two Warik warriors stepped into the hut. Their leader nodded at me.

"Hold her up."

They quickly untied my hands and feet from the pole and pulled me to my feet, one warrior on each arm. The grease from their arms turned my skin the color of soot where they rubbed me.

Kirutu stepped forward and I knew from the look in his eyes that he was going to try to destroy my womb now, as I stood before him.

I felt raw with panic. "The child is your blood, Kirutu," I said. My resolve began to crumble and my body began to shake. "Wilam is your brother...I beg you—"

His fist slammed into my belly like a battering ram. Pain bit deeply into my pelvis and spread up my spine. I instinctively gasped, but the air was already gone from my lungs. He hit me again, harder and lower this time, destroying what life might not have been broken with his first blow. My legs gave way, forcing the warriors to hold me up.

Kirutu hit me twice more while the muscles were still limp in my abdomen. I could feel the tissue tearing deep in my womb as his fist slammed into my gut. Horror washed through me. To have a wholly innocent and dependent child's life pounded from your belly by a man's fists is an offense impossible to describe. I could feel something wet flowing down the inside of my thighs. Urine, I thought, but it would soon be joined by blood.

I screamed my rage and my pain when breath finally came. With these blows Kirutu had crushed away not only my child's life but my own. I cried for Stephen, because in losing my second child I desperately wanted my first. I cried for Wilam, because our only child was now dead, murdered while his father lay asleep in his bed. I cried for all the Tulim, because their love of life was as great as mine, and soon that very life would run down my legs.

I cried because once again God had gone deaf.

Kirutu lifted my skirt, stared at me, then let the fabric fall. "Put her down."

They set me down against the wall, where I propped myself up with both hands to keep from falling over.

"Leave us."

The warriors left.

For a long while I sat gasping, unable to speak, mind swimming in revulsion. How could I possibly tell Wilam? The death of his coveted seed would crush him, and my torn womb would render me useless. Better for me to bleed to death on Kirutu's floor than to return home to Wilam and announce the death of his child.

"It is a terrible thing to lose a child," Kirutu said. "Among the Tulim, it is even worse to be barren. You will never bear another child. For this, Wilam will throw you away. His interest is only in what power you give him through your womb."

He was only reinforcing what I already knew.

I still could not comprehend how he thought the death of my child would compel me to kill Wilam. My determination to resist Kirutu was now un-shakable.

"You must understand that I do this for the sake of my people," he said. "Our ways have been pro-tected for generations by a perfect law. Wilam is soft. His interest in the wam will only breed more and our laws will soon be like grass in the wind. By killing this one life I will save many. Now you must do the same."

"I'll never kill Wilam!" I screamed.

"Then your child will die."

His words weren't making any sense to me. He'd just killed my child! A great weariness settled over me and I thought my arms might give way. I wanted to curl up and let darkness swallow away all of the pain.

"They tell me he was found on the banks of the sea, bound to a mat. The party that found him considered taking him to the foreigners, but an Asmat war party took him during a dispute. I paid a great price to acquire his life when I learned he was still alive. Now your son is mine. And if you do not kill Wilam, then I will return him to Wilam, who will be forced to kill your son."

My mind was reeling, hardly connected to his words. He was speaking as if he had Stephen, but my baby had died at sea six months earlier. Our boat had been smashed by the waves and I had survived only because I'd been trapped in...

An image of my baby tied to the seat cushion flashed through my mind. He'd been bound to a mat. How did Kirutu know about the mat?

"Bring him in."

One of the warriors entered. His fingers were

wrapped around the thin arm of a small, naked child tottering on wobbly legs. A white boy with shaggy chocolate hair and blue eyes that stared up at Kirutu's towering form.

The child turned to look at me and I stared into the eyes of my own son.

The confusion and terror that flooded me in the moment are difficult to describe. I was in no condition to trust my senses and my mind was telling me that Kirutu was playing a cruel game.

My mind told me these things, but my maternal heart was crashing in my breast, telling me that Stephen, my dead son, was alive and standing before me. And I could not temper my sudden desperation for that to be true.

Then Stephen's face wrinkled and he cried and he reached his hand out for me.

A groan filled the hut. My own. I lurched for him with both hands, but Kirutu had ripped the muscles in my abdomen, and they failed me. I fell to one elbow, screaming now, blurred eyes fixed upon my son. Even then it occurred to me that I might be dreaming, and if so, then in my dream I would sweep Stephen up in my arms and I would scratch out the eyes of any man or woman who came near us.

Then Stephen was walking toward me, crying.

He reached me and wrapped his small arms around my neck and I knew then, when his cheek was pressed against my own, that my son, who had been swallowed by the sea, was alive.

Leaning on one elbow for support, I clung to Stephen with my free arm, pressed him against my breast, and wept over his shoulder.

How he had survived I did not care. What horrors he had suffered these past months I refused to imagine. All that mattered was that he was alive. And he still knew his mother.

I was clinging to more than my son in that moment. I was holding life, that great mystery that binds us all. He was an extension of my own flesh—skin on skin, cheek on cheek, fingers digging into each other's back, weeping together. Perhaps only a mother can fully understand the sentiment that swept through my body when my son, who had once been dead, returned to me alive.

And then, as quickly as Stephen had come to me, he was dragged away by Kirutu. I screamed my horror, grabbing at thin air for his body.

"You will have your son," Kirutu said.

"Don't you dare touch him!" My voice was hysterical. "I'll kill you!"

"You will have him only if you kill Wilam."

Stephen was still crying, reaching for me.

"It's OK, baby!" I could hardly speak. "It's OK, Mommy's here now."

My eyes searched his body and face. He was over two years old but still such a baby! His hair was overgrown and tangled. He had a bad sore on his right shin and a dark bruise on his cheekbone. His nose was crusted with mucus. The Tulim would have washed and tended to one of their own, but Kirutu had left my child in this condition to inflict me with pain.

"Please," I begged. "Please..."

"Take him away."

Kirutu's intentions were plain to me, and there was nothing I could do to stop him. I did not cry out for my son as they swept him from his feet and took him away. I simply lay down on my side and wept.

When Kirutu spoke again his voice was matter-of-fact, even soft.

"Now you know I have your son. If Wilam learns that your son is alive, he is bound by law to put him to death."

"You're lying..."

"By law, any child from your womb must come only from his seed. You are his wife, your child must be as well. By blood. For you to have a living son not of Wilam's seed would remove him from consideration for power."

I had never heard of the law and the thought horrified me. I tried to dismiss it as another ploy by Kirutu, but even hearing it I knew the law made perfect sense to the Tulim way of thinking.

"If your son dies now, you are purified, so I will not kill him yet. Your only hope is to kill Wilam. Once he learns that you have lost his son, you will be worthless. I offer you the only way for you and your son to survive."

"You're lying to me!" I screamed.

But I knew he wasn't.

"If Wilam isn't dead within three days, I will return your son to Wilam to be killed. If you kill Wilam, I will take you and your child to the sea."

My mind was only a dim reflection of itself, unable to process my thoughts with any certainty, but one thing was perfectly clear: I could not let any harm come to my son. Never again. Nothing else mattered to me as I lay on Kirutu's floor, weeping.

"How?" I sobbed.

He stepped over to me and bound a thin roll of leaves into my hair, near my scalp where it would not be seen without a search. "You will put this in his food. Half will be enough."

"They will find it."

"Then you will find another way or your son will die."

Kirutu turned away and left me on the floor, a shell of myself.

I don't remember what passed through my mind as the warriors bound me up and carried me over their shoulders to the clearing several miles up the mountain. I could only see my son crying, reaching for me.

They left me under a tree in the middle of the same clearing where the anthropologist Michael had led me. I lay in a heap to be found by the Impirum.

CHAPTER EIGHTEEN

MY FIRSTBORN SON was alive. And my second child was dead.

The jungle around that clearing screamed its empathy as I huddled in anguish. I can't say that I grieved my forced miscarriage as much as I grieved Stephen's life. He, like me, had been saved from the sea only to meet a much crueler fate.

In my despair I cursed God for delivering me and my son to that fate.

I cursed the Tulim valley, not because I hated the people, rather because I hated their law. Stephen's life depended on the death of Wilam at my hand. My pain beside that tree wasn't caused by the cramping of my gut, nor by the vines biting into my flesh.

It was caused by knowing that God was mocking me.

For an hour I lay in a heap, unable to think clearly. My first instinct was to run to the Warik and rescue Stephen myself. But I knew it would be a fool's errand that would end only in more pain, perhaps pain to Stephen. Cutting off one of my son's fingers would mean nothing to Kirutu.

Gradually, as my tears ran dry, the simple truth of my predicament settled into my consciousness. I slowly pushed myself to a sitting position and stared at the jungle, mind lost to any danger it might pose.

I could not trust Wilam to find grace for Stephen. His conscience was tied to the well-being of his people, and to that end he would do whatever was necessary to take power. Every bone in his body rejected the suggestion that Kirutu would bring any good to the Tulim valley.

I couldn't let him know that Stephen was alive.

Neither could I tell him of my miscarriage. If he learned that Kirutu had savaged my womb, my status among them would be compromised. The trust I had earned might be lost, and my access to Wilam along with it.

I had to have access to Wilam. It was the only way to kill him.

My thoughts surprised me, but in that frame of mind I saw no other alternative. The only chance my son had for survival was through Wilam's death. Even then I would be at Kirutu's mercy, but I didn't have time to think about that.

I had to get back to the Impirum village on my own, before the sun rose. For the sake of Stephen, I had to muster the strength and do what was needed.

I pushed myself to my feet and staggered up the path leading to the north, no longer caring what kind of dangers lay along the way. All I needed was to put one foot in front of the other.

For Stephen's sake.

It was painful, but most of the aching was in my abdomen. I gathered moss to hide the bleeding. My legs were still strong, and months of walking on bare feet had toughened my soles.

The path led over low hills into steep crevasses before climbing again on switchbacks tangled with thick roots and mud, and I slipped often. But I knew the way.

My memories of Stephen's cry pushed me forward. The image of his sweet face, dirty and hurt, dragged me forward. I was going away from him, but it was the only way to him.

The journey was long, but my sense of time was off and I found myself at the creek just west of the main village as the horizon began to gray.

I had to wash away the blood. I had to cover my abdomen in pigment to hide any bruising that would show. I needed more moss—they'd never leave me unsupervised again. I had to appear normal, even refreshed, not puffy-eyed and destitute, and as to this I felt hopeless. So I madly searched for an explanation that would allow me to avoid questioning.

The washing came easily. The pigment almost as easily, because I had applied red mud from that very creek to my face and belly on more than one occasion with the children.

The mud was on my belly when it occurred to me that there would be no way to hide my abduction. They would find the guards who had been posted outside my hut dead, unless they hadn't been killed. It was unlikely but not out of the question that they had been a part of the plot.

My mind spun. I had to tell Wilam about the abduction. But I couldn't tell him about my miscarriage. How I could avoid the subject, how I could succeed in hiding it, I didn't know, but I would try.

I set out from the creek, intent on maintaining my poise.

I only made it halfway, to the edge of the large clearing just outside the village, before he came.

Wilam came.

I heard the sound of the warriors' thundering feet before they emerged from the jungle. They came down the slope like a rushing wind in the dim morning light, five hundred of the Impirum's most skilled warriors led by Wilam, whose blurred figure looked like a ghost to me. At first I thought they were Warik and that the warrior speeding toward me was Kirutu. But then I heard Wilam's thundering cry.

Here was my savior, whom I must kill.

Wilam sprinted toward me, spear in hand, like a god bent upon rescue. His muscles were strung tightly, his jaw was taut, his eyes blazed. They'd found the guards dead and my hut empty, and in a fury Wilam had gathered his warriors and struck out to save me.

My memory of that morning is still thin. I remember Wilam's hot, heavy breath as he pulled me close. I remember his arms, already wet with sweat, holding me. I remember a sea of bodies swarming around us. I remember Wilam's voice demanding to know if I was safe.

I'd had no idea how I would react when I saw him, but I only nodded and clung to his neck and wept.

They had already come to a conclusion.

"He's taken the son!" a warrior cried. "Kirutu has taken Wilam's son!"

Wilam stood and silenced the outcry with a raised hand. I had never seen a look of such rage as the one that settled in his eyes as they swept down my body. His chest rose and fell like a bellows fueling a hot fire.

"Tell me he did not succeed."

Every fiber in my body screamed for me to tell him why Kirutu had taken me, knowing the knowledge would send him and his warriors into the Warik village to raze it to the ground. He would be too filled with rage to consider sparing the innocent, much less Kirutu.

Or he would follow the law and do as Kirutu had said he would do. I could not sentence my son to death.

Tears flooded my eyes. "Please, Wilam, please take me home. I'm safe, just take me home."

I saw the darkness in his eyes and I wondered what power lay behind them.

"Tell me!" he said.

"He did not," I said. "I still bear your child."

"He tried."

"Yes. But my muscles are strong."

"You bled?"

"No. Only a little."

Telling him any less would make him wonder why Kirutu had let me go before seeing blood.

"How can you be sure?"

"I did not lose our son!" I cried, filled with a deep denial that shook me. "I know!"

Wilam stared, unmoving, considering the meaning of my words, undoubtedly judging their truth.

I put my hand on his neck and brushed his cheek with my thumb. "They took me in the night and beat me, but I did not lose our son. He means to draw your rage. I covered myself in mud to hide my shame for having disgraced you by being taken so easily. Forgive me, my husband. I beg you…"

For several long seconds he stood in silence. Then his spear slipped from his fingers and he sank to his knees. Tears filled his eyes and his mouth opened in a cry. The silence was quickly swallowed by a terrifying wail as he bowed his head to the ground and dug at the earth with his fingers. I had been too preoccupied with my own anguish to consider the full extent of his own.

Kirutu had taken his most prized possession and sent it back bruised. My value to him might be judged only by what I could produce for him, but it was value, and having it I couldn't dismiss it.

Wilam stood, reached for me, took my face in both hands, and buried his head in my neck.

"Forgive me, my wife, forgive me, my wife," he cried.

His words cut to my heart.

"I have let that beast hurt you. Forgive me, forgive me..."

Seeing such a powerful man so undone by his failure to save me filled me with a new and dreadful pain. I knew that I couldn't kill him easily if at all.

The circle of warriors had taken to one knee, watching their fearless leader express the appropriate outrage. They knew already—this would mean war.

With a sudden grunt Wilam seized his spear, leaped to his feet, and swung the spear at the tree to our right, shattering its fire-hardened shaft. He sprang to the nearest warrior, seized his bow, and beat the tree in a rage.

Surrounded by his splintered weapons, he faced his warriors, eyes fiery. Silence gripped the clearing.

When Wilam spoke, his voice was low and certain. "For this, Kirutu will give his one life," he said. "His spirit is full of darkness. We will send his body to join it."

Immediately a familiar chant spread through the warriors as their dark, steely gazes turned down the valley toward the Warik. "*Whoa, whoa, whoa...*"

It wasn't a show of bravado, only simple resolution to defend honor without consideration for danger or consequence. I could only imagine the kind of bloodshed a battle with so many warriors would bring.

I couldn't let that happen. My son was down there.

"No!" I cried.

Wilam turned to me, glaring. "No man may do this and survive. Any threat against my seed is a threat against my rule!"

"My husband, I beg..."

"Silence!" he thundered. The vitriol in his tone set me back. A new kind of resolve had steeled his mind. In another context I might have been honored.

Knowing what I knew, I felt only fear.

He turned to his army. "We meet them in the Tegalo valley in three days' time. They wear the black grease but we are stronger and our numbers are greater." He paused, stalking before me, fists clenched, muscles strung like cords.

"Last night Isaka passed from this life. I, the

rightful ruler of all Tulim, will burn his body when we have burned Kirutu's. Send word. In three days' time we take what is ours."

Then he swept his arms under my knees and my back and lifted me as if I were but a leaf. The sea of warriors parted for him as he struck out for the village.

CHAPTER NINETEEN

MELINO AND her servants swarmed around me the moment we entered the upper courts. She tended to me like a mother hen, snapping orders for hot water and herbs to speed my healing, muttering her curses at the Warik and the spineless purum Kirutu, who would feel the wrath of Wilam as no living being had yet felt it.

She kept asking me if I was OK, was I sure that I was OK, and I could only reassure her that I was, though my words were undermined by my own conflict.

I could not bring myself to speak of what had happened in Kirutu's hut. I dared not speak a word of Stephen. The thin roll of poison lay against my skull, a haunting reminder that I'd imagined none of what I had seen or felt.

My son was alive. I had seen his face, had felt his

arms around my neck, had heard his cry for me. My need to save him coaxed desperation from my heart like a winepress.

A woman who has been violated only wants to withdraw to a safe place in hope of recovering her dignity. But memory only withdraws with her, smothering her with every detail.

The true savagery of Kirutu's violation had nothing to do with my body.

When Melino had finished cleaning me, she demanded one last assurance from me that I was resting comfortably, then hurried the servants from my hut with the strictest orders that I be left alone to sleep.

The moment she was gone, I ripped the poisonous leaves from my hair and shoved them behind the thatched wall. Then I lay down, curled up into a ball, and cried. Exhaustion pushed me into a deep sleep full of horrible nightmares.

It was late afternoon when I awoke in a haze to find Melino sitting on the floor beside my mat. Only when sharp pain flared through my belly as I tried to stand did I recall the events of the previous night. I gasped as much from the memories that flooded me as from pain.

"No, you must sit," Melino demanded. "You must not move quickly if this wound is to heal. And it must."

I leaned back against a bundle of sago leaves. Her eyes searched mine and then fell to my abdomen. "You are sure the child is still with you?"

"Yes. Yes, I'm sure."

"Wilam questions, but I've assured him. What do men know of these things? A woman knows. And if the child doesn't grow, we will know."

"No," I said. "The child will grow."

"Yes. Of course it will." She offered an empathetic smile, then spat to one side and mumbled a curse.

"That beast will pay with blood. To kill the child of any prince is punishable by death."

Any child? I had to verify Kirutu's representation of their law.

I saw the opening and asked my question.

"Have any of the prince's wives given birth to children from other men?"

"This is impossible," she said. "No woman would be so foolish. The child would have to die."

I hadn't really expected any other answer.

"A prince would choose only a pure vessel, not a woman who has any living children," she continued.

I recalled her questions of me before Kirutu's wedding ceremony. She'd asked if my son was dead. The question was a part of her vetting.

"No, of course not," I said.

Melino poked the embers with a stick.

"I've never seen Wilam so distraught," she said. "He's thrown everyone but his three ranking warriors out of the Muhanim. He refuses to speak to even me." She paused. "I fear the valley will be filled with the blood of all the Warik. They underestimate the full wrath of my husband."

And this was the man I was to kill. My great defender, who would rend the heavens to save me and the child he had placed within me.

For a moment any thought of harming him fell from my mind. I wanted my warrior to rip the enemy limb from limb for what he had done to his cherished bride! I wanted him to descend on the Warik with a roar and sever Kirutu's head from his body with a single stroke. I wanted him to save my son and defend my honor.

But I knew that none of this was possible. I wasn't his cherished bride any longer—he just didn't know it yet. And he couldn't save my son—Stephen was a stain upon his honor. He just didn't know that either. Not yet.

Mistaking my anguish for self-pity, Melino placed her hand on my knee and offered me a faint smile. "You will heal and give Wilam a beautiful son, Yuli. You must not worry."

"How can you know that Wilam will defeat Kirutu?"

She studied me for a moment. "No one can know all things. But my husband would level these mountains to save his people. If Kirutu thought he could defeat Wilam, he would have tried many times. Many will die, but Wilam cannot be killed so easily."

I lay on the mat for hours after Melino's departure, drowning in a sea of misery. I tried to think of a way out for my son, but I couldn't. And as day gave way to dusk, my despair set its hooks into my mind, like a vicious cancer.

Wilam did not visit me. No, he would not, Melino said. His mind was on war. Lela did not visit me. No, she could not, Melino said. I was to remain sequestered with the lords.

I must heal. I must keep pure. I must not endanger myself in any way.

But how could I heal Stephen's broken heart?

How could I keep pure what was torn?

How could I remove myself from danger when I was already dead?

That night I could not eat. I could barely sleep, and then only when exhaustion drew me under.

The next day the village filled with the sounds of warriors running, eerily crying out the call to war. Where the sound of children's laughter and soft songs had once filtered through the jungle, I could hear only death's haunting voice.

It wasn't merely my own disposition, though I knew I was seeing through a dark glass. Fear had settled in the valley, so thick and heavy that no sound of joy could penetrate it.

And I alone held the truth secret in my heart, where none of them could know.

I was to blame. I was the stain. I was the ruined heap huddled in my hut, a fruitless bride who held no true value. A failed mother who'd delivered her own innocent children into the arms of a fiend.

There in that hut I cursed God, because any promise I had once clung to had proven false in this valley of death.

Three days, Kirutu had said. I had three days to kill Wilam.

Two of those passed, and as each hour crawled by, my heart slipped deeper into the abyss. I tried to smile when they brought me my food, and at times I think I may have, but their minds were on war and my deep melancholy was understandable, so they paid me little attention. I was only recovering from a terrible brutalizing.

The only way to save Stephen was to kill the man who'd saved me. I tried to tell myself that he hadn't saved me, only the person that he thought me to be: a pure vessel who carried his child. I was neither.

But my reasoning offered me no desire to kill him. I could not bring myself to murder another human being.

Wilam was, in fact, my only hope. He was the one who could kill Kirutu before my son was discovered. He was the one who might then offer me mercy and allow my son to live. He was the one who might yet find a love for me that extended beyond the laws that governed their beliefs.

I clung to that terrible hope alone, knowing deep in my soul that it was insanity. Wilam would not step beyond the beliefs and laws that had guided his understanding of all that was right, any more than I could rise up and walk on water.

By the time night had fallen, even that thin thread of hope had darkened. I lay alone in my hut long after silence had swallowed the village, and slowly settled into what can only be described as a living death.

Sleep.

And in that sleep, the dream that had first lured me from distant shores visited me once again, for the first time since I had left Atlanta.

Once again I was looking down at a large valley

filled with a tangle of trees, with vines the size of my forearms running all the way to the ground. Flocks of red-and-blue parrots took flight and flapped over an endless swamp at the valley's far end. The landscape was both savage and idyllic at once.

Once again a single sweet tone reached out to me, wooing me with its unbroken, haunting note. I looked around, wondering where the song could be coming from, but I could see no one. The singular, evocative tone grew in volume, and birds from all corners of the jungle took flight toward the sound, far before me.

And then I too took flight, sailing above the trees, up the valley. A low tone joined the higher one then, a deeper note that seemed to reach into my bones. I wasn't afraid—on the contrary, I found the sound exceedingly comforting. It seemed to wrap itself around my whole body and pull me forward.

Once again in that dream I was rushing, faster and faster, headed directly for a barren hill. It was there on that hill that I saw the figure who had so often stood there, calling to me. A nameless one. An exotic creature from another world, calling out to me in a voice that was deeply comforting.

Come to me, it sang without words. *Find me. Join me. Save me...*

And once again, before I could see the singer's face, the dream faded, leaving me to darkness.

I awoke with eyes wide open.

The morning had come, and with it a deep stillness. Still gripped by my memory of the dream, I wondered if I might still be sleeping.

And then the events that had delivered me into that hut deep in the jungle crashed into my mind. Wilam. Kirutu. Betrayal.

Death.

The reality of it all crushed any lingering memory of the dream.

I jerked upright from my mat and listened for any sound. But there was none. They had gone?

My heart hammered as I lurched toward the door, quickly removed the slats, and stepped into the sunlight for the first time in three days.

Distant birds called. Smoke coiled to the sky from several huts, and if I'd used my imagination I might have heard the sound of crackling fire. Otherwise the village was silent.

Empty. I was alone?

I hurried along the upper boardwalk, looking for anyone. But there was no one to be seen. Not even the elderly loitering near the doorways to their huts.

"Melino?"

My call was hollow.

I began to run along the boardwalk. I needed someone to shatter the illusion that I had been abandoned.

But there was no one. So I ran faster, calling out Melino's name, oblivious to the pain in my abdomen, all the way to the far end of the upper courts, which overlooked the massive clearing with the lone tree at its center.

I pulled up by the railing there and stared out at the sight that greeted my eyes.

The women, children, and elderly had gathered at the north end, near the trees, looking south. A sea of black men, Impirum all, filled the grassy slopes—thousands of warriors bearing spears and bows and axes, dressed in red bands and blackened pig grease that glistened in the dawn light.

The sight took my breath away. There were no guns or horses or tanks, only flesh and blood and bone. But the raw power and savagery amassed on that grass struck me as more threatening by far, for what are metal and bullets compared to feral muscle and sinew and honor and rage?

Wilam stood facing his army, dark and strapping, bands of red and blue and yellow on his biceps, thighs, and head. Stripped down for war, strapped with taut muscles.

My heart surged at the sight of him. My warrior, who had saved me and loved me.

My husband, who would kill my son and betray me for a throne.

It was their way.

Wilam thrust his spear into the air and cried for the heavens to hear. "The enemy of my seed must pay with blood! For law, for honor, for glory, we war!"

Then he turned and loped into the jungle.

The massive sea of dark bodies moved as one behind him, surging forward with a roar that rattled the leaves. I could feel their pounding feet in the soles of my own as they swept into the jungle, close on Wilam's heels.

In a matter of moments the field emptied of warriors, like a huge bowl spilling its wrath into the jungle, leaving only a vacuous silence to keep the women, children, and elderly company.

Would Wilam have gone if he'd known I was worthless?

I, the violated one with a bastard son—an outcast without value—had sent them to their deaths with my lie.

A deep and terrifying panic swarmed me. The die was cast. Kirutu would engage them with his dark ones. Michael had warned me that a struggle for power would rip the valley apart. I had never imagined how central my role would be. Truly I was only a pawn in their eyes. A wager, a pledge, a piece of property that would soon be thrown over the cliffs with my son.

I could not remain in the upper courts. Melino could not see me in such a distraught state. You see, even then I was clinging to the impossible hope that somehow, some way, I would wake from a horrible nightmare.

I spun and ran, not caring where I went. I only had to get out of the village, to a hiding place where no one could find me.

I let misery swallow me whole. The dream that had returned to me while I was asleep only stood in mocking contrast to the reality that faced me now. I had never found love, not from a father, nor a mother, nor a husband. The only great gift the world had ever given me was Stephen.

I had followed an absurd dream and now my son would go to an early grave for a second time, innocent as a dove.

Why? Because I was not worthy. Not as a daughter, not as a wife, not as a mother.

I ran up the path that led from the Kabalan into the jungle, and I did not stop when my abdomen screamed for mercy. It deserved none, for it had failed me.

I did not stop when I could no longer see the path through my tears. They streamed down my face like a river freed from its dam.

I slowed like a stumbling, lurching cow prodded to the slaughter when my legs began to give way, but I refused to stop.

I had to get out. Just out. It no longer mattered that the jungle would swallow me or that I would be killed by a wild beast. The jagged peaks to the north would accept my resignation. The swamps to the south would drink me like an offering.

It was over. I was nothing.

But the body has its limitations, and my weakened muscles found them. I don't know how long I managed to keep moving. Only that I had reached a grassy knoll topped by several craggy boulders that overlooked the valley when my strength finally gave way.

I sank to my knees facing the boulders, lungs heaving, vision blurred. It occurred to me then that I had run north while Stephen was south. I had run away from him because in going to him I would only ensure his death. But I had still run away.

Even in this I was a failure. Powerless.

I gripped my hair with both fists, allowed my head to sag backward, and wailed as my tears wet the dust at my knees.

And there I made my outrage known to God in no uncertain terms, not sure he cared.

The rage ran its course and left me defeated. At the end of myself, my cries became a whimper.

I begged. I pleaded. My tears were my blood offering—I had nothing else.

Please...

There was no more to say.

Only *please...please...* over and over.

And then nothing, because I was sure that God wasn't listening to this lone soul on a hill in the middle of the jungle so far from home.

I slowly settled to my side, curled up in a ball, and lay like a dirty, disposed-of rag.

The wind blew gently over my skin, unaware of its mocking caress. Birds called in the jungle, unmindful of the pain on the earth beneath them.

For a long time I was dead to the world.

It was then that I heard the gentle voice, like an angel from a dream.

"Wake up, my child," it said.

CHAPTER TWENTY

AT FIRST I thought it was only another dream.

"The day is bright," the voice said. "And yet you slumber."

I pried my eyes open and stared at the grass in front of me. The voice was real? The world before me looked cockeyed from that perspective, with my cheek flat on the ground.

"Wake up," the voice said yet again, low and soothing.

It was real and it came from my right.

I jerked my head up and pushed to my elbows, twisting. There, resting against the boulder, holding a bloodstained, bone-tipped spear, stood the one Melino had called the Nameless One, watching me with kind, gentle eyes.

A two-inch strip of fox hide cinched his hair

and forehead. Similar bands encircled his ankles, knees, wrists, and elbows as well.

The short lap-lap at his midsection was made from two swaths of tanned leather—of which hide, I couldn't tell. A large tribal tattoo, an *O* of sorts, covered the right side of his chest.

He looked at me without moving, and in those eyes I saw a vast understanding that drew me like a vortex. The warm breeze continued to sweep over my skin and lift my hair, but it seemed to move with purpose now, as if it too knew something.

For a few seconds I remained still.

"My name is Shaka," he said. "Some call me the Nameless One."

I didn't know what to say. It was the third time I'd seen him since coming to the valley, and the first time I'd heard him speak.

His voice seemed to reach into my bones. I'd heard it before, not spoken, but in song. I was sure of it. My dream. But I wasn't dreaming now, I was also sure of that.

I pushed myself to my knees and thought to rise to my feet, but somehow the thought of doing so felt presumptuous.

"You're too weak to stand?"

I cleared my throat. "No."

He pushed himself off the boulder and offered me his hand. I tentatively took it and he helped me to my feet. He wasn't Tulim. His cheekbones were slightly higher and his skin wasn't as dark, but he had the scars and lean muscles of one who had mastered the jungle.

"That's better." He offered me a kind wink, then turned to face the valley like a man eyeing the journey ahead. I followed his eyes and stared at the same jungle from which I had climbed. The Tulim valley consisted of several smaller valleys bordered by the tall cliffs and jagged peaks that protected it from invading tribes. Sweeping slopes thick with jungle descended to the southern swamps, which were just beyond view.

"You seem to have a problem," he said, keeping his eyes trained to the south. "But only because you think you do."

I turned back. I wasn't sure what to think, much less say. It occurred to me that Melino would be searching for me, frantic by now. The sun was already high in the sky. Wilam might be facing off with Kirutu in the Tegalo valley as we spoke. How many had already died?

"My problem is very real," I said.

"Is it?"

"Who are you?"

"The question you should be asking," he said, shifting his eyes to meet mine, "is who are you?"

"I'm Julian. Carter. Julian Carter." So many months had passed since I'd last spoken my own name.

"Julian." The man who called himself Shaka smiled. "A nice name for a costume. And who is Julian Carter's father?"

"Richard Carter," I said. "He died a year ago."

"No one dies," he said. "They only shed their costumes."

His reference immediately connected with me, because I knew some things about spiritual beliefs, both in major world religions and among the Tulim. He was calling my body a costume.

"Who are you?" I asked again.

For a long time he didn't answer. I forgot that I was standing on a hill deep in the jungle. I saw only him. Only Shaka. My heart raced.

It raced because I suddenly saw myself in the dream that had first called me to leave Atlanta. Could Shaka be that one who'd called to me with his haunting melody?

"You're confused, my child. It's OK—so is most of the world. You don't know who you are."

"I...I'm Jullian."

"No. This is only your costume. Your role.

Daughter. Wife. Woman…" He paused, eyeing me. "Mother."

An image of my Stephen sprang to mind. He was in Kirutu's arms, reaching for me. Crying.

Our predicament stormed back into my awareness. We were both the victims of a cruel world.

"I have a son…" I stammered, tears welling in my eyes.

A gentle grunt came from the man's throat, one of infinite patience that made me feel as though I knew nothing. He tapped the butt of his long ironwood spear in the dirt and stepped forward to the crest of the knoll, ten feet from where I stood by the boulder.

A single thick scar ran across his lower back, the mark of a battle with man, beast, or jungle. I walked up to him and faced the breeze, still disoriented.

"What I tell you today, you must never forget," he said. "The truth calls to all, but few hear. You've waited a long time for this day, so you must hear. You must see."

"Hear what? I've waited?"

"Hear that you are not wife, daughter, or mother," he said. "They killed the body of one who spoke this truth a long time ago. They refused to hear and hung him from a tree. It was he who said that you're not your son's mother."

I recoiled at the absurdity of his suggestion. Not only that I wasn't a mother, but at the suggestion that the Christian faith had ever suggested any such thing.

"Here in this world, in a much lesser way, I suppose you are a mother, but where it counts, you're not," Shaka continued. "When they brought the Master his mother, he said that his mother was all who had ears to hear and eyes to see. All, one mother. It was he who also taught that if anyone tries to find the narrow way and does not set aside who they think they are and what they think they need, they cannot follow."

Shaka raised his right eyebrow and peered at me. "You say that you follow this one? Our Master. Jeshua."

"I..." He was talking of my faith. "Yes."

He smiled. "The roles you identify with are not the true you, they are only the costume you wear for a short time. The time has come to put your eyes on the light of the world, which shines brightly. All who follow need not walk in darkness. They walk instead in that kingdom within, where there is no darkness, beyond the laws which bring suffering. This is the Way. On this path the yoke is easy and the burden is light. But that Way is hard to find. Few ever do."

I didn't understand all that he meant, but looking into his eyes I felt his deep sincerity settle me. Those kind eyes were the anchor in my stormy sea.

He put his hand on my shoulder. "Hear me, my child...you suffer now because you are blind to the light that shines even now. You look for your identity among costumes. These are not your true self, one with your true Father. Being his offspring, his love flows through you already. What love can you possibly need from the world if you are already full of his? None."

He removed his hand and lazily gestured at the horizon as if the world about us were only an afterthought.

"Once you surrender to this truth, you will see that all of your suffering is insanity. Until then you will be lost in darkness. Adrift in the black sea, trying to keep your head above the water so that you don't drown. You cannot drown. Nothing can threaten the child of God."

"You know about the sea?" I asked in a cracking voice. I swallowed. "That I was taken from there by the Tulim?"

"I do. I've been waiting more than two years, knowing you would come. I knew the moment he was born."

"Who was born?"

"Stephen," he said.

A hum ignited in my mind. So then...I was right. Shaka was the one from my dreams. In that moment, having suffered far too much, I felt my resistance drain from my bones. I still didn't fully grasp his entire meaning, but I felt no compulsion to do so. His words spoke to my heart more than my mind.

"How can you hope to save this son you call yours if you yourself are walking in blindness?"

New tears blurred my vision and a knot filled my throat.

Shaka looked at me tenderly, with bottomless understanding. "Do you see the light I speak of, or are you groping in darkness?"

He wasn't talking about any ideological condition of my soul beyond this life, but the here and now, that very moment, standing on that hillside.

"I'm in darkness," I whispered. My sense of loss and hopelessness swelled and I could not hold back my confession. "I'm lost in it." Tears slid down my cheeks. "I can't see, I'm dying. God has abandoned me."

"No, my child. God is no more capable of abandonment than he is of disappointment. He's not that small or threatened. The light of his smile shines on you now. You will see that when you surrender."

"Surrender to what?"

"Surrender your false self. Your costume. Your attachment to this world."

"My son…" I trailed off, thinking of his earlier words. Anger and confusion lapped at my mind. What he suggested seemed impossible to me.

Shaka shifted his eyes to the horizon again.

"From this valley comes a great calling that will awaken many so that they might see the light beyond the dim glass. They will hear the drum and come. They will step out of the law of death and walk in the kingdom within, that eternal reality filled only with light and love."

He said it with such confidence that I could not help but believe. Believe what, I didn't yet know, because understanding was still out of my reach.

"Stephen will live an obscure life, but he's destined to find and call all of those who would step out of the law and find the narrow path. Many will follow—some won't. He will be tested in ways that few have been, but he must be if he is to show them the Way. It begins here, today, if you are willing. You don't need to understand everything now, only that the path isn't difficult when you let your old costume pass away and allow all things to be new."

He was right, I didn't understand. But he was speaking of a path that I wanted to take because, if he was right, it meant Stephen could live. Shaka might not consider me Stephen's mother as such, but I wasn't seeing the world his way yet.

I had to save my son.

"Then show me," I said. "I'll do anything to save him."

"You can't save him."

"But you said—"

"You can save only his body. His costume."

Costume again. But I was understanding more. And I didn't really care what terms he used, I only wanted to save my son.

"Show me. I'll do anything."

He studied me for a moment. A tingling settled over the crown of my head and swept down my spine as his eyes searched mine.

"You must surrender. Everything."

"I will! I do."

"Nothing will be the same," he said.

"I don't want the same."

"It may seem difficult at times."

"Nothing can be as difficult as this hell."

"It may cost you your life—the one you presently wear."

He was saying that I might die. But in the wake of the life I had lived, I didn't care.

"Show me."

The Nameless One who called himself Shaka sank to one knee and pinched up some dust, which he sprinkled into his open palm.

"Everything you think you see now is far less than what is real," he said, rising. He spat into his hand. "You will know what to do. Do not forget." Using his fingers, he mixed his spit with the dust to make mud.

He lifted his eyes to me. "When the light fades, it's far too easy to forget—we are a narcissistic breed consumed with our costumes and our performances. Remember what you see. Know who you are. Tell only those who have ears to hear."

I felt my breathing quicken. Something was going to happen, I knew that as much as I knew I was alive. A tingling coursed through me as if the very blood in my veins carried electricity.

"Close your eyes, my child."

I closed them and held my breath.

He wiped his fingers across both eyes in unison, from the bridge of my nose to my cheeks, very quickly, as if wiping something off, not on.

"See," he said.

At first I saw nothing. Pitch-darkness. It took only a moment for me to realize that I couldn't hear either. It was as though I were in a void. No sound, no sight, no sensory perception at all.

And I thought, *I'm dead*!

I opened my eyes...but I still couldn't see anything, and for a moment I felt deep fear.

And then the sound came, low, the song that had first called to me in my dreams. Once again I was there above the valley, hearing the haunting call.

Once again I was flying forward as the call grew, higher and deeper at once. A chant joined the call deep down, like the chanting of the Tulim over and over as they danced.

My fear fell away as I became intimately aware that this was deep calling to deep—a call for love. I was being called...

And this time, when I approached the hill on which I'd first seen the form I now knew to be Shaka, I was suddenly there myself, staring out at the valley as if I *were* Shaka. Before me the jungle and hills fell away to a distant alluvial plain. The sound was coming from the jungle. From all of it. Not only from the trees, but from every living thing—beast and human—groaning for love.

The light of that love is coming, I thought. *It's coming to this world.*

The moment I thought it, a single ball of light streaked directly over my head like a meteor, roaring with power. It shot all the way to the alluvial plain and there ignited in a single flash, an expanding, concussive blue-and-white wave filled with a swelling music. The valley came alive with light.

And there, in the Tulim valley, I saw.

I saw everything. Not what it suddenly became, but what it had been all along. One moment I had been blind my whole life, and the next I could see with such vision and clarity that I gasped aloud there on the knoll of the hill.

And immediately I began to weep with joy. Because I saw, you see?

I *saw!*

I saw that it was staggeringly beautiful, brimming with iridescent red-and-green light seeping from every hill, every tree, every leaf. Even the air itself shifted in translucent golds and blues.

I saw that the valley was whole, a perfect stage streaming with brilliant colors and light that was only abstractly aware of the conflicts raging between the cliffs.

I saw that nothing could possibly threaten or present the vaguest challenge to the power flowing in, through, around, and from me. I saw that my body was only a costume to be worn.

I heard.

The song from my distant dreams. Music, riding the light with such exquisite power that I felt my every bone tremble with it. Deep tones that could not be pushed lower, high melodic strains that danced with ecstasy.

I knew.

I knew that time was an illusion because there is no future and there is no past. There is only now, and what is called the future is just another now.

I knew that my Father was perfect and that nothing imperfect could have come from that perfection, much less threaten it in any way. I was safe. Saved. Now.

I knew that I too was perfect, even as my Father was perfect, and that nothing could possibly threaten me now. There was no longer any separation between me and my Father.

Weeping with gratitude and relief, I became aware that I had dropped to my knees and was shaking as unending waves of power and peace coursed through my body. Fear was as foreign to me as the sky might be to a deep-sea fish; I was swimming in a lake of raw love, pulsing with light and ecstasy.

And within a very short time that might have been many years or only a moment, I knew what I would do.

CHAPTER TWENTY-ONE

IT TOOK ME two hours to reach the Tegalo valley, judging by the passage of the sun, which slowly dipped into the afternoon sky. But for me it felt like five minutes. Time was still strange for me, now that I had lived a lifetime in the color of that stunning world that was my own.

I know that any attempt to describe my experience on that hilltop can only be truly appreciated by those who have seen truth with their own eyes wide open, and I know that the memory of it easily fades, pulled away by the gravity of entrenched thinking and the law of this world.

Even as I rushed through the Tulim valley without regard for my safety, streaking for the shallow valley called Tegalo, where death was boldly flexing its shadowy, vacant muscle, I was still half-trapped in another vision of jungle around me.

More than green leaves and dark trunks, I saw the unfolding of all creation, welcoming me with open arms as if calling me: *Come. Come to me, come and be. Come and live.*

More than the birdcalls that I had become accustomed to over the months, I heard the song of angels. More than a path cutting into the valley of death, I ran down a street paved with love and light.

For I had touched the source of all bliss and he was my Father, who is God.

After an eternity on the hilltop, the light had faded. It had taken me a full ten minutes to reorient myself. Shaka was no longer with me, but I hadn't expected him to be. He had nothing more to say to me. I had heard all that I must.

I knew which path to take: the one that headed east of both the Impirum and Warik villages. To the valley of bloodshed called Tegalo, where the costumes of a deceived world clung to insanity and embraced hatred.

I ran on feet that hardly felt the roots and mud beneath them. It wasn't until I broke from the tree line onto a hillcrest overlooking the Tegalo valley that I heard the sound that stabbed my surety.

I pulled up sharply, staring up the at the grassy knoll before me, panting. A dull roar rose from the valley beyond, the sound of a monster with interminable breath determined to shake the heavens.

It was then that a small balloon of fear began to inflate deep in my belly. I knew the path that I would take, and any mother or father or wife or husband or child or woman or man might find my choice unthinkable for the pain and sorrow it promised.

For a few moments I stood there, heaving, aware of my swelling fear.

But having seen the truth, I also knew that I was not mother or wife or child or woman.

Shaka's words came to me again like a song spun from the light that swept through my mind.

The roles you identify with are not the true you, they are only the costume you wear for a short time. The time has come to put your eyes on the light of the world, which shines brightly. All who follow need not walk in darkness. They walk instead in that kingdom within, where there is no darkness, beyond the laws which bring suffering. This is the Way.

The fear ebbed.

I ran.

With each step the roar grew, as if it could hear me coming.

And then I crested the hill and the Tegalo valley

came into my sight, spread out in all of its own feigned glory.

Far below me a massive river of black bodies flowed in a circle of writhing flesh, brightly colored with red, yellow, and white feathered headbands and body paint. Ten thousand strong from all three clans formed the Tulim tribe in that distant jungle paradise, that hole ripped out of hell, hidden where no white woman in all the world had seen it except one.

Her name was Julian Carter and she thought she was me, but I was far more than her.

I say paradise because I knew that there was great beauty behind the seething anger; light hidden by the blood.

I say hell because they were blind to both beauty and light. Death had been conquered and its law abolished, but they were its prisoners still.

Chants, low and ferocious from the throats of thousands, punctuated the din—two choruses in as much conflict as the warriors' spears and arrows and blades. A large pyre of wood rose from the center of the circle, and heaped around it were the bodies of those already killed.

I saw immediately the method of their warfare. Rather than form two lines approaching head-to-head, they circled in a thick band from which individual warriors broke out to meet their enemies in single combat. The pace didn't slow when a warrior was gutted by his opponent's blade. His body was simply dragged and dumped by the piled wood, where it likely would be burned with all of the dead later, an offering to the spirits.

My heart hammered there on the hill as I stared down at the carnage. It was all so pointless. So misguided. Such insanity.

Then I saw Wilam, the husband who had claimed me for the son I would bring him. My heart surged. Such a magnificent man, spinning out from the thick band of fighters to meet a Warik warrior in the open.

Like a black stallion formed into a man, he loped toward one as strong and tall as he. The sweat on his dark skin glistened in the sun as he leaned into his gait, rushing headlong for his prey.

His opponent showed no sign of fear. Surely their hearts were pounding with terror, gripped by the certainty that one of them would lie dead within a matter of minutes.

The rest of the valley fell away from my consciousness as I focused on the imminent collision of flesh. Time slowed and I watched their precise movements.

Wilam held his spear wide like a sword in one

hand; a bone-handled club with a polished gray stone head was in the other. The Warik warrior ran crouched low like a lion, bearing a long bone dagger and shield.

They did not slow or feint or duck or jump.

They collided shield against body in open field, the Warik slashing up with his dagger, Wilam spinning from the blade. And as he spun, Wilam's cry of rage rose above the din. His extended spear cut through the air as he twisted beyond the man, spun through a full turn, and sliced back around to meet the Warik warrior from behind.

Astonished, I watched as his sharpened spearhead sliced through the man's neck like a sword and dropped him in a heap.

For a moment Wilam stood his ground, half-crouched, muscles taut, still crying his rage, glaring in the direction of Kirutu across the field.

I had the impression that all of this was preamble to a direct confrontation between the two brothers. And it occurred to me in that moment that Kirutu would prevail.

He had drawn Wilam to his death through the law so that he could emerge as the leader who had upheld the law without compromise.

But I was now the bearer of a new law.

Wilam broke from his kill and jogged back into

the thick of his men as their chants marked his victory.

Whoa, whoa, whoa, whoa...

Two Warik warriors peeled off the main circulating body, grabbed the arms and legs of the fallen man, hauled him like a pig to the center of the valley, and dumped him among the dead.

It was absurd.

It was insane.

It was the way of all humans.

And then, as if someone had spoken to them in a single voice, the huge band of Warik warriors slowed. Stopped. Stared down-valley. A cry rose from the Impirum, who quickly pulled up and turned to look down-valley with the Warik.

The form of Sawim, shaman of the Karun tribe, could not be mistaken. He walked slowly but deliberately using a cane, standing tall. From his shoulder hung a net bag. My heart lurched.

Sawim walked into the valley as one who cannot be touched, in much the same way that Shaka had once walked in to save me under the tree. Among the Tulim, power conquered—but not at the expense of the law, and the law was administered by the will of the feared spirits.

I wanted to run then, down into the battleground where my fate awaited me. But I knew that these three men—Kirutu, Wilam, and Sawim—all had to agree with what I would propose. So I waited high upon the hill behind them, allowing my blood to run through my veins like hot light.

I spent precious seconds remembering what I had seen. Hearing again Shaka's words and those I'd heard on the wind while my eyes were wide open. I fixed my eyes on the net bag Sawim carried so nonchalantly.

The circle had parted already, half with Kirutu, half with Wilam, both of whom had stepped away from the warriors and now stood waiting with heaving chests near the strewn bodies of the dead. I didn't know how long they'd been in battle—long enough to satisfy Sawim.

The shaman knew precisely what he was doing. As did Kirutu. Only Wilam did not know.

My heart broke for my husband. It hardly mattered that I had been taken by him as a person might take a loaf of bread. In their eyes I was his wife, and I had come to respect him as such despite all that I knew.

And now, knowing more, I loved him. Having seen, I found it nearly impossible to harbor any resentment for any of the Tulim. They were simply doing what they knew to do.

But I wasn't there for the Tulim. Not yet.

I was there for Stephen.

Sawim stopped before Wilam and Kirutu, and for a few long seconds silence hung over the valley. He wasn't wearing a mask, and even from that distance I could see that he saw me. It likely gave him some pleasure.

He slowly lifted his hand and spoke in a voice for all to hear.

"Beyond the valley given to all Tulim by the Creator of all, the wam wait for us to fail our ancestors by allowing evil into our hearts," he cried, turning slowly to address the whole crowd. "The law of our people must be fulfilled on this day or all Tulim will die at the hands of this evil. There is among us one defiled, out of the law, and this one must die."

He waited a moment for any challenge, but none came. Then he set the net bag on the ground and reached into it with both hands.

I began to walk then. On feet that were numb as much from what I was about to do as from the run, I strode down the grassy slope, eyes fixed on that bag.

Without fanfare Sawim lifted a small, sleeping child out of the bag and lifted him over his head.

Stephen's small naked body lay still in the shaman's boney grasp. They'd surely sedated him.

I knew that I was far more and far less than mother to him, but in that moment I wanted only to save him. It was now my sole purpose, mother or not.

Indeed, I had been drawn from American shores to this end. Of that I now had no doubt, not even a whisper of it.

"I give to you the son of the one taken by Wilam!" Sawim cried.

Dead silence. Wilam's back was toward me, as was Kirutu's, so I could not see their reactions. But the fact that Wilam didn't protest was reaction enough for me. He was bound by their law and that law would now be exercised.

"By our law Wilam must take the child's life, on the fire. In this way he will redeem himself for the grave error that he has made. Only in this way will he save himself from evil."

The breeze lifted my hair, a warm caress of assurance. I was only a third of the way down the hill, but I did not break into a run.

"As is the law, Wilam will take the life of this child now," Sawim said.

He stepped up to Wilam and held Stephen out. For a long beat Wilam made no move to take my son. But he would have no choice if he hoped to save his own life, much less his bid for the throne.

I knew what was going through his mind. Neither Stephen nor I could compare to his bid for power. He was destined to rule. In taking this white child's life, he would retain his honor and his bid for power to save the Tulim from Kirutu's rule.

He was likely thinking he would do what he must, and then, filled with rage, slaughter Kirutu before returning home to see his child grow in my womb while he ruled.

He didn't know that I had miscarried. Kirutu could make the claim, but for now, only I truly knew. And the bid for power was now, not when they discovered that no child grew in my womb.

Wilam slowly held out his arms and Sawim placed my son in his hands. The shaman held up his hand and a runner broke from the thick swath of Warik warriors, carrying a burning torch.

I was now halfway to them and I still did not run. I was only playing my part in a grand stage play unfolding in this valley. My heart was breaking, but I felt it as if slightly apart from my body. Because I knew then that it was my costume, not the true me, who was feeling deep sorrow and pain.

My pain wasn't necessarily bad or good. But in truth, I wasn't my mind, you understand? I wasn't my emotions or my body. These were only a part of my human experience confined to this life. This I had learned when Shaka had helped me see.

The runner handed the torch to Sawim, who held it high, then walked to the pyre and shoved the flame into the middle of it.

The wood caught immediately. They'd soaked it in resin.

Wilam held my son, stock-still, back still to me. Not a word came from the thousands gathered. They knew as well as he—this he must do to retain his honor.

"Cut the child's throat and burn his body," Sawim said.

Not until I reached them did the outer ring of warriors see me. They moved aside quickly, unsure of my presence, and I cut through them without a word, eyes fixed on Wilam as they parted. And then I was fifty paces from him.

Sixty from the blazing fire.

"Do what you must!" Sawim cried.

"No, Wilam." I did not yell, but my voice might as well have been a slap to his ear.

He twisted his head, and I saw his face for the first time. My husband was terrified but forcing himself to show strength before his people. I saw it in his wide eyes and the slight draw of his lips.

"No," I repeated, speaking directly to him. "You will not kill my son."

Kirutu turned as well, and I could see the smug

look of one who had achieved his goal. Had he known that I would come to save my child?

"A woman orders the prince?" Kirutu growled.

"I order no one," I said, louder now, approaching still. "I only make clear what is already known."

"A wam knows nothing of what is true," Kirutu said.

The dark shaman Sawim scanned the hills, not with fear, but with interest. Looking for something. For the one who would save me.

"I know that not even a prince may step beyond the law passed down from your ancestors," I said.

"Leave us!" Wilam snapped. "You are my wife! You carry my child. You have lost your mind to come!"

I stopped three paces from him and eyed him with compassion.

"I do not carry your child, Wilam." I spoke for the ears of Kirutu, Sawim, and Wilam alone.

Wilam blinked.

"I will never bear another child. I no longer offer any value to the prince of the great Impirum. I am no longer fit to be your wife. You must now throw me away, because Kirutu is right. I am mere wam."

The fire roared; sweat beaded Wilam's face. Though they could not know it, the Tegalo valley now lay on the fault line of a great shift.

"The Tulim will not respect any prince who clings to a wam merely for pleasure. You must throw me away," I continued. "You will no longer have a wife with a son of another man's seed. In doing this, you are not compelled to kill the child in your arms."

I could see the truth of his predicament settle into his mind. He'd descended on the Tegalo valley to defend his honor and claim his right to rule. He was now faced with an impossible choice.

"Did I not warn you, Brother? To defend your honor, you must now kill them both. No wam may influence the great Tulim."

I knew Wilam well enough to read the horror on his ever-sure face. So subtle on the surface, but beneath his skin he was screaming in pain.

Stephen's small chest rose and fell as he dreamed in deep sleep, far away from the valley. I was his mother and for that I would die, but I was also the keeper of a greater truth, and for that I would offer him life.

I stepped closer and looked up at Wilam.

"There's another way," I whispered. Only he could hear. "If you fulfill your law you will be retain your honor, I understand. But you do not have to kill us."

"You cannot know our law."

And yet I did, at least that which Shaka had shared with me after my eyes had been opened.

"I'm of no value to you now. I cannot be your wife, only your servant. Offer me to Kirutu in exchange for my son."

"There is no way for me to save this child," he said. "It is our law."

"Banish him," I said. "Turn him out of the law, to be banished forever."

Wilam's eyes briefly narrowed. "He would die in the jungle."

"Trust me, Wilam. Banish my son. Trade me to Kirutu for my son and banish my son from your law. He will be outlaw."

"I don't—"

"You can do this? By law?"

He hesitated. "Yes."

"And you would retain your honor in the sight of all."

He was at a standstill. He knew as well as I that trading me to Kirutu would end very badly for me. I saw his eyes soften.

"You love this child as we love our own."

"Yes," I said.

"He will only die in the jungle."

"Trust me," I whispered, laying my hand on his

arm. "Do this one last thing for the woman you once saved. Save my son. Give me to Kirutu."

"He will crush you in ways beyond your understanding."

"That is my burden to bear, not yours. You will save my son. I beg you. Do it now. Call it out for all to hear."

He searched my face, swallowing once deeply.

"Now," I said.

Wilam finally dipped his head so that only I could see, then turned with one hand raised high, cradling Stephen in his other arm.

"This woman is not my wife." His voice rang out for all to hear. "Her son is not my offspring. As is permitted, I offer her to you, my brother, in exchange for the child."

Kirutu looked momentarily stunned.

"She was yours to find." Wilam's voice, though softer now, carried. "Yours to bring. And I now return her to you in exchange for this child."

"The child cannot live among us!"

"If I keep the child, all of Tulim will judge me. I will not keep him."

"He may not leave the valley alive," Kirutu protested.

"Do I forget the law? Am I not my father's son? The child will not live among us. Take the woman you brought among us and give me her child so that our warriors will see that jealousy and spite don't rule your heart."

For a moment Kirutu stared, first at Wilam and my son, then at me.

"I accept," he said.

My pulse rose as I returned his stare. His eyes were holes into a world of rage and darkness. My life was at his mercy, though he knew none.

And then I remembered the world as it really was and I felt my fear dissolve. But there was still the matter of my only son, sleeping peacefully in Wilam's arms.

Trust me, Julian. Breathe.

"The boy cannot live," Sawim said. "He is yours to burn."

"I will not subject any child to the flame. Instead I will turn him out of our law and banish him forever as is permitted."

Trust me, Julian. Breathe.

"He is a child," Kirutu objected.

I was watching Sawim, and the moment I saw him go still I knew.

The warriors to my rear suddenly began to move, uttering surprise under their breaths. I turned my head and saw.

I saw them parting like waters, hurrying to escape the one who'd come into their midst. Some knew him only as Kugi Meli, the evil spirit. Some as the Nameless One.

I knew him as Shaka.

He walked toward us in even strides, undaunted and sure, face void of expression. His spear was his walking stick, and in his eyes he beheld the world as it truly was.

I faced Wilam. No words were needed. He knew immediately what I intended and I saw nothing but wonder in his eyes.

Shaka strode up to Wilam, eyes on Stephen. Sawim had taken a step back; Kirutu held his ground, bound by fear of a deeper magic.

Shaka lifted his eyes and stared at Wilam, who returned his gaze as if momentarily ensnared.

"I will take the boy," Shaka said in a gentle tone that carried. "He will not be seen among the Tulim. In your eyes he will be dead."

"This is not permitted!" Sawim cried. "No man may care for the child."

"The Nameless One is not a man," I said for all to hear. "You yourself proclaimed it."

Sawim hesitated, and in that long beat he sealed his own pronouncement. There was no way for him to backtrack. It would only compromise his own standing as one who knew the spirits.

"Yuliwam is right," Wilam said. "Sawim has declared this to be so. He is no man." He lifted Stephen high. "Today, for all to see, I turn this child out from among us and into the hands of he who comes. He is outlaw. To all Tulim, he is dead."

The valley was gripped by silence. None objected.

None could.

Wilam glanced at me, then handed Stephen to Shaka, who took my son in his free arm and offered Wilam a single nod. Shaka did not speak further. He directed no harsh glance toward Kirutu. He simply did what was required of him.

What he had come to the valley to do.

He was now my son's father.

I took Stephen from Shaka when he came to me, and I held him close to my breast. Silent tears slipped down my cheeks as emotions I did not understand washed through my heart and mind. I might not ever see my Stephen again, I knew that, but I also knew that he was safe in the care of a man who understood a mystery that few could comprehend.

I had never loved Stephen as much as I did in that moment.

"Write your story," Shaka said. He withdrew a hide-covered sheaf of old paper, which he pressed into my hand. "Write your story for your son and those who would know. I will find a way to retrieve it. Remember the light. Find us in your dreams. We will be there always."

He kissed my forehead.

"Surrender. And dream. You are with us always."

And then the one named Shaka took Stephen from my arms, walked through the parted circle of warriors, up the hill's crest, and vanished from our sight.

EIGHTEEN YEARS LATER

CHAPTER TWENTY-TWO

THEY STOOD side by side on the sheer cliff's edge high above the Tulim valley. Shaka and Stephen. Silent.

A thick white fog ran the length of the valley, like creamy milk that had settled in a basin, obscuring what lurked beneath. Not even a whisper of wind disturbed the placid haze. The scene stretching out before them was inordinately quiet, as if trapped in time itself.

Not knowing better, Stephen might have guessed that the whole world was in slumber.

But he knew better. The powers of insanity never slept, always vying for a voice that justified their lies.

Insanity. The insane self. The false self. The flesh self. The ego, the mistaken mind, the costume, the roommate...all names used liberally by Shaka.

And, as Shaka had so often said: *The insane self always speaks first, always speaks the loudest. It is suspicious in the least, vicious at worst, and make no mistake, it wants you dead.*

It wanted the *real* him dead. The one that wasn't body, or thought, or emotion, but soul. Essence. Being. Truth. I.

Still, something was in the air—a sense of impending discovery that was all too familiar to him.

Stephen stared ahead.

"Why have you brought me here, Shaka?"

His teacher and father, though not by blood, remained silent until Stephen turned his head to look at him.

"The time has come," Shaka said.

He'd spoken many times of the others who shared the world with them, but Stephen had only seen three others in his lifetime, each from a distance, each filling him with wonder. Perhaps the time had come to enter the world of others. Mystery filled his mind as he thought this.

"Time for what?"

"For what you make of it."

This was Shaka's way—always leading, never pressing.

"It?"

"Him."

Him. Another of Shaka's words for Stephen's body, mind, costume, self. The one called Stephen who shared a life with the real him.

"The insane one?" He looked at the man. "I already know him," Stephen said.

"Do you?"

Stephen smirked. "He's the one who tries to make me crazy and turn my head hazy. To do what I would not, and not do what I would." He crouched and made claws with both hands, eyes wild. "He's the beast that stalks in the fog of night and screams like a spoiled brat when I don't shiver with fear." Stephen slapped at his face with both hands, like a wild man. "Berserk, that's what he is. Plain insane."

Shaka regarded him with a cocked eyebrow. "Is that so?"

Stephen righted himself and smiled. "That is far too so."

Shaka nodded and returned his gaze to the valley. He was accepting, even encouraging of Stephen's antics. The spice of life, he called such things. The costume and all of its traditions, ways, and codes of behavior are best not taken too seriously.

"You think you know him," his teacher said. "And yet he hasn't fully shown himself to you."

Shaka's fingers eased their grip on the long spear in his right hand, then curled back around the wooden shaft. Though Stephen had watched his own body grow over the many years they'd lived together, Shaka did not seem to age. They were now the same height and, although Stephen's strength was now greater than his teacher's, both were equally proficient in commanding paths and trees and water and beasts with ease.

"I've seen enough of him to last me a lifetime," Stephen said.

"And yet so little of him for the life you've lived."

"He's dead," Stephen objected. "As a snake on the fire."

"And yet he writhes with fangs spread wide."

"Then we take the head off and eat it with sago."

"Might taste good," Shaka said. "Always loved snake head in a stew."

Stephen's mouth watered at the thought, not of the head so much as the flesh of snake, which tasted similar to bird.

"You have the head, I'll take the rest."

"Leave me the tail. Need a new whip."

"Done."

Shaka faced him, deep-set brown eyes gentle and knowing. The round emblem tattooed on his chest marked him with an eternal commitment. *Deditio.* A word in a foreign tongue called Latin that meant "unconditional surrender." They spoke in the tongue of the valley below, but Shaka had taught him a language called English as well. Why? Because it was a written language, and one day reading would be an important part of his journey. How, Stephen did not yet know.

"Tell me, where does Stephen live?" Shaka asked, serious once again.

Stephen hesitated, navigating the pathways to the true question behind his teacher's words. By Stephen, did Shaka mean his true self, or the one made of flesh and bone? The latter, he thought.

"He lives in the mountains above the Tulim valley in a world known as New Guinea."

"Where does he sleep?"

"He sleeps in a home next to the Wagali River." Stephen lifted his arm and stretched a finger west. "There, a short run though the thickest jungle." Then, in jest, "Longer for Shaka."

His teacher's mouth hinted at a smile and he offered a wink.

"You would like to see?" Stephen asked.

"Only five moons ago it would have taken you longer than me."

"I have little use for the past," Stephen said. "That past no longer exists. Nor did it ever. It was always and always will be just another now."

Shaka nodded. "And once again my own teaching shows me up. Then tell me about the present. What does his costume look like?"

Stephen glanced down at his form. Black bands woven from cured *angalo* fiber hugged his wrists and his arms just above both elbows. Next to Shaka's his skin was pale, marked with old scars on his right forearm, his knee, and one of his thighs, this last one from a boar. His hands were steady and strong, one gripping a hardwood spear slightly thicker than Shaka's.

Dark wavy hair held in place by a strip of red-dyed canvas hung to his shoulders. Otherwise they were dressed the same: fox hides around their hips, mud from the run to the cliff dressing their feet and ankles. A single bone knife was strapped to his waist.

The muscles on his arms, chest, and legs had grown with Shaka's never-ending physical challenges, all of which were designed more to assist him in stepping past the constraints of his body than to strengthen it. Still, there wasn't a beast alive that could put him down. None that he'd met, at least. A large crocodile, perhaps, but only if he was caught unaware and couldn't outmaneuver its powerful jaws.

"His costume is strong," Stephen said.

"And his mind?"

"His mind is quiet. My true mind is at peace."

"Why is this?" Shaka asked. The questions were a regular exercise.

"Because my true self is always at peace, dead to insanity. Only the insane mind offers any disturbance to the sound mind."

"And who gave you this sound mind?"

"The One from whom I come."

"What is his name?"

"He is called the One. The Way. The Truth. The One who first defeated death and is life. The One who is perfect and whole, one with God, the atonement, having made right all that was wrong. He has been called the second Adam. Jeshua."

"And you?"

"My true self is now made whole, holy, without any further blame, condemnation, or need for correction. I am dead to the old and alive in him. I am my Father's child."

"And what wars against this knowledge?"

"The knowledge of good and evil. Insanity. Also the costume."

"Which came how?"

"This is the most common knowledge, Shaka. Why do we repeat it again on this cliff?"

His teacher only cast him a sidelong look, which was enough. *Trust me.*

"By the eating of the fruit of the tree of this knowledge," Stephen said. "And yet there is in this same garden a tree of life. My insane mind dies at the foot of this tree."

"Can anything threaten you?"

"Nothing can separate me. As far as the east is from the west, so far has he removed any separation from him. I am blameless and nothing can remove me from my Master. It is impossible."

"Still, though dead, your insane mind speaks and causes suffering."

"Like a madman. Jabbering always, his mouth moves to a different beat. He likes to hear himself speak. *Jika, jika, jawa.* Madman coming."

"And sometimes you listen," Shaka said.

"Only when I forget he is dead."

"And when you do listen?"

"He tempts me to feel threatened. Less than whole and therefore needing more than I already have. Love. Joy. Peace. States of being, not simple emotion."

"And emotion is?"

"Sometimes pleasurable, sometimes not, depending on if I listen to insanity."

"Is your insane mind speaking now?"

Stephen considered the question, searching his mind for any disturbance, knowing that only radical honesty would suffice.

"He is saying that a breeze would be nice," he said.

"And this is insane why?" Shaka asked.

Stephen lifted his hand and slowly swept it through the hot, still air, aware of the sweat on his brow and chest. "Because the thought comes from a place of slight discontent with the heaviness of the air. My costume judges the air for not moving to cool the body, and in so doing judges me. As a result I suffer."

"Judge not lest you be judged," Shaka said.

Stephen lowered his arm. "And even now I release this insane judgment to what is."

"How do you release it?"

"By accepting the comfort sent by my Father and offering the world love instead of resistance."

"And the scars on your leg?"

"They are nothing! I forgive them as well. In fact, I love them. Are they not beautiful? Nothing poses even the slightest threat to me. I am made whole in him."

"Nothing can threaten you," Shaka repeated, turning to gaze down-valley. "Certainly not all of this hot air." His eyes twinkled at his clever pun. "And yet your costume feels threatened. Far too often. It is the only reason you ever feel fear of any kind."

"But I do not, Shaka. Only this air that—"

"He does, Stephen."

He. Stephen's false self. The one that died a long time ago, when the true Stephen first accepted the truth.

"He does," Shaka said. "And he has not yet walked through the valley of the shadow of death."

Stephen studied the valley below them, feeling no fear. Shaka had turned his attention to the Tulim valley more often of late, but the shift in his focus caused Stephen no concern. Evidently there was something down there that would test him further, and yet, knowing nothing of it, Stephen felt no disturbance. Only curiosity.

"Beneath the fog a struggle looms," Shaka said. "A grand stage for those threatened by death's shadow face every day. In this valley, insanity runs amok."

"I feel no threat."

"No. Not yet. Darkness has swallowed them, Stephen. They are blind. Captive in the night. And if you forget who you truly are, their insanity will call you into its dark pit."

He'd never heard his teacher speak so bluntly about the valley. Still, they were only words and they held no meaning for him and so he felt nothing.

"Get your bow."

Stephen spun, stepped to the ledge behind him, and snatched up the bow.

"One arrow," Shaka said.

He plucked up one of the reeds they'd formed into arrows over the night fires. Then returned to the precipice.

Shaka flipped a fist-size fruit—a guava—into the air, sending it far from the cliff.

"Through the heart," he said.

With practiced ease Stephen strung the arrow, calmly lifted the bow, made the appropriate reckonings for distance, wind, and trajectory, and released the string. The arrow sliced through the heavy air and struck the fruit as it fell. The impaled guava jerked away from them and dropped lazily toward the jungle far below.

"Bang! Dead. She falls into the abyss to be plucked by a lucky bird."

"What do we say of this?" Shaka asked.

"That I never miss my mark."

Shaka's brow arched. "Never? I've sent you chasing after a thousand spent arrows in my time."

"That was the past. It no longer exists. Now it's never." He could not hide his whimsical grin.

"Touché yet again. Clever boy. A miss means what?"

"To miss the mark is to be separated from the truth. In another land they call it sin. Evil. Missing the mark. If I separate myself even a fraction from my true identity, I suffer."

"It's harder to hit the mark when strong winds blow."

"True enough."

Shaka faced him. "You must know that a storm is coming."

Stephen dipped his head. "My heart will fly true."

Shaka studied him for a long moment, and for the first time since coming to the cliff, Stephen felt a prick of concern.

"Do you doubt me, Shaka?"

"The insane secretly crave suffering. It gives them an identity, however absurd."

"I am not insane."

"I don't doubt you, Stephen. The question is whether you will doubt yourself. For this day you were born. You are Outlaw, dead to the laws of separation and death that cause insanity. Soon those laws will try to reclaim you as they have the whole world. The storm will blow and your aim will be tested. Then you will be tempted to forget who you are and deny the truth."

"Never."

"But you will, Stephen. More than once."

He stared at Shaka, confused.

"But have no fear," Shaka said. "This too is necessary. Only by walking through the valley of darkness do you realize that death is only a shadow."

"I'm going to the valley?"

"I have raised you as a son, teaching you all you must know to be who you are. For this day I also came. And then my work will be done."

"Done? I will be alone?"

His teacher smiled. "Alone?"

This too was Shaka's way, always pressing for precision. In that place of knowing his true identity, there could be no true loneliness, because Stephen was one with his Father.

"I am never alone. Only my costume feels alone because he is afraid he is not enough. But I am complete. I will never be alone."

"No. In fact, you will soon be surrounded by many. Then you may wish you were by yourself. Which is only more insanity."

"Insanity. Always insanity. *Jika, jika, jawa.* Madman coming."

"*Jika, jika, jawa.* Madman coming." Shaka turned from the cliff. "The time has come." He strode toward the tree line thirty paces distant. A tangle of vines and thick moss was draped from heavy branches that blocked the fading sun's light from reaching the muddy trail beneath.

"It's time for you to see."

See what, Stephen did not ask, nor did he care to. His trust in Shaka had been forged over many years. Whatever his teacher wanted him to see or learn, he simply would, in its right time.

CHAPTER TWENTY-THREE

IT WAS dark when they broke from the trees and approached the clearing in which they'd constructed their three huts—one for cooking, one for sleeping, one for individual reflection if the training called for it.

It was in this third hut, which was built high on stilts, that Stephen had learned to be perfectly still for hours, sometimes days, searching the deepest parts of his mind. And then going beyond his thoughts to the place where the mind had to be stilled to truly *know*.

He was now twenty, Shaka said. He could recall being sequestered in the tall hut through the night at age six, feeling alone until that great warmth came to his soul and assured him that he was not alone. Rather he was in a world of light and color, oddly one with it, as if he himself were made of the same fabric as the light.

It was then, only after Stephen had informed Shaka of his experience, that his teacher had begun his bodily training, because unless one was connected with his true self, all else was futile, he said.

Stephen could not remember the last time he'd truly felt alone. Even when Shaka headed into the mountains, often for days at a time, Stephen felt no loss. The darkness offered him no threat, nor did anything.

He remembered the words of his teacher when he was only seven or eight years old:

"How big is God, Stephen?"

"As big as a bull," he'd cried, citing the beasts Shaka had told him about

"A bull. Fine, let's make him a bull. Can this bull be threatened by any other?"

"No, he's far too powerful."

"And evil...If we say that God is a big bull, how big is evil? What animal should we make evil?"

Stephen had considered this question for a moment.

"Like a mouse."

"Can this mouse threaten the bull?"

"He could bite it on the leg."

"And make the bull snort away in pain?" Shaka asked, brow raised.

Again Stephen had gone deeply into consideration for a solution, because he knew that God could not fear any threat.

"Then we must make the bull bigger," he said.

"How big?" Shaka asked.

"As big as the jungle. Then this mouse wouldn't threaten him."

"Why don't we make the bull as big as the sea?" Shaka asked.

"Yes! The sea!" Stephen had cried, thrusting both fists into the air.

Shaka had laughed, joining his delight.

"As big as the world!" his teacher said.

"The whole world. Then the bull would not even feel the mouse if it bit him on his leg."

Shaka had nodded. "The truth, my son, is that you still make your idea of God far too small. He is as big as the sun. As a thousand suns. As the universe. And this is only his mouth, which speaks all that is into existence."

Stephen had stared up into his teacher's eyes, lost in wonder.

"And the mouse?" Shaka asked.

"Is still only a mouse," Stephen said.

"And that mouse is like a speck that cannot

threaten, nor harm, nor even disturb such a bull."

Shaka had looked into the fire with glassy eyes, and Stephen thought he could see the sun in them.

"The people of this world make a god for themselves in their own image, and in doing so they make God far, far, far too small. His power is infinite. Evil is finite. Finite to infinite is like a speck of sand to a billion suns. This is your Father. You are his. In him, you cannot be threatened or harmed or disturbed. Your costume alone holds the illusion that such harm is possible and so it screams."

The truth of this had stayed with Stephen through many dark nights.

They subsisted mostly on fruits and vegetables taken from the jungle, small game, and boars. Occasionally crocodile meat and fish, but only when they headed south to the swamps, where Shaka first told Stephen about what it meant to be a Water Walker and then guided him in becoming one. By this he meant the art of forgiving. Of letting go.

Shaka dipped beneath the overhang of the cooking hut's grass roof and led Stephen into the small round room, lit by only glowing embers in the shallow pit at the center. Without a word he placed several large splinters of wood on the dying ash and gently coaxed the hot coals to life. The embers sprouted flame, fed on the fuel, and lapped hungrily for more wood, which Shaka supplied.

Stephen squatted across from him, arms on his knees.

Shaka looked up at him. "When two glowing logs are placed together?"

"They produce a greater fire than either alone."

"The nature of this fire?"

"Depending on the nature of the logs, love or hate," Stephen said.

Shaka nodded. He stood and crossed to the wall. Reaching up, he removed a small bundle wedged under the eaves. Stephen had never seen it before. This also was the common way of Shaka.

"You are that log, Stephen. I have been the second log. With me you have learned to burn bright. Now the time comes for you to join others whose fire is burned out or covered up."

So then he was going to the valley. His pulse quickened with curiosity.

"I will meet a woman?"

Shaka's eyebrow arched. "You will. Two. One to lead you in, one to lead you out. I trust both will be your salvation."

"What need is there for salvation when I am saved already?"

"You are saved tonight. When the winds blow strong, you may find yourself in need."

Shaka settled to the ground and began to unwrap the bundle.

"What did I tell you of your birth?"

"That I was born in a place where many have the color of my skin. I was taken from the sea and traded. You have raised me as your own son."

Shaka withdrew a black, hide-covered book like others he'd used to teach Stephen the art of reading.

"And your mother?"

"My mother? Her fate is unknown."

"Unknown, yes. But I have reason to believe that she's still alive."

The revelation was interesting. His mother, alive. But it sparked no great concern on his part.

"What does he think about this?" Shaka asked, eyeing him.

"He thinks that if she's alive, he could meet her one day. He is her son. But my true self knows that this is only a costume I put on. All are my mother, all are my brother. I am the son only of the One inside of me."

"True. I have decided that you are ready to face the crucible of the insanity in the valley where I last saw your mother. In which I believe she may still live."

"Which valley?"

"The Tulim valley."

So close? He'd never set foot in the valley nor seen the Tulim up close, and the thought of doing so once again quickened his pulse. Perhaps he would meet a woman. Such a curiosity. It would be a delight, he was sure of it.

"Your mother wrote in this book for you, so that you might know." He laid an open palm on the cover. "The time has come for you to see into her heart and know how you came into my hands through her doing."

Stephen stared at the book, unsure what to think.

"It is a thick book."

"I want you to read it."

"Then I will. When?"

"Tonight."

Stephen blinked. "The whole book?"

Shaka handed the book over and Stephen took it with both hands.

"All of it. Tonight. Read by the fire until you have read the last page."

Shaka stood and walked to the door. "There's plenty of wood to last the night. I will return in the morning."

"Yes, Shaka."

He turned at the door. "Every word, Stephen."

"Every word."

Then his teacher left the hut, leaving Stephen with the fire and his mother's book.

He peeled back the cover, tilted the first page so that he could clearly see the words by the flame light, and began to read.

THE CRICKET song had long fallen away; the fire had consumed most of the wood through the night; sleep had not called to him as Stephen read the handwritten account marked by his mother on the pages Shaka had given him. His fascination grew with each page. He was reading about a world as unfamiliar to him as sight to the blind.

Not because the writings of the jungle and its ways were new to him. He knew them as well as he knew his own breathing. New to him, however, was a world in which great importance was given to the roles of mother and son and lover and ruler and servant. All costumes. The wearing of flesh which, when mistaken for the real self, became a person's identity and inflamed insanity.

And yet he himself had been born into such a world, far from the jungle in a land called Atlanta. Born to a woman whose identity as his mother had consumed her to the exclusion of her true self and

driven her insane. In these last pages she was seeing the light, and for that he was glad.

The others—this Kirutu and this Wilam and all
those who fought to protect their own costumes—were not seeing so clearly. They continued
to live in suffering, captive in the hell of their own
insanity.

Why had no one told them the truth? Why had
Shaka not simply stood on that hill and told them
that they could be free by turning on the lamps of
their inner being and looking to the Master, who
had come to open the eyes of the blind and set the
captives free?

But he knew already—only those with ears to
hear and eyes to see would hear and see.

Stephen had been taken by Shaka for this? To
open their eyes?

Julian, the one who'd given him birth, had joined
with Wilam to produce another son. The vague notion of such a joining pulled at him in a way that
he could not explain. What would it be like to be a
father? To be with a woman?

And yet these too were only born of flesh and
costume—roles that were mistaken for true self.
Shaka had taught him as much a thousand times.

Still he read. Still the story unfolded, like a dance
with words sung around the fire, a play dressed

up in flesh, each page so fascinating that at times Stephen found his mind being pulled into it, as if it were real.

And it was, at least from her perspective.

Shaka's voice whispered through his head. *What does he think of the story, Stephen?*

He is full of fascination.

Does he like it?

He is very pleased with it. They gather in great numbers and dance around the fires in celebration.

Does it frighten him?

Stephen hesitated. He is only saddened that she was blind for so long. But I think it will end well for Julian. She is finding the truth of her freedom.

He lowered his eyes and continued to read.

The birds were already announcing the morning when he turned the last page and stared at his mother's final words.

Stephen, my son...

Six months have passed since I entrusted you to Shaka's care. I have painstakingly written all that I can remember to the best of my knowledge. I know that you are too young to read this, but hear in your heart that I love you deeply. My mind lingers on your face always. My dreams each night keep me strong when I have no will to live in this dark world. I am with you always.

You must promise me that you will learn to laugh. To scamper about the ground, chasing whatever amuses you. Eat plenty of fruit and meat. Grow strong, my son. Love and feel the light of the sun full on your face, for it is a small reflection of a far greater warmth that can be found within.

I sometimes forget who I am in that light, and then suffering tempts me in ways I had not thought possible. My body lives in a world that seems to grow dimmer with each passing day. Peace has not come to the Tulim valley. It is slipping into a darkness that few could fathom. When I forget the light, I fear dreadfully for the Impirum and the children. And then I remember what I saw on that hill and the light returns for a while.

I have found a way to pass this book out, hoping Shaka will find it. Hear my voice calling to you through these pages now. Come to your mother. I wait...

CHAPTER TWENTY-FOUR

A HUM awakened in the back of Stephen's mind. A whisper of concern for his mother's safety. The emotion swelled. Deep sorrow tempted him, not for himself but for the woman held in a place of such ongoing suffering.

Surely she had found a way to continue in the light without forgetting who she was.

But what if she hadn't?

He closed his eyes, took several deep breaths, and let the emotion pass without feeding it any resistance. Resistance only fueled deeper suffering.

The deep calm returned and he opened his eyes. He closed the cover and looked at the book. Shaka had marked the hide with a large *O*, the symbol for *outlaw* in the English tongue.

He understood now why knowledge of his mother would test him. It was the first time he'd been so directly confronted with another person's suffering. He had no context for Julian's role as his mother, but having read her story, he felt a deep compassion for her struggle. She'd seen the light and yet seemed to suffer still.

If his mother was still in the valley, perhaps he could go and set her free.

But of course! This was what Shaka must have in mind. This was his task now—to find Julian and help her see the light once again.

The thought swept through him and his body went rigid. He could not adequately or immediately describe the emotions swelling in his chest. They weren't negative. Eagerness, perhaps. Delight.

Stephen wrapped the book up in its cloth, set the bundle on the earth beside the thatched wall, and ran from the cooking hut to find Shaka.

Jika, jika, jawa...today was going to be a fine day.

He checked the sleeping hut and found it vacant. But this wasn't so unusual. Shaka often vanished early in the morning to find his way. Maybe he was in the tall hut. He dipped his head under the eaves and had one foot on the ground outside when he saw his teacher, watching him from the path at the edge of the clearing.

Shaka and one other.

A woman.

Stephen was so surprised by the sight that he jerked upright, hitting his head on one of the poles that supported the grass roof. He scrambled out and straightened, eyes fixed on the stranger by Shaka's side.

He'd never seen a woman. Shaka had explained the significant differences between male and female among humans, and he'd witnessed the polarities in the jungle among all creatures.

But he wasn't prepared for the fascination that swept through him upon seeing a woman in the flesh. And so close.

His first thought was of his mother. But Julian's skin was lighter, like his, not dark like that of the woman twenty paces from him.

Shaka took the woman by her hand and led her forward. Her round eyes were dark, not pale blue like his own. Her frame smaller by a third, thinner at her waist, which supported a short skirt made of woven grass. She had breasts for feeding an infant.

Woman! This was a woman and a fine, fine one at that, though he had no point of reference. All were fine. She was magical in every respect.

Stephen found that he was so taken by the sight of this woman that he could not move. But there was no need to. Shaka was bringing her to him.

And she seemed as fascinated by him as he was by her.

They came to a stop three paces away and for a while no one spoke. Shaka had told him that his affection for others might feel overwhelming. His heart was stripped of the judgments that many carried on their shoulders, he said.

Without any thought as to how the woman might react, Stephen stepped up to her and started to lift his hand, eager to make a connection with her. But he thought twice and glanced at Shaka.

"Can I touch it?"

"She's not an it, Stephen."

"No, no, of course not. It's a she." A small part of him began to feel awkward but he quickly allowed the feeling to pass. "I mean, she's a woman."

He returned his eyes to the woman, who was staring at him as if he'd fallen out of the sky.

"I only meant that you are very beautiful, and seeing as how I've never seen much less touched a female of my kind, I was wondering if I might touch your skin. Just to connect with you."

She said nothing. So he gently rested his hand on her upper arm.

"Your skin is very soft," he said.

She blinked but offered no other reaction.

"What is your name?"

"Her name is Lela," Shaka said.

Lela! The girl who had helped his mother!

"Lela," Stephen repeated. "I am Stephen."

His hand was still on her arm and he lowered it, thinking that it was making her uncomfortable. He had to remember that others' ways were not the same as his. He wasn't sure how else to be, so he shrugged and took a step back.

His teacher was watching him, wearing only the hint of a smile.

"What does he think?"

Shaka was addressing his costume again.

"He thinks he is very happy to see a woman," Stephen said.

"I'm sure he is. And he must know that this woman is not his."

"No, never. No woman could be his. He owns nothing, nor ever will. Nor does any man or woman own anything. These costumes only think to possess what cannot be possessed."

"Costume?" Lela said. Her voice was sweet, like a running brook, higher in tone and at once lovely to his ears.

"The name we use for body and mind," Shaka said. Then to Stephen, "She's only come to guide you."

"Of course, Shaka. To guide. Guide me where? To the valley?"

Shaka eyed him. "You read the book?"

"Every word. You would like me to go and find my mother as she requests?"

"I know your mother," the woman said.

"That's good!" Stephen said. "She is well?"

Lela seemed to have recovered from her initial shock at seeing him. She slowly stepped around him, studying his body. "I'm the first woman you've seen?"

He turned his head, following her with his eyes. "The first."

"You've grown into a strong man."

"I have."

Her brow arched. Why he found her so enchanting he wasn't sure, but his attraction to her seemed greater than any he'd felt. Or perhaps it was only different.

Her eyes darted to Shaka. "No man can confront Kirutu and survive," she said.

Stephen corrected her. "There's no need to survive when one cannot die."

He was only saying what he knew, but by the confusion on Lela's face it was clear that she didn't understand. She wasn't of this knowing.

"You're a naive boy who will die with me."

"Die? I cannot die. Neither can you."

"I am dead already!" she snapped, flinging out

her hand. "I came only because Shaka called me. Julian is there still, under Kirutu's rule of terror. Wilam is enslaved. If they discover that I've left the Tulim valley, they will put me to death."

Stephen looked at Shaka. "Why haven't you told me about this insanity before?" he asked.

"Because your time had not come," Shaka said.

"And my mother's time?"

"Has come as well," he said.

So then...it was as he'd guessed. Once again urgency raced through his mind. It was going to be such a day indeed.

"Then we should go and show them the way out of their insanity," he said. "We should leave immediately! Shaka, show Lela. Then we can enter the valley and show them all."

"Show me what?" Lela said. "That I'm to trust a child to protect me where he sees no danger? I would be better off returning alone." She made her plea directly to Shaka. "I beg you...come with us. Kirutu will only laugh at this one."

"It's his path to take. I wouldn't dismiss him so quickly."

She held his gaze for a long beat before he broke off and looked at Stephen.

"This isn't for me to show her, it is for you. And

only when you know it yourself, among those of your kind."

"You are my kind."

Shaka offered no agreement or disagreement.

"Lela has slept near the falls two nights, waiting. If you leave now, you will reach the valley by nightfall. Sleep before you enter it."

Two nights? Shaka had left him alone for a night three days ago. Now he understood.

"She'll show you the way to your mother. Find her, Stephen. She will know."

"Know what?"

"Find her."

"I will. You must not doubt this."

There was a thread of question in his teacher's eyes. He approached Stephen and took his hand. Smoothed his palm over his knuckles. When Shaka looked up into his eyes, that hint of concern had been replaced with a probing gaze of deep affection.

"The valley will be your great crucible, my son," he said softly. "Everything I've taught you must be understood among your own."

"Of course, Shaka."

"You will be tempted to forget."

"I will remember."

"Nothing can threaten you."

"Nothing."

"Do not forget who you are. That you need nothing more, nor anyone to be complete. In this way you disidentify with all labels. Remember the words I spoke to your mother on the hill before she made a way. Be, Stephen. Only be the light. Never forget."

The persistence of Shaka's warning surprised him, but he'd learned to listen.

"I will never forget."

"If you do, you will suffer. Many will suffer. The scales over Kirutu's eyes are thick. His ears cannot hear. His heart is imprisoned by hatred. He is enslaved to his costume. He is terrified of death."

"Darkness cannot exist where there is light."

"You will see this darkness in a way you never have. It will know you have come."

"My light will only chase it away."

Shaka's mouth slowly curved and a sparkle lit his eyes. "And how bright is your light!" He lifted Stephen's hand and kissed his knuckles. "Forget nothing."

Many times he had said this. Did he doubt what Stephen himself knew?

Shaka shifted his eyes to Lela, then stepped past Stephen to stand in front of her. He pulled her head close and whispered into her ear. Stephen saw her eyes soften over his teacher's shoulder. Tears misted her eyes.

Stephen gave them their space, stepping several paces away and squatting as Shaka spoke through her fear. She'd called him naive—perhaps it was best to be naive. Her suffering was unnecessary, this he knew, but he felt a deep compassion for her, because she was so bound by fear. Perhaps Shaka was helping her see even now.

Not so many years ago Stephen had faced dreadful fear alone in the swamps at night while Shaka watched unseen, ready to rescue him if he couldn't overcome the terror of death in the jaws of a crocodile or at a viper's bite.

From Lela's perspective Kirutu was that viper, poised to strike. She feared a future that by definition did not exist in the present and, therefore, was unreal. Her fear caused her to suffer unnecessarily.

Shaka kissed Lela's forehead and she nodded, then stepped away from him.

Stephen stood as she approached, eyes moist. He didn't fully understand what had pushed both Shaka and Lela into such a somber place, but this did not concern him.

Lela placed her hand on his chest and looked up into his face. "I will place my trust in you, son of Julian. Please, protect me. Keep me safe."

He glanced at Shaka, but his teacher was looking off to the horizon.

"I will," he said. "You have no reason to be afraid."

Her faced softened. She looked at his chest and brushed her hand over his muscled arm.

"Your mother's heart cries for you. She would be so proud. No Tulim could match your stature."

To this Stephen could not respond. He hardly knew what to feel. Pride, perhaps, but he had long ago learned the price of pride.

He could not deny, however, that her hand on him seemed to deepen his affection for her.

"You are very beautiful, Lela," he said. "No bird of paradise could compare to you."

"I didn't come for flattery from a young man," she said.

He did not know the nuances of the word *flattery*, but the rise in her energy pulled at him, so he said more, thinking to lift her joy.

"I am overwhelmed by you."

"And far too naive," she said, using that word again. He ignored it.

Lela reached up and pulled his lower lip open. Looked at his teeth. Satisfied, she gracefully turned toward the path.

"I will take you."

"I will follow."

"Stephen," Shaka said.

He turned. "Yes?"

"Take your spear. There are many boars in the Tulim valley."

CHAPTER TWENTY-FIVE

THE JUNGLE screamed with life; the sun beamed its unwavering approval; the streams ran with joy; the world was full of glory and making no apologies for its triumph. All of this presented itself to Stephen's awareness without interruption as the morning quickly passed, and with it the jungle that separated them from the Tulim valley.

But none of this awareness was so acutely focused as his growing appreciation for the wonder that walked beside him.

For the woman. Lela.

He'd long watched the splendor of the parrots soaring through the air, the flight of an arrow finding its mark through a steady breeze, the sniffing of mice seeking a morsel, the western sky painted in brilliant hues, announcing the close of the day.

But watching Lela—stepping lightly down the

path, leaping nimbly over fallen logs, glancing at him with her large brown eyes—made all he had yet seen lesser wonders.

He would remember what Shaka had said, always, and without pause. And now he hung on her every word as well. Hers was the first voice he'd heard other than his own and Shaka's.

The sound of her laughter after being startled by a slithering snake had so filled him with delight that he wanted to throw his arms around her and cry, "Me too, me too! I laugh with you!" Even her occasional *tsk*ing in disapproval at his veering the wrong way, or jumping to snatch a fruit from a branch for her, sounded like laughter in his ears.

"Quit showing off," she said.

He wasn't sure how to respond. And he found no reason to change his behavior.

They walked side by side where the path was wide enough, she in her grass skirt, he with his spear in his right hand and a single bone knife at his waist.

"Why do you smile this way?" she demanded. "Don't you know what awaits you?"

"I only see you now. And what I see pleases me."

She *tsk*ed. "A child in a man's body. I'm old enough to be your mother. Your own mother is in a pit and all you think about is the woman at your side. What kind of man has Shaka made you?"

She was too young to be his mother, but he let the comment pass.

"You too could be a child, if you choose. These are only costumes."

She shook her head. "You speak with words that have no meaning. A child cannot hope to save his mother from this valley of death."

"Then tell me what I will find."

She spit to one side, a curious behavior that he found interesting.

"Shaka tells me to say nothing. It is for you to discover if you can save her."

"You misunderstand. I would only find my mother so that she would know the truth. I cannot save her. She is safe already."

She pulled up on the path where it overlooked a shallow gorge suffocated with thick trees and vines. "Stop with this foolishness! Do you find this just a childish game? If your purpose isn't to save her, then why do I risk my life to bring you? Your mother has given her life for yours!"

Her words washed over him, and for the first time since leaving Shaka's sanctuary, he felt the gentle slap of offense. She was questioning his love?

He didn't know what to make of such an absurd accusation.

Do not forget, Stephen. Shaka's words whispered through his mind.

Do not forget that no man can possibly hurt one who is safe in the awareness of who they are. But Lela wasn't safe in any awareness. His objective must be to chase the fear from her heart.

He stared down the path, which vanished in a tangle of underbrush.

"Forgive me. I'm not accustomed to the ways of others. Fear doesn't stalk me. But this doesn't mean that I am weak. If I join your fear, I too would be lost in darkness. The blind cannot lead the blind."

She watched him, momentarily at a loss for words.

"This is a strange way," she finally said. "If not for Shaka, I would think you had lost your mind."

"But I have. Thankfully." He immediately realized that these words would mean nothing to her, so he clarified. "In a way of speaking," he said, smiling. "The mind cannot see the light as it is. The light allows me to see in a valley of darkness, yes? You must be patient with me."

"And you will see that all of your talk means nothing against his warriors. Every day people die. There can be no greater darkness."

"Then all the more reason for me to be the light," he said. "It is the only way that I can see truth."

"And what truth can you see now in this desecrated jungle?"

Stephen saw the opening to offer her courage and he seized it with a great passion. He took her hand and gazed at her face, her body.

"I see a shining star on the path before me, dressed in the red and golden feathers of a paradise bird. My heart leaps in my chest and cries out the glory of such a creation. Who could have created such a beautiful soul? Only the one through whose eyes I see this vision of splendor."

Her eyes softened.

"I see a soul that cries to be known as blameless. A soft heart that is cherished by its Creator. A gentle spirit full of kindness and love that her mind cannot yet recognize. But I see it. I see it all and I find more delight in you, Lela, than in any bird or tree."

"I am not a young woman to be chased by a young man," she said softly, but there was wonder in her eyes.

"I chase nothing. And you must know that however young, his body is strong." Stephen winked at her, a mannerism he'd picked up from Shaka. "He can face ten boars and bring them to the ground bare-handed. You cannot imagine what he can do with his spear."

This drew an unsure but unmistakable smile to her face. He grinned, delighted by his success in offering her this reassurance. So he continued.

"I can assure you, Kirutu will not stand against such a powerful sight. He will run into hiding at the sight of him."

She blinked, clearly in doubt. It made Stephen wonder what Kirutu was. He'd read his mother's account of battle with fascination, but without fear. Now a small voice in the furthest reaches of his mind tempted him with a whisper of concern.

What would it be like to face a hundred men intent on hatred and armed with axes?

But the whisper quieted as quickly as it had spoken. This wasn't his true self speaking. It was only a ghost of insanity, not to be feared.

"No man has ever defeated Kirutu," she said.

"And no man ever will. He defeats himself." But once again he was speaking in terms that she couldn't possibly understand. His words were falling on deaf ears. He would have to speak her language. Surely this was part of the challenge that Shaka had set before him.

"That's it!" he cried.

"What is?"

"Shaka's challenge. I must enter the valley and speak the language of the dead as a means for life. That's it! *Jika, jika, jawa!*"

"Jika jawa?"

"A word we made. Either way, so be it."

"The language of the mad."

She refused to find comfort, so he shifted his approach and acknowledged her misguided belief. She seemed obsessed with it.

"If I'm wrong, then only I will pay," he said. "I ask only that you trust Shaka's faith in me."

"If you are wrong, then I will pay with my life."

Her fear struck a chord of sorrow in his chest.

"No, Lela. I will protect you. There's nothing to fear by my side."

For a long time she just looked at him. But the lines of worry on her face had softened. She was starting to trust him, he thought. And for a moment he wondered if that was so wise. But he knew no other way.

"So be it," she finally said.

He smiled. "*Jika, jika, jawa.*"

Lela offered a nod, turned back down the path, and began to walk.

They traveled late into the afternoon, often cutting through the jungle on paths used only occasionally by hunting parties. Birds took flight above them, disturbed by the passage of humans below. Possums and snakes rattled the underbrush in hasty retreat.

It was at the Tengali River just east of the Tulim valley that his domain ended. He'd never been beyond. And yet he felt only eagerness to cross it. This day had brought him more wonder than any in recent memory.

The more questions they asked of each other, the more his fascination with Lela grew, despite her refusal to tell him anything about the Tulim valley. She was intelligent and tender, her fear aside, but this wasn't the reason for his interest. Her companionship, on the other hand, was exhilarating.

He embraced the realization that he was living and breathing and walking with the very form of God, made manifest in another besides Shaka. And he found himself touching her arm and her hair more frequently than she might have desired.

And yet with each passing hour her optimism rose. Or perhaps it was only his love for her, returned in kind. She liked him, he could not mistake this truth. He could see the sparkle of interest in her eyes, the curve of kindness in her lips, the intention to impress him in her gait.

He loved Lela, and she loved him. There could

be no insanity on earth in the presence of such love. It made him wonder if Wilam had loved his mother in this way. If so, then why had such insanity followed? Such beauty and yet so much suffering. It could not have been the same love he felt now.

Lela stopped by the exposed roots of a towering deciduous tree, winded from the long, arduous climb up the path that would bring them into the Tulim valley.

"There, over this summit," she said, shoving her chin at the forested crest ahead, "you will see all of the Tulim."

She'd often stopped to rest this past hour. Clearly she didn't have the same endurance as he or Shaka. It had been over a day since he'd slept, and only now was his body beginning to tire. How many times had Shaka urged him to climb faster, run longer, sleep less? *To discipline the body is to remind the costume that it is only something to be used and enjoyed*, Shaka often said. *Never let it use you.*

"Are you with a man?" he asked impulsively.

Her eyes darted up.

Perhaps he should clarify his question.

"My mother wrote much about the union of many to produce infants. You were to be with a man?"

"There is no love in this valley." She spat to the side. "I will gouge out the eyes of any man who attempts to force himself on me."

Her vehemence took him off guard.

"And yet you are from among the Impirum. Julian wrote of much beauty among your people."

She turned away. "There is now only Warik. Only hatred."

"With you I feel only love."

Tears misted her eyes. "It's been a long time since any man loved me," she whispered.

Those words broke his heart with compassion. How terrifying it must feel, not knowing that one was loved.

He thought to tell her that, in reality, she needed no more love than what was already offered inside of her, where the realm of the Master's love would rule, but again...she wouldn't understand. He could only serve her by speaking to her limited understanding.

He felt a strange kind of belonging next to Lela, an awakening of awareness that she, even by her simple presence at his side, fueled his own fullness of love. As did Shaka, when Stephen was with him. But with Lela that love felt different somehow.

He let a wave of emotion that cried for him to

pull her close wash over him, then let his affection be known by his words.

"You are loved by a man now," he said softly.

Lela seemed to soften, staring into his eyes. But she didn't seem able to accept the fullness of his love.

"By a child," she said.

His smile broadened. "By a child who knows how to love. And by far, far more."

She offered the jungle a blank stare. "I envy you, son of Shaka," she said quietly. "This kind of love is only a distant memory for me."

"I will help you remember," he said. "The woman who gave such love to my mother has forgotten far too much."

She hesitated, then swallowed deeply. "Come and see what I have forgotten."

Lela turned back up the path and led him to a cliff that fell away into a vast valley. Stephen pulled up and studied the view before him.

Many times he'd seen the valley from a greater distance, often enshrouded in a low-lying fog. But that fog had always been white and thick, not wispy with gray tendrils that clung to the entire lower reaches, stretching out to the swamps. In and of itself, this didn't matter one way or the other.

What did matter, however, was the fact that this mist seemed to be moving unnaturally. Shifting and circling over a focal point far south, as if of its own mind, alive and aware and gathering to defend.

What mattered even more was the faint, high-pitched whine that came from the valley. A barely audible scream behind a low hum.

Fear sliced through his mind as he stood on the cliff, spellbound, struck by the impression that the ground in the valley was groaning and the mist above shrieking its torturous pain.

This was more than a valley blanketed in fog.

"There," she said, pointing to the south. "The Warik."

Stephen could make no sense of the dread reaching into him. There was nothing here or anywhere that could threaten him. Everything he'd learned from Shaka made this plain.

Why did he feel this strange fear?

"Below the mist?" he asked.

She looked up at him. "Mist?"

So then Lela couldn't see what he saw.

You will see this darkness in a way you never have, Shaka had said. *It will know you have come.*

Do not forget.

He did not.

Immediately the mist began to fade. And with it the faint whine and the low hum. Only a thin layer of smoke rising from cooking fires remained.

He slowly exhaled through his nostrils, breathing out the balance of his concern. What his hearing and seeing meant, he didn't know, but the threat was gone. Defeated already.

"The smoke," he said, nodding at the section of jungle far south.

"Yes, below the smoke. They'll see us before we arrive. Kirutu's spirits see always. His warriors roam the valley."

A barely discernible hum of anxiety tempted his mind again, whispering of the unknown.

"How far?" he asked.

"We won't make it by dark."

"No."

The apprehension that crossed his mind wasn't in itself a problem. That he wasn't able to dismiss it easily, however, might be one.

"You're frightened?" she asked.

He turned his head. She was with him, and he drew comfort from her presence. Perhaps it was why Shaka had brought her for this final quest.

"I've never been to this valley," he said. "It's a strange place of men, unknown to me."

"Now you doubt?"

He tried to consider his feelings, but he wasn't quite sure what to think.

"No." And he didn't. But he couldn't dismiss his unease, however slight.

"We can sleep here tonight," he said, "and go together when the sun rises." Then he added, for good measure, "Don't worry. We are safe."

CHAPTER TWENTY-SIX

The sense of caution that had presented itself to Stephen on the cliff vanished as darkness fell. He concerned himself then only with making Lela as comfortable as possible, because she couldn't dismiss her fear of what the morning might bring.

In her presence he felt no fear.

They both needed food, preferably meat to eat with the sago Lela carried in a net bag at her waist, but she insisted they not build a fire—it might be seen. So they ate raw strips of a small snake he killed near their camp. She wasn't accustomed to eating uncooked meat. He'd settled her fears by stuffing his mouth with far more than it could comfortably hold and showing great pleasure with every chew until the juice ran down his chin. Smiling, she first nibbled, then ate, strips of the flesh with him, although she insisted the Tulim were a more refined people.

"You killed this snake with your spear?" she asked, staring at the severed head.

"Yes," he said.

"It has a small head, and yet you struck it."

"I used the spear as a blade. Better to keep a spear close to be used again than throw and chase it."

"Shaka taught you how to fight?"

"Shaka taught me all that I know."

"You may need these skills when you meet Kirutu."

The thought hadn't occurred to him and he rejected it outright.

"Hurting Kirutu would only inflame more insanity."

She grunted her disapproval. "Then you should kill him."

He would never do such a thing, but Lela wasn't able to understand the teachings he'd learned over so many years, so he just smiled and let the statement pass.

They rested on a bed of grass, side by side, and in that time beside her warm body, he felt a great comfort that filled him with awe as sleep coaxed him into dreams of running through fields of flowers with Lela at his side, laughing with delight. All was well.

How could it not be?

Stephen woke Lela before dawn to begin the journey into the Tulim valley. The insanity he'd seen the day before was long gone. Even the memory of it had faded, because he had little use for memories that might bring fear into the present.

And in the present he was with Lela, fully grateful for her as he watched her walk down the path, amazed at her every movement and her repeated urging that he take their approach to danger more seriously.

By the time morning dawned, Lela had led him down the mountain to a worn path, headed south.

The jungle in the lowlands was thicker in some respects, crowded with mangroves and casuarinas and broadleaf grasses of endless varieties. Here the animal life was more abundant than in the highlands—snakes, possums, bats, lizards, marsupials, many species of which Stephen recognized by sound alone. But there were too many to be known fully. More than seven hundred kinds of birds lived in this jungle, Shaka said. And more insect species than could be counted in a full year. It was a land of abundant life.

Thinking of that, Stephen thought the jungle

seemed oddly quiet. The birds' calls seemed to lack their full delight. Rodents took to hiding long before Stephen and Lela came close. Only the insects seemed unperturbed by the humans' arrival, singing without reprieve as they always did.

Stephen was at peace and fully aware that only his costume passed here, delighted to be in the company of another.

They walked for a long while, ever closer to the area where he'd seen smoke. All was well. Today he might bring his peace to his mother.

All was well, but then suddenly it wasn't.

They had just stepped from the trees onto a grassy knoll that gave them full view of the jungle when the high-pitched whine Stephen had heard on the cliff returned.

He pulled up, intrigued by the sound. Above, a gray sky. Ahead, the knoll, which fell into dense forest. At the bottom of the valley, smoke from morning fires, drifting up through a heavy canopy.

The whine was slightly louder, like a chorus of insects unknown to him—a vast army spread across the jungle, too small to be seen but making its presence known in this unending scream.

"What is it?" Lela asked, on edge, looking back at him. She followed his eyes, scanning the jungle ahead. "What do you see?"

"I hear."

"Hear what?"

"The sound of insects, high and low at once. A kind I haven't heard."

She listened for a moment. "I hear nothing new."

"Then you shouldn't worry."

But it was too late, Lela's fingers were trembling already.

"These are the evil spirits!" she said. "You hear death with the ears of the shaman!"

Stephen thought she might be right, but he could find no words to express what he did not know. He could only assure her that all would be well.

"How far to the Warik?"

"I told you, the whole valley is Warik," she said. "The main village is just beyond this draw where the land has been cleared to the swamps. Down this path." She motioned to a narrow trail fifty paces ahead.

"Then follow me."

He passed her and headed down the path, unable to dislodge the whine from his hearing, eager to discover its source. Even more willing to root the sound out of his mind.

Do not forget who you are.

He did not.

"Stephen…"

He turned back and saw that Lela was staring at him, still rooted to the ground.

"There's nothing to fear," he said, stepping back to her. "Trust me. Stay close to me."

She glanced at the jungle beyond him, then walked forward.

He smiled and continued down the trail, spreading his arms. "You see? Nothing to fear."

Behind him Lela said nothing.

They made their way back into the trees and down the mountain along a switchback that led them into another clearing.

"You see?" he asked, stepping out. He scanned the trees that surrounded the clearing. "There's nothing to fear here. Nothing but trees."

"Kirutu sees everything," she whispered.

"Then he sees only what cannot hurt us," Stephen said. "I will keep you safe."

The high-pitched whine did not abate. Instead it grew, and this caused him some concern, but not enough for him to redirect his course. If he was meant to do anything other than face the fear that presented itself, Shaka would have told him so.

The only way to overcome fear is to walk through it and learn that it is but a shadow of death.

TED DEKKER

So he walked on, one foot in front of the other, straight toward the trees on the far side of the clearing. Spreading his arms once again to reassure her.

"You see? There is nothing to..."

But then there was something. The distinct sound of a long shaft hurtling through the air. An airborne spear to his right.

He instinctively dropped to a crouch.

Heard the unmistakable *whump* of wood connecting with bone just behind him. And with the *whump*, the sudden termination of the whining in his head.

Stephen spun back as Lela's body fell heavily to the ground, bounced once, and then lay still, head bloodied by a blunt spear, which rolled into the grass three paces from her.

Silence settled over the clearing. She'd been struck by the spear. Her chest still rose and fell with breath.

For a long moment Stephen didn't seem capable of processing any thought. Shaka had talked about war and he'd read his mother's account, so he knew of the violence that humans took upon themselves, but seeing it now he wasn't sure how to process what he was seeing. What to think about the blood seeping from the wound on her head.

He turned his head to the right and blinked. There, between two towering trees, stood a man wearing only black and red markings on his face, and yellow bands on his arms and legs. Staring at Stephen nonchalantly, without threat in his eyes.

A dozen warriors silently emerged from the trees and stood in a line, watching with only casual interest.

He looked back at Lela's unconscious body. Her jaw was broken. Blood seeped from her mouth. What manner of insanity could possibly lead to such a brutal attack? He couldn't bring himself to understand.

And then he did understand something. Or rather feel it. A terrible sorrow that reached up through his chest and threatened to swallow him whole.

Here lay Lela, collapsed as though dead with one blow. Lela, who had done nothing except trust him.

In a flurry of thoughts, memories of their journey swept through his mind. Of laughing and touching and sleeping side by side with such contentment.

Trust me, Lela. I will keep you safe.

And yet there she lay, bleeding on the ground.

Stephen slowly straightened, suddenly ill. He felt

his spear slip from his fingers and fall to the ground.

Do not forget.

He lifted his head, breathing deep, aware of the scent of blood in the air. Even more aware that forgetting now could throw him into a pit of fear.

Shaka had known?

The warriors were approaching, twelve abreast, cautious now, each holding a spear or a long blade made of steel. Machetes, Shaka had called these. Two carried long bows.

They thought to hurt him? But they couldn't reach him easily. The jungle was open behind him and on either side. If he wanted to, he could easily slip away.

Only then did he see the others, emerging from the trees on all sides, no fewer than fifty warriors approaching their single prey.

Do not forget. But in that moment Stephen forgot what he shouldn't forget. Because the warriors were suddenly jogging forward, closing in on him like a noose. His mind had gone blank and all he could think to do was what he'd come to do.

Find his mother.

If these men took his life now, he wouldn't be able to do that.

He turned toward the only gap in the closing circle and he ran, moving with the same instincts that had often kept him safe.

His mind calculated distances and speeds on the fly: thirty-five long paces to the trees; fifty paces for the closest warriors.

You're leaving her, Stephen. You're running from Lela, whom you love.

Yes, but he knew nothing else to do. The warriors wouldn't leave Lela to die—they would want to find out what she knew. He couldn't protect her by staying at her side. Not now.

Now he had to find his mother.

He heard the sounds of flying projectiles behind; saw their trajectories with a slight twist of his head; made a small adjustment to his course to avoid three spears that sped harmlessly by and clattered into the branches ahead.

He was already halfway to the trees, and although many of the warriors were now sprinting, they wouldn't reach him in time. Once in the dense vegetation he would be as difficult to track as a boar on the run. The leader always had the advantage once aware. It was why stealth was so critical in hunting.

The wind was at his back. They wouldn't be able to track him by scent. Could Tulim warriors even track by scent? It had taken him many years to refine his senses to Shaka's satisfaction.

All of these thoughts whispered around the edges of his mind. At its core only one thought spoke clearly.

Run! Find your mother. She will know.

Two hastily slung arrows slapped through the brush to his right as he planted his right palm on a massive fallen tree and catapulted his body up and over the timber. A third arrow angled toward his body before he landed beyond the log.

This one he swatted away like a fly with his left hand.

He landed on his right foot and threw his weight forward, then to his left, around the trunk of a tall sago palm. Within five strides he was beyond their line of sight.

Stealth, not speed or strength, was now his greatest ally. They would stop to listen and follow any sound he made, but he would offer them none.

It occurred to him only then that he could just as easily turn and attempt to deal with them head on.

He'd no sooner allowed the thought passage through his mind than Shaka's teaching came to him.

When the evil man comes against you, do not resist him. Doing so will only strengthen his power. Among men, resistance always draws equal and opposite resistance.

You're forgetting, Stephen. Already.

He shoved the thought from his mind and stumbled forward, aware that he was making far too much noise. He took a deep breath, calmed his nerves, and continued on lighter feet, using fallen logs and stones as his path through the understory.

Down into a narrow creek bed. Across to the slope beyond.

The telltale sound of crashing in the brush behind and to his right pushed him up the slope to his left.

South, he thought. *My mother is there, south.* So he angled farther to his left as the crashing behind faded.

The distant whispers in his mind were still there, laced once again with a thin, high-pitched whine. He felt no need to pay the sound any mind.

He was distracted, instead, by a new concern: the continued presence of those other small voices—the ones that said he'd abandoned Lela after promising to protect her. The thoughts that entertained, if only for a moment, the impulse to resist the warriors directly.

The thought that he was running toward, not away from, danger.

But he knew nothing else to do. This was the valley Shaka had sent him to. Death was only a shadow here. He could learn this only by walking through it now, undeterred by the insane mind, which had forgotten that it could not be threatened except by its own insanity.

Truly, the Tulim valley was his own mind.

Stephen was so distracted by the reflections warring in his mind that the sudden appearance of a well-worn path took him off guard. He pulled up hard in the middle of a wide trail pounded barren by constant foot traffic.

With a single glance he knew where the trail led. And without allowing himself further contemplation he followed the voice that assured him he'd find his mother at the end of the path.

He would go of his own accord, not herded or bound by the Warik.

Stephen turned up the path and jogged forward, eyes fixed on the corner ahead.

The whining in his head rose to a bone-clawing screech, but he still paid it no mind.

Move forward, Stephen. Run.

He ran. One step in front of the other, pounding the soft earth underfoot.

Find your mother, Stephen. Bring her peace.

He rounded the corner, took three long strides, then pulled up sharply. The path opened up to a huge, grassy field that sloped down to a ten-foot-high fence made of erect, sharpened timbers bound together with vines, extending far in either direction. A massive gate made of two swinging sections beneath a round beam waited at the end of the path.

Beyond the gate a sea of brown grass-roofed huts stretched into the jungle, some within his view, most undoubtedly not. Hundreds—perhaps thousands—of dwellings made up the Warik stronghold, split down the center by a wide swath of earth that ran up to a large complex near the center of the village.

But it was the bodies of two impaled natives suspended on tall sharpened poles, one on either side of the outer gate, that rooted him to the ground. This and the hundreds of bleached skulls set upon the beam over the gates and along the fence running east and west.

Confusion swarmed his mind. How could this happen? And who were those who could do such a thing? He could feel as much as see the carnage.

And with that feeling, another whispered that he was a stranger here, alone in his own distant existence. This was the rest of the world? He did not belong here.

No, that couldn't be true. He simply belonged where he was at any given moment. And yet he felt at impossible odds with the sight spread out before him.

And he'd abandoned Lela.

Shaka's words returned in force—the ones he'd spoken on the cliff before giving Stephen his mother's book.

Darkness has swallowed them, Stephen. They are blind. Captive in the night. And if you forget who you truly are, their insanity will call you into its dark pit.

Immediately the thin screams that had hung in the air faded to silence. To the extent that he retained faith in his true identity, he would not be pulled into their insanity. Nor would he be alone, for his true self was never alone.

My mother waits in the valley of death.

He strode forward like a dead man walking, because he was dead to their world.

CHAPTER TWENTY-SEVEN

STEPHEN HAD covered only a quarter of the long slope that descended to the village when he heard feet pounding on the path behind him. But he held his pace—the warriors would allow him to walk. His mind returned to the prospect of walking into this place so at odds with the high mountain on which he'd lived.

The jungle seemed to have stilled for his arrival. He placed one foot before the other, aware now of the others running to his left. In his peripheral vision he saw a dozen warriors jog by, eyeing him curiously.

Another dozen passed to his right, two of these carrying Lela's limp form between them.

For the space of two breaths his eyes blurred and the sky screamed, and he knew that their world encroached on his own, daring him to resist. But he knew this ploy already and he let the desperate emotions pass through him. Lela was not his to save now.

His mind went silent.

He could see. The village growing nearer with each step as he approached the towering fence. Smoke from a hundred cooking fires coiling lazily into the air. The warriors jogging through a doorway in the fence to the right of the gates, carrying Lela like a pig.

He could hear. Birds calling from far away and chirping from the nearby jungle. His breath being pushed in and out of his lungs. His heart pounding steadily in his chest.

He could smell. Woodsmoke laced with the scent of cooked meat. Feces and mud. Rotting flesh.

He could feel. The worn grass under his feet. The still, humid air pressing into his skin, filling his nostrils.

The slight tremble in his right hand.

Father, save me.

He could see some things more clearly now. The bodies of the two naked natives—one an elderly man, the other a young woman—dead on their perches on either side of the gate. He found that he couldn't process this madness with reason, so he released his attempt to do so and walked on.

Down the hill. All the way to the gate, keeping his eyes forward so that he wouldn't have to look at the dead body on either side.

He was wondering how he would enter the village when the gates began to swing out, each pushed by a warrior. Like a blossoming flower, the Warik stronghold opened to him.

And yet there was no beauty here that he could see.

Still he walked, arms limp by his sides, breathing deliberately as he passed through the gate and into the village.

The wide path was packed down the center, muddy along the edges. Round huts had been built on stilts in rows set back ten or fifteen paces. At least one human skull bleached by the sun hung above the entrance to each hut.

A long line of warriors had stationed themselves on either side of the path. All were armed with spears or axes, some with steel machetes. Their faces were painted in blacks and reds and they wore bands on their foreheads, arms, and legs. To a man they stared at Stephen with round, white eyes, as though dead.

They didn't show any signs of hostility. They did not scowl or shout or lift their weapons. These were warriors enslaved by fear and uncaring of all but their own survival. They were only funneling him toward the one he'd come to see.

Kirutu.

And his mother.

Slave of Kirutu.

He was seeing a part of himself, he thought. This place was only a much larger version of his own costume, determined to protect what it understood as life.

This was darkness. And yet he couldn't identify with the darkness. He felt misplaced. A bird in the sea.

Villagers stripped of hope were exiting their huts and loitering, watching. Hugging their bodies, as if this too might offer them some protection.

Did they know who he was? Had they seen other white men or women in the eighteen years since his mother had given her son to Shaka and herself to Kirutu?

Stephen wasn't sure what he was meant to do, so he did nothing but walk. Forward. Headed directly for a second fence that surrounded a tall structure at the end of this long warrior-lined path.

Lela had been right, he thought. They'd known he was coming.

A small naked child hanging on to the thigh of one of the warriors pointed her stubby finger up at Stephen and asked a question, which the man ignored. Several other children were hurrying through the village behind the warriors, eyes wide with wonder. They were too young to realize that they were enslaved.

Like a child, Stephen, Shaka said. *Always, like a child.*

These were the first he'd ever seen. Such wonder in tiny bodies, clinging to innocence, still unaware of the madness lurking in their own minds, waiting to overtake them.

He walked on feet of clay now, separate from all that his eyes saw. Many women of all shapes and heights gathered, some supporting children hanging off their bodies, others peering around huts, afraid.

An older man with graying hair and a toothless smile squatted between two huts. Stephen stopped. Here he felt a momentary bond. The man's grin was, like Stephen, an anomaly.

One of the warriors grunted and waved his ax at the looming fence fifty paces on. They wanted him to keep moving. He was expected.

He resumed his walk, feeling more disconnected from the strange forms around him with each step. And he began to understand why Shaka had said this would be his most difficult test.

To walk among men. For this task Stephen suddenly felt unequipped.

A dead body hung from a tree limb—a young man, limp at the end of a rope that had been tied around his neck and pulled over a thick branch high above.

At the base of that tree sat a man who was missing an arm. The stump was wrapped in bloodied leaves. And yet the children near him paid neither the wounded man nor the limp body any mind. They were interested only in Stephen.

He swallowed back a flood of emotions and walked on.

The space between the huts began to fill with more onlookers staring dumbly at him, the white man dressed in a lap-lap, bearing no weapons, walking freely to his fate at Kirutu's hand.

But Stephen did not belong to their master—he had his own. And Kirutu had no power over his.

The Tulim village his mother had written of had been orderly and beautiful, abounding with laughter and song, clean and ornate. That world was gone.

Instead he was surrounded by death, the smell of feces and rotting flesh ripe in the air. Somewhere deep within his mind, the sound of distant screaming returned and with it a single, simple question.

What if I do forget?

And then another question, even as he approached the second fence that circled Kirutu's stronghold.

Forget what exactly? Which part?

Because suddenly there was so much to remember.

The gate to the second fence swung open, and Stephen was greeted by the sight of a wide, manicured courtyard. It surrounded an expansive rectangular structure built of hardwoods, roofed with thatched palm leaves.

These were the grounds of royalty.

No fewer than two hundred warriors stood around the footing of what could only be Kirutu's palace. Another twenty lined each side of the path leading up to the structure.

Stephen walked through the gate, heard it latch behind him, and stopped. Ornate carvings of faces and spirits, many stained in reds and blacks with touches of yellow, covered the building's hewn timber walls. A dark entrance opened into the structure at the top of sweeping steps.

All of this Stephen saw at a glance, but it was the warriors who drew his attention. To a man these were stronger than those outside the courtyard. The red and black markings on their bodies and faces had been drawn with more care, and many wore colorful feathers in their headbands.

They did not look at him, they glared. They did not merely stand, they were poised, tall, with deeply defined muscles. They did not speak, they screamed, not with their throats, but with their hearts.

They screamed fear. And hatred.

This challenge could break you, Stephen.

The thought surprised him. Nothing could break him, of course, and yet he felt that this challenge might, and this more than anything disturbed him.

Do not forget, Stephen.

Forget what?

Who he was...but who was he here? A boy in a man's body, momentarily lost in a sea of rage and insanity. Why had Shaka sent him here?

To find his mother. She would know what to do.

Or was he to tell her what to do?

Stephen took three more steps before a warrior to his right stepped out of line, closed the distance between them, and struck him on the shoulder with a club, jarring his bones.

He staggered to the side and righted himself, momentarily stunned. The man glared at him as if expecting him to speak.

But to speak what?

Another blow struck him—a warrior from behind had swung a stick at his lower back. Pain swept up his spine.

He turned to the man, wondering why they were hitting him. Was he doing something they disapproved of? He posed no threat to them.

"Do you stand like a god in his courtyard?" the second man who'd struck him yelled.

Another stick slammed into the backs of his legs, just below his knees, and this time Stephen's instincts got the better of him. He leaped forward, spinning to ward off any further blows, thinking the next one might snap his bones.

They reacted to his movement immediately, ten or more of them leaping forward, clubs swinging already. The impulse to defend himself loomed large for an instant before his training kicked in. To resist would only bring greater force to bear against him.

So he let the blows fall, a pounding of staffs and clubs that thudded against his back and shoulders and head, forcing him to his knees. They were yelling, crying out his insubordination and threatening to kill him, the wam, the worm dragged from the jungle to be fed to their pigs.

Shaka had taught him to disassociate from physical pain, thereby robbing its power to control his body, and he was able to do so now.

But he was aware of another impulse that lapped at his mind—offense at being so forcefully rejected by others of his kind. He was human, they were human, and yet they clearly did not want him.

Was he not acceptable to them? His skin was the wrong color, perhaps, or his presence threatened them, though he meant them no harm. He'd only come to meet his mother.

A single hard blow landed on the back of his head and the world started to fade. He felt his body toppling forward but broke his fall with his right forearm. All that remained was a throbbing pain that spread down his neck, fueled by those screaming demons of fear that taunted him.

If the warriors had wanted to kill him, why hadn't they done so in the field? Instead they'd attacked Lela. His mind swam in a sea of confusion.

"Bring him!"

He lifted his head and stared up the path. Slowly his eyes found focus.

There at the bottom of the steps that lead to the darkened entrance stood a man. A tall warrior with sharply defined muscles, older than some, more powerful, even in his harsh eyes, than any of the others.

This was Kirutu, ruler of all Tulim. Stephen

knew it immediately by the scar running down his chest, described by his mother.

Hands dug under his arms and pulled him to his feet. But he didn't need their help. His strength had returned as quickly as the blows had robbed him of it.

They shoved him forward, cuffing at his shoulders and his ears with cupped palms, quiet now in the presence of their leader.

"Release him."

They let him go and backed away, leaving Stephen to stand three paces from Kirutu, who studied him with dark eyes set deeply in the shadows of a chiseled face. Here Stephen did not see fear. Only rejection.

For a long time the man didn't speak.

Don't forget, Stephen.

His mind was vacant. Perhaps his mother would know what to do.

"Who are you?" Kirutu asked in a low voice.

"My name is Stephen."

Kirutu stared at him.

"Answer my question. Who are you?"

He hadn't heard? Or didn't understand the word—Stephen wasn't a Tulim name.

"I'm the son of Julian, the woman you took as your own," Stephen said.

The ruler's face darkened.

"You refuse to speak the truth in my presence? When I ask who you are, you will speak only what is true."

Stephen hesitated, then said what he thought the man wanted to hear.

"I am Outlaw."

"You are *nothing*!" Kirutu hissed. He stepped forward, circling to Stephen's left, speaking in a low, gravelly tone that was neither gentle nor accusing, like a man simply reporting the truth.

"You have no place...no home...you do not belong to anyone."

He walked behind, rounding him, speaking matter-of-factly.

"In this way you are lower than the wam, viler than the serpents who slither in the grass. An outcast who dares enter the Tulim valley with hopes of finding a home. So then I will help you understand."

When he came to a stop he was only a pace from Stephen. His skin smelled freshly washed and rubbed with oil from the angalo flower, which offered a sweet scent. When he spoke, the scent of rapina bark carried to Stephen on his breath.

"You are Outlaw and dead to this world. Tell me this is so."

He thought about it and found the words true.

"I am Outlaw and I am dead to this world."

"It is the only reason I am bound to let you live. You are dead to me. Knowing this you come. Why?"

"To speak to my mother."

The brow over Kirutu's right eye rose and a smile slowly twisted his face.

"And yet you have no mother. You are alone, never to belong. If you were not dead already, I would kill you now."

For a long moment Stephen stood still, hardly aware of the meaning behind those words. And yet something in him had shifted. The sounds of the jungle had faded, as had the faint, high-pitched whine that had come and gone with his remembering and forgetting.

Slowly a new awareness grew in his mind. An isolation that he'd never contended with. The dawning realization that Kirutu was right. He was alone. He didn't have a mother. Hadn't Shaka taught him this very thing?

Hadn't Shaka said that his identity with and in the things and relationships of this world only distracted from his true identity and could thus be his downfall?

He looked at the warriors staring back at him with vacant, dark eyes. He knew that he was forgetting something—being one with his Father—but he now felt oddly disconnected from that truth.

Here in the flesh, in the real world, he saw only rejection. And he felt only isolation. The feeling threatened to bring fear with it, so Stephen shut his eyes and took a deep breath.

It's OK. It's going to be OK.

When he looked back at Kirutu, the ruler wore a knowing grin.

"I don't belong to your world," Stephen said. "It holds no power over me."

"No? And I say that every pig will root in the mud until he finds food. Perhaps if I show you that food, you will pretend to be alive. Then I will have reason to kill you as well."

What he could mean, Stephen didn't know.

"Bring her!" Kirutu ordered to one side, expression now flat.

Two warriors emerged from around the corner, supporting a hooded woman who struggled feebly in their grasp. She was one of them and her hands were tied behind her back.

They stood her up next to Kirutu, who kept his eyes on Stephen.

"All of this valley and everything in it belong to me," the ruler said. "What I do to one, I can do to whomever I choose."

He waited a beat to let his words carry, then issued an order.

"Remove her hood."

One of the warriors jerked the hood from the woman's head. Stephen's mind put reason to what he saw before his heart could react.

Here stood Lela, hair still matted with blood. She was awake and her eyes were round with fear. If not for a gag, screams might have accompanied the tears running down her cheeks.

But he didn't need to hear her screams, he could hear her heart already. *Save me*, she was crying. *You said you would protect me.*

Before Stephen could react, Kirutu stepped behind Lela, grabbed her hair, jerked her head back, and ran a sharp bone knife across her exposed neck.

He held her still for a moment, then released his hold. Lela collapsed to the ground. Dead in her own blood.

Stephen recoiled.

Do not forget. Do not forget.

"She means nothing to you because you are dead," Kirutu said. "And yet you show fear because you mistake yourself as one who deserves a woman. You deserve nothing but your own misery. In this too you are alone."

Shaka's teachings flowed through his mind,

longing to be absorbed but finding no place to rest. In their place a larger realization swelled: Lela had accepted him where these others did not. She had trusted him. He'd failed her.

"Take her!"

The two warriors grabbed her arms and dragged her around the corner, leaving Stephen numb on the path.

"In the Tulim, life is mine to give and take," Kirutu said. "I have taken the place of the shaman who once spoke the ways of the spirit. I am now ruler of this valley. The woman you call your mother believed that by giving me her life, she spared yours. But she only sentenced both of you to death. Now you both live at my whim."

"No," Stephen said.

Eyes fixed on him, Kirutu lifted his hand and motioned with two fingers. "Come."

A woman slowly stepped into the daylight from the dark entry above Kirutu. A white woman dressed in a top and a short skirt, both woven from strands of palm thread. Her skin was luminous and her dark hair long, and Stephen knew immediately that he was looking at his mother.

She stood on the landing, tall and brave, arms at her sides, staring down at him. He hadn't prepared himself, not knowing what to prepare for, but looking at her now, he could see his face in hers. His skin on her body. His eyes in her face.

Eyes that brimmed with tears as she gazed down at him.

His mother slowly descended the steps, walking upright, holding her head steady. There was a bruise on her right arm...two more on her legs. No cuts that he could see.

Her fingers were trembling as she set her feet on the path and stepped forward. Stephen stood still, at a loss. But he didn't have time to consider the matter because she was suddenly rushing forward.

Her face twisted and tears streamed from her eyes as she reached him. The woman who was his mother threw her arms around him, pressed her cheek against his chest, and clung to him as if he were her flesh.

"Thank God...thank God...you're alive. You're alive. You're alive."

She was speaking in the language Shaka had taught him. The tongue of his mother.

She pulled back and looked up into his eyes. "You're alive." She touched his arms, his shoulders, his neck, drew her thumb over his cheek, nearly frantic in her thirst to know that her eyes did not deceive her.

He'd never felt so treasured as he did in that moment. It was as though she lived only for him. And now he stood before her, flesh of her flesh.

"You're healthy?" she asked. "He took good care of you?"

Stephen wasn't prepared for the emotions that rose through his chest at her question. A whole new world blossomed in his consciousness. Where he'd felt a desire to be close to Lela, he felt perfectly as one with this woman.

She was the one who'd given him birth. Who'd submitted herself to life under Kirutu's brutality so that he could live.

So that *she* could live through him.

And yet upon her seeing him alive, her only concern was for him.

The details of her story, merely fascinating only two nights ago, now flooded Stephen's mind with vibrant life. In that moment he became his mother's son. Wholly and without reservation.

"I'm your son," he said, speaking her tongue.

She blinked, eyes wrinkled with smiling gratitude. "You remember me?"

He somehow did, if not in his mind, in his bones.

"I read what you wrote."

"So you know."

"You will come with me?" he asked.

"No." Fresh tears spilled from her eyes. "No, I can't come now. In their eyes you are Outlaw."

Stephen felt the crushing weight of that single word as if it were a boulder dropped from heaven. He felt his fingers tremble at his sides. Why, he didn't know. She was his mother; he was her son. Yet he was Outlaw. Unworthy to be with her.

"You are well?" he asked.

"Don't worry about me," she said.

But the bruises on her body suggested he should.

She glanced over her shoulder at Kirutu, who seemed content to let them speak, which confused Stephen in the wake of his harsh words.

His mother turned back, speaking now in a whisper. "I have dreams, Stephen. I can only remember parts of them when I wake, but they keep me alive. They are something beautiful. A great love. Shaka taught you how to love?"

"He taught me many things…"

"You must remember his words! They're from beyond all that you see, like Shaka himself. You must not give in to the thoughts that will tear you apart."

She knew, then.

"There isn't time, sweetheart." His mother placed her hand on his chest and gazed up into his eyes. "Promise your mother you'll remember. Promise me."

"Enough," Kirutu said.

Enough? Fear swiped at Stephen's mind, threatening to pull him into its prison.

"I beg you, Stephen. You have to remember, because I can't. It's the only way."

"Enough!"

She backed away from him, eyes pleading. "Don't give in to the fear. I beg you!"

Kirutu stepped up from behind and struck her jaw, sending her staggering.

"Enough!"

He grabbed her hair and pulled her up against him.

"Find the light," his mother said.

But Stephen could see no light now.

The warriors on either side closed in next to their ruler. Kirutu brought his knife up to her exposed throat and pressed the blade into her skin, deep enough to draw blood.

"You have no mother because you are dead. The dead feast only on bones. It would be this woman's bones that I feed you."

The world had darkened and his mind was spinning, taunting him with a terrible fear. He couldn't leave her in this monster's house.

Three paces to Kirutu's right, Lela's blood still soaked the ground. The bodies he'd passed upon entering the compound still hung from their perches. Tulim was a valley of death, and the mother who had given her life for him was in its grasp. She too would die. Of this Stephen suddenly had no doubt.

"You will leave this valley and the mountain on which you hide, never to return. Know that she will serve me as I see fit, as she has. She too is dead."

Stephen's self-control was slipping, he could feel it, like silt being drawn by a deep current, pulled toward open waters.

A very faint voice at the back of his mind suggested that Kirutu was playing him, taunting him, daring him to react. But the warning was already distant, a voice far out from the shore. And then gone. In its place Stephen heard only the rush of blood in his ears.

Kirutu lifted his blade and swiped it against his mother's cheek, leaving a bleeding gash in her flesh.

She gasped with pain, and Stephen felt something in his mind snap. Only one thought remained.

Save her.

And with that thought, a hundred emotions he'd long mastered overtook him. To save his mother he had to terminate the threat against her.

Kirutu. And the warriors at his side. Those who'd subjected her to endless abuse because she'd given herself to save her son.

All of this came to him in a single blink of his eyes, exploding into his awareness like a ball of fire that consumed his mind.

With that awareness, only one impulse.

To kill.

CHAPTER TWENTY-EIGHT

HIS BODY moved without forethought, overtaken by the instincts that Shaka had nurtured in him. Exact movement and calculation of forces, isolating muscles for their most efficient purpose, directing nerves to trigger with precision.

Since being taken by Shaka as an infant, Stephen had been in contact with no other man, much less lifted a hand to harm one. But these were no longer men in his mind. They were simply forces of darkness aligned against his mother. Black bodies inhabited by evil.

They were death itself, and his mother was in their grasp.

He had taken three long running steps directly toward Kirutu before he realized that he was moving. But Kirutu couldn't be his first target. The man had his mother by her hair and a knife at her throat.

If directly threatened he might kill her. If not he would keep her alive as leverage. Stephen needed his mother alive. And he needed a weapon.

He didn't know how this logic came to him—he was simply aware of it, knowing Kirutu's animal instinct as well as the air he breathed.

Already at a full sprint, he veered sharply to his left, directly toward two warriors already throwing their spears. Stephen saw the shafts leave their hands and he saw it slowly, the way Shaka had taught him to watch thousands of his own projectiles travel to their intended targets. If properly focused, the mind could more accurately perceive.

See it differently, Stephen. See it in each moment, bending to your will. See it stopped in time.

He saw. The spears were already airborne, five paces distant.

As was he, hurtling forward in a low dive, eyes on the spears' long shafts, spinning through slow, wobbly rotations as they flew. Their trajectory was fixed.

His was not.

He tucked himself, rolled once on the soft ground, and came around as one of the spears sped past him.

The one he would take for himself.

Using his momentum he came up, hand reaching for the butt of the shaft already. He closed his fingers around the wood, took three bounding strides toward the two empty-handed warriors, planted hard, and spun, swinging the spear in a full circle by the end of its shaft.

The spear was capped with a bone head sharpened to a blade on both sides, slicing through the air eight feet from the end of Stephen's extended arms. The head completed its arc at three times the speed of his rotation and hardly slowed when it cut through the first warrior's neck.

The second warrior had time to pull back, but not far enough to avoid the spear's tip, which tore out his throat.

Four seconds since Stephen had first moved.

Two warriors lifeless.

One spear in hand.

Stephen didn't pause to consider—his mind wasn't thinking so much as reacting. And the ease of his first success only fueled his determination to save his mother. To slaughter the whole compound if required.

The speed and precision of his attack gave the Warik pause. The entire compound came to a standstill, all eyes locked in wonder at the feat they had just witnessed. Even Kirutu, who was clearly not accustomed to being questioned, much less bested, was still.

While his attack still had them set back on their heels, Stephen tore forward. Straight for Kirutu, spear cocked already. The man's head was to his mother's right now, a hand's span between them. It would be like striking a coconut on the run.

He'd hit a thousand coconuts on the run. And his arm was already in forward motion when the Warik warriors recovered. Not only a few, but all of them at once, moving as one large body, like a school of fish or a flight of birds.

They roared and launched themselves forward, swarming around Kirutu in one black mass, cutting Stephen off from their ruler.

His attack had made them stronger, not weaker.

He knocked two spears from the air with a swipe of his arm and was at the throats of the leading men with his own shaft turned wide. The long hardwood shank struck three men broadside and shoved them back into the others, momentarily stalling the surging warriors.

"Stephen!" His mother's voice screamed over the din of crying warriors. "You can't——"

Kirutu had shoved his mother off to four men, who gagged her as they hauled her up the steps.

Stephen's path to her was cut off by the encroaching warriors.

He skipped backward on bare feet, twirling his spear in both hands, aware of his control over balance, speed, angles of attack, and escape.

But none of these promised a route to his mother.

His heart pounded, not from exertion, but with emotion. Rage. Fear for his mother. He could feel her years of suffering wash through his body as if it had replaced the blood in his veins.

And that blood was as black as midnight, swelling in him still, blinding him to everything but the desperate need to save her.

The warriors were closing in on him now, twenty of them abreast, forming an arc. He could tear through them, he was certain. Would tear into them. Wanted nothing more now than to rip them apart, a notion that roared through his mind like a rabid beast and left him trembling.

Only then did he see the flood of warriors pouring through the gate. Like dark waters they spilled into the compound and spread wide in both directions along the fence with the intention of sealing him in.

There was only one way to reach his mother. Kirutu had to die. Without a leader the Warik would offer no threat, like a headless snake.

Stephen slowed his retreat. The warriors, emboldened by the flanking maneuver of those streaming through the gate, slowed, clearly sure in their numbers.

The body follows the head, Stephen. Control your mind and you will own your body.

The ruler stood near the foot of the steps, at ease, watching without concern, bearing only the single knife. He lifted one hand to his mouth and issued a shrill whistle. Then threw his head back and laughed, a madman relishing his power.

Hatred swallowed Stephen whole. It wouldn't suffice to kill this man. Kirutu deserved to be crushed by the same brutality that had fed him for so many years.

Stephen grunted through clenched teeth and sprinted directly at the line of warriors closing in on him. Beyond them: Kirutu. He held the spear loosely in one hand, like a javelin. They'd seen what he was capable of, and they second-guessed themselves as he'd known they would, pulling up sharply.

All hesitated but two, who increased their pace. Both were armed with axes, no match for the spear in Stephen's hand. Did they still not know his reach? No, how could animals such as these learn so quickly? So then, these two would be the first to pay for their ignorance.

Three spears angled for him, thrown from the line to his right. He sidestepped two of them easily, snatched the third from the air with his left hand, took a stutter-step, and sent it forward, screaming full-throated.

The spear struck one of the axmen as he turned to evade, and plunged deep into the man's bowels.

The other came on without missing a step. The man's audacity darkened Stephen's vision, focused his rage. The world was slow before him—he could feel each footfall like hammers on the earth; hear each pump of blood as it rushed through his brain; see the man's bared teeth and defiant eyes. This single warrior embodied the evil that had tortured his mother.

The valley was shrieking, roaring, rushing with a wind that swept black streaks of vapor overhead—this he saw and heard only as a distant distraction. This and the thunder of the warriors' feet as they flooded the compound with shrill cries.

His own scream joined theirs as he came under the man's swinging ax like a battering ram, headfirst.

The impact of his skull against the warrior's chin offered up a loud, crushing crack that sent a jolt of pain down Stephen's spine. He didn't so much collide with the man's head as hammer through it, leaving the warrior's skull shattered and his body lifeless before it hit the ground.

Stephen was much heavier and stronger than the warrior, and his momentum carried him through without breaking his stride.

Kirutu would die. If so required, Stephen would tear the house apart board by board to reach his mother. Nothing else mattered now.

But when he lifted his head, he saw that the balance of power had changed. No fewer than fifty of the warriors who'd poured through the gate were closing in on Kirutu's position directly ahead, forming a circle around him.

The ruler of this realm stood with arms still spread wide, relishing his power, untouched by fear.

Stephen took two more long strides before a single thought penetrated his darkened mind. Kirutu knew that every warrior in his command would die to save him. They feared him more than they feared Stephen.

On the heels of this realization, the fear that wouldn't find a home in Kirutu's mind found one in Stephen's.

They were too many. He was throwing himself into certain death. If he died now his mother would have no savior.

An arrow sped past his head and he narrowly avoided a second by pulling up sharply. It had been shot from the left, where the compound had been empty.

With a single scan of the field, Stephen saw what he hadn't seen before. The warriors were still entering through the first gate, streaming along the fence to form a perimeter and cut him off. But many more were now entering through a second gate at the opposite end. Hundreds.

A thousand, like bats flowing into a massive cave, cutting him off from any hope of escape, even if he did reach his mother.

Panic set into Stephen's mind. And with it a terrible desperation he'd rarely felt. The need to breathe, to fight, to destroy, to save, to protect his life because he couldn't die now. Not while his mother was enslaved by a ruler who fed on the fear of others and crushed any who challenged him.

The warriors were holding back now, focused entirely on surrounding the compound and sealing him in. Kirutu grinned wickedly, surrounded by his men who bobbed up and down, taunting, slightly crouched and ready.

If he'd had a bow ... but he didn't.

He took three long steps forward, drew the spear he still held in his right hand back, and put his full weight into his throw, directing it at the body of a warrior who stood in front of Kirutu, protecting him.

The spear flew as though on his breath, straight and true, streaking with a speed that denied the wind whipping past its shank. The sharp head struck the warrior protecting Kirutu, broke through his lungs, and reached the ruler before losing its momentum.

Movement in the compound stalled save for the rushing of warriors along the fence. Kirutu stepped back, touched his ribs, and slowly lifted a bloody hand.

His eyes lifted to meet Stephen's, and he stepped forward to show his body. Pierced and bleeding, but the wound was only superficial.

"For this you will burn alive with your mother!" Kirutu's vitriolic voice carried over the warriors' cries.

He extended his bloodied hand toward Stephen, fingers spread wide and trembling.

"Take him!"

A thousand warriors had entered Kirutu's sanctum and formed a broad ring around the entire field. With a roar that overpowered the shrieking sky, they surged forward, closing in on Stephen like a massive constricting snake.

He did not calculate. He did not think. He did not embrace his survival instinct as much as become it. His mind collapsed in on itself and he found identity only in survival.

To this end, speed and momentum would be his only advantage. If he could not escape the compound, both he and his mother would be burned.

They would expect him to run. He stood still.

They would expect him to rush them as he had before. He took a knee. And he waited.

His body was trembling, he could feel it in his fingers as he planted one palm on the earth, readying himself. Fear crashed through his mind like a thundering boar. He couldn't escape it.

So he used it, tensed and coiled.

You will burn alive, Kirutu had said. If not for that cry, they might have sent a thousand arrows into his body.

The warriors on the leading edge were covered in sweat that beaded on their oiled bodies. Stephen fixed his gaze beyond them on those who trailed, ten deep.

He didn't think of them as armed men, but as a thick veil of evil that he had to escape if he was to save his mother.

Twenty paces, and still he didn't move.

Fifteen, and he dug his fingers into the earth and shifted his weight to give himself maximum leverage.

Ten, and they began to pull up, their prey at their feet, captivity now assured.

Five, and Stephen launched himself.

His movement was again so sudden that he'd taken three full strides and was already in a full sprint before any could react.

An ax was arcing toward him when he reached the line, but he managed to slow its drive with his right forearm. The ax head glanced off his shoulder, leaving a bloody gash.

Then he was past the warrior and crashing through a gauntlet of bunched, sweating bodies. Their spears were useless in such tight formation. Some swung their axes, but there was too much flesh in close quarters for any weapon to effectively find his body.

Fifteen battering strides and Stephen slammed past the last of them, sending a smaller man flying onto his back. Blood flowed from his shoulder, but his body was fueled with enough adrenaline to suppress any pain.

He sprinted across the open field, knowing that spears and arrows could still reach him. He veered to his left, away from the back gate, which still accepted a steady stream of warriors. He struck for a vacant section along the wooden fence, fifty paces distant.

All that mattered now was reaching that barrier.

He shut down his hearing and paid no mind to the pursuit.

They were coming after him, a herd terrified of failure. He could feel the ground shaking under him. Arrows sailed past; a spear clipped his right elbow.

None of this mattered. Only the fence.

Twenty meters.

He adjusted his approach and angled for a sapling that grew along the enclosure.

Ten meters.

Stephen left the ground at five paces, planted one foot on the tree's supple trunk five feet above the ground, and used the sapling's recoil to spring him higher. His progress catapulted him to the fence's crossbeam—barely.

He crashed into it, threw his body into a forward roll, and toppled over the fence.

Stephen landed on his feet in a crouch, facing a single terrified warrior next to a hut. He wasn't sure where his next impulse came from, and he felt no need to temper it.

He closed the distance to the warrior in two even

strides and shoved his palm up into the man's jaw with enough force to shatter his teeth and crack his skull.

And then he was running through the village for the jungle.

CHAPTER TWENTY-NINE

THE WARIK'S pursuit pushed Stephen deep into the jungle. They posed no real threat to him once he cleared the village. No one could hope to catch him in the trees.

They posed no threat, but their madness had overwhelmed him. He knew this, but he seemed powerless to change it. The peace he'd guarded so closely as he'd entered their village had fled. He was now host to a barrage of emotions no longer abiding in the peace of his Father. Chief among them: a terrible fear that he'd condemned his mother to a funeral pyre.

With that fear came a sickening sense of loss and abandonment. The only person in the world who was flesh of his flesh—the mother who'd brought him to life and sacrificed peace for his sake—

suffered in the heart of the Warik village without hope.

Nothing mattered now more than rescuing her. If required he would kill a thousand Warik to save her. The impulse pounded through his skull. She was hopelessly lost without him. He owed her his life.

He rushed through the jungle and doubled around, searching for higher ground. Within the hour he reached a knoll that offered him a clear view of the valley.

He peered down at the village, panting and drenched with sweat. From his vantage he could see the full scope of their resolve. Five thousand warriors had found their way into Kirutu's compound now and flowed like a river around the towering structure that held his mother.

Another five thousand ran back and forth just outside the main gates that led into the fenced village. There was no way into the stronghold. And if by some impossible means he did manage to reach his mother, ten thousand strong would smother them both.

He too, then, was held captive. He too was in the heart of darkness, lost and trembling. He could feel her desperation—layers of it, thick like so much black mud deposited over so many years. How she'd endured it he could not fathom, but she'd somehow clung to life, fed by dreams of being rescued by him. Dreams that were now failing her. She was too weak. It had been too much.

And he would fail.

Stephen sank to his knees, limp and powerless.

He tried to still his mind, but new voices had taken up residence, whispering pain and anguish, his mother's and his own. His mother had brought him to this distant world knowing the danger, subjecting him to isolation from the rest of his kind. Now he was left to live his life in this jungle alone?

There would be no home among the Warik. He couldn't live on a mountain his whole life. He needed companionship, the kind he'd been allowed to feel with Lela, if only for a day.

The memory of Kirutu slashing his blade across her neck sliced through his mind.

Every bone in his body demanded he rush down the mountain to save his mother. To reclaim Lela. Both were impossibilities. They were dead and doomed already and he was alone.

Abandoned.

He would rather be dead. And now he saw that Kirutu was right: he was dead already, with his mother in her grave.

He was falling apart and he didn't seem to be able to find a way clear of his desperation. Tears filled his eyes as he stared down at the sea of pulsing flesh.

He had to find Shaka. There was no other way. He had to return to the mountain and fall at Shaka's feet and beg his teacher to show him a way he could save his mother. And in saving his mother, save himself from this pain, because he was her son, born of her flesh, one.

Stephen staggered to his feet, turned his back on the Tulim valley, and ran.

Each step took him farther from her hole of misery and this alone terrified him, but he could see no other way. Shaka had negotiated his release from Kirutu many years ago. Surely he could do the same for his mother now.

The miles fell behind and still Stephen did not slow. Under any other circumstance he would have jogged lightly for such a long run, but the world had changed. There was no time. He ignored the pain in his shoulder and the crying of his lungs and he ran, leaping over fallen logs, rushing up steep inclines, often cutting directly through the brush when he knew the switchbacks would only slow him.

The sun was setting when he finally burst into the familiar clearing he'd called home for so long.

"Shaka!"

At first glance there was no sign of him.

"Shaka!"

He ran up to the cooking hut and shoved his head inside. "Shaka."

The fire was out and the ash smokeless. Two partially burned sticks of wood stuck out of the cold coals where he'd left them when he'd finished reading his mother's story two days earlier. The fire hadn't been lit since then. There was no sign anyone had been in the hut since he'd last left it.

Stephen hurriedly checked both of the other huts and found them both vacant. The roll Shaka typically kept at the head of the sleeping hut was in place, which meant he hadn't left with the intention of sleeping elsewhere, as he sometimes did.

Stephen tore out of the hut and cried out. "Shaka!" In every direction he repeated the same call. "Shaka! Shaka!"

Only birdsong answered him. How could his teacher have left him alone, knowing what he would find in the Tulim valley?

He paced, fighting back an uncommon fear, staring at the jungle, willing the familiar form of his teacher to appear as it always did.

But no. The jungle sounded oddly vacant. And he was alone, high on the mountain.

The cliff? It was where Shaka had first spoken of this quest.

Stephen ran, his mind lost to desperation. He wasn't aware of the path, or the way, only of the one question that drummed through his mind.

What if he's not there?

He came out of the jungle at a fast jog and bounded up a ledge on the highest part of the cliff.

"Shaka!"

A hawk perched on the far edge of the cliff sprang off the rock face and glided into the abyss below. The valley lay in near darkness, lit only by a sliver of gray light on the distant horizon.

Stephen stood on the ledge, breathing heavily from the run, staring at the setting of all light in his world.

It was as if the sun itself were shrinking, conspiring with all the world to abandon him in his darkest hour of need.

He tightened his fists as a ball of rage rolled up through his chest, and he screamed the name of his teacher into the falling night.

"Shakaaaa!" Then again, face flushed with heat, jaw strained wide. "Shakaaaa!"

The cry went out into the void before him and was swallowed by a heavy, mocking silence.

Shaka was cruel. In the valley far below, his

mother lay crushed. Here on the cliff, Stephen stood powerless.

He stepped out onto the ledge on numb feet and walked out to the edge of the cliff, pulled by the notion that jumping from this precipice would be his deserved end. Perhaps only in his death could his mother be safe. Kirutu would keep her alive indefinitely as a means of drawing Stephen in. If he died now, he could never again threaten her life.

The rocks below would crush his costume and save his mother's.

Costume.

Yes, these thoughts, all of them, were those of his costume—so he had learned. And now he was learning that he *was* his costume. All of Shaka's words to the contrary mocked him.

Remember, Stephen…

Remember that he was a Water Walker. His true self could jump off this cliff and float down the mountain, unaffected by the pull of gravity, as much as his Master had once walked on water, knowing that he would not sink.

So perhaps he should jump. His costume would die, of that he was certain. And why not?

Remember, Stephen…

He *was* remembering! He could hear all the

words drilled into him for so many years. But those words did not save his mother. Nor convince him that she didn't need saving.

All that Shaka had taught him seemed to fail him now. That promised power of security and beauty and peace and joy only ridiculed him.

In this way too Shaka had been cruel. To promise so much and deliver so little in the time of need. Where was he now?

Stephen stood on the cliff for a long time, at a loss. The last of the light vanished and tonight even the crickets were silent.

He didn't know what to think, much less do. Every time he tried to go beyond his thoughts, they quieted for only a brief moment before whispering of hopelessness once again.

He thought he might return to the huts but saw no point in sitting alone in an empty home. Returning to the valley wasn't an option.

So he finally sank to a sitting position, wrapped his arms around his knees, lowered his head, and rocked.

Save me. Save me...

He prayed to his Master, whom he had accepted as the truth, but he heard only silence.

He begged God, the Creator who had sent his Master, to save him.

He begged his Spirit to fill him and wash away the anguish that tortured his mind.

None of them answered his call.

Time slowed as waves of sorrow washed over him. He let them come, one after another deep into the night, until his mind finally surrendered itself and left him vacant. Hollowed.

Numb.

"Tell me, where does Stephen live?"

He heard the voice in his mind—his mother's. And he answered in a whisper only to answer himself.

"He lives in the mountains above the Tulim valley."

"Where does he sleep?"

Stephen hesitated. "He sleeps in a home next to the Wagali River."

"And how is his costume now?"

He'd heard these same questions only two nights ago, spoken by Shaka on this very cliff. His mind was replaying the discussion. But not all was as it had been.

"His insane mind screams of failure."

"And his true mind?" his mother's voice asked. She spoke with Shaka's inflections but in a higher tone. More soothing.

"It's at peace," he said, but he couldn't believe it now because he felt none of that peace.

"Why is this?" she asked.

"Because my true self is always at peace, dead to insanity. Only the insane mind offers any disturbance to the sound mind."

"And who gave you this sound mind?"

He blinked. A hint of calm, barely discernible, edged into his awareness.

"The One from whom I come."

"What is his name?"

"He is called the One in me. Immanuel. The Way and the Truth. The One who defeated death and is Life."

"And you?"

Stephen spoke aloud now, eager for the comfort that came with his speaking these words, however little.

"I too am now made whole without any further blame, condemnation, or need for correction. I am dead to that which makes me less than whole. I am alive only in my Father."

"Then can anything threaten you?" his mother asked.

"Nothing can separate me from his love. As far as the east is from the west, so far has he removed any true thought of my separation from him. I am blameless and nothing can remove me from my Master. It is impossible."

"Forgiven."

"Forgiven," he said.

"And yet, though dead, your insane mind speaks."

"Only when I forget that my insane mind is dead."

"And then?"

"And then he tempts me to feel threatened; separated from my true self in him. To feel less than whole and therefore needing of something other than the knowledge of my Master's love, which is already in me."

The voice waited a few moments before coming again.

"And yet now you think that you need your mother."

The truth of those last words grew in his mind like a balloon. He blinked.

A hand rested on his shoulder. "This is the grievance you cling to, my son. This is the god you look to for your salvation."

He jerked his head up and twisted to his right. His mother stood beside him, dressed as she'd been in the Tulim valley. Not merely an image of his mother, but her, in the flesh, hand on his shoulder, looking out at the abyss.

She turned her head and offered him a gentle

smile. "You forget your true Master, Stephen. Only he can save you. And he already has."

Stephen scrambled away and clambered to his feet, expecting the vision to vanish when he lifted his eyes.

But his mother was still there, looking out over the cliff again as a slight breeze lifted her hair.

"It's almost finished," she said.

He tried to speak but found his throat knotted.

"We are so close."

"Who are you?" he stammered.

"You don't recognize me? We know each other so well. You're forgetting."

She had to be a vision. She was speaking exactly as Shaka would have spoken, full of surety and confident knowledge, using his inflections. Stephen was hallucinating.

His mother, who could not be his mother, turned and stepped up to him. Took his hand and kissed his knuckles. Placed his fingers on the side of her face.

"Who do you feel?"

He could not deny touch.

"My mother," he whispered.

"And who are you?"

"Your son."

She smiled and drew her fingers through his hair.

"Mother and son. But only in the flesh, and this is a small thing. This is why our Master said that we must hate our mother, father, spouse, child if we are to follow him and find his narrow way. He meant that we must not cling to them. Most can't fathom his meaning. If you look to anyone to satisfy your longing, you will think you need something more than him and what he has made you to be complete and at peace. The expectation of fulfillment in relationships will always fail you, and you will hold grievances that darken your world. You will become blind to the light that guides to the narrow path. You were taught this on the mountain alone, and yet among others you forget."

The truth settled over him. His suffering was due to his attachment to his own mother. He had allowed himself to need her. The feeling had felt so natural, but it wasn't his Master's way.

And yet...

"She needs me," he said.

"I do?"

He was still confused by the nature of her presence here on the cliff. Was this his mother in the flesh? Shaka, showing himself as his mother in a vision? His mother showing herself in a vision?

"I...she's suffering."

His mother nodded, thoughtful, then turned back to the valley.

"Like you, I'm of two minds, one that sees clearly and is at perfect peace, the other that holds grievances against those who I think have wronged me. All human suffering comes from grievance. The inability to forgive that which offends us and turn the cheek. And yet we have the power to forgive and receive forgiveness. We are just blind to it most of the time."

"Kirutu..."

She faced Stephen, face serene. "My costume despises Kirutu most of the time, except when I sleep, as I do now. When I'm awake, I would scratch his eyes out and shove a dagger in his throat. I try to love him, but I hold terrible grievances against him."

His mother paused.

"The truth is, all costumes are incapable of true love, and most keep their grievances in hiding, under the dark clouds where they can't see the light. Only love will change the heart. Kirutu's heart. We came to the valley for this end, Stephen."

Her words rushed through him, as if they were more than mere waves of sound. The peace he'd forgotten was now thick in the air. A familiar tingle rode up his spine as he remembered. Truly remembered.

"I don't need to be rescued, my son. I'm whole already, in perfect peace with my Father. I know this when I sleep. When I dream, as I dream now. But when I awake, I forget most of what I know when my mind is silent. Then I see only my own terrible misery."

"You're dreaming? Are you here?"

She looked at him, eyes bright with a deep certainty that filled him with mystery.

"I've been with you all along."

She meant in spirit.

"Spirit is reality," she said, as if hearing his thoughts. "Flesh is only costume. Remember?"

He did. Perfectly.

"And yet we continue to listen to our costumes," he said. "They want to be God."

"I suffer when I'm awake because I've forgotten how to see when I'm awake. If Shaka hadn't come to my dreams so long ago, I might never have seen with eyes wide open. If he hadn't touched my eyes on a hill eighteen years ago and shared such truth, I might still be in blindness. What he shared with me, I forget when morning comes. Then the song fades and with it the full truth. And I feel terrible remorse and fear."

The story she'd written filled his mind. "Shaka called you to this valley."

"Shaka," she said. "But whenever I slept, I was with you."

She faced him. "So you see, Stephen, I never left you. I saw you as I dreamed. I still do, even now, this moment. This was the gift given to me so that I could find courage for so long."

"And who is Shaka?" he asked impulsively.

"I don't know. Perhaps an angel." A coy smile toyed with her lips. She glanced over his shoulder. "Ask him yourself."

He twisted around and started. Standing three feet from Stephen, staring out over the cliff, stood Shaka.

His teacher winked. "Hello, Stephen. I hear you got lost."

Stephen spun back to his mother.

But his mother wasn't there.

Or was she? He slowly faced his teacher, filled with wonder.

"You..."

"Some things will remain a paradox, my son. He works in mysterious ways, and there is no mystery greater than the reality beyond flesh and bone."

"You're an angel?"

Shaka smiled. "Some might call me by that name. Words fail these mysteries. But know that you've never been alone or in danger. Ever. Only madness believed that you were."

With those words the last thread of doubt fell from Stephen's mind and he became fully aware that he was whole. Complete. Atoned for. Loved. He was love itself. As was his mother.

His body began to tremble as waves of infinite awareness and power rolled through him.

"Now you know more than you once did," Shaka said. "The crucible of all transformation is renewing your mind as it relates to others. Love surrenders all expectations, all grievances. Forgiveness is the path. Acceptance the gateway. Even as you have been forgiven, go now and release all your expectations and grievances."

Stephen thought to speak, to say that he understood. To make Shaka aware that he was seeing it all now. This was why he and his mother had been drawn to the Tulim valley—for this day. To be called beyond the laws of this world and to live as Outlaw. To find true love through forgiveness and to spread it throughout a hidden valley lost in darkness.

This was the darkness he'd seen over the village. The same madness that he'd embraced. Shaka had called both his mother and him to bring the light into this valley.

He thought to say as much, but his throat was stuffed with emotion and his chest was bursting with gratitude. He could hardly breathe, much less speak.

"Deditio," Shaka said. *Surrender* in Latin, one of his favorite expressions. "Trust only in his Way, his Truth, his Life."

"I will," Stephen managed.

"Yes. You will. It's the only way."

Shaka stepped up to him, stared into his eyes, and offered him a consoling smile. He lifted his hand and clasped Stephen's neck, then pulled him forward and gently kissed his forehead.

"I treasure you, my son. When the way seems dark, only remember to surrender to the Truth beyond the law of this world. You are Outlaw. You and all those who follow that narrow way."

"I will," Stephen said. His voice came out weak, strained by the power sweeping though him.

Shaka took Stephen's hand and placed a medallion in his palm. It was a tribal stone with a large *O* carved on the surface and the word *DEDITIO* engraved within the circle.

"Keep this with you always as a reminder."

Stephen swallowed deeply. "Thank you."

"Close your eyes."

He did. Felt the pressure of his teacher's thumbs

on his eyelids for a moment before Shaka swiped them away.

"Open them."

He opened his eyes.

"What do you see?"

Nothing had changed.

"I see you."

"Yes. You see me. But you will see more when the time comes. You will see the narrow path inside of you that very few find and even fewer follow. Very few. It is your destiny to take this path. Follow where it leads you."

Yes. Yes of course, he should. Already he knew where it would lead him.

"What if they kill us?"

Shaka smiled. Winked.

"We don't really need these costumes, now do we?"

"No."

"No. And you will not see this one again. Come to me. Your fate awaits."

And then Shaka walked away and vanished into the darkness. There was nothing more to say. Nor to see, as it pertained to Shaka.

Stephen turned. There was no sign of his mother either.

The wind whispered softly. The night was dark. He was by himself.

But he was not alone.

His mother was dreaming in peace. He too would sleep.

And then he would follow the narrow way into the Tulim valley.

CHAPTER THIRTY

THE SUN SHONE bright and hot over Stephen's head as he ran in a steady cadence, planting one foot before the other without breaking stride, gracefully avoiding obstacles. The drumming of each footfall on the earth provided a simple guide—three for each pull of breath—which kept his mind fixed and his resolve sound.

It was true, as Shaka had taught him, that in life there was nowhere to go, only a place to be. But in the world of flesh and bone, he ran for the Tulim valley, his mind disregarding any trouble it might bring.

Because now he remembered, without doubt, that there were problems only in the world of madness, from which he'd been rescued long ago.

He was the child of his Father. Nothing could possibly threaten his Father. Therefore, abiding in his Father, he could know no threat, much less any real problem. Wasn't this the lesson he'd learned in Shaka's illustration, in which God was as big as a million suns and could not be threatened by a mere mouse?

Only yesterday he'd forgotten and feared that mouse. Thinking now, he couldn't help but chuckle.

And so he ran, one stride followed by another in perfect rhythm, three footfalls for every breath; two heartbeats for every footfall.

The sun was already low in the western sky when he reached the cliff from which he and Lela had gazed into the Tulim valley. He pulled up on the rock ledge, chest heaving like a massive bellows.

He'd half expected to see the black fog, the madness that had imprisoned the Tulim. But the valley was perfectly clear, without a hint of low cloud or mist. He thought it was because he wasn't bothered by the valley's threat.

But the moment he thought this, a black mist began to materialize, first above the distant swamps, encroaching up-valley.

He watched in fascination as the low-hanging fog formed out of thin air on all sides, flowing like long reaching fingers that coiled and flowed of their own accord, as though alive.

They joined to form a seamless river of darkness that blanketed the lower Tulim valley, where the Warik gathered for their feast at Kirutu's feet.

A feast?

Yes. At which his mother would be sacrificed to that darkness.

Fear whispered through his mind. It was then that Stephen realized his task might be impossible, and the thought made him shiver.

He closed his eyes. Breathed. Set his mind at the feet of his infinite Father. Saw that there was no snake to threaten such vast love and power. As far as the east was from the west—as far as one end of infinity was from the other—this was how far his Father had removed the threat of separation from him. It no longer existed, not even in the mind of God, for even to think of a threat is to be threatened. The infinite did not contemplate any such thing.

Peace washed over him like warm water, and he breathed it deep.

When he opened his eyes, the fog was gone.

"You see, Stephen. Madness has no power over you," he whispered.

A long call cut the still air and he spun to see its source. The call was coming from another bluff some distance off. It was uttered by a warrior just visible between the trees, calling down into the valley.

The cry echoed, then fell away, followed by another, this one from much farther down in the valley, barely heard, answering or passing on the first call.

He'd been seen by Warik scouts. They were sending word down into the valley. So then...they would be ready for him.

But he'd expected no less. Kirutu was no fool. The ruler knew now that the white son raised as Outlaw was a highly skilled warrior not easily killed.

And this was Kirutu's clear intention. To kill him.

Stephen knew this as well, and being reminded of it now gave him pause. But he allowed the concern to pass quickly. His place wasn't to outwit or best Kirutu. Not this time. Nor ever.

It would take some time to reach the village, and darkness would be falling. They would be waiting and he wouldn't disappoint them.

He ducked back into the jungle and ran. Through the trees, down the switchbacks that took him lower, always lower, then over a creek and up a rise, the view of the valley now hidden by the jungle.

Still he ran, closing the distance between himself and Kirutu.

His mother would be awake now, he thought. She probably wouldn't remember what had happened in her dreams, much less realize that they, not her waking hours, held the Truth of awakening. It could be said that his mother was only truly awake while sleeping. During the day she lived a nightmare, separated from the Truth. Only the remnants of her dreams continued to give her hope.

He would quicken that hope. Like a burning log, he would join her and their fire would burn brighter. Where two or more gathered, there was always more light, Shaka said.

Exactly how he would do this when he arrived at the Warik village, he didn't know yet. In truth he knew far more what he would *not* do when he arrived than what he would.

He would *not* entertain any grievance against Kirutu or the Warik.

He would *not* allow his costume to wail of its need or shout with any grievance.

He would *not* resist.

He was dead to this flesh, to the law of the world. His costume might not know it, because it was only flesh and bone and brain, but his true self, long ago made whole, did.

He was only a short way from the knoll that

overlooked the village when he heard the sound of crashing through the understory to his right. His first thought was that he'd disturbed a boar.

He pulled up and scanned the forest. This was human. And now he could hear the unmistakable sound behind and to his left as well.

They already had him surrounded, just beyond the trees. The thought that he should evade them again skipped through his mind, but he immediately let it go. He'd been raised in this jungle for this day. Resisting his destiny on any level would only trigger his own madness once again.

So he ran on. They herded him forward. He could easily escape. Kirutu would know that. They knew he could just as easily turn and kill any number of the warriors who trailed him in the bush—perhaps it was why they didn't attack.

Run, Stephen. Run to your mother. Run to Kirutu. This is your path now. Run.

He ran. Closer. Very close. Close enough to hear a low chant rising from the valley ahead.

Whoa. Whoa. Whoa.

Like a slow drumbeat that pulsed through the trees and reached into his bones. They were waiting.

Stephen did not slow. Neither did he press forward with more speed. He simply ran to his destiny. To whatever awaited, without judging what that might be. For this he had been brought to the jungle.

For this he had been saved.

And then he was there, bursting from the trees out onto the knoll that overlooked the Warik village, which sat half a mile down the wide, grassy slope. He pulled up hard, taken off guard by what he saw.

A thick slab of black cloud hung low over the village, creating a ceiling that no light could penetrate. The ominous sky shifted and flowed, perfectly flat and silent.

It had no reason to shriek or thunder—that power had been passed to the sea of flesh below.

The warning calls he'd heard on the cliff had reached the village long ago, and Kirutu had gathered his Warik into a massive show of force, ten thousand strong outside the main gate. Warriors all, blackened skin glistening in the light of a dozen fires. They formed a wide arc, perhaps several hundred men wide, fifty deep, and faced the hill on which he stood.

Facing *him*.

Chanting, armed with bows and spears, dressed in bright paint and feathers—the only color besides the light of the fire and the whites of their eyes.

Whoa. Whoa. Whoa.

And with each chant their feet and the butts of their spears came down hard on the earth, ten thousand crushing hammers that sent a tremor through the earth.

A chill rode Stephen's bones, unbidden by his will.

Before the sea of Warik warriors stood a large pyre of wood stacked around a post. And strapped upright to that post...

His mother.

Ten paces to her right, Kirutu stood tall and broad-chested, glistening with greasy, blackened skin. He stared up the hill at Stephen.

Somewhere at the edge of the inexhaustible reservoir of peace and wholeness, Stephen's costume began to scream. And for a long moment that stretched out with each rumbling chant from below, he wondered if he could do what he was meant to do, not yet even knowing what he *was* to do.

Surrender your own understanding. Trust only in the truth. See the narrow path. Follow him. This is the Way.

And that Way would lead him down the hill to that black sea. It was no different from stepping off the shore and walking out on the black waters in the dead of night. Hadn't the Master been a Water Walker? Wasn't he still?

Stephen looked over his shoulder. The jungle behind him was lined with a hundred armed warriors, staring at him with fixed resolve. They did not approach, they did not speak, they only stared, and in their eyes he could see fear.

Fear. They knew that if they attacked, he was more than capable of taking any number of lives before vanishing into the jungle.

These warriors were only doing what Kirutu demanded of them.

Stephen faced the gathered host and walked forward, one foot before the other, down the slope, into the reverberating chant.

Whoa. Whoa. Whoa.

Now his breathing was shallow and his pulse deep. And his costume began to ask its maddening questions, innocuous at first, then with an edge of fear.

Why has Kirutu gathered so many in such a crushing show of power?

"Because he is terrified, deep inside, where a voice asks him why even such a skilled warrior would return to certain death in a hopeless attempt to save his mother."

Did you come to save your mother?

"I came for Kirutu, who holds my mother's costume in his claws."

And how will you defeat Kirutu?

"I won't."

You've gone mad! What can you possibly do?

His mind went blank. One foot in front of the other.

"I will remember. I will surrender. I will be what I am and surrender all else."

And if you fail to find that place of infinite power inside you, they will kill you.

"They cannot kill me. My life is eternal."

They will kill me!

"I don't need my costume."

I do! I need your costume! I am your costume!

Stephen hesitated. "Be quiet," he said aloud. "You're already dead."

Their chanting, delivered in perfect unison with hammering feet and pounding spears, shook the earth as the slope gave way to level ground. The blazing fires that stretched east and west before the Warik sent sparks to the black-capped sky with each stomp.

He glanced behind and saw that the warriors who'd herded him here followed, fifty paces to his rear.

The only thing Stephen knew to do was walk, as

he had once before, this time knowing that he was walking into the arms of a crushing force.

Two others stood near his mother's pyre. An emaciated man who wore no paint nor dress of any kind. And to his right, one step behind, a frail-looking woman wearing only an old grass skirt. Death had hollowed out their stares. They watched Stephen without expression. He thought it might be the prince of his mother's story, Wilam, and his wife, Melino. Stephen couldn't be sure.

Kirutu had strapped his mother to the post at her ankles and bound her arms behind the pole to keep her upright. A dirty brown sack covered her head.

They will burn her.

She is safe.

They will burn you.

I am safe.

There's no way out!

There is *the* Way. And it is *in*, not out. Shaka said I would see it.

Shaka has gone mad!

You are madness.

Stephen came to a stop twenty paces from Kirutu, who stared at him, hand wrapped tightly around his spear. His chest rose and fell slowly as the thundering chant made his power plain. His mouth was flat, his face resolute. But Stephen saw something else beyond his eyes.

Fear.

Uncertainty. Terror, beneath layers of power and years of brutality, but hiding there still, in the deepest caverns of his mind.

A strange calm settled into Stephen's mind. Who was Kirutu but another deeply wounded man who didn't know what else to do but protect his costume?

The ruler was used to an enemy who would resist him, and he'd learned to crush any such threat. Now came one from Shaka who walked willingly to his death without fear. Kirutu could not understand this. And what he couldn't understand, he feared.

Stephen felt the world fall away. The chants faded, the air thickened. He experienced no grievance, no judgment, no blame—these things were not his concern. And in that place without grievance, he saw no threat. Before him stood a child, crying out for what he had long forgotten.

Screaming out for a love he had never known.

Compassion swallowed Stephen whole and a knot rose into his throat. What was inconceivable to flesh and bone became perfectly clear to him. There were no words to explain it.

Kirutu lifted his hand, a casual gesture that was immediately taken as a command. The chanting ceased. The earth stilled, leaving only the crackling of fire and the anguished sound of a woman trying to hold back her sobs.

His mother was crying under the hood.

Stephen held his eyes on Kirutu, pulled by his mother's fear.

Deditio. Surrender. Remember who you and your mother are. There is no threat. None.

Kirutu stepped forward, brazen before a people who could not see the fear in his heart. Blinded to it himself.

He stopped two paces from Stephen and ran his gaze down to his feet, then back up to his eyes.

"You wish to die," he said in a low, graveled voice.

"You can kill my body, but not the love inside it."

"And this childish love for a mother will end only in the burning of your flesh with hers."

"I did not come to save my mother," Stephen said.

Kirutu watched him, unblinking.

"I came for you."

"For me. You would cut off the head of the snake, but this snake does not die so easily."

"I didn't come to kill you. I came to set you free."

The man's jaw tightened. "And yet you kill with ease."

Yes, he had killed, and the memory of that now filled him with a deep sorrow.

"Forgive me. I had gone insane."

"This madness has not left you. You see as an infant. This woman you call your mother is a slave who cannot be saved. So you come to die with her. You are mad."

It was a natural conclusion, but wrong.

"You are the slave," Stephen said quietly, riding the waves of compassion that rolled through his mind. "Hatred rules your heart and puts you in a deep pit of suffering where you live alone."

The man wasn't able to quickly respond, so Stephen told him more.

"Your power in this valley is unquestioned—no man can live without your approval. Even the trees bow to your will. There's no more to be gained and yet you suffer, secretly hating all that you are and all that you've done. That is your pit. But you can be free."

For a moment Stephen thought Kirutu was listening on the deeper level of his soul, no longer deaf to this hidden knowledge. And maybe, for a moment, he was, because his face seemed to soften and a hint of wonder relaxed his eyes.

But as he watched, Kirutu's face began to change. His jaw tightened and his lips twisted into a snarl. His people couldn't see the shift, because Kirutu had his back to them, but they'd surely seen rage consume their leader a thousand times.

Stephen looked at the warriors' faces, all of them full of desperation. They too were enslaved by Kirutu's hatred. But he also saw wonder in their stares. The powerful man from Shaka's mountain could stand before their tormentor and his full army without fear.

There was surely a place in the heart of all Tulim that desired liberation from Kirutu's tyranny. Kirutu couldn't allow his people to see Stephen stand before him without fear.

A quiver had taken to the man's hands. Stephen was about to speak, thinking he should tell Kirutu that he didn't need to fear the loss of his power—instead he would gain a greater power—when the man turned, walked up to his mother on the post, and ripped the bag off her head.

Stephen now saw his mother's face, filthy, stained by the tears that had raked her cheeks, still matted with blood from the cut above her jaw. Her eyes were bright with fear as she jerked her head to take in the scene. They fixed on Stephen and her face twisted into an unspoken plea for help.

Kirutu grabbed her hair and spun back to Stephen.

"This is the pig who bore you! She is the one I have crushed." His voice cut like a spear, and, seeing his mother's anguish, Stephen felt the dark sky above him reach for his soul.

"You come to my house to save her?"

Kirutu jerked his mother's head to one side by her hair. She screamed: the sound of it sank into Stephen's mind like a talon.

"Save her," Kirutu mocked. "Show me the love of a son and save this wretched woman!"

His mother was beyond herself now, lost to terror, weeping loudly. He felt her anguish as if it were taking up residence in his own flesh. He was slipping.

"Save her!"

Kirutu glared, muscles drawn taut, made of rage and undone by it at once. His mother was shaking on the post, neck twisted to the breaking point, wailing—the terrifying keen of a dying animal.

Darkness pressed in and Stephen felt the first tendril of rage slip into his gut.

Kirutu lifted his right arm and brought his fist down on his mother's face as he held her hair. The impact of bone on flesh produced a sickly *thunk*.

His mother's body went limp, but that didn't stop

Kirutu from striking her again, as hard, pummeling the helpless to show his strength.

He released her hair and she slumped forward in her ropes, head hung low, unconscious.

The tendril of rage coiled into a ball and rose through Stephen's chest. He couldn't stand in the face of such brutality without resisting. Without extracting revenge. Without crushing the oppressor.

Without engaging Kirutu, even knowing that this was Kirutu's ploy. The ruler could not abide an enemy that did not fear him in front of his people.

Which was why Stephen could not attach himself to the anger rushing through him. He could neither react to nor resist it without also fueling it.

His breathing thickened and he felt as though he might break. And if he did, both he and his mother would die.

They would die anyway. It was already over. There was no way out.

No, Stephen. There is the Way.

A narrow way, already misted over with forgetfulness. A realm seen only dimly through the fog.

A chill washed over Stephen's crown as his mind flopped between assurance and the desperation that tempted him. He was going to fail. He'd come in trust, leaning only on the understanding that came from beyond his mind, and yet there was his mother, bleeding on the post, and he, powerless before the people.

Kirutu closed the distance between them in three long strides, face dark like a storm.

He could save his mother now. He could kill Kirutu with the man's own dagger. In the space of one breath he could twist out of Kirutu's way, slip the bone knife strapped to his thigh from its sheath, and bury the blade deep into the back of his skull, forcing upon him the full meaning of *surrender* as used in conquest.

Deditio.

Stephen caught himself.

Deditio. This was his way.

He stood still, allowing the fear to wash through him. The terror was only his costume in full protest. He had to stay surrendered to the Way in which—

Kirutu swung his hand and slapped him, a slicing swipe that crashed into Stephen's jaw and jerked his head to one side. For a brief instant the world became perfectly dark and silent, a void with no valley, no Warik, no body. Only stillness.

But only for a split second and then he was back, in the flesh. Pain ballooned in his skull, and with it the terrible fear that his body and his breath weren't only his costume. His very life was being threatened. He had to save himself!

But he couldn't. Not now.

"You have no will to stand like a man?" the ruler bit off. He slammed his fist into Stephen's gut. And as Stephen folded forward, Kirutu brought his knee up into Stephen's face—a glancing blow that struck his cheekbone and sent him staggering back.

Once again the world sputtered to darkness and silence. A void. The end of existence.

Once again that void vanished and he returned to the place where he was being beaten while his mother hung limp on a post. Panic welled up and screamed his name. *Live, Stephen! You can't die…not now.*

"Fight!" Kirutu stepped to him and swung again. When his fist connected with Stephen's head, Stephen dropped to a sitting position. Blackness swirled through his mind and he felt the world slipping. On the edges of his consciousness the loud demand that he protect himself persisted. He must kill this man and save his mother.

But he could not. Would not. His whole life was staked on this truth that his Master had taught: *When the evil man comes against you, do not resist. You are not your body. Walk on water, Stephen.*

He felt himself sinking into darkness, like a rock into a pool. Over him Kirutu, enraged and roaring, beat him. He was aware that he was lifting his arms to ward off the blows. Aware that a heel had slammed into his rib cage with a crack. Aware that he was curling into a ball to save himself. Aware that he was being beaten to death.

The world suddenly blinked off. And this time it stayed off. The rushing of blood through his head fell away. He wanted peace to flood him but he felt none.

Instead he felt alone in the darkness, and so deep was that darkness. Isolated, lying on his side, quivering.

Abandoned.

In that moment he felt like a child, powerless to protect himself. He had failed again. The world had been rolled onto his shoulders and he'd been crushed by its weight.

He only wanted to die now. It was too much.

"It's alright, darling. It's only our costumes they take."

Stephen heard the voice, clear and present, and he snapped his eyes wide.

The first thing he saw were the bands of color flowing through the air. The darkness was gone, replaced by a sky that streamed with light, and wide bands of red and orange and blue.

He jerked his head off the ground and stared. He wasn't in the valley. He was above it, far away, on the cliff overlooking it. The trees glowed with life under the flowing, colored sky, and with a single draw of breath, the truth returned to him, as if living in the air itself.

All was well.

All was perfectly well.

"It's going to be alright. They can't hurt us, Stephen."

He turned his head and saw that his mother stood two paces from him, gazing out over the valley, hair lifting with a gentle breeze.

This was real?

The colored world suddenly blinked off. He was back in the valley, cheek pressed against the cool earth. Being beaten by Kirutu, who landed his heel on his side. He heard himself grunt.

His mother hung forward against her restraints on the post. Unconscious, as though asleep.

Dreaming of another place. A place on the cliff, above all of this savagery.

They can't hurt us, Stephen.

The words had been his mother's, spoken in the other place as she dreamed, and his memory of them turned off the night.

He was suddenly there, back on the cliff under

brightly colored ribbons of light, looking up at his mother, who was walking toward him, then kneeling. Smiling softly.

She lifted her hand and stroked his hair. "You're going to be alright. We have no reason to fear."

He saw her words. They came not only with sound, but with color like the bands in the sky, flowing from her mouth as she spoke. They washed over his face, waves of intoxicating power that flooded him with overwhelming peace and love.

"We've always been together and always will be," she said, and again the words flowed from her in waves of raw color that stroked his soul. "Here there's nothing to fear. We are one."

He wanted to wrap his arms around her. He wanted to rest his head in her lap and let her hold him close.

But the gratitude smothering him had turned his muscles weak.

"I love you," he said. And the words came from his mouth in another wave of colored light. They streamed to her face and he watched as she breathed them in. She smiled, intoxicated by that love. "I'm with you always," he said.

Tears misted her eyes. "Always."

Here there was no problem. No darkness. No time. No pain.

Here there was only infinite love and power.

And there?

The words Shaka had spoken after touching his eyes returned to him like a soft echo. *You will see more when the time comes.*

This is what he'd meant?

"When you speak, I can see color," he said.

She looked at him. "Color?"

"Like the color above us."

She glanced up at the sky. "I see only the bright sky."

And then he knew what Shaka had meant.

He stood up and helped her to her feet. All around there was color. He could see it with each of her breaths, very faint, but there. She was inhaling and exhaling more than air.

"I see it, Mother," he said in wonder. "I see it everywhere!" He blinked and looked out over the cliff. "You're dreaming now on the post. It's the same gift that first drew you to this valley."

He looked back and saw that she understood.

"You see clearly when you're asleep."

She offered a gentle nod.

"And when you're unconscious. Like you are now."

"Yes. Yes, you're right."

"And now I can see as well. And what I see is

more." He took her hand. "There's power in your words, Mother. Great power. When you speak I can see it. I can feel it. But when you wake up, you forget who you are and fear fills you."

"Yes. I try..."

"But don't you see, Mother? It's *your* love that Kirutu must see. The forgiving of all grievance from the woman he has crushed."

"But when I wake..."

"Not when you wake, this is too much for you. But now, while you embrace that love completely, reach out to him."

Her eyes were wide.

"I see it now," he said with rising passion, watching his words wash over her. "I see that I was brought to the valley to help you love him. Now. They are down in the valley, killing our costumes, but we are here, and here we're swimming in power and love. Can you forgive and love him?"

"Now?"

"Yes, now."

"Yes," she said. "Now I see his costume as nothing more. There's no need for any grievance."

"Then speak to him now."

She blinked. "How?"

"How were you called to this valley?"

"A song," she said.

"Then sing as Shaka sang to you. Draw him where soul calls to soul, as you were called."

She stared out over the valley, awareness dawning in her eyes. "Yes," she whispered.

"Yes," he said. He lifted his hand and caressed her cheek. "Sing to Kirutu, Mother. Sing to him now, while you can. Let that song hold you in its embrace of love and call to the one you would forgive."

A tear broke from her eye.

"Forgive him," Stephen said. "He is only a broken child who doesn't know love."

A slight smile nudged the corners of her mouth. "Yes," she said, and wiped the tears from her cheek. "Thank you, Stephen. Thank you."

Then his mother turned to face the valley, stared into the colored light for a moment, closed her eyes, and began to sing. A simple long note, pure and crystalline. It streamed from her mouth into the air, bearing more power than had ever been known in all of the Tulim valley.

CHAPTER THIRTY-ONE

THE WORLD shifted, and Stephen found himself on the ground at Kirutu's feet. Two things he knew before he had time to open his eyes. The first was that nothing had changed in the valley, because only a moment had passed, not enough time for Kirutu to land more than one blow.

The second was that everything had changed in the valley. He could hear the sound, very faint, only at the very edge of his consciousness. It was a note and it came from his mother.

He opened his eyes and saw her in his direct line of sight, hanging from the pole, head slumped, hair draping her face.

And now he knew a third thing. He could still see. A very faint wisp of color drifted from his mother's mouth, eked out by a note so thin that perhaps only he could hear it.

He lifted his head off the ground. The sky above was still dark, yes, but from his mother on the post, color was coming into the valley.

"And now you will watch her burn," Kirutu was saying.

He landed another blow to Stephen's face, but this didn't bother him. His eyes were on his mother and his heart was one with hers.

"Sing, Mother," he whispered.

He watched in amazement as a red wave left his mouth, closed the distance to his mother, and washed over her body.

He said it with more power. "Sing."

Another blow from Kirutu landed on his body.

"Sing…"

She sang. Eyes still closed, head still hanging, she sang from her soul, a long note that streamed with increasing volume and color.

"Sing…"

The note came pure and long, a haunting tone that could not be denied.

Stephen shifted his eyes and saw that Kirutu had hesitated. The soft song was now just audible above the roaring flames—he'd heard it. Surely he had.

The man twisted his head and stared at the slumped form on the post.

There was his mother, hanging as though dead,

and yet from her mouth came a beautiful song that defied her state. They could all hear it and they'd all gone still.

And as Stephen watched, his mother's head began to rise. Her eyes were still closed, but her mouth was parted and the colored light that streamed from it shot past him, up the hill, into the night sky far behind him.

Kirutu slowly stepped back, away from Stephen, fixed by what he heard and saw. Not the color, surely, but to hear such beauty from such a desolate victim...

"Sing," Stephen whispered. "Sing."

Her head came all the way up and she sang to the distant mountains, now with even greater volume and growing intensity. Light streamed from her face, shooting deep into the night sky.

Stephen was just twisting his head to see where the light was going when the first band of color from that distant horizon swept through the sky above him.

Her simple call for forgiveness was being returned, not as another streak of light, but in thick ribbons pushed by a wall of light that rolled into the valley.

A thundering, concussive tsunami of brilliance that rushed toward the valley. The ground shook with its power as it approached, moving fast.

Cries of alarm spread. The Warik weren't looking at the sky—they couldn't see the light. But they could feel the earth trembling and it sent them scattering, running for their very lives.

Still the light came, hurling down the valley like a rolling mountain of color, threatening to crush everything in its path.

Still the Warik fled in terror before the thundering sound and bucking earth.

Then the light reached his mother and blew through her, lifting her hair from her shoulders.

She sang on, one long crystalline note returned by crushing power.

The flames of the fires bent low, bowing toward his mother under the power of the wave.

Still she sang, as the light streamed past the fence, through the village, and flowed toward the lowlands beyond.

This was the song his mother had first heard in her dreams, now made manifest in the Tulim valley. This was why she'd come.

This was why he'd been saved. So that they too could be saved.

Her song remained unbroken and beautiful until Stephen wondered if his own body could stand the power sweeping through it. Her hair streamed backward as the light rushed past her, but her face glowed in perfect peace, like that of a child singing through a dream.

For an endless breath that robbed Stephen of his own, she sang, face full in the rushing color.

And then, when Stephen thought his own lungs would burst, she closed her mouth. Her song quieted and the rumbling earth settled. But the silent, colored light did not abate. It flowed through her, filling her with its infinite life. She hung from her pole, head erect, bathed in power.

The Warik warriors who'd fled crept back, eyes on his mother, as the earth stopped shaking. Villagers—women and children and the aged—rushed out of the gates and pulled up short at the sight before them.

His mother's eyes opened. She stared ahead for a moment; then, as if knowing precisely what she must do, she slowly turned to look at Kirutu.

For a long time she said nothing. When she spoke, her words flowed as light.

"Let me speak to you, my husband."

Her light reached out to Kirutu and flowed through him, and although he couldn't see what Stephen saw, the power of her love was affecting him already. He stood rooted to the ground, unable to comply or refuse. The night seemed to have stalled completely.

His mother turned to the man who stood next to the emaciated woman. "Cut me down, Wilam," she said softly.

A tear glistened on Wilam's cheek, but he showed no other outward signs of emotion. He looked at his brother, who made no move to stop him, walked over to a warrior, took the man's knife from his hand, and stepped up to the pole.

Stephen pushed himself to his feet, watching with vision blurred only by emotion.

With one last glance at Kirutu's wide eyes, Wilam cut the grass ropes—first the ones at her feet, so that she could reach the ground, then the ones that bound her hands behind the pole.

His mother stepped away from the pole slowly, on light feet, as if still in a dream. She took Wilam by the hand and led him halfway toward Kirutu before releasing him and crossing the rest of the way alone, eyes fixed on the man who had tormented her for so long.

Kirutu might have objected, Stephen thought, but here with a full army in the face of no threat, doing so might be seen as weakness. And more, there was a place in his wounded soul that surely cried to be free of the prison he'd lived in for so long.

Or perhaps there was another reason—Stephen didn't know—but Kirutu made no move.

She stopped in front of him and searched his eyes.

"You are a great leader, my husband. And I am your humble servant."

The words streamed into Kirutu's face, unseen by all but Stephen yet felt by Kirutu to his very core. His eyes were wide.

"In any way that you have hurt me, I remember it no more." The tangible power of her words reached Stephen as a warm wave that swept over his skin. She was speaking to them all, he knew. And to the whole world.

"My heart cries with you and your people. Like children we long for love. Know my love for you. Know that your Maker would see only the love in your heart. Hear his call, Kirutu. Hear his song calling your name and know that he will remember no blame on your part."

Kirutu's hands were shaking. He might have been trying to stem the tears that filled his eyes. If so, he failed miserably.

She stepped up to him, lifted her hand to his face, and brushed away his tears with her thumb.

"The heart of all Tulim cries for a great love that would make you innocent of all but love," she said. "Hear my words and see this same love now. It is my gift to you."

She took his hand and kissed his knuckles.

The first sound of crying came from the woman who'd stood by Wilam. His wife, Melino, stood thirty paces away, weeping softly, unabashed. And Wilam too was quickly besieged by tears, his silent. They had suffered too deeply and for too many years to hold steady in face of such beauty.

His mother leaned forward and whispered something to Kirutu that only he could hear. But its power became immediately evident.

Even as she spoke, Kirutu began to shake from head to toe. And the moment she pulled away he sank to his knees. He sat back on his haunches, let his arms drop by his sides, and began to weep with his head hung low.

The sight of their powerful warlord so overcome by kind words swept away the last bonds of fear that had kept his warriors in check, and now the soft sound of crying could be heard spreading through their ranks.

Stephen slowly scanned the scene before him. He had a few broken ribs, and his head had taken far too many blows, but the pain sat at the edge of his awareness, only a minor disturbance.

The Warik, on the other hand, had suffered a lifetime of cruelty. They looked like lost children, some confused, some weeping, some only standing with vacant eyes. Their minds could not begin to understand the full implications of what they were witnessing, but in their hearts they knew that something had changed in the Tulim valley. In time to come they would find a new life. Then they would understand more.

It was for this that his mother had been called. It was for them that she had suffered.

Stephen looked at the sky. Stars shone brightly. The bands of light were no longer visible, not because they weren't there, but because he no longer needed to see them with these eyes, placed like buttons on his costume.

Why should he? The full power of the light lived inside him already.

His mother was walking toward him, eyes swimming in the sea of such love and power.

She took his hand.

"Come with me, my son."

And she led him away from the Warik so that they could be together.

CHAPTER THIRTY-TWO

One Week Later

THE TULIM valley lay in all its lush splendor beneath a bright blue sky helmed by a crystalline
sun. From this vantage high upon the hill, where
Shaka had first called to his mother in her dreams
and later opened her eyes to see what few ever saw,
the endless swamps glistened with reflected light
where the canopy thinned to expose the still waters. A flock of red-and-green parrots flapped over
the jungle below Stephen. He could barely hear
their call.

"It's all so clear now," his mother said, gazing
out over the expansive scene. "This was what I saw
in my dreams on the night you were born." She
faced him, eyes round. Such a beautiful woman, his
mother. A woven yellow headband crowned her as

the queen in this valley, though she was the servant of all.

"I couldn't see who was calling to me, but I knew, where deep calls to deep—I had to come. Even as I know now that I must stay."

Stephen looked into her eyes, then offered her a gentle smile. He turned back to the valley without speaking. They'd spent a week on the mountain where he'd lived with Shaka, speaking little at first. Whatever could be said in the wake of such a powerful encounter with love was best left to the heart, not the mouth. As Shaka had often said, sometimes words diminished the greatest truths and experiences.

Then they'd slept and bathed and eaten and been, just as he and Shaka had been for so many years. They hadn't discussed the awakening in the Tulim valley until the second day, and then only in simple terms, because they already knew what had happened.

Strangely, his mother seemed to know much of how he'd spent his life on the mountain, as if she'd lived there with him. But then, she had, in a manner of speaking. She recalled it all as she might a dream, distant and slightly out of focus, but remembered. Even so Stephen had taken great delight in recounting those years for her. Once they began, their talk went all day, filled with wonder and laughter. In some ways they had many years to catch up on; in other ways none.

She'd gone down to the valley on the fifth day, and two days later he'd met her on the hill where they now stood. She'd had to see the people, she said. It was her place to do so, alone. She'd found the Warik still in a daze. Confused. Stripped of all the brutality that had ordered their world for so long. Kirutu had not come out of his house once since that night of power. He'd wept like a child when she went in to see him.

"So you will stay," Stephen said, eyes down-valley, "and I must go."

"Yes."

He felt some apprehension at the prospect of leaving, but he knew that his time here was finished. He had come for two reasons: to be raised on the mountain with Shaka, and to help his mother bring light into the valley. He was ready to take that same light to a faraway land so that others might awaken as well. He couldn't deny the eagerness he felt in setting out for that discovery. This was his purpose in life.

This and to walk in the light himself.

"I've lived my whole life with you and Shaka," he said. "It will be a new thing."

"It will, and I will miss you more than I can bear to think about at times. But I send you gladly."

She stepped up to him and took his hand in hers. Kissed his fingers.

"I'm so grateful for you. Proud beyond any mother's right to be. You're such a man. The world needs the light you have to share."

She was a foot shorter than him, so he tilted his head to look into her eyes. "And what would I be without your sacrifice? Is there another woman like you on this earth?"

She chuckled. "Many. They just don't know it yet."

"Then I'll help them learn."

"I'm sure you will. And break a few hearts along the way."

"Break them?"

"Just an expression, dear. Unknowing hearts are fragile and easily broken. Wasn't mine?"

She had a point.

His mother stepped away, crossed her arms, and faced a slight breeze that shifted her hair. "It's quite ironic, isn't it? I left my home to bring God's love to this dark valley. Now you will leave this valley to bring that same love to others. Full circle."

He nodded. "There's a part of me that would like very much for you to come with me. Not in a sad way, just in a hopeful way. We'll see each other again, won't we?"

"Of course we will! Often, I hope." She took a deep breath and let it settle. "My work isn't finished here, Stephen. They need me more than before now. They have so much to learn about the source of the power they saw. So many questions about the path to forgiveness, so little understanding about the Master's Way." A pause. "Besides, I know this valley better than I knew my own home. I belong here."

"And Kirutu? You'll still be with him?"

"I don't know. We will see. It'll be mine to decide, not his."

He understood this. Some might think staying with such a tormentor unwise, but Kirutu had only done what he knew to do. Love would change his heart and his costume.

"What about Wilam?"

"I don't know. The children need me most. I am mother to them all."

"And I am son to all mothers."

"And how fortunate they all are," she said with a smile.

Her eyes lowered to the medallion on his neck—the tribal carving that Shaka had given him with the word *DEDITIO* at its center. He'd tied it to a leather thong. She reached for it and ran her thumb over the smooth surface.

"You are Outlaw still," she said softly.

"As are you," he said.

"Beyond the law that brings death, into the law that is life."

"Found on the narrow way that few find and fewer follow," he said, recounting Shaka's words.

She smiled. "My place is to help the Warik become Outlaws, all of them. Your call will take you to places few have seen."

"Beyond the Tulim valley."

"He told me on this hill that you will live an obscure life. That you're destined to find and call all of those who would step out of the law of death and find new life."

"Then I'll fill the world with Outlaws."

She released the pendant. "Many will follow. All Outlaws, just as our Master was one."

"As we will be, always."

That brought a smirk to her face. "It's now what? Nineteen eighty or so? Dear me, I've lost track of the years. It seems I'm destined to grow old in this jungle."

"Your costume ages," he said.

"Yes. My costume. Older than yours, but I'm sure we both still have so much to learn."

"More to learn?" This confused him. What more could there be to learn that was not already known? The ways of the foreign lands he would see, perhaps.

"Yes, Stephen. More. You will be tested in ways we cannot foresee. As will I. The temptation to forget is woven into the fabric of these…costumes. Even our Master felt great fear, even up to the day he sweated drops of blood before the world killed him. If our Master felt such fear to the end of his life, I'm sure we will as well. We take courage from the one who rose from that grave of death and fear."

She had quickly adopted his language. But then, it was hers as well, from her dreams. Hadn't she been one with Shaka? The notion of that singular truth was still bound in mystery. Stephen wouldn't try to understand—leaning on that understanding only inflamed the costume's need to know what it could not with its limited mind.

Allow for mystery, Stephen. Shaka's teaching. *Lest you think you would be the greatest of all, feeding always on the tree of the knowledge of good and evil. This is Lucifer's complex. Instead, trust in the One who gives you true life.*

So he would trust. And be. As he was, saved from the ravages of the law that had thrown the world into chaos. Outlaw.

"This life will give you much and then take it all away," she said, "and yet you will gain and lose nothing you don't already have. In so many ways your journey is only beginning, however complete it already is."

She paused and a shadow crossed her face.

"Many people won't understand you. Some will find great courage in your gift, others will try to kill you. When the voice of doubt cries the loudest, remember your Master's journey. Remember mine. Eighteen years here, and now it's only been one night. And this too will pass. If you wander the earth for as many years or longer, remember…it's already done. Just walk the Way, abide in the Truth, and embrace the Light."

The Way, the Truth, and the Light. She was speaking to him both as mother and as the voice of God.

He felt compelled to step up next to her, take her hand as a son, and gaze out over the valley with her. The breeze whispered its contentment.

"Yes, Mother."

A long beat settled between them.

"Thank you, Son," she said.

And then they said nothing for a while.

"Now what?" he finally said.

"Now I go to the Tulim to bring healing and you leave this jungle to be Outlaw."

She took a deep breath and let it out slowly. Then faced him with a bright twinkle in her eyes.

"But first, would you like to meet some beautiful children?"

He grinned wide.

"I would love nothing more."

AUTHOR'S NOTE

Some of my readers know that I was born and raised the son of missionaries in the jungles of Irian Jaya where this novel is set. I didn't grow up among the Tulim people, because they are a people of my making—rather I grew up among the Dani, a tribe of cannibals north of the Tulim in *Outlaw*. Indeed, my first language was Dani, the native language which I borrowed for the story you have just read. Yes, "wam" really does mean "pig."

In many ways, this novel represents broad swaths of my own heritage and upbringing in a land so foreign to the west that most attempts to explain it to Americans returns only blank stares. My hope is that through the power of story you have been able to peer into a culture that, for all of its vast differences from your own, is the same in every respect that makes all humans, human.

Although the Tulim is a fictional valley as are the Tulim people, all of their customs, beliefs and practices are real somewhere in the world, in some tribe, collected here in a fictional setting that mirrors reality. If the people seem real to you, it's because they essentially are, written by one who knows, from first hand experience, how such a people would believe, feel and live.

In the end, *Outlaw* is the same journey of awakening and redemption that we may all take, regardless of where we live. It's the story of losing the world we think keeps us safe to gain our true selves as we were created to be—a lifelong passage that often takes us to the very limits of our understanding only to discover a far richer, and far, far more powerful awareness of love, life and purpose in this thing we call life.

Thank you for taking the journey with me.

Ted Dekker

ABOUT THE AUTHOR

TED DEKKER is a *New York Times* bestselling author with more than five million books in print. He is known for stories that combine adrenaline-laced plots with incredible confrontations between unforgettable characters. He lives in Austin, Texas, with his wife and children.

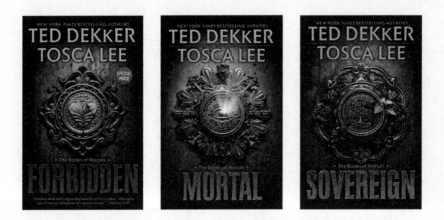

TELL THE WORLD
THIS BOOK WAS

Good	Bad	So-so

JG good

Weird ant
ridiculous !
FM

HK